One

*C*ool wet fingers of fog brushed against his face as Matt Winters walked up the hill to his San Francisco apartment building. At the sound of a siren, he automatically stiffened. He'd been chasing ambulances for so long he couldn't help but wonder what new story was developing, what tragedy was unfolding, what family was about to receive an unwelcome late-night phone call.

As the siren drew closer, he glanced down the street behind him. All was quiet. Parked cars, shadowy buildings, the light from the street lamps broke the darkness, but nothing looked out of place. Still, Matt felt the prickles of uneasiness stab the skin on the back of his neck. He felt like someone was watching him, and his instincts screamed caution even though his brain couldn't figure out why.

Taking one last look down the street behind him, he moved to unlock the front door of his apartment building. He frowned when he saw that the door was ajar and the lock appeared to be jammed. Matt wasn't particularly concerned about his barely furnished apartment or even his own safety. He'd lived in places far more dangerous than this. The broken lock aggravated his sense that something was wrong, but a quick look around the lobby revealed nothing amiss.

With a weary sigh, Matt pressed the elevator call button and rubbed a hand across his tired eyes. He hadn't slept more than three hours in a row in the last seventy-two. He'd been chasing a news story, following a money trail that had led him straight up the steps of City Hall. Tomorrow the rest of San Francisco would read about the corruption of one of its supervisors in the morning edition of the *Herald*.

His mission accomplished, Matt should have been feeling satisfied. Instead he felt restless, once again reminded that no matter how many truths he unveiled, no matter how many mysteries he solved, he couldn't solve the one that mattered most.

Matt pressed the elevator button again, hating himself for not being able to let go of the past. How ironic that he lived his life in search of the truth, yet couldn't seem to accept it when it stared him in the face.

That need for closure, the desire to stop the endless hunger, the unquenchable thirst for answers had brought him back to San Francisco, the place where it had started and where it had ended.

Finally, the elevator doors opened. A minute later, Matt stepped onto the tenth-floor landing and walked down the hall to his apartment. He let himself in just in time to catch the phone before the machine picked up. "Winters," he said abruptly.

There was no reply, just the sound of someone breath-

"PLEASE. I DON'T KNOW ANYTHING ABOUT BABIES."

Matt looked into Caitlyn's eyes with a hopeful expression. "I only moved to town a couple of months ago, so there's no one else to call."

"I've been manipulated by the best," Caitlyn said dryly, "so I can recognize a sob story when I hear one."

"I really would appreciate your help. This isn't an area I know how to control."

And she had a feeling there wasn't much in his life that he didn't control. "You're pretty good at getting what you want, aren't you?"

"That depends on your answer," he said, turning on that killer smile.

With the baby and Matt both looking at her with their big brown eyes she was completely lost. She handed Matt the baby and put a hand on his arm. The heat between them suddenly seemed to sizzle. He looked into her eyes and she felt her stomach clench. She'd meant to offer him a gesture of comfort, but instead the touch had created awareness between them, a connection, a sexual attraction.

Oh Lord. What had she gotten herself into?

Other Avon Books by
Barbara Freethy

ALMOST HOME
ASK MARIAH
DANIEL'S GIFT
JUST THE WAY YOU ARE
ONE TRUE LOVE
RYAN'S RETURN
THE SWEETEST THING

BARBARA FREETHY

Some Kind of Wonderful

AVON BOOKS
An Imprint of HarperCollinsPublishers

AVON BOOKS
An Imprint of HarperCollins*Publishers*
10 East 53rd Street
New York, New York 10022-5299

Copyright © 2001 by Barbara Freethy
Excerpts from *An Offer From a Gentleman* copyright © 2001 by Julie Cotler Pottinger; *True Confessions* copyright © 2001 by Rachel Gibson; *Some Kind of Wonderful* copyright © 2001 by Barbara Freethy; *Here and Now* copyright © 2001 by Constance O'Day-Flannery; *The Wedding Wager* copyright © 2001 by Catherine Maxwell; *The Prince's Bride* copyright © 2001 by Cheryl Griffin; *The Truest Heart* copyright © 2001 by Sandra Kleinschmit
ISBN: 0-380-81553-2
www.avonromance.com

First Avon Books paperback printing: September 2001

Avon Trademark Reg. U.S. Pat. Off. and in Other Countries, Marca Registrada, Hecho en U.S.A.
HarperCollins ® is a trademark of HarperCollins Publishers Inc.

Printed in the U.S.A.

10 9 8 7 6 5 4 3 2 1

To the Ladies at the Peninsula Tennis Club,
who provide great tennis, great ideas,
and great friendship

ing. A prank call, an informant, a threat? He didn't know which.

"Matt?" It was barely a whisper, so hushed he couldn't tell if it was a female or a male.

"Who is this?" No answer. "Look, I don't have time to—"

The sound of a click, then the dial tone, told him the caller had hung up. Out of habit, he wrote down the caller ID number. It wasn't one he recognized, but he'd check it out later. He was simply too tired to deal with one more thing tonight.

Tossing his car keys onto the dining room table, he headed into the kitchen, wondering if by some impossible chance there was actually something edible in the refrigerator. Unfortunately, it boasted nothing more than a couple of beers, some wilted lettuce, and molding tomatoes. Popping open one of the beers, he took a long grateful swallow, then walked back into the living room.

It wasn't much of a room for living in at the moment. There was an old black leather couch along one wall and a matching overstuffed armchair, an oak coffee table that held his array of newspapers and magazines, a stereo system, because he couldn't live without music, and a punching bag hanging from a hook in the ceiling, because he didn't know a better way to relieve stress than to beat the hell out of that bag. Boxing had gotten him through some tough times, given him a sense of control over himself and the chaos that had once been his life.

At some point, he'd have to invest in some furniture—or maybe not. Who knew how long he'd stay in San Francisco? Who knew how long he'd stay anywhere? His life had been a series of entrances and exits, new places, new faces.

The phone rang again and Matt's muscles tensed. For a second he was tempted to let it ring, but he'd never been one to run from a fight or avoid a confrontation, although there had been plenty of people in his life who had told him to do just that. He reached for the phone again and said, "Winters."

"Congratulations," David Stern replied.

Matt relaxed at the sound of his editor's voice.

"I can't wait until the morning paper hits the streets," David crowed. "Your story will rock this town."

"As long as Keilor doesn't file a libel suit."

"Let him try. You covered your ass quite well."

"Yours, too," Matt reminded him.

"That's why I pay you the big bucks."

"Yeah, right." Matt walked across his living room with the portable phone in one hand. "What's next?"

"Why don't you take a break? You've been on this story nonstop since you landed in town six weeks ago. Take some time off. A few days in Lake Tahoe wouldn't do you any harm."

Matt didn't want a few days off. Vacations were for people who wanted to relax, to think, to philosophize, and he wanted to do none of the above. Too much time on his hands would only make him feel that much more restless.

"I'm fine. I don't need a break," he said.

"I figured you'd say that. By the way, that P.I. friend of yours stopped by the paper today. Want to tell me what you're working on?"

"It doesn't involve the paper."

"So it must have something to do with why you surprised the hell out of me by actually accepting my job offer and leaving Chicago," David said, obviously fishing.

"Could be."

"We've been friends a long time, Matthew. I'm going to have to pull rank on you and insist on the truth."

Matt laughed. "You can try."

"I can do my own investigation."

"If you were any good at investigating, you'd be writing the stories instead of editing them."

"Now that hurts. Did anyone ever tell you that you wield honesty like a blunt instrument to the head?"

"And your point is?"

Matt's attention drifted as David launched into a long-winded reminder of how any investigation Matt was involved in could ultimately affect the newspaper. Matt didn't bother to interrupt. He simply stared out at the lights of San Francisco weaving like drunken sailors up and down the city hills. It was a staggeringly good view, but most days he wondered what had possessed him to take this tenth-floor apartment in Pacific Heights. The burnished hardwood floors, the big bay window, the ultramodern kitchen felt wrong. This wasn't him. He was back alleys and bad neighborhoods, Chinese take-out and cigarette smoke. But somehow David had convinced him that a new location might change his perspective.

"How's Jackie?" Matt interrupted, knowing if there was anything guaranteed to distract David, it was his wife.

"Whining about getting fat. She asked me today if she looked like a glowing pregnant woman or a fat penguin."

"Tell me you chose glowing pregnant woman."

"Glowing penguin wasn't good enough?"

"I hope you like sleeping on the couch."

"It's warmer than our bed these days. Sometimes I wonder why I ever wanted to have a kid."

"Well, you'll need someone to mow the lawn someday."

"Thanks for the reminder. That might get me through

tonight's cravings. Jackie usually gets hungry just about the time I'm falling asleep." David paused. "You know, I must have babies on the brain, because I can almost hear one crying."

Matt frowned and turned his head toward the door as the crying grew louder.

"It's not your imagination. I hear it, too." Another shriek made Matt pause. "I'll talk to you later." He put the phone down and walked to the door. The only other tenant on this side of the L-shaped building was a single woman he had yet to meet. He opened the door, but there was no one there. Actually, there was someone there, way down there . . .

On the floor, in a car seat, was a tiny baby with a few strands of fuzzy black hair on its head, red cheeks, teary eyes, and a mouth that screamed in fury. "What the hell?" Matt looked around the empty hallway, wondering where on earth the baby's mother was.

"Okay, just be quiet for a second, would you?" He squatted down next to the baby and patted the baby's head, which only seemed to make him—or was that her?—more angry.

"Where is your mother?" Matt asked, the uneasy feeling returning to his gut.

He looked at the door across the hall and hesitated. There appeared to be a light on, but it was almost midnight. Still, what choice did he have? Leaning over, he pounded on the door. A moment later, a female called out, "Who is it?"

"It's your neighbor."

"I can't see you," she said warily.

Matt stood up and looked straight into her peephole. "I'm here."

"What were you doing on the floor?"

"Looking at your baby."

"My *what*?"

"Open the door, would you?"

"I don't think so."

"Look, we have a problem out here. Someone left a baby in the hall."

Silence followed, then she said, "All right. But I have my phone and I've already dialed 9-1, so if you're trying something funny—"

"I'm not."

Another brief pause, then the door opened the width of a security chain. A woman's face appeared in the crack, a vision of blond curls, white lace, and some sort of filmy veil.

Matt blinked rapidly, wondering if he'd conjured up a bride to go with the baby on his doorstep.

The woman pulled the veil away from her face, and he saw that her cheeks were flushed, her brown eyes overly bright. "What do you want?" she asked, a breathless note in her voice.

"Your baby is crying." He pointed to the infant, who made a liar out of him by sitting quietly in the car seat, considering the two of them with a confused expression.

The woman peered around him. "I don't have a baby."

"You must. It sure as hell isn't my baby."

"Who are you?" she asked suspiciously. "Why are you trying to get rid of your baby?"

"It's not mine," he repeated. "And I live there." He pointed to his door. "I'm your neighbor."

Her wary gaze traveled slowly down his body, and Matt became very aware of his dirty black jeans, sweat-stained gray T-shirt, and black leather jacket. Putting a self-conscious hand to his face, he could feel a beard grazing his cheeks.

"I just got off assignment," he said. "I don't usually look like this."

"What do you usually look like?"

"Well, not like this," he said in exasperation. "Look, I need some sleep, and you need to take care of this kid."

"That's not my baby. I don't know what you're trying to pull, but—"

"Hey, wait." He instinctively stuck his foot in the space between the door and the wall as she tried to retreat, wincing when she hit it with the door. "I really am your neighbor. Matt Winters. I've got ID." He reached for his wallet and pulled out his driver's license, holding it up so she could see it. "I'm a reporter for the *San Francisco Herald*. And I'd be happy to give you references if you'd just open your door and help me figure out whose baby this is."

"That address says Chicago."

"That's where I lived until recently. Come on, you must have seen my name on the mailbox over yours. The landlord's name is Rick Shrader. I can give you his phone number. Help me out here."

She stared at him doubtfully, then the baby let out a howl of protest. A second later the woman released the chain and opened the door, allowing Matt his first full glimpse of his neighbor. Barefoot, in faded blue jeans, a short-cropped bright yellow sweater, and a lacy white veil, she made quite an impression. But it wasn't just her crazy attire that caught him off guard, it was her gold-flecked brown eyes and the sun-streaked blond hair that cascaded halfway down her back when she self-consciously pulled off her veil.

"It's not what you think," she murmured.

"I wasn't going to ask."

She gave him an embarrassed half smile. "Good."

"So, wedding night fantasy with the boyfriend?"

"I thought you weren't going to ask."

"Sorry."

She stepped around him and knelt down next to the baby. "Oh, you sweet little thing. Who are you?"

The baby began to cry louder, tiny fingers closing into fists as it squirmed in its seat.

"I think it wants to get out," Matt said.

The woman undid the straps and slowly pulled the baby into her arms, a somber expression in her eyes as she looked at the infant, then at him. "Are you telling me that this baby was just left here in the hall?"

"It sure looks that way."

"I don't understand."

Matt shrugged. He certainly didn't have an explanation.

"She's so precious," the woman murmured as the baby nuzzled into her chest.

Matt cleared his throat as he realized he was staring at his neighbor's breasts with fascination, and she was once again regarding him with suspicion.

"Are you sure you don't know who she is?" the woman asked.

"I wasn't even sure it was a she."

"Pink sleeper, pink blanket, pink socks. I think it's safe to say she's a girl. Maybe one of your girlfriends left her for you."

Matt stiffened. "No way. That baby is not mine. I can guarantee you that."

The woman patted the baby's behind. "One thing is for sure. She's soaking wet. You should change her."

"Or you. After all, she's in the middle of the hallway, maybe even closer to your door than to mine." He inwardly groaned at his lame comment. "Didn't you hear her crying? Why didn't you open your door?"

"I was listening to music. I didn't hear a thing," she explained. "Fine, I'll change her, but you're not going anywhere," she added as she saw him edging toward his apartment.

She stood up with the baby in her arms. "Rick Shrader did tell me you were an okay guy, so I guess you can come in. But I'm warning you I've taken self-defense. So don't think you can try anything with me."

Matt had to bite back a smile. She was barely five foot three if she was an inch. He had almost a foot on her, and he didn't doubt for a second that he couldn't take her anywhere he wanted to go. But judging by the fierce expression in her eyes, he'd be better off agreeing, so he simply held up his hand in submission.

"All right, but you know Tae Bo aerobics doesn't really qualify for self-defense," he drawled.

"Just bring the car seat and the bag with you."

Matt followed her into her apartment, expecting to see something similar to his place, something clean and utilitarian with perhaps a feminine touch. What he saw was sheer chaos, layers and layers of white fabrics, silks and satins adorning the couch and the love seat, spools of threads, stacks of lace, a sewing machine in one corner, and a mannequin in the other. There were bridal magazines on the coffee table, boxes of pearls and beads, and swatches of ribbons on the floor in a discarded heap. It was a single man's nightmare. Maybe that was it. Maybe he'd fallen asleep on his feet. Maybe he was dreaming.

"I have to wake up," he said. "Just wake up."

She stared at him uncertainly. "Have you been drinking?"

"No."

"Really? You look like you have a hangover."

"I haven't had much sleep the last three days. I've

been too busy pulling a city official's hand out of the till. You can read about it in the morning paper, by the way."

"Oh, I don't get the newspaper," she said with an off-hand toss of her head.

"You don't get the paper?" Everyone got the paper. It was part of life, a ritual as important as eating and drinking and sleeping. "Why don't you get the paper?"

"The news depresses me. Can you see if there is a diaper in that bag?"

"The news may be depressing, but it's important. How can you manage your life if you don't read the paper, if you don't know what is going on in the city you live in, the world that surrounds you?"

She cleared her throat. "Okay, I lied. I read the paper every morning."

"Now, you are lying. What is wrong with you?" He didn't understand how anyone could not read the newspaper.

"Right now I'm holding a stinky baby. That's what's wrong with me. Did you find that diaper yet?"

Matt set the bag down on the floor and dug through it, wishing he'd never come home at all. He'd been looking forward to peace and quiet, some downtime after the stress of the last few days, but here he was right back in the middle of somebody else's mess. Relieved to find a disposable diaper in the bag, he pulled it out and handed it to her.

She cleared off the end of one couch and laid the baby down, then quickly changed her. She didn't seem to have any problem with the baby's flailing legs and arms or the shrill crying that continued until she fixed the last piece of tape.

"You look like you've done that before," he commented.

"A few times. I baby-sat when I was a teenager." She picked the baby up and offered her to him. "Do you want to hold her now?"

"No. No." He shoved his hands into his pockets and took a step back, almost tripping over a large spool of lace.

"Sorry about that." She gave the spool a nudge with her foot. "I'm on deadline."

"For what? Are you getting married in the morning?"

"I'm doing the alterations on a wedding dress. I have a bridal shop on Union Street. Devereaux's is the name. Do you know it?"

"I don't make a habit of knowing where the nearest bridal shop is."

She offered him the first genuine smile he'd seen all night. "I bet you don't."

"What is your name anyway?" he asked, realizing he couldn't keep thinking about her as "that woman."

"Caitlyn Devereaux."

"So why isn't all this stuff at your shop?"

"Because Tiffany Waterhouse moved up her wedding date. It turns out she's pregnant, and she absolutely cannot go down the aisle looking like a watermelon—her words, not mine. I brought her dress home to finish because she's getting married at eleven o'clock tomorrow morning instead of in four weeks as she'd originally planned. And her family is very well connected, so I don't want to disappoint her."

Matt looked at the yards and yards of material draped over the couch. "She must be really fat."

"That's just her train, a six-foot trail of lace that goes down the aisle after her," she added at his blank expression. Caitlyn moved the baby from one shoulder to the other. "She still isn't happy. I wonder if she's hungry."

"I wonder who she is."

"We should call the police."

"I suppose." Even as he agreed, he felt the same prickly uneasiness he'd experienced earlier. Why would anyone leave a baby in his hallway?

"She's so young," Caitlyn murmured, caressing the baby's head with her fingers. "She can't be more than two months old. How could anyone just put her down and walk away? Especially her mother." She shook her head in bewilderment. "How could they do that?"

Matt had a hundred answers, but there was something about Caitlyn—an innocence, maybe—that made him instinctively want to shield her. Hell, it probably had something to do with all the white lace in the room.

Before he could reply, Caitlyn walked up to him and pushed the baby against his chest. "Hold her for a second. I want to look through that bag and see if I can find a bottle or instructions or something."

Before Matt could protest, he found himself wrapping his arms around a tiny baby who felt so small, so fragile in his arms, he thought he might break her. And when the baby began to squirm and whimper, Matt awkwardly shifted his feet and patted her back. He looked to Caitlyn for relief, but she was still digging through the diaper bag.

"Hey, I could use some help here," he said.

"I found some formula . . . and a bottle," she added triumphantly, holding it up like a trophy. "A little water, and I think we can make her a lot happier."

Matt followed her into the adjacent kitchen. No way was she leaving him alone with the baby. He found her kitchen to be as chaotic as the living room—cookie jars with faces on them, pasta noodles in colorful glass containers, magnets of every shape imaginable on the refrigerator, and a couple of potted plants on the windowsill, some looking half dead despite the freshly watered soil. Apparently, Caitlyn didn't like to throw anything away.

With the clashing bursts of color, the room felt warm and cozy, inviting. Probably too inviting, Matt decided. Definitely too inviting, he added silently as Caitlyn came over to him. As she put the bottle into the baby's mouth, her blond hair drifted against his chest and arm. She was so close he could smell flowers in her hair and mint in her breath, then her breasts grazed against his arm as she maneuvered the bottle in the baby's mouth, and his heart skipped a beat. Her femininity called out to him like a siren, and he felt his body harden, a completely unwelcome reaction considering the fact that he was holding a baby and Caitlyn was a perfect stranger. Perfect being a big part of the problem.

"Here you go, sweetie," Caitlyn cooed. "Take a sip. There's a good girl."

"Don't you want to hold her?" Matt asked, feeling more uncomfortable by the second.

Caitlyn hesitated, then said, "I don't think so."

"Are you sure you don't know who this baby is?" he asked her again as they returned to the living room.

"Of course I don't. Why would you ask that?"

"She seems to like you."

"Well, I'm a nice person. Babies can sense goodness."

"Then I must be a nice person, too. She's not crying anymore."

"We'll have to see how she feels about you when she's done sucking on her bottle," she said with a wry smile. She knelt down on the floor next to the diaper bag and began searching through it, much the way he had done a few minutes before.

"There's no note in the bag. I already looked," he told her.

After a minute, Caitlyn sat back on her heels and frowned. "What mother leaves her baby without even a note?"

Matt pulled the bottle out of the baby's mouth as she stopped sucking and appeared to be done. "What do I do with her now?"

"Put her over your shoulder and pat her back until she burps."

"I think you ought to do that."

"Fine. Let me grab her blanket. She might be getting cold." As Caitlyn pulled the baby blanket from the straps of the car seat, something fluttered to the ground.

"Oh!" She reached for the piece of paper, then looked into Matt's eyes. "There *is* a note."

Matt felt his body tense. "What does it say?" he asked shortly, having trouble getting the words out of his mouth. He had a bad feeling about this—a very bad feeling.

Caitlyn read silently, the tension growing with each passing second.

"What the hell does it say?" he demanded.

She looked up at him through troubled eyes. "Someone named Sarah wants *you* to take care of her baby."

"Sarah." He breathed her name like a long-forgotten scent.

"Who is Sarah?"

He stared at Caitlyn, knowing she'd asked him something, but he couldn't concentrate, couldn't focus. Sarah? How could it be? He remembered the eerie sensation he'd felt walking up to the apartment building, as if someone was watching him. And the phone call, the woman's voice . . . had it been Sarah? My God! Had she actually been standing outside his apartment?

Matt strode across the room, thrust the baby into Caitlyn's arms, then dashed out the door.

"Hey, where are you going?" Caitlyn cried. "You can't leave me with your baby."

Two

"You can't leave me with your baby," Caitlyn repeated helplessly, but Matt was gone, and she was alone. She took in a deep breath and let it out, glancing down at the baby's cherubic face. "Well, this is something, isn't it? What are we going to do now?"

The baby smiled up at her, and Caitlyn felt her heart melt at its sweet innocence. A tightness came into her chest, making it difficult to breathe. This baby, this darling baby, reminded her of everything she'd ever wanted, and it was suddenly too much for her.

"Oh, God," she whispered. "You have to go home."

The baby squinted, her little mouth turning down into a pout just before she let out a wail.

"Okay, maybe not yet," Caitlyn said quickly. She put the baby up on her shoulder and patted her back, bouncing her up and down until she heard a small satisfying burp. Then all was quiet. She lowered the baby into the cradle of her arms and walked over to the couch to retrieve the blanket. By the time she wrapped the child up in a tight cocoon, the baby had drifted off to sleep. Setting her back in the car seat, Caitlyn picked up the piece of paper and reread the note that had sent Matt rushing out the door. The words were scrawled in a shaky hand, the ink not fully completing each letter.

Matt,

I can't believe I've found you again. When I read your name in the newspaper, I knew it was a sign. Please take care of Emily. I have no one else to ask, and I'm desperate. I'll call soon.

Sarah

Sarah. Caitlyn sat down on the floor next to the sleeping Emily and leaned against the couch. Who was Sarah? An old girlfriend, an ex-lover? Matt had taken off in such a hurry. She'd never seen the blood drain out of anyone's face quite so quickly.

Matt must have loved this woman once. He'd looked stricken at the sound of her name, shocked to the core. It appeared that maybe Matt *was* the baby's father.

Caitlyn stood up and walked around in an aimless circle, wondering what she was supposed to do now. When was Matt coming back? She deserved an explanation. It was after midnight, and she was now baby-sitting for a man she'd met twenty minutes ago!

He certainly wasn't what she had expected when she'd heard a newspaperman was moving in across the hall. She'd pictured someone older, with glasses and a serious expression, wearing loose suits and ties that didn't match. She certainly hadn't expected a sexy hunk of a man in tight-ass black jeans and a leather jacket. He looked like someone who'd be more comfortable out of an office, maybe on the back of a Harley or in a smoky nightclub someplace where men drank Scotch and no one asked for last names.

Caitlyn shook her head in derision at her own wild imaginings. Her curiosity and overly active imagination had gotten her into trouble plenty of times before. But she couldn't seem to stop herself. Dreaming and drawing were as vital to her as eating and breathing.

Instinctively, she reached for the sketch pad on the table, and within seconds, her fingers flying over the page, she had sketched the face of Matt Winters. She studied it for a second, tilting her head in critical analysis. No, it wasn't quite right. His jaw was strong and square, his features more ragged. His wasn't a traditionally handsome face, but rather an interesting one, with the lines of life etched in his forehead and around the corners of his eyes. And those eyes, a deep, rich brown that reminded her of semisweet chocolate. But whoever had said the eyes were the window to the soul hadn't met this man, for Matt's eyes hadn't revealed one tiny clue to who he was or what he was thinking.

No, his eyes had guarded every last secret of his heart. Yet despite his wariness, his expression had changed when she'd placed Emily in his arms. He'd softened, as if something untouchable deep within him had been touched, some long-forgotten core of tenderness perhaps?

As Caitlyn stared at her sketch, she realized it wasn't nearly good enough; it really didn't resemble him at all. And she was once again confronted with her inability to get it right. Why couldn't she put down on paper what she saw so clearly in her head? In the past few months there seemed to be a short circuit in her brain between the thought and the execution, a block she couldn't hurdle or climb over or even push aside.

She started to erase the sketch, then quickly tossed down the pad as heavy footsteps drew her attention to the doorway. There would be time to have a heart-to-heart conversation with her muse a little later. She got to her feet as Matt entered the room. His face was still ashen, his eyes bleak.

"I couldn't find her," he said heavily. "God dammit, I couldn't find her."

"Maybe tomorrow," Caitlyn said uncertainly, not sure how to react to the intense pain in his expression.

"No, not tomorrow, not ever! I can't ever find her. I've been looking for years, everywhere I go."

"Who is she?" Caitlyn asked in confusion. "An ex–girlfriend?"

He shook his head. "No. She's my sister."

"Your sister?" It wasn't the answer she'd been expecting. Caitlyn sat down on the arm of the couch. Not having siblings, she had no idea of the intensity of a brother-sister bond, but Matt's emotion seemed unusually deep. "Well, maybe someone else in your family knows where she is," Caitlyn offered when Matt remained silent.

"I have no other family." He paused for a long, tense moment, then said, "Where's the note?"

"Here." She picked it up off the coffee table and handed it to him, watching him read each word at least twice.

"The newspaper," he murmured, looking at Caitlyn with a new light in his eyes. "She must have read my by-line in the paper. That's how she found me." His mouth turned grim. "But I'm still no closer to finding her. Why didn't she just knock on my door? Why didn't she ask me to help her?"

Caitlyn shook her head, because she couldn't imagine what had driven this Sarah to leave her baby unattended in the middle of the hallway. "It's a good thing you were home."

"The phone call." He snapped his fingers. "I thought it was a wrong number, but she said my name. That was her. That was her," he said again. "Sarah. She spoke to me."

"But you didn't know it was her?"

"No. She hung up. But I wrote down the number." Once again he was out the door before she could stop him. He returned almost as quickly, a piece of paper in his hand. "Can I use your phone?"

She waved her hand toward the phone on the table by the door. "Go ahead."

Matt dialed the number and waited. After a moment he hung up. "No answer, no answering machine. I'll have to see if I can trace the number."

"You can do that?"

The light in his eyes dimmed. "Well, not right this second, unfortunately. Damn." He let out a sigh. "Do you have anything to drink?"

"Lemonade, diet Coke, some tea?" she offered.

"I was thinking more along the lines of a good bourbon."

"Sorry. I'm not much of a drinker. Why don't you sit down?" She jumped up and swept a pile of fabric off an armchair. "Relax for a minute and think about what you want to do next."

Matt did as she suggested, resting his elbows on his knees as he stared across the room at the baby. "Sarah's little girl," he murmured. "It doesn't seem possible."

"Why not?" Caitlyn asked, reclaiming her seat on the arm of the couch.

"Because Sarah was nine years old when I last saw her."

"How long ago was that?"

"Thirteen years, four months, three and a half—well, it's been a long time."

For a few minutes the only sound in the room came from the slight snores issued by little Emily. Caitlyn didn't know what to say—or what to do, for that matter. The baby was obviously meant to be in Matt's care. A quick glance at her watch told her time was passing quickly and Tiffany's wedding was only hours away.

"Do you want me to help you carry Emily's things over to your place?" she ventured.

He looked taken aback by the suggestion. "What do you mean?"

"It's late. I have work to finish, and Emily is asleep."

"What if she wakes up?"

"There's more formula in the bag and diapers, too."

"I can't take care of her by myself." He jumped to his feet, running a hand through his hair. "Why the hell did Sarah leave me with a baby?"

"I don't know the answer to that, but I do know that she's your responsibility, and you need to take her home now."

He stared at her, his hands on his hips. "Maybe . . . you could watch her tonight?"

She immediately shook her head. "No."

"I'll pay you."

"It's not the money."

He thought about that for a second. "I'll write an article about your wedding shop. I'll get you publicity."

"No."

"You must want something. You must have a price."

"You think everyone can be bought?"

"Yes."

Her jaw dropped open at his blunt answer. "Well, I can't be bought."

He stared at her for a long moment, his gaze so intense she had the feeling he could see right into her head, and she didn't like it.

"Would you do it just to be nice?" Matt asked. "To be a good neighbor? Because I really need your help. I don't know how to take care of a baby."

Caitlyn licked her lips, feeling a stab of guilt. She could help him, probably should, and it was those words that always drove her into turmoil—*could, should, ought to*. Matt was smart enough to see that if money didn't work, guilt probably would. But this time she held on to her resolve.

"She'll probably go to sleep now. Just change her and feed her when she wakes up. I'm sorry, but I have to finish this dress, and you have to go back to your apartment. Frankly, you look like you could use some sleep, maybe even a shower."

He snapped his fingers. "I can't leave her alone while I take a shower. What if she woke up? What if she was scared or hungry? What if she somehow got out of the car seat and hurt herself?"

Caitlyn sighed, sensing the battle was not yet over. "Is the word *pushover* written that clearly on my forehead?"

"It's not there yet, but I'm still hoping."

"Emily can stay here while you take a shower, a quick shower. Then you come back and get her. Understand?"

"Thirty minutes," he said.

"Ten."

"Fifteen."

"Not a second more, or I'll be knocking on your door."

"Deal." He paused, looking into her eyes. "Thanks."

"No problem. Just come back soon. I really can't take care of *your* baby."

"Stop calling her mine. She's not mine." He closed the door firmly behind him as he left Caitlyn's apartment. For a brief second, he was tempted to run, but deep down inside he knew he couldn't.

Ten minutes later, Matt stood under the showerhead, hoping the hot water would ease the tension in his shoulders. Unfortunately, the knots kept tightening every time he thought about Sarah standing outside his building, taking the elevator, walking down the hall. He'd been just a few feet away when she'd left her baby by the door. Just a few damn feet away. And he hadn't known it, hadn't sensed her presence. Why? Why?

The question screamed at him again and again and again. He'd searched for Sarah for so long. Why couldn't she have knocked on his door? Looked into his eyes? Asked for help?

Because she'd been afraid he would say no? Instinctively, he knew that was the truth. He'd let her down before. He closed his eyes against the pain of his memories. It was a mistake, because then he could see her in his mind.

Sarah sat on the curb, her raven-black hair drifting past her waist as she stared up at their apartment building, at the orange-red flames that leaped out of their windows, and the smoke billowing around them, reminding them that if they hadn't been in hell before, they certainly were now. Clutched in Sarah's hand was a stick with a picture of a doll face on the end. She called the stick EmmaLou and pretended it was her baby. It was the only thing she'd grabbed on their way out of the building.

"It's just going to be for a little while," Matt told her

with every last ounce of his sixteen-year-old bravado. "They will find a place where we can live together, you and me."

"Don't forget EmmaLou," she'd said in her quiet, thin voice, and then she'd looked up at him with a sadness that broke his heart.

"EmmaLou, too. I'll take care of us, Sarah. No one will hurt you. I won't let them."

"Where's Mommy?"

"I don't know." He looked helplessly down the crowded street where residents were huddled together praying the fire that had started in their apartment wouldn't consume the other buildings on the street. He should have stayed home tonight instead of going to work at Jack in the Box, then he would have been home. He could have made sure Sarah didn't get a hold of the matches. Suddenly anger and an overwhelming tiredness overcame him. "Why the hell did you have to play with those matches, Sarah? I've told you a hundred times to leave 'em be. Now we have nowhere to go, no place to live."

Sarah looked stricken at his words, and he wished them back, but it was too late.

"I'm sorry, Mattie." Sarah put her thin arms around his neck and hugged him with all her might. "I'm sorry."

"God," Matt muttered as he opened his eyes and stared at the water dripping down the shower wall. "Come back, Sarah, give me another chance. Just one more chance."

By the time he finished dressing, he was twenty minutes past the fifteen he'd promised Caitlyn. Knowing he couldn't stall a second longer, he walked across the hall and found her door unlocked. He walked in, steeling himself for another glimpse of Sarah's baby. At least everything was quiet.

In fact, it was too quiet. He'd expected to see Caitlyn at her sewing machine, but in fact she was asleep on the couch, one hand flung over the side, resting on Emily's tiny chest. The baby lay fast asleep in her car seat, which sat on the floor next to the couch.

He studied them both for a second, caught by an unbelievable rush of emotion. Caitlyn was just a woman. The baby was just a baby. He didn't know either one of them, didn't care about them at all, but still the sight unsettled him, made him remember a feeling he'd tried hard to forget—the feeling of family.

Clearing his throat, Matt debated his options. They both looked comfortable—happy, in fact. If he moved the baby, she might cry. And if he didn't move her, maybe he could get some sleep before she woke up. Caitlyn, on the other hand—his gaze drifted over to his neighbor—would probably prefer he take the baby home. But then again, she was asleep. That wasn't part of their deal.

Ignoring his conscience, he backed toward the door and quietly let himself out. He'd be worth a lot more to both of them after a few hours sleep. Yeah, that's what they all needed, sleep. It was the perfect solution.

The dream was back. It began with the fireplace and the Christmas tree, the twinkling lights, red, green, blue, gold, and the matching sparkle of her engagement ring, promising a lifetime of holidays as special as this one. Then the colors faded to white.

For a moment Caitlyn imagined her wedding day, her satin dress with the lace bodice and tulle skirt that would twirl when she danced. It was picture-perfect, a beautiful dream.

Then the white dress turned into puffy white clouds and powdery white snow. The warm fire turned to ice,

hard, cold, unforgiving ice. Caitlyn yearned to get away
from it all. And suddenly she was flying, images of speed
and space surrounding her, until she crashed into a world
where nothing would ever be the same. She cried out
against the unbearable, heartbreaking pain, but it
wouldn't stop—not the pain, not the screaming.

Caitlyn wrestled against the bonds of sleep. Finally, finally, she fought her way out, and with a jerk she sat up-
right, her heart pounding, her blood roaring in her ears,
her face dripping with sweat.

"Oh, God," she murmured, feeling shaken, the way
she always did when the memories returned. Then she
suddenly realized that something was different. She
wasn't asleep and she wasn't crying. Emily was crying.

Emily! She automatically reached for the infant, who
was trying to squirm out of the car seat. Caitlyn undid the
straps and picked the baby up. Then she glanced at the
clock on the wall. Six forty-five in the morning!

"Oh, my God!" she cried. "Where is your . . ." Her
voice trailed away as she tried to remember the connection to Matt. "Your uncle?" she asked triumphantly. Her
minor victory faded as the baby continued to scream and
Matt did not materialize.

"I'm going to kill him," she told Emily. "He was supposed to come back and get you, so I could finish—" She
stopped abruptly, the reality of her situation getting
worse. "Oh, no! Tiffany will be here in an hour, and I
haven't finished her dress."

First things first, Caitlyn decided, striding to the doorway. She marched across the hall to Matt's door and tried
the doorknob. It was locked. The bum. She knocked, then
pounded, then pounded some more. Finally, she heard
swearing and the door opened. Matt appeared bleary-
eyed, dressed in a pair of gray sweats and a tank top. He

was a grumpy, sexy, irritating male. And the fact that she had the nerve to actually consider him sexy at all only made her more angry.

Caitlyn thrust Emily at him. "You creep."

"Wait a second."

She ignored him, heading back to her apartment.

"You were asleep," Matt said, following her into her living room before she could slam the door in his face.

"You still could have taken Emily to your place. I didn't finish the dress. And it's all your fault."

"Hey, you fell asleep. You wouldn't have finished the dress even if Emily wasn't here."

"I would have been done if you'd never knocked on my door."

"Maybe not. Maybe—"

"Oh, shut up," she snapped, then grabbed the baby formula out of the diaper bag. "You change her. I'll get a bottle started. Then you are going to leave so I can try to save myself from disaster."

"I'm not sure I can change her," he said doubtfully.

"Try." She stormed into the kitchen to mix the formula with water and heat it up.

As she tapped her fingers impatiently on the countertop, waiting for the water to turn hot, she heard Matt talking to Emily, whose cries had diminished to whimpers.

"Let's see if we can figure this thing out," he told Emily. "I'm not sure which is the back and which is the front, but maybe it doesn't matter since you're a girl."

Caitlyn felt the anger slowly seep out of her body. She tried to fight the weakening, determined not to let his total ineptness charm her. But she had to admit there was something about a man and a baby that got to her. Damn! Don't go there, she told herself.

"Whoa, you peed enough to sink the *Titanic*," Matt continued. "This sucker must weigh five pounds."

A smile broke across Caitlyn's face with his last comment. Well, the baby had slept a good six or seven hours, she calculated. Quite a long time for her age. Emily must have been exhausted, poor thing. Who knew when she'd slept before she'd arrived. Sarah certainly had some explaining to do.

The water warmer, Caitlyn mixed the bottle and walked out to the living room to see Matt holding Emily aloft with a proud smile on his ridiculously attractive face.

"I did it," he said.

"Not bad for your first time." She handed him the bottle. "Here you go."

"That wasn't my first time," he confessed.

She raised an eyebrow. "Really?"

"No, but it's been a while." Matt put the bottle into Emily's greedy mouth, and for a moment they simply watched the baby suck on the bottle, her little hands trying to grab it as if she were afraid it would disappear.

Caitlyn felt a catch in her throat, a fluttering in her stomach. It was happening. She was getting attached, the way she always did, a soft touch for babies and animals and anyone in need. But she couldn't let herself get attached. She had to stay cool, calm, collected.

Turning away, she fixed her gaze on Tiffany Waterhouse's wedding dress and tried to focus on her priorities: work, work, and work. If she just thought about her business, everything would be fine. It was the mantra that had driven her life for the past eighteen months.

Taking a breath and letting it out, she walked over to her sewing machine. She still had one seam left to stitch, then she would be done.

Grabbing the material, she sat down at her machine and maneuvered the settings to where she wanted them. She felt Matt's eyes on her and looked up. "You can go, you know."

"I'll let her finish eating," he said, sitting down on one of the chairs by her kitchen table.

"Then you'll go?"

"You don't like my company?"

"I have work to do."

"So do it."

"You're staring at me," she said pointedly.

"I've never seen anyone sew before."

Caitlyn raised an eyebrow. "Oh, come on, your mother must have sewed a hem on your pants at one time or another."

He shook his head, a dark look in his eyes. "No."

Matt didn't elaborate, and Caitlyn couldn't bring herself to ask what he so obviously didn't want to share. Besides, she had more important things to worry about, like Tiffany's dress. She was only a few stitches in when a knock came at her door. "That can't be her," she whispered, staring at the door in dismay.

"You going to find out?" Matt asked with a lazy drawl.

"She's not supposed to be here for an hour. What am I going to do?"

"Tell her it's not done."

"You don't understand. She paid extra for the rush job. I promised her it would be done by this morning."

His raised eyebrow told her she must look as wild and worried as she felt. Caitlyn glared at him. "This is all your fault. And that sister of yours. I'd like to give her a piece of my mind."

"Hey, lay off Sarah," Matt said sharply, protectively.

"She left her baby in a hallway, and you're defending her?"

"Sarah left her baby for me."

"Then why are you in *my* apartment?" she cried in frustration as the impatient knock came again. Putting the dress aside, she walked over and opened the door.

"Hello," Tiffany sang out. "I'm here." She walked into the apartment, her face glowing with excitement and love.

Caitlyn hated to see that glow fade, but she had a feeling it would only take a couple of words. "You're an hour early. Your dress isn't ready yet," she burst out.

"But you promised! You said you'd work all night. I gave you a thousand dollars."

Caitlyn cleared her throat. "Something came up."

"More important than my wedding?" Tiffany's face was a picture of shocked hurt.

Caitlyn knew that this spoiled socialite had never once considered that someone or something could be more important than her.

"I'm sure Caitlyn didn't mean it that way," Matt interrupted.

Tiffany's gaze swung to him. "Who are you?"

"A neighbor."

"Well," Tiffany sputtered, her glance lingering on Matt far longer than it should have for a woman about to be married in a few hours.

Caitlyn frowned. Seeing Matt flash a smile in Tiffany's direction made her once again aware of just how ruggedly handsome he was, especially this morning. His just-gotten-out-of-bed look, the ruffled hair, and the muscle T-shirt were enough to put any woman's motor into overdrive. Not that her motor was humming. That wasn't attraction, that was anger, frustration, and not to be confused with any other emotion, she told herself firmly.

"I think this is so unprofessional," Tiffany continued, evidently unwilling to let even Matt's presence foil her hysterics. "I'm going to tell all my friends how disappointed I am in you, and I have a lot of friends. You let me down, Caitlyn."

"I'm sorry," Caitlyn said helplessly as Tiffany began to sniff back tears.

"Why don't you let Caitlyn finish your dress? After all, you're an hour early." Matt patted the seat next to him. "Come and tell me all about your wedding plans and your husband-to-be. You must have a few minutes to spare."

"I guess," she said slowly, softening under Matt's irresistible smile.

"Sure you do. Does your fiancé know how lucky he is to be marrying you?"

Caitlyn's mouth fell open. She wouldn't have figured Matt for charming, but apparently he could be when he wanted to.

"I have to be at Antoines at eight, though," Tiffany said sharply to Caitlyn. "That's why I came early. My hair appointment got moved up, and *no one* is late for Antoine."

Caitlyn nodded. "You'll make it. I just have a little left to do." She sat down in front of her sewing machine and readjusted the fabric. She couldn't quite believe Matt had come to her rescue, but this was hardly the time to ask him why or if he had an ulterior motive. Which he undoubtedly did.

"Is this your daughter?" Tiffany asked Matt.

"My niece. Her name is Emily."

"She's beautiful."

"Would you like to hold her?"

"I would love to, if it's all right with you."

"Sure thing."

All right with him, Caitlyn fumed, as she finished stitching the seam. Matt Winters had a way of enticing every woman he met into taking care of the baby.

"I'm expecting myself," Tiffany said. "I can't wait to have a baby."

Caitlyn forced herself to concentrate on the dress and not on their conversation. Fifteen minutes later, she was done. The dress was fussier than one she would have designed, but it seemed to suit Tiffany and was consistent with her big hair, big diamond ring, and big need to stand out. Still, Caitlyn thought something off the shoulder would have shown off Tiffany's figure. Not that she'd been given the opportunity to offer her suggestions. Like many of the women who visited Devereaux's, Tiffany had wanted a big-name designer gown over anything more personal, and it had been left to Caitlyn to make only basic alterations.

It was probably just as well, Caitlyn thought with a sigh, since she hadn't been able to complete one design in the last eighteen months. Initial response to her first collection three years earlier had begun to fade without any follow-up collections. She had the terrible feeling that if she wasn't a flash in the pan already, she might be soon.

She simply had to get back to her sketch pad, find her creative muse, and rekindle her dreams of her own line, but first she had to get Tiffany on her way.

"It's done." Caitlyn got to her feet and held up the dress for Tiffany to see.

Tiffany put a hand to her mouth in awe. "It's spectacular, isn't it?" she murmured, her voice choked with emotion.

"Not yet, but it will be when you put it on," Caitlyn said softly.

"Do you really think so?" Tiffany asked with a hint of insecurity.

"I know so." This was the part Caitlyn liked best, watching a bride see herself in a dress that captured every last one of her daydreams.

"Do you want to try it on one last time?" Caitlyn asked.

"No, I better not. I don't have the time, and I weighed myself this morning and I've actually lost a pound, so I'm sure it will be fine."

"All right." Caitlyn carefully placed the dress on a hanger and wrapped it in a plastic sheath so it would transport easily.

Tiffany handed Emily back to Matt and took the dress. "Thank you, Caitlyn. I'm sorry that I got crazy before. I'm just nervous about everything being perfect."

Caitlyn simply nodded and smiled and shut the door behind Tiffany with a sigh of relief.

"Do all your customers give you that kind of shit?" Matt asked.

She whirled around, her momentary pleasure fading as she was reminded of why she'd gotten that "shit" in the first place. "All brides are nervous, especially when their gowns aren't done by the morning of the wedding. Now, I'll just pack up Emily's bag and you two can go home."

"Not so fast. I saved your butt just now."

"You want a thank-you—thank you."

"I don't want a thank you. I want a babysitter."

"No way."

"A couple of hours. I need to start some people looking for Sarah, and it would be a lot easier if I didn't have to take Emily with me. Just think, the sooner I do that, the sooner this will be a child-free floor once again."

She had a feeling that arguing would only delay the inevitable. "How long? I have to go into the shop by eleven."

"No problem. I'll be back before you know it."

"That's what you said last night," she reminded him as he handed her the baby.

"And I came back, but . . ." He sent her a slow, lazy smile that completely unsettled her. "Did anyone ever tell you that you look beautiful when you're asleep?"

"I already said I'd baby-sit; don't push it. You better be back by eleven, Matt. No excuses."

He hesitated, a serious expression on his face. "I can trust you, can't I? You won't call the cops on Sarah? You won't start thinking that some social worker would be better for the baby than me?"

Caitlyn could tell from the expression on Matt's face that having to ask such a question pained him, and she wondered what had happened to separate him from his sister.

"Can I count on you, Caitlyn?" he persisted.

She suspected that trust did not come easily to this man, and she found herself wanting to reassure him. "You can count on me. I won't do anything without talking to you first."

His eyes searched hers for a long minute, then apparently reassured by what he'd seen, he said, "Thank you."

When he was gone, Caitlyn let out a breath, suddenly realizing how tense her body had become under Matt's piercing gaze. It occurred to her that no one had studied her with such thoughtfulness in a very long time. She'd have to be careful around this man. He was probably better at uncovering secrets than she was at keeping them. And that could be disastrous.

 *Three*

*A*t half past eleven, Caitlyn realized that Matt Winters's time was obviously different than Pacific Standard Time. In other words, he was late again. Pacing hadn't accomplished anything, so she'd finally packed Emily up, hopped into her car, and prayed she wouldn't get into an accident on the three-mile trip to the shop.

It was amazing how complicated things had become since Matt had knocked on her door. To think she had actually been miffed that she hadn't caught a glimpse of her new neighbor in the six weeks since he'd moved across the hall. Not that she was seeing much of him now, just his baby, his darling, irresistible baby, who was reminding Caitlyn that the future she'd once planned wouldn't happen.

Since she'd banished both her wedding dress and thoughts of happily ever after to the bedroom closet eighteen months ago, Caitlyn had managed to pretend that her life was fine, that she could live without the things she'd always wanted most: a husband, a child. Women did it all the time. They found joy and peace in their work, in their friendships. She could do the same. Only getting caught up in little Emily was putting that resolve into question. Instead of working on new sketches, she had spent the morning watching Emily try to grab her toes with her fingers. So much for staying focused.

She didn't want to get involved with Emily or Matt. She didn't want to think about what her life would have been like if the bottom hadn't fallen out of it. She'd put off thinking about that just about every day of the last year and a half, no mean feat considering she worked in the wedding business and was constantly faced with beaming brides and anxious grooms, eager to begin their own happily ever after. But she'd managed—until now.

Caitlyn parked behind the store, glanced at Emily, sitting so happily in her car seat, and sighed.

"You're going to be a big hit in the store. All those brides dreaming of babies. They'll go crazy." She shook her head. "But it's not that simple, you know. Sometimes life is complicated." She paused, considering the circumstances. "Maybe you do know. After all, you're here with me, probably wondering who the heck I am and where your mother is. I'm wondering the same thing myself, because I don't know how anyone could bear to let you go."

Caitlyn blinked back the annoying moisture in her eyes. "But I will let you go, because you're not mine. You're someone else's baby, and I won't forget that. You and me—we're not going to be friends. So don't get too comfortable, okay? In fact, you can call me Ms. Devereaux. Caitlyn is only for close family friends."

Emily gurgled a half smile and Caitlyn couldn't help but smile back. "All right, you can call me Caitlyn, but that's as close as we're going to get. And no matter how good-looking or desperate your uncle is, I will not let him talk me into any more baby-sitting."

Caitlyn got herself and Emily out of the car. The baby squinted in the morning sunlight, giving a coo of pleasure when the air hit her face. It was a nice day, Caitlyn thought as she walked up the quiet street to Devereaux's. San Francisco in the spring was usually cool and windy, but today the breeze was mild and the clear blue sky dotted with only an occasional puffy white cloud.

Her store was located in Cow Hollow, a neighborhood that had once been rural. But today the streets resembled nothing close to a cow pasture. The blocks were lined with old Victorian houses transformed into shops and cafés along one of San Francisco's most popular shopping streets, Union Street.

Caitlyn still couldn't quite believe she owned her own business. She'd dreamed about designing wedding dresses since she was a little girl. After getting a degree in fashion design, she had worked for several clothing manufacturers, but found herself doing more filing than designing. Finally, a seamstress position with the wedding designer known simply as Annabelle had opened up, and Caitlyn had spent the next three years learning everything she could.

Although she'd enjoyed working for Annabelle, Caitlyn had longed for the opportunity to create her own line of dresses. That's when Jolie had come in. Her cousin, Jolie Palmer, had caught her millionaire husband in the back seat of their Mercedes with a floozy blonde and a pair of pink panties in his hand. Jolie had gone on to divorce her husband and divest him of a good deal of his income. Looking for a new start, Jolie had convinced Caitlyn that this was the perfect time to start their own business, and what better irony than to use her divorce money for a wedding business.

Jolie was a big fan of irony and not at all romantic. She saw the wedding business as a financial gold mine and figured she might as well cash in on all those starry-eyed dreamers while they were still starry-eyed.

Familiar with Caitlyn's lifelong dream, Jolie had suggested a retail wedding shop with racks of gowns from the top designers and a special collection by Caitlyn. Touched by Jolie's incredible belief in her talent, Caitlyn had jumped at the chance to do what she'd always wanted to do, and together they'd opened Devereaux's.

Word of mouth, excellent service, and a booming trend in big weddings had helped them turn a profit the first year. Jolie's practical business savvy and Caitlyn's romantic artistry had made a perfect combination. They'd believed they were on their way—until the accident.

Caitlyn was beginning to realize that she could divide her life into two sections, before the accident and after the accident, before Brian and after Brian, before innocence and after regret.

Before the accident, she'd designed an entire spring collection and had been ready to show it the following January. Then with the accident in December everything had been put on hold. Not only would she not show that collection, she would be unable to complete another design in all the weeks and months that followed. She'd told herself it would happen; she just needed to recover. But the days continued to pass, leaving her with the helpless overwhelming sense that her dream was vanishing.

To her credit, Jolie tried not to nag. "There's always next season," she'd say. And Caitlyn always hoped that next season would be different. That somehow, some way, she would find her passion again, her creativity . . . her soul.

But it probably wouldn't be today, she thought realistically as she switched the car seat from one hand to the other and looked down at Emily.

"Today, we just deal with you," Caitlyn said out loud, knowing even as she said it that Emily was another excuse in a long line of excuses.

Caitlyn could just imagine what Jolie would say when she saw Emily. It would go something like, "Caitlyn, have you lost your freakin' mind?" For Jolie, a thirty-year-old statuesque redhead with an hourglass figure that drove most men to incomprehensible babble, was as blunt as she was honest. She'd grown up with Caitlyn and was used to speaking her mind, even if her opinion wasn't asked for.

Caitlyn opened the front door to Devereaux's and walked up the stairs to her second-floor shop. The bridal salon took up the entire top floor of the Victorian, with bridesmaid, mother of the bride, and flower girl dresses in the front, wedding dresses and three large dressing rooms in the back. In a small alcove on the side, Jolie had also set up an accessory business, with wedding favors, invitations, and a video library featuring local wedding vendors.

Caitlyn smiled at a few of the women browsing through the racks in front and headed directly to the large oak desk by the bay window that overlooked Union Street. Jolie sat behind the desk, adding up receipts on her calculator. She didn't even bother to look up, so Caitlyn set Emily's car seat down on one of the comfortable leather chairs.

"Just a sec," Jolie said.

Caitlyn was happy to wait just a second. Emily was not. She took that moment to open her tiny angel mouth and let out a scream worthy of any horror movie heroine.

Jolie looked up in surprise, her eyes widening when she saw Caitlyn and the baby. "Who is this?"

"This is Emily." Caitlyn reached into the bag for the bottle she'd prepared and put it into Emily's mouth, effectively ending her scream. She'd already learned one thing—when Emily got hungry, she got mad.

Jolie stared at Caitlyn in amazement. "Who does she belong to?"

"My neighbor."

"You live in a no-children-allowed building."

"It was until last night."

"And you're baby-sitting?" Jolie ventured.

"For the moment. Matt was supposed to be back by eleven, but I'm beginning to realize he's habitually late."

Jolie shook her head in bewilderment. "Are you out of your freakin' mind?"

Caitlyn smiled. "I knew you would say that. You are so predictable."

"And you usually are, too. You should know better than to take care of a baby."

"Why?"

"You know what happens to women in their late twenties. The baby clock starts ticking off like a time bomb. Instead of concentrating on your wedding sketches, you'll be dreaming about pink baby booties, and you'll be impossible to live with."

Caitlyn immediately shook her head. "It won't happen to me. I'm focused on the business. You know that."

"So you say," Jolie replied, sending her a suspicious look. "But I remember all those times you made me play house, so this dramatic turn into career woman has me a bit confused. I thought maybe you were just cooling off after Brian and your broken engagement, but . . ." She paused. "You have changed, Caity, and I'm not sure I like it."

Caitlyn shrugged. "Everyone changes, even you. You're not the same girl you were before Mark cheated on you."

"Is that what Brian did to you?"

"I thought you'd decided to stop asking me that question."

"I thought maybe you'd finally tell me. I've been very patient."

Caitlyn adjusted the bottle in Emily's mouth as she started to whimper. "Do you think she's taking in air?"

"How would I know that? Unlike you, I've never been a baby person."

"I wish Matt would come back." Caitlyn checked her watch again. "We'll only get busier as the day goes on."

"Who is Matt again?"

"My neighbor. His sister dropped the baby on his doorstep late last night. It was all very mysterious. And Emily was in trouble, so I helped."

"Emily is his sister?"

"No, Emily is her," Caitlyn tipped her head toward the baby. "Sarah is his sister."

"Sarah? I'm totally confused now."

"Bottom line, Matt didn't know what to do with a baby. It was after midnight, and Emily needed someone to take care of her, so I decided to help. She is beautiful, isn't she? Sweet innocent perfection."

"Speaking of perfection, your mother called this morning. You weren't here, so she gave me an earful."

"Really? Why?" Caitlyn felt her whole body tighten at the mention of her mother.

"She feels it's time you pull your head out of the sand and get on with your life."

Caitlyn sighed. That sounded familiar. Her mother, Marilyn Devereaux, a brilliant professor of mathematics, had never been one to let the grass grow under her feet—or under Caitlyn's feet, for that matter. When Marilyn saw something that needed to be fixed, she fixed it. It was probably one reason why she was an excellent mathematician: every equation in her life added up.

While Marilyn's motives were always born out of love, Caitlyn bore the scars from most of those so-called repairs. Memories of the summer vacation her mother had sent her on, which had turned out to be a fat camp, reminded Caitlyn of just how far her mother's obsession with fixing could go.

"You don't have to say anything more," Caitlyn said.

"Brian," Jolie said anyway. "Have you checked the calendar lately? His fellowship ended last week. He's back, Caitlyn."

"Are you sure? I thought he might stay in Boston." Actually, she'd been *hoping* he'd stay in Boston, because dealing with Brian, dealing with everything that went with Brian, made her very uncomfortable.

"Nope. He called your mother last night looking for you. He was very surprised you had moved out of your parents' house. Your mother gave him your phone number, by the way. Is that all right with you?"

"I don't know," Caitlyn said helplessly, not sure how she felt about Brian anymore, not sure how she should feel. He'd been a friend, a lover, a fiancé, and now he was . . . she didn't know what he was.

"Well, you better figure it out fast, because I think she gave him your address, too. He wants to see you." Jolie cleared her throat. "Apparently he wants to get your relationship back on track."

Caitlyn sank down on the empty chair in front of the desk and adjusted the bottle in Emily's mouth, grateful to have something to do so she wouldn't have to look into Jolie's inquisitive eyes. "He's been gone over a year. How can he possibly think that he can come back and we'll just take up where we left off?"

"I have no idea what Brian thinks. For that matter, I have no idea what you think," Jolie said pointedly. "The only thing I do know is what your mother told me. Your parents are *very* excited to welcome him home, and they're interested in having him work with them at the university. He is the son they never had, and if you think they aren't hoping you'll get back together, you are sorely mistaken. They want you and Brian, love and marriage, and the baby carriage. You know how the song goes."

"Well, I'm not singing that song."

"Because?"

"Because I'm not," Caitlyn said firmly.

"You know you can shut me up with that, but your mother won't give up so easily."

"Why can't she just let me live my own life?" Caitlyn complained.

"Because she doesn't think you're doing a very good job." Jolie leaned forward, waiting until Caitlyn looked at her. "I'm surprised she gave you this much time. And we both know that while you may have moved out of your parents' house, you haven't completely moved on."

"I'm trying."

"Are you? Because there is that little matter of your blank sketch pad."

"That has nothing to do with Brian. I'm an artist. I can't create on demand."

"You can't create at all . . . and I'm not asking you to tell me why," she added quickly as Caitlyn tried to interrupt. "I'm just worried about you. I know the accident set you back, but it was months ago, and something is still wrong. I want to help. I wish you'd let me."

Caitlyn wished she could, too. But some things were too private, too painful. She took the bottle out of Emily's mouth and pulled her out of the car seat so she could burp her. When she glanced back at her cousin, she saw Jolie shaking her head in disbelief. "What?" Caitlyn asked.

"Career woman? Yeah, right. Look at you, you're in heaven."

"I'm baby-sitting," she said defensively.

"Sure you are." Jolie got to her feet. "I'm going to sell some dresses while you take care of someone else's baby. Now, do you see anything wrong with this picture, Miss Career Woman?"

"It's just for today, a few hours."

"Tick, tock, tick, tock."

"It's not like that."

"Maybe it's a good thing Brian is back. Maybe it's time you looked at some of the choices you're making, because it's been months since I've seen you so content. Holding a baby is definitely a good look for you. As your business partner, I'm not encouraging it. But as your cousin and your friend, I have to admit that—"

"Don't say it. Emily is just temporary. Tomorrow I'll be a career woman again, I promise."

Caitlyn sighed as Jolie walked away. She couldn't believe Brian was back in town. She wasn't ready to see him, to look toward the future, to make decisions. She'd been comfortable in her safe, secure, bland life of the past year. Now, she felt suddenly overwhelmed, and as she looked down at Emily, she wondered if Sarah had felt the same way. Had Sarah been so burdened with motherhood that she'd simply run away from it? Because Caitlyn could understand that desperate need to flee. She felt it right now, so much so that her toes were tingling.

She looked up as the door opened and Matt walked in. Wearing worn blue jeans, a brown aviator jacket, and a pair of dark sunglasses, he looked stunningly male. So much for bland. This man was anything but.

"It's about time," she said, deciding her rapidly beating pulse had to be due to anger and not, not, God forbid, attraction, because she certainly wasn't in the market for any spine-tingling, palm-sweating moments. She had enough problems.

Matt walked over to her. "I went to your apartment, but you'd already left."

"Thirty minutes after you were supposed to come back," she reminded him.

"I got hung up."

"Did you find your sister?"

"Not yet." He took off his glasses, and the worry in his eyes stopped her from giving him a harder time. It was obvious he was concerned about Sarah, and she could respect that.

"Maybe she'll call or come by," Caitlyn said. "You should be home just in case. I'm sure she won't leave Emily with you for long."

"I'd like to believe that. But I don't know Sarah anymore. She was a little girl when I saw her last."

Caitlyn hesitated to press for more information, but she desperately wanted to understand. "May I ask what happened to your parents?"

"My father died right after Sarah was born. Some

years later there was a fire. My mother disappeared, and my sister and I were sent to foster care."

"That sounds like the short version."

He shrugged. "It's what happened."

"I'm sorry." She couldn't imagine the horror of being abandoned. Not that she wouldn't mind a bit more distance from her own family, but not total abandonment. "Your mother just disappeared? Why?"

"I don't think she wanted to be a mother," Matt said, surprising her with more information. "I guess she tried—sometimes." He stared out the window, lost in thoughts that turned his face to stone. "Maybe Sarah turned out just like her," he murmured. "Maybe she isn't coming back for her baby either."

"Don't say that. It's not like Sarah left Emily on a street corner. She left her with you." Caitlyn didn't know why she was trying to make Matt feel better, except that he seemed to need it. And making people feel better was ingrained in her. It was the way she compensated for her shortcomings, the way she drew positive attention to herself instead of negative. When people were happy, they were usually less critical, a truth she'd learned from living with the high expectations of her family.

"At any rate, I have a private investigator looking for Sarah," Matt continued, turning to face her. "Now that we know she's somewhere in the city, we should be able to find her. I guess I'll take Emily back to the apartment and wait." He shook his head with impatience. "I hate waiting."

"Emily will keep you company."

Matt sent her a doubtful look. "I hope she doesn't start screaming again. Will you come by when you're done here?"

Caitlyn hesitated. "Uh, I don't know."

"Please. I don't know anything about babies. And I don't want to do something wrong or hurt her in any way." He paused, looking into her eyes with a hopeful expression. "I only moved to town a couple of months ago, so there's no one else to call. I don't really have any friends. . . ."

"Yeah, yeah, you're breaking my heart," she said dryly. "I should tell you, Matt, that I've been manipulated by the best, so I can pretty much recognize a sob story when I hear one."

"I would appreciate your help. This isn't an area I know how to control."

And she had a feeling there wasn't much else in his life he didn't control down to the last detail. "You're pretty good at getting what you want, aren't you?"

"That depends on your answer," he said, turning on the killer smile he'd used on Tiffany earlier.

If Caitlyn had any sense, she'd say no. Just say no, she told herself. It's an easy word, just spit it out. But with Emily looking at her with her big brown eyes and Matt looking at her with his big brown eyes, she was completely lost.

"I'll come by," she said. "For a few minutes, just to check on you. But no disappearing on me."

"Deal."

She handed Matt the baby, who didn't seem to mind cuddling up on Matt's strong shoulder. Emily apparently sensed that he was one of the good guys. And something inside of Caitlyn told her the same thing. She put a hand on his arm, and the heat between them suddenly seemed to sizzle.

He looked into her eyes, and she felt her stomach clench. She'd meant to offer him a gesture of comfort, but instead the touch had created an awareness between them, a connection, a sexual attraction. Oh, Lord. Another complication! She dropped her hand from his arm. "You better go," she said abruptly.

He stared into her eyes as if he were seeing her for the first time. "Yeah," he said somewhat gruffly as he bent over to put Emily in her car seat. He awkwardly fiddled with the straps as she began to squirm. "Shit. Can't she just sit still?"

"You have to show her who's the boss."

He rolled his eyes as he looked up at Caitlyn. "I think we both know she's the boss."

"Maybe. By the way, I almost ran into Mrs. Pederman on my way out this morning. I had to hide in the laundry room so she wouldn't see the baby."

"Mrs. Pederman?"

"The nosy old lady who lives by the elevator and asks who you are every time you walk in the front door."

"Oh, her."

"She takes a nap between one and three every day, so you should be okay, but maybe you should leave the car seat in the car and—"

"And do what, smuggle her in under my jacket?"

"I don't know; you're the investigative reporter. Figure something out. But whatever you do, don't let her see the baby or we'll both be in trouble. I do not want to lose my apartment."

He frowned. "This isn't going to work."

"It will if Sarah comes back today."

"*If* being the operative word. The women in my family have a history of disappearing."

"She said she'd be in touch. Have some faith."

"I'm trying, but I don't have a good feeling about this."

Neither did Caitlyn, but she hoped she was wrong, because getting Matt and Emily out of her life as soon as possible suddenly seemed desperately important.

The Reverend Jonathan Mitchell stared down at the broken glass. The small window by the back door of the church had once again been broken, the third time this month. He hated to give in to cynicism, to hopelessness, but even he could take only so much without losing patience. He might be a minister, but he was also a man.

Pauline Evans, the church secretary, an African American woman in her mid-fifties, clucked disapprovingly as she saw the damage. "I think it's time to put a board over that window," she said.

"It's bad enough we have to lock the church at night. If we start boarding up all the windows, we might as well lock God into a safety-deposit box."

"It's just another homeless person looking for a warm place to sleep," Pauline replied. "Or a runaway."

"But if they come here, maybe they're not just running away, maybe they're running to something."

Her stern expression softened. "I know there's always hope, but honestly, Jonathan, I think sometimes you're too optimistic. You have to face facts. There isn't enough money in the church budget to keep replacing broken windows."

"Then maybe we should just unlock the door," he said with a smile.

She shook her head. "And what will they do to the inside of the church, to our sanctuary?"

"But that's just the point, it isn't our sanctuary, it belongs to everyone."

"You're young, you'll change your mind. The Reverend Wallace locked this church up twenty years ago, and it's the only reason it's in as good a condition as it is."

Jonathan was tiring of the constant references to Reverend Wallace, whose place he had taken a year earlier when the good minister had finally decided to retire at seventy-nine. At thirty-three, Jonathan was much younger, and he knew he had a lot to learn, but he also knew he had a lot to give, if he could just figure out the best way to give it.

"You know the church board will use this broken window as one more reason to close the church," Pauline pointed out.

He sighed, knowing she was right. With the neighborhood deteriorating around them and the low attendance at Sunday services, there was growing pressure to close the church and sell the land for a profit that could be used at other churches within the ministry.

Jonathan didn't want to see his ministry closed. The people in the community needed the church; he just had to make them realize that. Sometimes the task ahead of him seemed impossible. Maybe if he was a different kind of preacher, more like his father, with fire and brimstone and passion in every word, he'd draw in the masses. But he wasn't his father, and he had to stop making the comparison, even if he couldn't stop others within the religious world from making it.

Just the other day one of the board members had suggested he ask his father to visit, to come in and preach a sermon that would have the rafters shaking with the force of his personality, with the passion of God's word delivered in a way that only William Mitchell could deliver.

But Jonathan didn't want to ask for his father's help, didn't want to admit that he needed the help. It was selfish on his part, and he prayed for forgiveness every night. He wanted to make it on his own. He wanted to find his own way to serve God, not just follow in his father's overly large footsteps.

"Why don't you call someone to fix the window?" he suggested to Pauline, forcing himself to concentrate on the task at hand.

"Are you sure you don't want me to go inside with you? Lord only knows who's in there."

"That's exactly true, Pauline. The Lord knows. That's why I'm not worried about going in by myself." Jonathan smiled at Pauline's disapproval of his sometimes irreverent humor. Ah, well, they'd figure out a way to work together. Because deep down they both wanted the same thing.

As Pauline left to call for a window replacement, Jonathan let himself into the church. All was quiet, nothing out of place, nothing damaged. His practiced eye noted all the details at the altar, then he walked down the center aisle, looking into each pew. It wasn't until he came to the last one that he saw her—fast asleep.

She looked like a tiny broken bird, a raven—with straight black hair down to her waist, pale white skin, small bones, old clothes that hung big on her frame. She shifted on the bench, obviously uncomfortable. It was then he caught sight of her face, her swollen cheek, black eye, cut lip. Each wound made his fingers clench tighter in his fist.

Someone had hurt this beautiful creature and hurt her badly. His gaze traveled down to her hand, to the sharp jagged cuts that could have been made only by shattered glass. He'd found his trespasser. Was she just another down-on-her-luck story or was she something more?

He caught his breath as her eyelids flickered and slowly opened to reveal eyes as dark and as deep as a starless sky. She saw him watching her and sat up abruptly.

"Are you all right?" he asked quietly.

"I'm leaving now. You don't have to call the cops." She tried to stand up, but swayed, then sat back down. "I feel a little dizzy."

"What's your name?"

"Why?"

He smiled gently. "Maybe I can help you. But first you have to tell me your name."

She hesitated for a long, long moment. "Sarah. My name is Sarah."

Four

"Sarah." Jonathan offered her a gentle smile. "It's nice to meet you. I'm Jonathan Mitchell, and this is my church."

"You're the minister?" she asked uncertainly.

"That's right."

She licked her swollen lip, drawing his attention once again to her injuries. He instinctively raised a hand to her face, and she flinched as if he were about to strike her.

"I won't hurt you," he said quickly.

She didn't look like she believed him. Nor did she appear to have any reason to believe him. For someone had definitely hurt her and broken whatever trust she'd had. Sarah looked past him, her gaze darting to the door, seeing her escape route, her way out, but he couldn't let her go, not in her condition.

"Let me help you, Sarah."

Her mouth trembled, but she didn't speak; she simply shook her head.

"Please?"

"It's too late," she said in a breathy whisper, as if she were afraid to say the words too loudly.

"If it were too late, I don't think you'd be here now. I think you came to church looking for something. Maybe you found it."

Her dark eyes clung to his for a long moment, a glimmer of something in their dark depths. Then she glanced away. "I was cold. That's all. I saw the broken window, and I thought I'd be gone before you found me."

"So you didn't break the window?"

"I'm not a thief."

"That's not what I asked you." He wondered then if his pity was misplaced. Had he been taken in by what looked like innocence but was nothing more than practiced ingenuity? For surely she was lying. There was blood on the floor from where she'd cut her hand.

Sarah tried to stand up but swayed once again, and Jonathan grabbed her arm to steady her.

"Ow," she said, grimacing with pain. He looked down at her arm and after a second's hesitation pulled the sleeve of her sweater up until he could see the dark purple bruising on her forearm. At least there were no needle tracks.

She pulled away from him, pushing her sleeve back down.

"Let me help you, Sarah. I've got a house next door, a bathroom where you can clean up, and we can wash some of those cuts on your face."

"I can't tell you anything. I won't," she warned him.

"I wasn't going to ask—yet."

As they faced off, Pauline came into the church, brandishing a large wooden broom in one hand. She lowered it when she saw it was just the two of them.

"You were gone so long, I thought maybe there was trouble." Her voice faded as she took in Sarah's condition. "Oh, my, someone did a real number on you, didn't they?"

"This is Sarah. She's coming next door to get cleaned up," Jonathan said.

"I'll call—"

"No," he said, cutting her off.

She raised an eyebrow. "No?"

"Not yet." He sent her a silent plea to let him play this one his way. There would be time to call in the appropriate social services, but right now he wanted to ease some of Sarah's pain. He wouldn't be able to do that if she tried to run. And there was no doubt in his mind that she would run.

"All right," Pauline murmured reluctantly. "You come with me, and we'll get you fixed up. Maybe some food, too? Are you hungry?"

Pauline moved forward, then stopped, her gaze suddenly fixed on Sarah's chest. Sarah placed a defensive hand over her breast, but it was too late.

"Oh, honey." Pauline shook her head, her eyes worried. "Where's your baby?"

Jonathan realized then that Sarah's shirt was wet, stained with milk.

"Sarah?" he questioned. "Do you have a baby?"

"No. I don't have a baby," she said flatly. "Not anymore." She broke away from both of them, startling Jonathan with her quickness. One second she was there, barely able to stand, and the next she was disappearing through the door.

He finally got his feet to move and rushed after her. He caught a glimpse of her as she turned the corner in front of the church, but by the time he reached the same corner she was gone. He turned and walked slowly back to the church.

Pauline met him on the sidewalk. "She's in trouble."

"It looks that way."

"You should have called the cops as soon as you found her."

"So they could throw her in jail?"

"Maybe she should be in jail. Because that girl had herself a baby and not too long ago. So where is it?"

"It could be any number of places, all legal."

"Or not." Pauline looked at him through troubled eyes. "They found a baby in a Dumpster by Golden Gate Park, barely alive, just last week."

Jonathan's gut told him it couldn't have been this woman who'd left her baby in a trash can. She hadn't seemed defiant, only hurt. Then again, maybe she'd felt she had no way out.

"You should call the police, Jonathan."

"I will report the break-in, Pauline."

"You know that's not all you should report."

"Someone hurt that girl badly." He found his fingers curling into fists, which disturbed him, for violence was not supposed to be a part of his nature. Yet there were times like this when his civilized Godly demeanor wore thin. He hadn't always been a man of the cloth. He'd once been just a man.

Pauline studied him with the wisdom of her years. "I know you're the reverend, and I'm the secretary, but I've seen some things in my life. You can help a lot more people if you stay on top of the cliff throwing down ropes, rather than climbing down into a hole to save one soul and maybe never coming back."

Jonathan looked down the empty street, knowing that Pauline was probably right.

"Anyway, I don't think she'll be back," Pauline said, turning toward the small house next door to the church where he resided and where the church office was located.

"I hope you're wrong," he said.

She stopped and looked at him. "I'd like to believe that girl hasn't gone and run herself right back to the man who beat her up. But I'm not sure I'd be right. I just hope . . ."

"What?"

"I pray that baby of hers doesn't bear the same scars."

"I pray that, too," he murmured heavily. But this time he wanted to do more than just pray.

It was past six when Caitlyn finished work. After a long day of anxious brides and controlling mothers, she was more than ready for a quiet evening at home. But as she walked down the hallway to her apartment, she was reminded of Matt's plea for her help.

She hesitated outside his door, listening for Emily's cry. All was quiet. Well, as long as she wasn't crying, Matt didn't need her help, which was a good thing. She didn't need to get further involved in their problems, she had enough of her own.

And she was determined to pick up her sketch pad tonight and try to draw something. Besides, it wasn't as if Matt had made any attempts to get to know her before Emily's arrival. He had wanted to be a silent neighbor, and that's the way she preferred it, too. Why let Emily's arrival change their relationship? It was better this way. The whole situation had heartbreak written all over it. And Caitlyn wasn't about to let a handsome reporter and his mysterious sister drag her to a place she didn't want to go.

Deliberately, she turned toward her apartment and slid her key into the lock. She had barely touched the knob when Matt's door flew open. His hair stood on end, as if he'd raked his fingers through it a dozen or more times, and his eyes had a wild look in them.

"Where are you going?" he demanded.

"Into my apartment."

"You said you'd help."

"I don't hear Emily crying."

"That's because she cried herself to sleep," he said, waving his hand in the air. "She screamed every second of the last two and a half hours. Her face turned purple. I thought for a minute she had killed herself when she finally fell asleep."

Caitlyn tried not to smile, because in truth, a desperate, barefoot Matt Winters was pretty irresistible. "Well, she's asleep now. You should try to get some rest, too."

"You can't leave me alone with her."

"I think I can."

Matt grabbed her arm, his eyes filled with desperation. "I'm going crazy, Caitlyn. She hates me. Nothing I do is right. She hates the way I hold her, the way I talk to her, the way I feed her. I'm doing everything wrong. You have to help me."

"I'm sure she just misses her mother. It's not you."

"It is me. I was never good with babies. Kids that can talk are okay, but babies are like little aliens to me."

She felt herself weakening. "I can't. It's been a long day, and I'm tired," she said, removing her arm from his grip. There—she'd done it. She'd said no.

"I'll make you dinner." He snapped his fingers, a new light in his eyes now, one of determination. "Or I'll order out. That would probably be safer for your stomach. I'm not much of a cook. And we can have some wine. Do you like red or white?"

"White, but that doesn't matter. I'd like to help you, but I—"

"But what?"

"It's too hard," she said helplessly, knowing he wouldn't begin to understand and she couldn't begin to explain.

"I know it's hard. That's why I need your help," he said, misunderstanding her reluctance. "I've been playing music to cover up her crying, but I'm afraid if she keeps on screaming, someone in the building will come looking for a baby, and then what will we do?"

"We?" she asked pointedly. "I don't think it's our problem, I think it's your problem."

"If you want to split hairs," he said with a shrug.

"I'm hardly splitting hairs. She's your niece."

Before he could reply, Emily let out a glass-breaking shriek from inside the apartment.

"See," Matt said. "She's awake and mad. I think she needs a woman's touch, something soft and gentle. Like you."

Matt looked into her eyes, and Caitlyn felt the breath flee her chest again. He was really, really good at getting past her defenses, and he didn't even know it. So intent was he on securing some help that he had no idea he was affecting her in a basic man/woman way that reminded her this situation was dangerous on many different levels.

Before Caitlyn could offer up another protest, Matt pulled her into his apartment. Emily sat in her car seat on the floor by the couch. And it was her tiny, puckered, angry face that drew Caitlyn to her side. Undoing the straps, Caitlyn picked Emily up and cradled her instinctively against her chest.

Emily's tiny mouth turned immediately toward Caitlyn's breast, seeking nourishment, love, nothing that Caitlyn could give her, and that tiny gesture almost broke Caitlyn's heart.

"Get me a bottle," she ordered Matt. "Do it now."

Matt stared at her, then moved into the kitchen, where she heard him running water and hitting the buttons on the microwave.

"It's okay, baby," she whispered. "Your food is coming."

Emily whimpered and squirmed and grabbed Caitlyn's hair. Her little fingers tugged at the strands so tightly tears came into Caitlyn's eyes. But at least this pain was real and not the phantom that haunted her dreams.

"Here you go," Matt said, returning to the room with a bottle.

She put the nipple into Emily's mouth and the baby sucked greedily. Caitlyn sat down on the couch so she could make Emily more comfortable.

"Are you crying, Caitlyn?" Matt asked.

She shrugged off his question as she blinked the telltale moisture out of her eyes. The man saw too much. "Emily pulled my hair. It's nothing."

"Are you sure?"

"Yes."

"Look at me."

She didn't want to; she really didn't want to. But the silence between them lengthened and she found herself lifting her head and gazing into his eyes. They were perceptive eyes, shrewd, seeing right into her, and she didn't like it one little bit. "You must be a good reporter," she murmured.

"Why do you say that?"

"Because I find myself wanting to confess, and you don't even have a lightbulb over my head."

"Confess what?"

"Nothing," she said hastily. "I said I had the urge to confess, not that I had something to confess."

"But you do."

"No, I don't. You're the one with the secrets." She hoped to turn his attention away from her.

"And you're trying to redirect. I applaud your technique."

"Did you find out anything about your sister?" she asked, ignoring his perceptive comment. She had to keep her distance, and sharing secrets with him wouldn't accomplish that.

"Nothing yet. I wish I had more to go on, a description, a picture of what she might look like now."

"Maybe like you?"

"More like my mother than me probably. I took after my father. Sarah's hair was darker than mine, black as ink. She used to wear it so long she could sit on it. And her eyes were black, too. They always seemed big for her face. Or maybe it just looked that way because her skin was so white. She bruised easily. One touch and she'd have a purple mark for a week." He paused, obviously caught up in his thoughts. "Sarah was a scrawny kid, her ribs always poking through her shirt. I knew she needed more to eat, but I couldn't always get it."

"And your mother wasn't around?"

"Not much. She was a mess most of the time. Hell, why am I telling you all this?"

"Maybe it's easier to tell a stranger."

"I was hoping you'd stay a stranger," he said bluntly. "I'm not much for nosy neighbors."

"Have I acted like a nosy neighbor?"

"Well, not until about five minutes ago, when you started giving me the third degree."

"Because you pulled me into your apartment," she reminded him.

"You're right." He sat down in the chair across from her, resting his elbows on his knees as he watched Emily suck on her bottle. "A neighbor used to call the cops on us. Mrs. Malkovich. She was a mean old woman, used to chain-smoke in the hallway until you couldn't see past your nose. I'd have to lie, make up some story about where my mother was, and hope she'd come back before they did. It worked, too, until the fire, until we had nowhere to go. Then Mrs. Malkovich got even by telling everyone that our mother was never coming back. The next thing I knew we were put into separate foster homes. They wouldn't even let us stay together."

"How old were you?"

"Sixteen. And Sarah was nine."

"Did your mother ever come back?"

"No." Matt stood up and paced around the apartment. "I have to find Sarah. I've looked a hundred times over the years, but the records were sealed, locked away for our own protection, or so they said. As if I needed to be protected from the only person who ever gave a shit about me."

"I'm sorry, Matt. That's so horribly unfair."

He shrugged. "Whoever told you life was fair?"

"What happened to you after they split you up?"

"I went to a foster home for a few months, then another and another. I was mad at the world. No one wanted a part of me. On my eighteenth birthday I was told to get out and move on."

"What did you do then?"

"You're certainly full of questions."

"Just passing the time, unless you'd like me to leave you with Emily?" she asked pointedly.

"No, you just sit there and relax," he told her hastily. "I hung around San Francisco for a while, picked up odd jobs, eventually moved around the country, got into the newspaper business."

She waited for him to embellish, but he remained frustratingly silent. "Just out of curiosity, do you write in more depth than you speak?"

His mouth curved into a reluctant smile. "When I'm not talking about myself, I can be quite articulate."

"Thank heavens." She glanced down at the baby in her arms. "Tell me more about Sarah."

"It was so long ago."

"You must remember something."

Matt thought for a moment. "Angels. She used to see them dancing on her ceiling at night. I didn't want to tell her it was just the streetlight throwing shadows." He paused, lost in thought. "People always say you can't miss what you don't have, but I think Sarah always missed it. She'd get this yearning look on her face, as if she were trying to see something that wasn't there. She kept wanting to light candles to make things brighter. She was a sad little girl. That's what I remember about her most. I remember her being sad." He took in a deep breath and let it out. "I have a feeling she's still sad."

Caitlyn nodded, her own emotions stirred by the pain in his words. It didn't sound like Sarah had had much to smile about in her life, Matt either, at least not during their childhood. "What was your dad like? Was he as bad as your mother?"

"No. He was a pretty good guy," Matt replied, a rough edge in his voice. "He kept my mother sane, I think. He was a cook at a restaurant on Fisherman's Wharf, and even after a long day he'd come home and cook for us. When he died, my mother fell apart. Sarah was just a baby, but that wasn't enough to pull my mother together. She took sleeping pills and pain pills and God knows what other kind of pills and drank 'em down with a shot of whiskey." He paused, looking Caitlyn in the eye. "I kept thinking she'd change, get better, but it never happened. I was a fool."

"You were a child," Caitlyn replied.

"It doesn't matter anyway. What really worries me now is Sarah," he continued. "What if she turned out like my mother? What if she's cut and run on her kid the way my mother did to us?"

"She said she'd be back."

"I've heard that before. I've learned to take promises with a grain of salt."

"That's sad."

He shrugged. "I think it's practical."

"What if Sarah doesn't come back? What will you do with Emily?" The question slipped out before Caitlyn could stop it. It was none of her business what Matt did with this baby. In fact, she was supposed to be pulling away, not digging in deeper, but despite his bluntness, or maybe it was because of his bluntness, he was easy to talk to, and different from most of the men she'd met in her life, men like Brian, who always spoke from some elite intellectual plane.

"I don't know," he answered. "I hope it doesn't come to that. I'm not exactly a family man. I work long hours. I travel . . ." His voice drifted off as he seemed to consider her question even further. "I'm not sure I'd be a good father. I screwed up with Sarah."

"You weren't her father. You were a sixteen-year-old boy."

"Yeah, well, hopefully Sarah will come back and it will be a moot question."

"I think you'd be a good father, Matt. You've done pretty well so far."

"Why do you say that? Because she's still breathing?" He smiled. "That might just be luck. And you've been pretty helpful."

"That's true. But Emily is just a little baby. She doesn't need much more than something to eat and someone to love her." Caitlyn looked around the barely furnished apartment. "Which is probably a good thing in your case."

"I haven't had time to get settled yet."

"Do you ever get settled? Or do you just move on?"

"Most of the time I move on," he said with a small nod at her perceptive statement. "I've always traveled light. It's easier that way."

From what she'd heard of his past she could understand his thinking. But there was something about the way Matt was looking at Emily that told Caitlyn he might have just found a very good reason to acquire some baggage. Because she couldn't believe that a man who cared so much about his missing sister would abandon his niece to strangers no matter what he said.

"Hey, are you hungry?" he asked. "Because I'm starving. Do you want to share a pizza?"

"That sounds a little too neighborly for me."

He flung her a grin. "Yeah, I know. But since you're feeding Emily, the least I can do is feed you."

Caitlyn hesitated. It was tempting, too tempting, because she wasn't just liking Emily, she was starting to like Matt, too, and that was even more dangerous.

"I don't think so," she said firmly. "In fact, you should take Emily now and finish this feeding." She stood up and handed Emily to Matt, bottle and all.

He reluctantly took Emily, adjusting the bottle in her

mouth as she started to squirm. "Was it something I said?"

"I have things to do."

"Well, this certainly isn't your problem. I can't blame you for wanting to get on with your life."

Exactly. Only when he said it like that, Caitlyn felt guilty. She hated to let anyone down, an unfortunate trait ingrained in her by her mother and father, who had always expected and demanded so much from her.

"I'm not going to feel bad," she said out loud.

He raised an eyebrow. "Did I say you should?"

"You're very good at the subtle implication."

He laughed at that. "No one has ever called me subtle."

She couldn't help but respond to the sexy grin that spread across his face. On the surface he was such a dark man, in features and in expression. But when the smile broke out, his whole face changed, softened, and was incredibly appealing. He wasn't for her, she told herself firmly. And she wasn't right for him. He was a man who needed love and family in his future to make up for all he'd missed out on in his past, and she was concentrating on her work now, leaving love behind and everything that went with it.

"I'm leaving now," she said.

"You said that before, but you haven't quite reached the door."

Caitlyn deliberately walked over to the door and opened it. "Better?"

"No." His dark gaze held hers in a connection that was far too strong. He wasn't touching her, but he was pulling her in all the same, something in him calling out to something in her. It was more than attraction, more than simple desire, more like a deep aching need, and it scared her. How could she suddenly feel so much for someone she had just met? Someone who was completely wrong for her in so many ways? Was it just chemistry? Hormones? Or something more? She'd been touched by his story. Maybe that was it. She felt sorry for him.

But no, that didn't ring true either; Matt wasn't a man to feel sorry for. He'd pulled himself up out of the gutter and made something wonderful. He was smart, handsome, funny, sexy. No, she didn't feel pity, not one little bit. She only wished she did. That would be a much easier emotion to deal with.

"Caitlyn?" His voice held the same question.

"I have to go," she said softly. "Let me."

His gaze didn't waver for a long, searching moment. "Sure, go. I'll see you around sometime."

She grabbed on to his casual note as if it were a lifeline. "Yeah, I'll see you around."

As she opened the door and stepped into the hallway she saw a man get off the elevator. Her first instinct was to hide, and she dashed back into Matt's apartment just as her name rang through the hall.

Dear Lord, it couldn't be Brian, not now, not at this moment, when she was already feeling confused. But she could hear his steps moving impatiently down the hall. That was Brian, impatient, purposeful, and apparently back in town.

"What's going on?" Matt asked.

Caitlyn couldn't answer. She wasn't ready to see Brian. She'd sent him away eighteen months ago, but now it seemed like only a minute had passed. "I—I . . ." She turned her head as Brian called her name once again. Obviously he'd seen her dash into Matt's apartment. Darn.

"I think someone is looking for you," Matt said. When she didn't move, he walked over and opened the door.

Brian stood in the hallway looking confused.

"Caitlyn?"

Both men said her name at exactly the same time. Caitlyn was caught between them, foolishly wishing Emily might cry and distract Matt at least, but the baby was still cradled in Matt's arms, blissfully sucking on her bottle.

"Hello, Brian," she said, finally looking into the face of the man she had once hoped to marry. He hadn't changed at all, still tall and lean, sandy brown hair cut just above his collar, and a neat beard to match. He wore tan trousers and a cream-colored sweater vest over a knit shirt, looking very much like the intellectual he was.

"Caitlyn," he said again. "I hope this isn't a bad time."

"You might have called first."

"I did call." He cleared his throat somewhat awkwardly. "When you didn't call me back, I thought I'd come over. Your mother said you'd made some changes in your life."

"I—I have," she replied.

Brian's gaze drifted to Matt, who was unabashedly listening to their conversation. Suddenly, he turned pale, a disbelieving light coming into his eyes as he looked back to her. "My God, Cait, is *he* the change your mother was talking about? And is that—is that your baby?"

 *Five*

Brian's question knocked the breath right out of Caitlyn's chest. How could he think that she could have gone from him to another man so quickly and had a baby . . . it was unbelievable, unthinkable.

"How could you even ask me that?" she demanded. "Do you remember what I looked like when you left? Do you?"

Brian stared back at her for a long minute. "Sorry," he muttered, pressing a hand to his temple as if he had a throbbing headache. "I don't usually jump to conclusions. I just don't know what to think."

"This is my neighbor, Matt Winters," she said tightly. "And his niece, Emily. This is Brian Hastings."

Matt looked at them both with a speculative gleam in his eyes. His reporter instincts obviously sensed a story, but Caitlyn had no intention of sharing this one with him.

"Nice to meet you," Brian said.

"Yeah," Matt replied.

"Can we talk, Caitlyn?" Brian asked. "In private?"

Oh, how she'd love to say no, that she was too busy right now, that it would have to wait until tomorrow or next week or next year, because she still didn't know what to say. Unfortunately, she didn't think she could put him off. He had that look in his eyes, the one he wore when he was determined to find the correct answer.

"All right." She walked across the hall and opened the door to her apartment. As Brian walked inside, she glanced back at Matt. "I can see why you don't like nosy neighbors."

"Who is that guy?"

"None of your business."

"Do you want me to stick around?"

"I'm fine."

"Are you sure? A minute ago you looked like you wanted to find a dark hole to hide in."

"I'm okay." And with that, she took a deep breath and shut the door, leaving her with one problem instead of two.

Brian stood in the middle of her apartment, looking dazed by the feminine surroundings and bridal accessories. "Well," he said. "It's different."

"I've been swamped with alterations," she explained. "This is the big wedding season. Everyone wants to be a June bride." She cleared her throat, wondering why she was talking about weddings with her former fiancé.

"Why didn't you stay with your parents? I thought it was easier for you to concentrate on business when you lived there."

"I'm twenty-eight, a little old to be living with my parents." She could have told him that after the accident it wasn't just physical space she had craved, but emotional space as well. But that would only open up the can of worms called their past that much sooner.

Brian didn't seem to know what to say.

During the ensuing quiet, Caitlyn looked at him, really looked at him for the first time, and saw the familiar features, the errant curl by his ear, the shoulders upon which she had once rested her head, the arms that had held her so close. It was good to see him. It was disturbing, too. It had been far easier to keep her emotions at bay when he was living on the other side of the country.

Brian looked back at her with the same curiosity in his eyes, but there was a wariness there as well, a cautiousness that she didn't remember being a part of his personality, at least not with her. He'd always been the take-charge one in their relationship, so smart about everything, so certain of what they should and shouldn't do that it had seemed natural to follow his lead. But that had been before the accident, and she'd changed in so many ways since then.

"So," he continued. "My fellowship ended last week. I must say it's good to be home."

She nodded. "The time went quickly."

"In some ways. You look wonderful, Caitlyn." He offered her a tentative smile. "Not even a limp?"

"Only when it rains or when I'm tired."

"That's good to hear."

Another uncomfortable silence fell between them. Brian shifted his feet. Caitlyn glanced around the room, wondering what to do next. If he'd called first, she could have gotten herself together, but as it was, she was rattled at seeing him again and she didn't know what to say. Finally, she came up with, "Are you planning to stay in San Francisco?"

He looked surprised by her question. "Yes, of course. This is my home. I've already submitted my résumé to several universities. I'm hoping to work with your parents, but that remains to be seen."

"They'd love that."

"What about you? How would you feel?"

"I'd be happy for you. It's what you've wanted, what they've wanted."

"Caitlyn . . ." he started, then stopped, then began again. "What's going on?"

"What do you mean?"

"I don't know where we stand. I don't know why you didn't call or write."

"You didn't call or write either."

"I did in the beginning."

"One letter."

"One letter that you didn't answer. I knew then you were angry. Why did you tell me to go if you didn't want me to go?"

"Because you wanted to go," she said simply, the words coming to her so quickly they slid right out of her mouth.

"That's true. I did want to accept the fellowship. But I didn't understand the choice was the fellowship or you. By the time I came to that realization it was too late to back out. I just hoped that once you were recovered and I was home we could work things out. That's why I'm here now." He sighed, his face filled with confusion. "I seem to continually get into trouble for taking a woman's words at face value. You said to go, but what you were really saying is if you go, it's all over."

He was right. She had sent him mixed signals. She'd told him to go when deep down inside she'd wanted him to stay, to tell her she was the most important thing in the world to him.

Or maybe that wasn't even the whole truth. Sending him away had gone hand in hand with sending away so many other troubling emotions.

"Besides the fact that I left, I think you blamed me for the accident," Brian continued when she didn't reply.

She shook her head. "That's not true. I didn't blame you."

"You weren't ready for that ski run. I pushed you into it."

He *had* pushed, but she'd gone along, pretending to be someone she wasn't, someone he would love more, someone as in tune with nature as he was. She'd seen the need in his eyes and, as always, had wanted to fill it. But she'd fallen hopelessly short. In fact, she'd fallen halfway down a mountain. They'd spent Christmas in the hospital, instead of by a hot fire in a beautiful lodge the way they'd planned. And after the immediate crisis of saving her life had passed, she'd been transferred to another hospital in San Francisco, sent home to spend the weeks and months recuperating from her injuries.

"Well, *I* blame myself," Brian said heavily. "And my life hasn't been the same without you in it. I would very much like another chance with you, Caitlyn. What do you say?"

What did she say? A million words came to mind, but they were so cluttered and disorganized she couldn't get a single one past her lips.

"Are you with someone else? Is that why you're hesitating?"

She wanted to say yes, she was with someone else; then he'd go away again and take the rest of the stuff she didn't want to deal with away with him. But she couldn't lie. "I'm not seeing anyone else."

His blue eyes lightened. "Will you let me take you to dinner?"

She hesitated. "I don't know. I have so much work to do."

"You have to eat."

Right now she felt more like throwing up. The turmoil of seeing him again, of being taken back to a place she'd never wanted to revisit, had completely unsettled her.

Brian had no real idea of what she'd gone through that year. She'd made her noble gesture, and he'd grabbed it, disappearing through the hospital doors before she had a second to have second thoughts. Now he was back, asking her to dinner as if nothing had happened between them, and yet everything had happened.

"I don't think we can go back to the way we were," she said slowly.

"We could try."

"Why? Because I'm healthy now?" she asked.

"And because now I can be here for you all the time. I want a chance to make things right again."

"I doubt that's possible." She paused, gathering her courage. "It wasn't just your leaving that split us apart. I heard you, Brian. I heard you that night when I was waking up from surgery."

"Heard what?"

"You said I was—I was damaged beyond belief," she whispered, barely able to get the sentence out.

His mouth dropped open. "My God, Caitlyn. I never meant for you to hear that. I was shaken. I didn't know what I was saying. I was horrified by how badly hurt you were."

"You were right. I *was* damaged, Brian." She took a breath and continued. "I'm still damaged. Maybe you can't see the scars, but that doesn't mean they're not there."

"Let me make it up to you. Let me prove to you that I'm not as selfish or as heartless as I must have appeared to be when I left you behind."

She saw the sincerity in his eyes and weakened. "I don't know."

"Think about it. Think about all of it. Remember what we were to each other. How we felt."

"Don't you understand, Brian? The last thing I want to do is remember the days I have tried so hard to forget. I spent a lot of time in a lot of pain." She walked over to the door and held it open. "I think you should go."

Brian hesitated, then walked slowly toward her. "I'll go for now, but I'm not giving up on you, or on us." He ran a finger down the side of her cheek in a familiar caress. "I want the future we planned, you and me together, a family. It's what you wanted, too, and I can't believe that you could change that much." A gleam of triumph lit up his eyes as she couldn't deny his words. "I'll see you at brunch tomorrow. Your parents invited me over."

Her heart sank. "Brian, this is too fast. You're gone . . . now you're back. I can't change channels that quickly. I'm different now. So are you. We have lives that haven't included each other for a while."

"Then we'll get to know each other again. I'm not giving up, Caitlyn. You told me to go before, and I believed you, so I went. But I learned my lesson. This time, no matter what you say, I'm staying, because I think that's really what you want."

And as she shut the door behind him, Caitlyn had the terrible feeling she'd created a monster. She needed to learn how to say what she meant and mean what she said. But she was feeling as confused and conflicted now as she'd felt eighteen months ago.

At one point in her life she'd been certain she could stand by Brian for all time. She'd been prepared to take vows to that effect. What kind of a woman was she now to not even consider giving their relationship another chance when she'd once invested so much of herself in it? Didn't she owe him something? Didn't he owe her? Or would they both be better off by calling it even and calling it over? If only the answers would come as easily as the questions.

Matt heard Caitlyn's door close and had to resist the impulse to look through the peephole. Caitlyn and her Abe Lincoln boyfriend were none of his business. He certainly wasn't surprised that she'd hooked up with some bearded intellectual type. He probably read her poetry and took her to museums.

Although . . . Caitlyn hadn't looked that happy to see him, and the fact that the guy had jumped to a big conclusion about Caitlyn and himself made Matt suspect they'd had a breakup of some sort.

Damn! Why was he thinking about Caitlyn again? He needed to concentrate on Sarah, on trying to figure out where she might have gone and how he would find her. It was unbelievable how many searches he'd conducted over the years, always coming up empty. Even with all his resources, he'd struck out. But Sarah had somehow found him and decided to leave her baby with him. It still blew his mind. How did Sarah know she could trust him? He could have been anybody now. So could she. That's what worried him the most, that Sarah could have inherited their mother's genes. He wanted to believe she was coming back. But he'd been wrong before.

Restless again, Matt stood up. It was too quiet. He almost wished Emily was still awake, but she'd finally dropped off to sleep after he'd made her comfortable in the middle of his king-size bed, placing cushions all around her to keep her from rolling about. He'd put her on her side and hoped that was right, but that hadn't stopped him from checking on her every few minutes. He didn't know how he would sleep tonight. Who would watch her when he was asleep? The responsibility of parenting suddenly overwhelmed him.

What would he do with Emily if Sarah didn't come back? Could he really be a father?

He shook his head, knowing he couldn't think about that right now. One step at a time. Matt just wished the damn phone would ring, or a knock would come at his door and Sarah would magically appear. He glared at the phone, which remained ominously silent.

But in the quiet came the sound of another door closing—Caitlyn's. Matt didn't stop to think before he moved, so desperate was he for a lifeline. He was in the hall before she'd gotten halfway to the elevator.

"Caitlyn," he called out.

She stopped and turned slowly, as if she wished she'd been able to escape. "What?"

"Where are you going?"

"Is it any of your business?"

"Tell me anyway."

She sighed and pointed to her running shoes. It was then he realized she'd changed into a mint-green jogging suit that was the color of his favorite ice cream. "I need to get out."

"It's after eight—it's dark out there."

"And your point would be . . ."

"That you shouldn't be running alone after dark."

"I'll be fine. I need some air. And I can't stand all the tension in my body."

He had a hunch he knew who was the cause of that tension. "I have an idea."

"No, I do not want to hold Emily."

"That wasn't what I was going to say."

She sent him a suspicious look.

"Two words. Punching bag."

She stared at him for a long moment. "You're talking about that thing you have hanging in the corner of your living room?"

"Exactly. It's great at relieving tension. Frankly, you look like you could throw a few good punches right now."

"I don't know how to box."

"I thought you'd taken self-defense."

"My mother signed me up," Caitlyn admitted. "She was determined I should know how to defend myself before I was allowed to go on a date. I spent most of the time in the bathroom. The guy in the pads scared me."

He tried to fight back a smile, but her honest admission only made her that much more likeable. "Then you should definitely learn how to throw a punch, especially if you want to go running at night. It's easy. I'll show you."

"This is just a trick to get me to help you with the baby again."

"You are so suspicious. Emily is fast asleep."

Caitlyn walked toward him, until she was standing a foot away. She studied his face for a long minute. "You hate being alone with her, don't you?"

"No."

"That little baby has got you freaked."

"I'm perfectly calm. Feel my pulse." He held out his hand to her.

Caitlyn put two fingers on his wrist, and the heat of her touch sent his pulse on a sprint. When he looked into her eyes, he saw the same sudden leap and felt a surge of pure male satisfaction, quickly followed by dismay. He could not be attracted to his neighbor. He could not have a thing with Caitlyn. No way in hell. The idea was unthinkable.

He never brought his relationships home, and he certainly didn't start relationships at home.

Jesus! He was already thinking of this as home. Maybe he needed to throw some punches himself.

Caitlyn dropped his wrist. "I was never very good at finding a pulse," she said, pretending that whatever had jumped between them hadn't happened. "I really should run."

He knew it would be smarter to let her go, but these days being smart didn't seem to be an option. "Just give the bag a chance. It can be a great workout. Trust me."

She hesitated. "All right. I guess I could try it."

He ushered her into his apartment. "Emily is in the bedroom. Do you want to check on her?"

"We should leave well enough alone."

"Okay." He walked over to the hall closet and pulled out two boxing gloves. "These should work."

Caitlyn looked doubtfully at the enormous gloves. "I don't think those will fit."

"We're not going for style, just protection. Put 'em on."

Caitlyn took off her jacket to reveal a body-hugging white T-shirt that had Matt clearing his throat. He'd always liked curves on a woman, and Caitlyn had some dangerous curves, the kind that made a man want to hold on for dear life.

"I feel ridiculous," she said as she slipped on the bulky gloves.

"No one is watching."

"You are," she said pointedly.

Matt forced himself to concentrate as he walked over to the bag and braced it with his hands. "I'll hold it steady. You take a swing."

She paused once more, offering him an apologetic

glance. "I don't think I can do this. I've never hit anyone in my life."

"No siblings to fight with?"

"I'm an only child."

"No bully in the third grade?"

"I went to Catholic school. The nuns didn't put up with bullies."

"What about in the neighborhood?"

She shook her head. "My mother screened my play dates."

Good grief! Only child, Catholic school, play dates— if he'd had any doubts that they came from different sides of the tracks, they were gone.

"You must know someone you've wanted to hit. Think about it." He watched the muscles in her face draw tight. "Maybe starting with the guy who just left," he ventured. "Bradley, right?"

"Brian. And I don't want to talk about him."

"Did I ask?"

"You were about to."

"Take a swing, Caitlyn."

Caitlyn pulled her arm back, then took a soft feminine punch that didn't even move the bag. Matt shook his head in disgust, telling himself he could not possibly be turned on by her completely sissy punch. But there was something incredibly feminine about her. "You hit like a girl."

"I am a girl."

Didn't he know it! "Try again. See if you can actually make the bag move."

"What if I miss the bag and hit your hand?"

"With the force you just used, I think I'll live."

"You're making fun of me, aren't you?"

"Does that make you mad?"

"As a matter of fact . . ." She took a better punch this time and smiled with satisfaction. "That felt good."

"Do it again."

"Once was probably enough."

This woman had a lot to learn. As far he was concerned, once was never enough. "You're just getting started. Think about something that makes you hot under the collar."

"I'm usually even tempered."

"Think about me leaving you with the baby when you were supposed to be finishing that wedding dress."

"Oh, right." She took a much harder punch, pushing the bag back against his chest.

"You're a quick study. Now, what about that guy who just left, the one who thought Emily was yours. How did that make you feel?"

Caitlyn's expression turned to stone. "I told you to mind your own business."

"You didn't look happy to see him."

"I wasn't."

"So who was he? A boyfriend?"

She hit the bag again, even harder this time. "He was my fiancé, if you must know."

Another punch glanced off the bag, and her expression turned fierce as she lost herself in a memory.

"He broke up with you?" Matt couldn't quite imagine a guy walking out on Caitlyn.

"Not exactly," she said, her punches accenting each word. "He had a job opportunity that took him back east for a year, and I told him to take it. But I was a little surprised by how fast he got out of there." She danced around the bag, taking punch after punch until a line of sweat broke out across her brow.

"Out of where?"

"The hospital," she said breathlessly.

"What is he—a doctor?"

She took another wild punch. "Astrophysicist, Ph.D. He has a genius IQ and ambition to match. The fellow-ship at the McClellan Institute allowed him to study with one of the top men in his field. It was a once-in-a-lifetime proposition. And he couldn't let anything slow him down, especially someone who . . . who . . ." She stopped, her chest heaving as she caught her breath.

"Who what?" he prodded.

"Who might not ever be able to walk again," she blurted out.

"What the hell are you talking about?" he asked in amazement.

"I had an accident—two broken legs, a crushed pelvis, and a couple of broken ribs. Oh, and did I mention a se-vere concussion and twenty-seven stitches in my scalp? They had to put me back together with pins and screws. I wasn't a pretty picture."

"And the asshole left you like that?"

"I sent him away. I was damaged, horribly damaged." Her voice caught in her throat. "If you could have seen me then, you would have thought the same thing." She shuddered at the memories washing over her.

"I still can't believe your fiancé would leave you in the hospital and take a job on the other side of the country."

"I told you, it was a big deal. And what could Brian do for me anyway? He could barely stand to look at me. He probably wondered how he could ever love me again." Her eyes flooded with a sudden onslaught of tears. Matt dropped the punching bag and took her in his arms. He pressed her trembling body against his chest, smoothing her hair under his chin as sobs rocked through her.

"Sh-sh," he whispered.

She struggled to catch her breath, to stop crying. "I'm sorry," she said with a small hiccup. "I don't know why I'm crying. I haven't cried in a long time, and now I can't seem to stop," she said with a sniff. "I'm as bad as Emily. You're surrounded by crying females."

Normally, he would have shied away from her. He'd never had much patience with female dramatics, a left-over discomfort from the days spent with his weepy mother, but Caitlyn's sorrow was so deep, he felt only helplessness that he couldn't make it go away. There didn't seem to be any words he could offer, none that didn't sound trite and unsubstantial.

Caitlyn pulled away from him with a self-conscious swipe across her wet cheeks. "I'm okay, you know. Seeing Brian again brought it all back, but I'm fine."

"How did you get hurt so badly?"

"We were skiing. Brian is a great skier. He loves the mountains, and we were on vacation in Sun Valley. He wanted to do this challenging run with one of the faculty members from UCSD. The professor's wife was going along and thought it would be fun for the four of us to ski together. I didn't want to hold Brian back."

"He must have known you couldn't handle it."

She shrugged. "I told him I could."

"And he wanted to impress his friends more than he wanted to keep you safe."

"I don't think he thought of it that way. Really. It was all just an accident. It wasn't his fault."

"Right. So then. you're lying in the hospital with a dozen broken bones and he tells you, Hey, honey I got a great job offer, so see you later."

She frowned. "He didn't say it like that, and I told him to go, so I can hardly complain that he went, can I?"

"But you didn't want him to leave."

"I thought he'd argue, offer to stay," she admitted. "But I got what I asked for. End of story."

Matt shook his head in disbelief. "You were injured. You weren't thinking clearly. What was his excuse?"

"It was a fabulous opportunity."

"More important than his fiancée?" The question slipped out before Matt had a chance to consider how badly it might hurt. When Caitlyn's face turned pale, he realized his mistake. "I'm sorry."

She drew in a deep breath and let it out. "You know, I don't really want to talk about this." She slipped off the boxing gloves and handed them back to Matt. "Thanks. That was fun."

"Yeah, next time we have this much fun, I'll bring a bigger box of Kleenex."

The smile broke across her face like the sun coming out from behind a cloud. "I probably should have just gone for the run, but my body still doesn't care much for jogging. Although being told at one point that I might not be able to walk without a limp made the joy of running a lot sweeter."

"That was rough, what happened to you."

"I survived. I was lucky."

"Optimist, huh?"

"Most of the time. You probably can't tell that by tonight, but I usually don't feel this sorry for myself."

"No, you just pretend the bad stuff isn't there, don't you?"

She made a face at him. "You're so smart. You have me completely figured out, don't you?"

"I doubt that," he said dryly. "Figuring women out is not my forte."

"That's what Brian said. He doesn't understand why

women say go when they want you to stay, or say stay when they want you to go."

"What did you tell him this time—go or stay?"

She didn't answer, her eyes somewhat guilty.

"You told him to hit the road, right?" he persisted. "You didn't give him a second chance?"

"Well, I did tell him to go, but—"

Matt groaned. "I knew there was a but."

"It's complicated, Matt."

"You're making it complicated."

"But," she repeated, "I don't think he believed me when I told him to go."

"Should he?"

"I don't know. I'm confused."

"He left you when you were hurt. What's confusing?"

"I loved him. I said I would marry him. I still have my wedding dress hanging in the closet. Don't I owe him at least some consideration?"

"No, absolutely not."

"It's not so black and white, Matt, not to me."

Matt started as Emily's abrupt wail rang through the apartment, reminding him he had a more pressing problem to deal with than Caitlyn's love life. Which didn't concern him anyway. But he was still fighting the urge to shake some sense into her. From what he'd heard, Brian didn't deserve a second chance, and Caitlyn was being too soft. Although he had to admit her softness was one of the things he really liked about her.

"Emily is awake," she said with a commiserating smile. "Do you want some help? After crying on your shoulder, I owe you." Caitlyn moved across the room, pausing at the bedroom door. "By the way, you're a good neighbor."

"Yeah, good neighbor," he muttered as she went into

the bedroom to rescue Emily. He wondered why he suddenly wanted to be so much more than a neighbor. Caitlyn wasn't his type. She was white lace and promises. He ought to have his head examined. Unfortunately, at the moment he was not thinking with his head.

 *Six*

"*J*ust think," Sarah muttered to herself as she hovered in a doorway on Seventh Street, just south of Market, in San Francisco's downtown business district. The Greyhound Bus Station was across the street. She could walk over and use her last twenty dollars to buy herself a ticket somewhere. But what if she couldn't get back to Emily? What then?

Maybe Emily would be better off without her, the poor baby. She hadn't asked to be born into this mess, getting a horrible mother, an even worse father, and nothing much else. Sarah was completely overwhelmed by her situation. She sank to the ground, the weight of the world pushing on her shoulders. She was only twenty-two years old, but she felt like a hundred.

"Hey, move along," a man told her as he came out the door of the tobacco shop behind her. "You're scaring away customers." He took a good look at her face, which she instinctively tried to hide behind a shield of hair. "Go on, now, find yourself somewhere else to sleep tonight. If you're here in the morning, you'll be sorry."

She was already sorry, Sarah thought as she wearily stood up. Sorry she'd ever been born, sorry the monsters under her bed had turned out to be real, sorry she'd ever believed in a promise. And sorrier still that she'd brought a baby into her life. Maybe that's the way her mother had felt, like she had no way out, no chance of making it.

The feeling that she was just like her mother scared Sarah to death. She didn't want to be that way, yet here she was alone, her baby left behind with Matt, a brother she hadn't seen in years. What had she done?

The only thing she could do, she reminded herself. Seeing Matt's name in the newspaper had been a sign. She had wondered about him for years, dreamed of seeing him again, and then just like that, when she'd needed him the most, she'd seen his name in the paper. It had been easy to find his office, and when she'd gone to the library to look him up through the Internet, his phone number and address had popped right up. It was almost too easy—as if someone had paved the way for her to find him.

An angel maybe? The whimsical thought was ridiculous. There were no angels. A sudden breeze blew against her face; she shivered, and goose bumps slid down her arm. Maybe it was being back in San Francisco that made her feel like she wasn't alone. It was here in this city that she'd been loved, once, a long time ago. Coming back had been the right thing to do.

But now what? What was she supposed to do now? Was seeing the Greyhound Bus Station a sign that she should leave Emily with Matt? And go where? Could she really abandon her baby? What kind of mother did that make her? One like her own mother? The maddening, horrifying refrain went around and around in her head. She tried to run away from it by walking more quickly, but it followed her through the darkening city streets.

As she walked she wrapped her arms around her waist, trying instinctively to protect herself from the night and the rest of the world that couldn't get out of that night. She'd slept outside before, hidden away in the shadows, praying for safety, but she hadn't been able to do that with Emily.

She wondered for the thousandth time if Emily was all right, if Matt was loving her. She remembered how Matt had taken care of her before the fire. He was the only father she remembered.

Her real father had died when she was only a few months old. Her mother had fallen apart after that, but Mattie had been so responsible, always worrying about her. He'd seemed old at the time, but now she realized how young he'd really been. It was her fault they'd been separated, another reason why she hadn't found the courage to talk to him. She still remembered the look on his face as they'd watched their apartment burn. In that moment he'd hated her.

She'd always messed things up, but this—this was the biggest mess of them all. There had to be a way out. She just had to find it. But she'd spent all day trying to get a job without any luck. No one wanted to hire a woman with a battered face, little education, and no job references. The familiar feeling of hopelessness enveloped her like a warm sweater that she couldn't bear to take off.

After a dismal morning of job hunting, she'd spent the afternoon in Union Square, listening to a sidewalk street musician sing the blues, wondering why she couldn't just get up and go somewhere. But it always came back to where. She'd almost chosen the liquor store. She'd stood outside of it for almost ten minutes, looking at that pure gold liquid in the window, remembering how it had felt sliding down her throat, making all the bad things disappear.

Oh, how she'd wanted a drink, and how afraid she'd been that one drink would lead to a bottle, and she'd never have to be sober again. It was a tempting thought. She'd spent most of her teenage years in just such a place. Emily had straightened her out. When Sarah had found out she was pregnant, she'd quit drinking, and she hadn't had a drop since. But now she really wanted a drink, wanted it so bad she could almost taste it.

No! Taking a deep breath, Sarah reminded herself to think clearly, think about Emily. But she was scared. It was getting late, and the people on the streets could be dangerous. She wondered about a shelter. Maybe if she could sleep, she could decide what to do next. But where was a shelter? She had no idea.

She walked and walked and walked, losing track of the streets, not even sure where she was going until she saw the steeple of the church. It was the sign that had called to her the night before. As a child she'd seen that steeple out of their fourth-floor apartment, just two blocks away. Every Sunday she'd heard the bells ring and the angels sing, and they'd given her hope. But last night, while sleeping in the church, she hadn't felt any hope, nor had she seen any angels, so why had she come back again?

They'd probably reported the broken window. It wouldn't be easy to get back inside. Everything would be locked up tight. Still, Sarah lingered on the corner, wondering why she couldn't seem to move away. An old woman came around the corner at the far end of the church wearing a large straw hat on her head despite the rising moon and darkening twilight. She held a watering can in one hand, but instead of walking toward the strip of flowers that graced the walkway, she came toward the sidewalk, dousing the weeds that grew along the curb with water.

Sarah watched her in fascination. There was something about the woman that seemed familiar, and a memory tugged in the back of her mind. She found herself moving forward, but the woman walked away from her, crossing the street to the other side, muttering something to herself as she went.

Sarah shivered as a cool evening breeze seemed to blow through her. She turned to leave and saw him standing there, watching her.

Startled, she wondered for a split second if Gary had come after her. Then she realized the face belonged to the man she had met in the church earlier, a man with blue-gray eyes that reminded her of the sky just after sunset.

"Hello, Sarah," the man said quietly. "I was hoping you'd come back."

"I—I didn't."

"And yet you're here."

Sarah silently kicked herself for being so dumb. Why couldn't she think of the right thing to say at the right time?

"You remember me, don't you?" he continued. "I'm Jonathan Mitchell, the minister here."

"You don't look like a reverend," she said, taking note of his casual gray slacks and dark sweater. In fact, not only did he not dress like a man of the cloth, his features were too pretty, with his wavy brown hair and long, thick eyelashes that any woman would have killed for.

"What's a minister supposed to look like?"

"Old."

He smiled. "I'll get there one of these days, probably sooner than I'd like. Are you hungry, Sarah?"

"How do you know my name?"

"You told me earlier."

And he remembered? Gary hadn't remembered her name the first few times she'd slept with him.

"You made quite an impression," he told her.

"Did you call the cops?"

"No."

She stared at him uncertainly. She wanted to believe him, but he had to be lying. She'd broken into the church, caused damage. Why wouldn't he call the cops? "I have to go," she said abruptly.

"Don't."

"But—"

"My housekeeper makes a wonderful beef stew. There's more than I can eat. I hate to see anything go to waste."

She wondered if he was referring to her. Because there was an expression on his face, a worry in his eyes, and it scared her to think that she wanted to trust him. No one worried about her. He must have an ulterior motive. Most people did.

"Do you get points for how many homeless people you get off the street each night?" she asked brashly, a tiny spark of her old street courage coming back to her.

"Are you homeless?"

"No. I live in one of those mansions up on the hill."

"Then I guess I'll have to look elsewhere for my points," he said with a dry smile.

"I'm fine, you know. And I don't believe in God, so if you think you're going to save me or have me be born again, you can forget about it."

"It's already forgotten. Look, Sarah, I'd like to help you. I think you've been hurt and maybe you could use a friend."

"What do you get out of it?"

"Maybe I could use a friend, too."

His kind words stole the toughness away and reminded her of how tired she was and how much she really did need a friend. But could she trust him? He was a stranger. He might still call the cops. Then what would she do? They'd find out she was a terrible mother and take her baby away the way they'd taken her away from Mattie.

"I can't." She turned blindly away, the tears already filling her eyes.

He caught her by the arm and held on, a strong, masculine grip that hurt her already bruised skin. He must have seen the pain in her eyes, because he immediately let go. "There's a shelter three blocks from here. The Samaritan House, on Fourteenth and Stringer. They won't ask you any questions, and you'll have a safe place to sleep."

She nodded, trying not to break down in front of him.

"I want to help you, Sarah."

"Why? I'm nobody to you."

"But you're somebody to someone. Aren't you?"

Sarah thought of Emily and the tears streamed down her cheeks as she shook her head. "Not anymore."

"I don't want you to go," Jonathan said, surprising her with the intensity in his voice.

She looked into his eyes and saw more than a minister; she saw a man. Is this what he wanted, then? Her body in exchange for his help? She couldn't even imagine why he would want her body. She hadn't washed in a couple of days. She looked like a poster girl for abused women. Not that a man necessarily needed a pretty face; a female body would often do.

"It's not like that," he said. "I won't hurt you."

"I've heard that before."

"Come back tomorrow. Just to talk. Maybe I can help. Maybe you'll be able to trust me more in the daylight."

She wanted to say yes, for as she looked at the church, at the familiar steeple, she felt a tiny glimmer of hope. Maybe it was a sign after all.

It was almost eleven, long past the time to go home, but Caitlyn couldn't make herself get up and go. The couch was comfortable, the baby was asleep, and the man . . . well, Matt was something else, stirring her senses in a way that made her want more—more of everything: his husky voice, his male scent, his wry smile. She'd never been so aware of a man, but here in his apartment with so little furniture, so little of anything but him and her, she felt an intimacy that was completely at odds with their relationship.

Their friendship was barely twenty-four hours old, if you could even call it a friendship, more of a chance relationship based on circumstances beyond their control. If Emily hadn't arrived, Caitlyn had no doubt that Matt would have stayed forever on his side of the hallway, and she would have done the same. But Emily had come. And so had Matt, a man she couldn't quite figure out.

The little he'd told her of his background had colored him as dark, rough, edgy, intense. Yet with Emily he was tender, kind, patient. She wondered which was the real Matt Winters. And she couldn't help speculating how he would be with a woman he was interested in. Would he be passionate and impulsive or slow and deliberate?

Caitlyn felt an uncomfortable uneasiness run through her as she watched Matt clear up the remains of their pizza. His blue jeans fit him like a glove, outlining his strong, fit body. He had a great ass, she thought, suppressing a small giggle at the trail her thoughts were taking, a trail she wouldn't mind taking with her hands. Okay, enough, she told herself firmly, setting her wineglass down on the coffee table in front of her. She had to get a grip. She had no business ogling Matt's buns or any other part of his anatomy.

"More wine?" Matt walked over with the bottle of red he'd opened up for her earlier that evening.

"Did I drink all that?" she asked with a frown as he poured the last few ounces into her glass.

"Looks that way," he said with a smile.

"If I finish that, I'll be asleep."

"Well, it is that time of the night."

"You don't look tired," she observed.

"I'm a night owl, and I'm also a little wired with my new houseguest."

"You should try to sleep while she's sleeping."

"I probably should, but I don't feel like sleeping." He walked back to the window, a trip he'd made many times over the past few hours.

"Thinking about Sarah?"

"I can't help it. She's out there somewhere." He waved his hand toward the city lights. "Temperature dropped today. She must be cold."

"Maybe she's inside."

"I hope so. I feel helpless. I'd much rather be out there walking the streets than sitting in this apartment wondering where she is."

"You're doing more than sitting. You're taking care of your sister's baby. That's pretty important. In fact, I can't think of anything more important."

He looked back at her, his gaze connecting with hers for a long minute. "Thanks. I think I needed the reminder."

"You're welcome. And I'm not even taking it personally that you'd rather be anywhere else than here talking to me."

He smiled at that. "I didn't mean it that way."

"I didn't take it that way." She patted the couch beside her. "Why don't you sit down? You're making me nervous."

"My mother used to say the same thing. Mattie, can't you just be still for five minutes," he mimicked.

Caitlyn smiled at the note of unexpected tenderness in his voice. "You loved her, didn't you? In spite of everything."

He looked shocked by her suggestion. "No. I didn't love her. How can you love someone who doesn't take care of you, who abandons you?"

"Because you can. Because love doesn't always make sense."

"Well, that's true," he said, digging his hands into his pockets. "But I didn't love her."

"Have you ever been in love with anyone—you know, crazy, head-over-heels in love?" she asked him.

"No."

"Do you want to think about it for ten seconds?"

"No," he said with another small smile.

"That's too bad."

"Why do you say that? It doesn't look like love got you anywhere." He shot her a curious look. "Are you going to see Bradley again?"

"Brian," she said with annoyance, somewhat irritated by his perceptive remark. Although, hadn't she come to the same conclusion, that love wasn't all it was cracked up to be?

Still, she hadn't really given up on love, she realized. How could she? Her entire business was driven by the emotion. If she didn't believe in love, how could she design dresses for the most important day in the life of two lovers?

Maybe that was the problem. Maybe that's why she couldn't draw anymore. The answer was suddenly glaringly clear. She couldn't draw because she couldn't feel. Her designs had always come from her heart, but her heart had gone out of business.

"Wow, I think I just had an epiphany."

Matt raised an eyebrow. "About what?"

"About myself, about love, about my inability to draw wedding dresses." She shook her head. "It's a long story, but I've had a mental block every time I've tried to design something, and I think I just realized why."

"I take it you're not planning to share it with me," he said after a moment of silence. "Does it have something to do with Bradley?"

"Partly. I did love Brian once, but so much has happened. I don't really know how I feel anymore. But one thing I do know is that Brian is going to get everyone riled up. They won't wait for me to make up my own mind, they'll drive me crazy until I become convinced that getting back together with Brian is the absolutely right thing to do and, in fact, was my idea all along."

"Who's they?" Matt asked, joining her on the couch.

"My mother, for one. She loves Brian like the son she never had. She's already given him my phone number, my address, and invited him to Sunday brunch tomorrow. I'm sure she intends to have me re-engaged by next Friday and married the week after."

He raised an eyebrow. "Your mother would encourage you to get back together with that idiot who left you on your sickbed?"

"She doesn't know the whole story."

"Why don't you tell her?"

Caitlyn shrugged, not willing to admit that she hadn't told anyone the full story, not even him. In fact, she could barely tell it to herself. "You don't know my mother. She always wants what's best for me. At least that's what she tells herself when she decides it's time to haul me in for repairs."

"What kind of repairs?"

Caitlyn waved her hand in the air. "Oh, you name it, I've had it—braces, contact lenses, laser eye surgery, fat camp, hot wax."

"Ouch."

"You don't even want to know what it feels like to have hot wax dripping down your thigh—"

"Don't go there," he interrupted with an outstretched hand. "How women can do that to themselves, I do not understand. Nor do I understand how your mother could possibly look at you and see anything that needs fixing. You look pretty damn good to me."

His gaze traveled from her face down her body and up again, drawing a hot blush to her cheeks. The sparks smoldering between them suddenly burst into flame. Caitlyn couldn't seem to look away from Matt's eyes. She saw his pupils dilate, watched the gleam of desire awaken and stretch like a slumbering lion ready to pounce. And if she'd had any sense, she would have run like hell, because she had absolutely no business leaning forward, and neither did he, but the distance between them vanished like a puff of smoke.

Matt's breath touched her lips first, teasing her with his scent; then his mouth covered hers, drawing her into a deep, heart-stopping, soul-shattering kiss that might have lasted for seconds or minutes or hours. Caitlyn was so immersed in the texture and taste of his mouth, the scent of his skin, his fingers running through her hair and trapping her head so she couldn't move that she lost all track of time. It was a kiss that completely consumed her, and it was only ended because of the shocking cry of a very small baby.

They broke apart in breathless amazement, their eyes connecting on the same note.

"What the hell was that?" Matt asked her.

She shook her head, unable to release a coherent word of explanation. Matt looked from her to the crying baby and back again. "I—"

"Have to get Emily, I know," Caitlyn finished, finally finding her voice. "I must have had too much wine."

"You're going to blame it on the wine?"

"I'm thinking about it," she admitted.

Matt leaned over to pick Emily up off the floor. "What's wrong now, sweetheart? Hungry, wet, what?"

Emily answered him with a downturned mouth that turned into a scream.

"Okay, I get the picture. You're mad."

"Probably hungry, too. I'll fix her a bottle," Caitlyn said, anxious to get to her feet, to move away from Matt, to give herself a chance to regroup.

"I'll change her," he said. "Might as well take care of both ends."

And for a few minutes, they focused only on Emily's needs, the air bristling with electricity, unanswered questions, and unsatisfied desire. When Emily had settled down with her bottle, comfortably tucked into the curve of Matt's arm, Caitlyn decided it was time to leave.

"I'll see you later," she told Matt, staying a safe distance away from him.

"You don't want to talk about it, do you?"

"It was just a kiss, nothing to get too excited about."

"Really? You weren't excited at all?" he asked with a skeptical raise of his eyebrow.

She felt the warmth cover her cheeks again. "I told you, it was the wine."

"It wasn't the wine. It was you and me together, going up in spontaneous combustion. I've been around the block a few times, and believe me that rarely happens."

She cleared her throat. "Yes, well, there might be an attraction—"

"Might be?"

"That doesn't mean we have to do anything about it."

"I think we already did."

"I mean again."

"Well, it could get awkward," he conceded. "I don't usually kiss my neighbors."

"You don't usually talk to your neighbors."

"Exactly."

"We'll just forget it happened. Chalk it up to . . ."

"The wine," he finished. "But I didn't have any. So what's my excuse?"

"You were temporarily insane."

"I suppose you could drive a man to insanity."

"Very funny. But I'm not like this, Matt."

"Not like what? Beautiful, smart, sexy?"

She swallowed hard as his gaze swept over her once again, making her tingle all over as if he were touching her. And she wanted him to touch her. Wanted the kiss to start over again. Wanted to do it in slow motion this time so she could feel every second. She cleared her throat, trying to clear her head at the same time. "I don't usually kiss men I don't know very well, especially a man I'm not even dating."

"I did buy you dinner," he said pragmatically.

"And I saved you from a screaming baby." She tucked

a piece of hair behind her ear. "This isn't even a romantic situation. I don't know what came over me."

He smiled at her, a slow, sensuous, knowing smile that didn't just come from his mouth, but his eyes. "It's okay to want someone without having a good reason. Men do it all the time."

"Well, I'm not a man."

"Thank God!"

She smiled and shook her head at the teasing note in his voice. "You're not making this easy."

"Do you want me to?"

"Yes."

"Okay, it was momentary insanity."

"And it won't happen again," she said firmly.

"I don't know if I can promise that."

"Matt!"

"All right. I don't think it will ever happen again."

She supposed that was as good as she was going to get. She turned to leave.

Matt's voice caught her at the door.

"Caitlyn," he said.

"What?"

"You don't need any fixing. You're fine the way you are."

"You don't know the half of it," she muttered as she shut the door. Out in the hall, she leaned against the door and drew in a deep breath. "No one does."

 *Seven*

After fitfully trying to get to sleep, Caitlyn was not happy to hear pounding at her door just after she'd finally dozed off. The angry shrieks that followed could belong to only one person—Emily. Caitlyn rushed out of her bedroom in her oversized T-shirt, stubbing her toe on the way into the living room. She opened the door with a curse on her lips.

Matt's shirt hung open, his jeans missing the top button, as if he'd thrown on his clothes in the dark. Emily's face was red, sweat dampening her face, mixing with the tears running down her cheeks.

And besides the din of Emily's cries, Matt had his stereo cranked up full blast.

"Why on earth are you playing that music?"

"I'm trying to cover up her screaming. She won't stop crying, Caitlyn," Matt said, panic in his voice. "It's been hours. What are we going to do?"

If it hadn't been two o'clock in the morning, and she

hadn't been so exhausted, she might have found the "we" in his statement endearing. "We could try giving her a bath," she suggested.

"A bath? Are you crazy?"

"It's just a thought."

"You want me to strip her down and put her in a tub of water? I don't think that's going to make her happy," he said with a wave of his hand.

The movement sent a flutter of air between them, and for a moment Emily gasped and stopped crying, then immediately started again.

"I have an idea," Caitlyn said. "Go get the comforter."

"Why?"

"Just do it. Jeez, you ask a lot of questions. And turn off that music, too."

While Matt was gone, Caitlyn grabbed her overcoat out of the closet and threw it on. Then she met him in the hallway, which was thankfully a bit more quiet, although Emily was still crying. "Are we going somewhere?" he asked.

"The roof."

"What?"

"Come on." She led the way to the stairwell at the end of the hall and up the flight of stairs to the roof. She opened the door and stepped out onto the flat landing. The air was bracingly cold and stopped Emily in mid scream.

Caitlyn waited for a second, which turned into a minute, holding her own breath and hoping, just hoping, that something she'd read about babies liking to be outside was true.

"I think she stopped," Matt whispered in amazement.

"Don't jinx her. She might just be catching her breath."

Both Caitlyn and Matt stared at Emily as she blinked suspiciously at them both.

"Let's walk over there," Caitlyn suggested, heading toward the railing. She'd discovered the roof a few months earlier when her father had told her to find a good spot to watch an eclipse. Since then she'd come up a few times to clear her head, to soak in the great city view, or just to get away from it all. There was a large step-down at the far end of the roof that made a nice bench. Caitlyn sat down with Matt and helped him adjust the comforter around Emily.

It was a clear night for a change, the fog remaining safely offshore. Caitlyn took several deep breaths, her pulse attempting to settle down now that Emily was quiet.

"This is incredible," Matt said. "I think she's falling asleep."

Caitlyn watched as Emily's eyes blinked once, twice, then her lids settled with a soft sigh.

"Now what?" Matt asked.

Caitlyn sent him a smile. "I have no idea. I guess maybe we could go back inside, see if she stays asleep."

"Let's give her a minute, make sure she's really out." He sighed. "I never appreciated the quiet until just this second. I wonder if Emily cried this much with Sarah. I can see how the constant crying could drive you nuts."

"She might have colic. One of my friends had a baby who cried all the time, especially at night. She used to try everything to get her to calm down."

"Like going up to the roof at two o'clock in the morning in a nightgown and overcoat?" he asked with an appreciative grin.

Caitlyn pulled her coat more closely around her shoulders. "You're not supposed to be looking at me."

"Why not? The view is good from where I'm sitting."

His voice held a note of genuine appreciation that sent an unexpected thrill down her spine. So much for forgetting about kissing him and ignoring their attraction. A few hours into their agreement, and she was already wondering just how hot his lips would be in the cool night air.

"Say something," Matt commanded her.

"Like what?"

"Doesn't matter. Just something to distract me from . . ."

"From what?"

"You."

She swallowed hard, searching for something to say to deflect his attention from her. The answer was in the sky overhead. "Did you know that there are eighty-eight constellations that you can see from Earth?"

Matt shook his head with a wry smile. "I had no idea."

"It's true. Although the constellations are somewhat arbitrary depending on where you are." Caitlyn tilted her head back, studying the stars. "It's not as easy to see them here in the city, but when you go up in the mountains away from the lights, you can see things you'd never imagine."

Matt looked up at the sky overhead. "I know nothing about the stars. The way I grew up, it was more practical to keep your eyes on the ground, watch where you were stepping or who you were tripping over."

"That's kind of sad."

Matt shrugged. "There are a lot of sad things in the world. Oh, I forgot—you wouldn't know about them, because you don't read the newspaper."

She shrugged off his teasing jab. "I keep up with what I need to know, but I think you can drown in the bad stuff if that's all you ever hear about. It's like a traffic accident. I don't have to look when I go by. I don't have to see the mangled metal car doors and the bloodstains on the ground to figure out something nasty happened. But that's what the news gives us, every last icky detail."

"Which fascinates most people, by the way. That's why the traffic comes to a dead stop when there's an accident. Everyone wants to see."

"Well, I'd rather not."

"You'd rather bury your head under the covers."

"Or look toward the stars," she told him. "Come on, you have to admit the universe is awe inspiring."

"I guess," he said grudgingly, following her gaze toward the heavens.

"My father—an astronomy professor, by the way— would love to get on the space shuttle and fly to the moon. He has always been mesmerized by the limitlessness of space. Infinity is his favorite number. He's a real dreamer, the quintessential absentminded professor."

"It sounds like you take after him."

"Maybe a little in the dreaming department. It's funny, though, how different he and my mom are. They're both smart as can be, but my mother has to be in absolute control of everything in her life, and my father is like a leaf on the wind, drifting down, then up and away. I'm never quite sure when he's going to touch down."

"Doesn't sound like he was there much for you," Matt observed.

She shrugged. "He loves his work. So does my mother. She's a math professor."

"You're surrounded by eggheads."

"Geniuses," she agreed. "All mentally gifted. Brian, too. Sometimes, I think he should have been their real child. He fits in so perfectly with them. They rarely know what to do with me."

"I don't think you're a dummy, Caitlyn."

"Maybe not a dummy, but I wasn't a good student. I used to daydream and doodle all over my papers. My parents would get so frustrated with me. And when I said I wanted to major in fashion design, they almost collapsed. I think when I brought Brian home, they breathed a sigh of relief, because now they could be with me but have someone sort of in between us to be a bridge, a translator, whatever you want to call it."

"That's why you got engaged to the guy?" Matt asked, a note of amusement in his voice.

"No," she said firmly, shooting him a dark look. "I got engaged to him because I loved him. Having my parents love him was an added bonus—at the time, anyway. Now it's more like a nightmare."

"You could just take him back. That's what he wants."

"I could. Probably even should. Don't you hate that word, *should*? It seems to drive my life. What I should do always seems more important than what I want to do."

"Duty versus desire," he said, rolling his tongue around the word *desire* in such a way that made her shiver.

Just the night air she told herself, another lie in the growing attraction between them. Because if Brian was duty, then Matt was definitely desire. But she wasn't choosing between them, for heaven's sake. Matt was her neighbor. She couldn't even call him a friend. How could she desire a man she didn't know anything about?

But that was the problem, their whole relationship thus far had been one of intensity, unusual depth, telling each other things usually reserved for best friends. Why? Why did she feel comfortable with him one second and edgy the next? How did Matt arouse feelings in her that had taken Brian months to get to?

"I've known Brian for a long time," she said out loud, trying to remind herself of that fact. "We dated for almost three years before he asked me to marry him."

"Fast mover, huh?"

"Some decisions should be made carefully."

"If you say so."

"I do. And since you've never been in love or engaged, I think I have more experience than you do in this matter."

"Okay," he said agreeably, too agreeably for her taste.

"You're laughing at me."

"I'm not. Do you always worry this much about what people think of you?"

"Yes."

"You shouldn't."

She groaned. "There's that word again. I know I'm a mess, Matt. I can't make heads nor tails of my thoughts. If someone looked into my brain right now they'd run screaming into the night."

Matt laughed out loud. "Shush, don't give Emily any ideas."

Caitlyn smiled back at him. "Sorry."

"You can't please everyone. Why try?"

"I'll probably die trying. I've been surrounded my whole life by people who are highly intelligent, incredibly focused, and totally obsessed by what they do for a living. There hasn't been much room for flexibility or understanding." She cast him a curious glance. "You're like that, too, aren't you? I bet you go days without sleeping or eating when you're on a story."

"Sometimes. It's not a bad thing."

"It can be lonely for the people you leave behind."

"I don't leave anybody behind," he said flatly. "There's never been anybody there."

"But there could be now. There's nothing to stop you from getting married, having children. You could have as big a family as you want."

Matt glanced down at the baby in his arms, his expression suddenly somber. "Children are a big responsibility."

"That's true. But you seem to be a responsible guy to me."

He thought about that for a moment. "I've spent so much time looking back, searching for Sarah, looking for the family that I once had, that I haven't spent much time thinking about the future. But . . ."

"But," she prodded, feeling a terrible need to push the point, even though she had a feeling she wouldn't be that happy with his answer.

"I might like to have kids," he admitted. "Someday, but I'm not sure I'd be a great father."

"Sure you would. Look at how Emily trusts you to take care of her."

"Only because you got us up here on the roof. She was pretty pissed off at me before."

"I made a lucky guess." She leaned back on her elbows and looked toward the sky once again.

"What about you, Caitlyn?" Matt asked. "What's in your game plan?"

"Building my business, starting some new designs, having my own collection."

"So you're saying you're also driven by work," he teased.

"I guess. It used to be when I'd sit down to sketch that I'd lose all track of time. It could have been a minute or an hour that passed. But the creative juices have left me, and I don't know how to get them back. It's like my muse has gone on an extended vacation. Does that ever happen to you when you write?"

"Never. The stories happen; I tell 'em. Now, maybe if I were writing a book I'd get stumped on what to say next. But I simply record the facts as they happen."

"And nothing but the facts," she said with a grin.

"That's right."

"Unfortunately, I can't draw dresses by the numbers."

"Maybe you need a new approach."

"Or a new head."

"Bradley really did a number on you, didn't he?"

"Brian, and it wasn't just him," she murmured.

"Then what? What happened that took away your creativity?"

She looked into his eyes and found herself wanting to confide in him. But the words wouldn't come, couldn't come. She'd never let them hit the surface of the air, never let them come to life, and she couldn't allow the quiet intimacy of the night to lull her into sharing secrets she didn't want to share.

"What are you hiding, Caitlyn?" Matt persisted.

She looked away from his invading gaze. "Nothing. What you see is what you get."

"You want to know what I see?"

"I don't know. Do I?"

"I see a beautiful woman with a big heart who can't resist helping someone in need. She has a bit of a temper, especially when someone is a little late, but—"

"Perpetually late is more like it."

"But she can also be hard on herself, and I have a feeling she's hiding something, a secret that is eating away at her."

She shivered at his words, words that hit too close to home. "That sounds mysterious," she said, forcing some lightness into her voice. "You should write a novel someday. You've got a great imagination."

"Am I wrong?"

"Yes."

"I don't think so."

"Well, I think Emily is fast asleep, and we can go inside."

"Did I also mention that you have an annoying habit of running away just when things are getting interesting?"

"Thanks for the psychoanalysis. How much do I owe you?"

"Five more minutes. I'm not quite ready to test Emily yet."

"It's late, Matt."

"It's nice out here. Peaceful. Do you think that blinking light is a plane or a star?"

"A plane."

"Damn. So where's the Big Dipper or the Little Dipper or whatever they call it?"

"Over there," she said, pointing out the Big Dipper to him.

"So your father is an astrologer?"

"He's a professor of astronomy. Astrologers do your horoscope."

"Oh, sorry."

She smiled at him. "But there are all kinds of incredible stories tied to the stars."

"Stories or facts?"

She ignored that. "My favorite is the story of the Milky Way."

"The candy bar?"

"No, the Milky Way in the sky. Do you want to hear it?"

"Do I have a choice?"

"Not if you want my company."

"Okay, shoot."

"You have to promise not to laugh or be cynical."

He shot her an amused look, and she shook a finger at him. "That is exactly the expression I am not looking for."

"All right. I'll be serious," he said in a deliberately low voice. "Proceed."

"Okay." She tilted her head toward the sky, letting the

stars weave their magic spell over her. Her father's star lore had always fired her imagination. And there was a design in the back of her mind, a design for a wedding dress with tiny shimmering sequins that would look like stars dancing in the moonlight. Someday maybe she'd actually draw it, or make it, but it would have to be for the right bride, someone who could appreciate pure and utter romance.

"I'm waiting," Matt said. "Or have you fallen asleep?"

"No, just trying to remember the right way to tell it. There are a couple of versions, but this is one. Once upon a time there was a weaver fairy who lived in the sky. She used to weave silken robes for the other fairies, but one day she fell in love with the buffalo boy—"

"The buffalo boy—doesn't sound like a good match for a fairy."

"Sh-sh," she said. "Anyway, the buffalo boy lived on the earth, herding buffalo and playing his flute all day. For a time, the weaver fairy lived on the earth with the buffalo boy, but she was forced by her father, the Jade Emperor, to return to the sky. She pleaded that the boy be allowed to stay with them. Her father finally agreed, but only if the boy tended the herds of buffalo that lived in the sky and she returned to weaving silk robes. For a while, they were happy, but so wrapped up were they in each other that they began to neglect their duties. The emperor punished them by putting the fairy and her loom on the east bank of the Silver River and the boy and the buffalo on the west bank. They begged for one more chance. The Jade Emperor reluctantly allowed them to meet once a year, on the seventh day of the seventh month. Every year they do so, and they are so happy that their tears of joy fall to the earth. That's why the two stars Vega and Altair come together during the summer months, and sometimes there is a summer rain, but the rest of the year they are kept apart by the Milky Way." She glanced over at him. "What do you think?"

Matt's face was turned toward the sky, his profile strong, sexy. Then he looked at her, and her heart flipped over.

"It just goes to prove opposites attract, but they can't live together," he said.

She knew she was treading in dangerous waters, but she couldn't stop herself. "Do you think we're opposites?"

"Don't you? If I were speaking celestially, I would say you're the bright-eyed smiling face of the sun and I'm the dark, dangerous side of the moon."

She smiled. "Not a bad analogy for a man of the earth, but I'm not sure either one of us is all one or the other. You think I hide from the truth, but I think you do, too. You want to be tough and uncaring and cynical, but there's a part of you that really liked my romantic story. Come on, admit it," she prodded.

He gave her a reluctant grin. "I would never admit that."

"And I am much more dark and dangerous than you could even imagine."

"Oh, yeah, bad to the bone, huh?"

"I fed coins into the parking meter without moving my car today, even though you're not supposed to do that."

"No way. I am shocked, Ms. Devereaux."

"See, I told you."

"You're not like other women," he said, surprising her with his comment.

"Is that a good thing?"

He shook his head as if he hadn't quite figured it out. "I'm not completely sure. I guess I haven't taken the time to really get to know a woman in a while."

"In a while or ever? Because I get the feeling that your mother did such a number on you that you don't really feel comfortable letting another woman into your life. You're not sure you can trust another female."

"What about you? Are you afraid deep down that no guy will ever love you more than his job?"

"Why are we being so philosophical all of a sudden?"

He laughed. "I have no idea, maybe because conversations at two in the morning are half incredible insight and half utter nonsense."

"But which is which?"

"Beats me. I liked your story, Caitlyn. I especially liked the way your eyes got all dreamy when you told it."

She punched him lightly in the arm, careful not to disturb Emily. "You sound like a fifties song."

"But . . ." He paused, waiting until she looked into his eyes again. "I have to tell you, after listening to your tale, that if I wanted a woman, I wouldn't let anyone keep us apart, not even a Jade Emperor."

Her breath fled her chest at the suddenly purposeful look in his eyes. "Uh, I, well . . ."

"Kiss me," he whispered.

"I don't think so," she whispered back.

"One kiss. I can't even touch you, not with Emily in my arms. Just your mouth on mine."

"Why?"

"Because I want you."

It was wrong, it was foolish . . . it was inevitable. She leaned over and pressed her mouth against his, closing her eyes, losing herself in his warmth, in her need, in his want. The cool night air surrounding them made the heat between them only that much hotter. She didn't touch him anywhere but on the mouth, but she could feel him all over, in every nerve ending, in every part of her body.

She forced herself to pull away from what was fast becoming an addiction. He was under her skin. He was in her blood. He was becoming too big a part of her life, too fast.

"That was the last one," she said firmly. "We have to be sensible."

"That doesn't sound like a sentence that should be delivered by a woman who believes in fairies and their star-crossed lovers."

"That was a story. This is real life." Getting to her feet, she said, "Time for bed." She shook a finger at the gleam that flitted through his eyes. "Don't even say it."

"Are you sure Emily will stay asleep?"

"I'm not sure of anything, except that I have to get up in a few hours and it's time for us to call it a night."

"I appreciate the help—again," he said, carefully getting to his feet, making sure not to jostle Emily. "You've been a lifesaver. I just wish I could do something for you."

A sudden terrible idea occurred to her. She couldn't possibly ask him. Still . . . Matt would be an incredible distraction, not to mention Emily. "You really want to help me?" she asked impulsively.

He gave her a wary look. "I think so. What do I have to do?"

"Come to brunch at my parents' house with me tomorrow."

"Oh, no, I don't think so."

"You owe me, Matt."

He groaned. "Why would you want me there anyway? I'm no egghead."

"You can run interference. My mother has the ability to steamroll me into doing anything. I need a blocker. With you and Emily there, she won't be able to push me into Brian's arms."

He frowned at her. "You could just say no. And besides, I thought you were considering actually getting into Brian's arms."

"I need more time to think about what I want to do. And you haven't met my mother. No one just says no. What do you say? Will you come to brunch?"

"I should stay home in case Sarah comes looking for me."

"We can leave a note on your door."

"What if Emily cries the whole time?"

"Then we can leave early," she said, feeling even more optimistic. "It's the perfect plan. My mother won't be able to pressure me with you there. Of course, if she thinks Brian is out of the running, there is a remote possibility that she might consider you husband material, but—"

"But what?" he asked in dismay.

"You can always just say no," she told him sweetly. "Tomorrow you'll see just how easy that is."

He was preaching to the choir, literally, Jonathan thought cynically as he finished his Sunday sermon for the ten people in the church and the group of teenagers in his choir. Where was everyone? He looked to the altar for guidance. Why am I here, Lord? he asked silently. What possible good can I do when so few people come to hear me, to hear you?

His father's churches had always been filled to the rafters with life, crying babies, young families, the old faithful. They'd sung out every hymn with the choir, rejoicing in the word of the Lord. His father had a gift for creating a passion for prayer, a gift he had not passed on to his only son.

Mrs. McInerny's cane hit the floor with a bang, jolting awake Mr. McInerny from the slumber he'd fallen into shortly after entering the church. It seemed as good a time as any to end the service, and with a final blessing Jonathan dismissed the congregation.

Pauline stood up and followed him out to the front of the church, where they said their good-byes.

"That was good, Reverend," she said, patting him on the shoulder. "Every Sunday you get better and better."

He felt like a young boy being encouraged by his mother to finish the race, when they both knew the race was long over. "Thank you," he said anyway, appreciative of her support.

"Mary dropped off a casserole for your Sunday supper," Pauline said. "If I can't convince you to join my family . . ."

"I'll be fine."

"I don't like to think of you eating alone. You need a family, Jonathan, a wife, children."

"I haven't had time for all that. And with my job, a woman would have to understand that the church comes first." How many women could accept that? His own mother had complained endlessly about the constant parade of people through their house, the late-night phone calls from the sick and the troubled, until she'd finally called it quits. Jonathan didn't think she'd ever reconciled with the fact that her husband was loved by so many people while she was barely loved by two.

"There's a woman out there who will understand your devotion, and she'll love you for it," Pauline said. "You're young. You have time."

"Maybe not enough time." And he wasn't talking about marriage, he was talking about the church. "We need a congregation."

"Folks around here don't venture out much, even in the daylight, especially to church. The neighborhood has been going down for years. You came in at the wrong time, I'm afraid. It might not be the worst thing for you to get reassigned. It might be better for your career to be in a place where you can get recognized for your efforts."

"But it wouldn't be better for the neighborhood. I feel like a failure." And he hated that feeling.

"Some mountains are just too high, Jonathan," she said with a shrug of her world-weary shoulders.

"For some men," he murmured.

"You'll find a way to make a difference. I have faith in you."

"Thank you. That means a lot."

After seeing Pauline safely to her car, Jonathan returned to the church. As he entered the sanctuary, the sun came in soft shining beams through the windows, creating a heavenly light, and it made his nerves tingle. He wasn't alone. The Lord was with him.

"I'm trying," Jonathan said out loud. "I'm trying to save this church for the community." Even as he said the words, he felt a tiny stab of guilt. Was he trying to save the church for the neighborhood, or was he trying to save it for himself? Deep down he knew that a failure here would give everyone yet another reason to wonder if he could live up to his father's reputation.

But whatever his personal ambitions, he couldn't put them ahead of what was right. He *had* to find a way to succeed.

"Reverend?" The halting voice spun him around, but he knew who it was even before he saw her.

"Sarah," he said softly. Her name had run around in his head all night long. He'd wondered if she'd found the shelter and if he'd see her again. He'd hoped that she would trust him enough to come back, and here she was. Maybe he was doing something right.

"I . . ." She hesitated, clearly uncomfortable with her need. "I don't know why I'm here."

"I'm just glad that you are." He walked toward her and waved a hand toward a nearby pew. "Will you sit down?"

Sarah did as he asked, sliding down, leaving several cautious feet between them as he joined her on the bench.

"Can you tell me what has gone wrong in your life? What has brought you such pain?" he asked.

She didn't say anything for a long moment, her face turned toward the ground, her long hair providing a curtain to guard her expression. Jonathan didn't move. He didn't press. He just waited, hoping the quiet of the church, the spiritual strength of their surroundings, would give her the courage to speak.

"I made a big mistake," she said finally.

"What kind of a mistake?"

"My baby."

A sense of dread filled his soul. He prayed that he wouldn't hear she had harmed her child. For how could he protect her from the consequences of such a horrific deed?

"What happened to your baby?" he asked slowly, trying not to let any emotion show in his voice. He didn't want to scare her or threaten her; he wanted her confidence.

"I left her with someone without even asking. I couldn't stand her crying, and I wasn't sure I could keep her safe or provide for her."

Jonathan let the breath out of his chest with a feeling of relief that the baby was alive and, he hoped, well. "Why don't you start at the beginning, Sarah?"

"Where is that?" she asked in bewilderment, raising her head to look at him.

He saw the confusion in her eyes and a hopelessness that touched him deep inside. Sometimes he wondered how he could counsel those who had suffered so much more than he had suffered. How could he understand their pain? How could he reach them when he'd never been to that place where they lived, that bleak, despairing, hopeless place? He was a minister who had grown up in the suburbs, who had never known hunger or thirst, never had to wonder where he came from or where he was going. Sometimes the responsibility of his ministry overwhelmed him with feelings of his own inadequacy. But he couldn't give up. He had to try, even if it meant floundering like a bull in a china shop.

"Start wherever you want," he said to Sarah, hoping it was the right thing to say. For he wanted to help this young woman, wanted to help her more than he'd ever wanted to help anyone.

She looked away from him toward the altar where the candles from the service still burned brightly. She seemed suddenly mesmerized by the flames.

"Fire," she murmured. "I think it started with the fire."

"What fire?"

She started at his question, a shutter coming across her eyes, closing him out, and he silently cursed his own impatience.

"It doesn't matter," she said.

"Is your baby safe, Sarah? That's the most important thing. You must tell me if the child is all right."

She nodded tightly. "She's safe."

"A girl?"

"Yes. Her name is Emily." Sarah's face softened with the love that filled her eyes. "She's a beautiful baby. I never thought I could have anything so perfect."

He smiled gently. "Emily is a lovely name."

"I used to have a doll named EmmaLou. She was my best friend. She wasn't a doll really, just a stick with a doll face on the end of it. Mattie made it for me one day when I was crying because I wanted a dolly, and we didn't have any money to buy a real one." She jerked again, hugging her arms around her waist, as if afraid she had told him too much.

Jonathan had the urge to touch her on the shoulder or the hand, a gesture of comfort, but he held back, afraid even the simplest touch would send her running. She reminded him of the animals at his grandfather's farm, the skittish horses, dogs, and cats who had been mistreated elsewhere, then rescued by his grandfather and protected at his farm. Saving people and animals was a family tradition. His grandfather had had the touch with animals, his father with people. And Jonathan was still trying to find his touch, his way.

"I'd like to talk to you some more, Sarah. Why don't you come next door with me? We can have lunch. I promise it will be good, because I didn't make it."

Sarah didn't respond at all to his encouraging smile. Instead, she bit down on her bottom lip, which he could see she'd already worried into tiny red blisters. "Will anyone else be there?"

"Just me."

"I don't know. I don't even know why I came here. I can't seem to stay away."

"That's why I'm here, Sarah, to talk to people who need to be here. You can trust me. I won't hurt you."

"I don't trust anyone," she said quickly.

"I'm sorry to hear that. Will you come anyway?"

Her face suddenly crumpled and tears slid down her cheeks in quiet agony. "I'm so tired and hungry and scared. I don't know what to do. I don't where to go."

"I can take care of the hunger and the tiredness," Jonathan said decisively. "And I can promise you that you'll be safe." He stood up and held out his hand to her.

"Come with me, Sarah." He had to help her. He had to save her. If he could do that, maybe he could be worthy of his calling.

She hesitated, then slowly took his hand. Her palm was ice-cold, and he felt chilled at the touch. At the same time, her hand felt completely right in his. She needed his warmth, and he needed, God help him, he needed her soul.

 *Eight*

*M*att stepped out of Caitlyn's car and stared at the large expanse of manicured green lawn leading up to a stately Spanish-style house with white stucco and a red shingled roof. The house was in St. Francis Wood, a San Francisco neighborhood he had never seen. And what a neighborhood it was, with large homes set on even larger lots, an unusual occurrence in a city where most houses shared walls and backyards. But these homes were set apart, as if daring anyone to compare them to each other. And this was where Caitlyn had grown up.

Matt had never really felt a class distinction with a woman before, but he had to admit that he felt like he should be using the servant's entrance. He glanced over at Caitlyn, wondering if she, too, was having second thoughts about having asked him to come to brunch, but she was busy unhooking Emily's car seat.

His breath caught in his chest at the sight of her feminine form, alluring in a tantalizingly thin floral dress the color of pink roses. Her legs were bare, her feet encased in thin strappy sandals, and her long blond hair was pulled back in a gold clip at the base of her neck. She was pretty, a ray of sunshine, a golden girl. He took a breath of much-needed air and wondered what the hell he was doing with such a girl.

"I've got her," Caitlyn said with a smile, holding the car seat aloft. "I think Emily has gained weight. She feels heavier."

"I'll take her," he said gruffly, still annoyed with himself and his ridiculous attraction to someone completely wrong for him.

"What did I say?" Caitlyn asked.

Once again she surprised him with her perceptiveness. Didn't she ever miss anything? "Nothing. Let's get this show on the road."

"All right, but you'll have to lose the scowl first."

He forced a phony smile on his face. "Better?"

"Not much. Relax, Matt. They're not that bad."

"Tell me again who will be here," Matt said as they walked up the flower-lined path.

"My parents, Marilyn and Colin, my cousin Jolie and her parents, Sharon and Brady, my aunt and uncle, and maybe the Myers, their best friends."

"And Brian."

"Yes, at least that's what he said. No one else saw fit to mention he had an invitation. They must be going for the surprise attack."

"My favorite kind." Emily made a little gurgle, and Matt flung Caitlyn a grin. "Speaking of surprises, I doubt they're expecting the two of us. Don't you think you should have called?"

"There's always enough food to feed an army. Don't worry. No one will care that you've come with me."

"Oh, I think they'll care. And so do you. That's why you brought me."

She put a hand on his arm, her brown eyes suddenly serious. "I brought you because I really need a friend today. And while Jolie is my dear, dear friend, she's always torn between the family commitment and the friendship thing. Since you don't know any of them, you'll have to be on my side. I know we're not really friends, but maybe just for today you could fake it?"

She seemed unsure of his answer, and it surprised him, reminding him that this beautiful, bright woman had demons of her own to fight. "I'm on your side, Caitlyn. And I won't be faking it."

"Thanks." Caitlyn led him up the front steps. She took a deep breath, then rang the bell.

"Don't you have a key?"

"I don't like to use it. When they have to answer the door, it reminds them that I don't live here anymore, and I don't have to do everything they want me to do."

"Honey, if you're relying on a doorbell to state your independence, I think you've got a ways to go."

"It's a start. Mother!" she exclaimed as the door opened to reveal a stunningly beautiful blonde in a turquoise linen dress.

Matt had to stop his jaw from dropping. From Caitlyn's description, he'd been expecting someone formidable, stern even, but this woman was laughing and smiling and offering her daughter a hug. Then she turned her bright blue eyes on him with genuine curiosity.

"Hello," she said.

"This is Matt Winters," Caitlyn said. "My mother, Marilyn Devereaux."

"It's a pleasure," Marilyn said. "And who is this darling with you?" She leaned over and took a deep breath. "I love the smell of babies. Isn't she just precious?"

"This is Emily, Matt's niece," Caitlyn explained. "He's baby-sitting for a few days."

"How wonderful. I love a man who is good with children. I'm afraid Caitlyn's father was always a bit too vague to be trusted with the details," she said with a charming laugh. "But come in, please. We're so happy to have you here. Any friend of Caitlyn's is a friend of ours."

Matt stepped through the front door, feeling like Alice going down the rabbit hole. The house was exquisitely decorated, hardwood floors, antiques, mirrors . . . it all passed in a blur as they walked through the living room, dining room, and family room to the backyard, where a redwood deck spanned the entire length of the house. The rest of the group was sitting at tables on the deck, drinking what looked to be champagne cocktails. The gathering was rich, sophisticated, and out of his league. What on earth would he say to these people?

Fortunately, he didn't have to worry about conversation, because Emily proved to be an incredible icebreaker. After the introductions, he set her car seat down on the table, and the ladies in the group immediately encircled the baby, each pleading with Caitlyn for a chance to hold Emily. She laughingly told them to take turns, sending Matt a warm smile of her own. Caitlyn was pleased that the baby was getting all the attention and so was he.

Caitlyn's father had barely said hello to Matt. Colin Devereaux was engrossed in a conversation with someone named Jack Myers about the temperature conditions on a distant planet and an experiment to be conducted by astronauts aboard the space shuttle. The man didn't even notice the people moving around him, the other conversations, the housekeeper serving appetizers, the music playing softly in the background. No wonder Caitlyn had said her father lived on another plane.

"So you're Matt," a woman said, speculation ringing in her voice as she stopped next to him.

Matt glanced warily at the beautiful redhead with the stunning figure. She seemed to be the only female in the garden unaffected by baby mania.

"I'm Jolie," she reminded him. "I'm Caitlyn's partner in crime, or at least I used to be. You seem to have taken my place."

"Only temporarily," he said hastily, not sure he liked the inquisitive gleam in Jolie's eye.

"That's a shame. I haven't seen Caitlyn smile like that in a long time."

He followed her gaze, watching as Caitlyn swung Emily up into her arms as naturally as if she were Emily's mother. It struck him how good she was with the baby, how suited she was to motherhood. She was meant to be married, to be loved. He could easily see her with a bunch of kids running around her legs, laughing, squealing, loving her. And this setting fit her perfectly, too, the gardens, the champagne, the beauty of it all. Maybe Caitlyn was right. Maybe she didn't need to read the newspaper. Maybe she didn't need to know all the bad stuff.

They might live in the same apartment building, but they did not live in the same world, and he couldn't start thinking they did. Caitlyn wasn't his girlfriend, and hell, Emily wasn't even his baby. He had to remember that, remember all of it, before he got sucked into wanting all of this to be his.

"I'm surprised Caitlyn brought you," Jolie added, drawing his attention back to her.

He folded his arms across his chest, trying not to look any more uncomfortable than he felt.

"Don't worry, I know which fork to use."

"Ooh, touchy, aren't you? I just meant that Caitlyn doesn't usually bring eligible men anywhere near her mother," Jolie said. "Marilyn is like a shark. She can smell fresh blood from a mile away."

"I'm not eligible."

Jolie raised an eyebrow, perusing him in such a way that another man might think she was actually interested in him, but he had a feeling she was more interested for Caitlyn's sake than for her own.

"You look pretty eligible to me," she purred. "I don't see a wedding ring."

"That doesn't mean I'm available."

"I don't see a girlfriend either."

"That is none of your business. And Caitlyn and I are neighbors, that's it."

"Whatever you say."

She didn't believe him, and to tell the truth, he wasn't so sure he believed himself. It certainly didn't explain why he felt like kissing Caitlyn every other second, or why watching Caitlyn with Emily made him feel protective of both of them.

"How long will you be watching your niece?" Jolie asked.

"I'm not sure."

"Then you and Emily will be quite a distraction for our Caity. She loves kids, always has. How about you?"

"I—I never thought about it."

Matt looked up as another man stepped onto the deck—Brian. He wore slacks and a sport coat almost identical to the one Caitlyn's father was wearing, Matt realized. In fact, as the younger man greeted the older one, they could have been mistaken for father and son. Caitlyn's father's face lit up as he drew Brian into his conversation. It was quite a different response than Matt had received, although he supposed an astrophysicist had more in common with Colin Devereaux than a newspaperman who spent more time investigating the underworld than the heavenly sky.

"Ah, that's the reason you're here," Jolie murmured. "Caity suspected a setup." She nodded approvingly. "Good for her. Better to attack than to go on defense. Don't you agree?"

"That's always been my motto," he said, deciding he liked Jolie despite her prying. She struck him as a woman who'd seen a few games played in her life and had figured out a way to win. She also appeared to be loyal to Caitlyn, although Matt knew that alliances could be deceiving.

"He's here," Caitlyn said tightly, joining Matt and Jolie, having successfully handed Emily over to her mother. "Look at him, he's the prodigal son come back."

"Maybe if you told us all what happened," Jolie said pointedly, "we could treat Brian accordingly."

Matt shot Caitlyn a curious look. Why hadn't she told her parents and her best friend that she'd been devastated by Brian's departure when she was still in the hospital? Was she protecting him? If so, why? Because she still loved him? Because she was thinking of going back to him? For some reason the thought of that disturbed Matt more than he cared to admit.

"Oh, dear, I hope this won't be awkward," Marilyn Devereaux interrupted as she joined them with Emily in her arms. "I thought it might be nice for you and Brian to meet on neutral ground, Caitlyn. I didn't know you were bringing another man."

"This is hardly neutral ground, Mother," Caitlyn retorted. "And you might have consulted with me first."

Good for you, Matt silently cheered her on. Despite Marilyn's charming manner, he had a feeling this was a woman who had her iron fist hidden in a velvet glove.

"I'm sorry, dear. I've been so worried about you. You haven't been yourself. And I hate to see you just drifting along. You haven't even been able to draw lately. And you know how much you love to draw." Her expression changed to inquisitive as she turned her attention to Matt. "Are you an artist, too, Mr. Winters?"

"I'm a reporter for the Herald."

"How fascinating."

He suspected that the fact he was with Caitlyn was what made him most fascinating to her.

"And you're single?" Marilyn continued.

"Mother!" Caitlyn protested.

"I'm just interested, Caitlyn."

Emily started to squirm, and Marilyn Devereaux wrinkled her nose as the four of them were suddenly assaulted by a distinctive odor. "Oh, dear, not exactly conducive to brunch."

Matt took Emily into his arms. In truth, he was just as relieved to have this female to deal with; at least she couldn't ask personal questions or examine him like a bug under a microscope.

"Why don't we take Emily inside and change her?" Caitlyn suggested.

"You should speak to Brian, Caitlyn," Marilyn protested. "He's trying so hard to understand you, dear. Please give him a chance. I think it would be good for both of you."

"I spoke to him last night. Didn't he tell you?"

"He told me that you think it might be better to stay

apart." Marilyn shook her head at her daughter. The expression in her eyes expressed frustration and disappointment. "He still loves you, Caitlyn. I'm sorry if that makes you uncomfortable," she said to Matt, who was trying to bounce Emily into better spirits. "I don't mean to intrude into whatever relationship you and Caitlyn have. I'm just very concerned about my daughter."

"I'm fine," he said shortly. "Don't mind me."

"Caitlyn and Brian were engaged, and they broke it off at a very difficult time, due to circumstances beyond their control," Marilyn continued. "I think they should talk."

"I'm standing right here, Mom," Caitlyn said with annoyance.

"I can see that. But I'd like you to be standing over there." Marilyn tipped her head toward Brian.

"I'm going to get the diaper bag," Matt said, eager to get away.

"I'll come with you," Caitlyn replied. "I'll talk to Brian later."

Matt followed her to the French doors leading into the family room. They were almost home free when Brian stepped away from her father with a wary smile and greeting.

"You remember Matt and his niece, Emily?" Caitlyn said politely.

"Yes," Brian said with a nod, not looking at all pleased to see Matt again. "He's your . . . neighbor."

Matt didn't like the way Brian said the word *neighbor*, as if he were spitting out something distasteful. "Honey, I think we should change the baby," Matt said, deliberately implying that Caitlyn was more to him than a neighbor. He didn't know why he did it, because he certainly hadn't intended to give Caitlyn's family the wrong impression, but there was something so smug about Brian that his competitive instinct immediately sprang to the fore.

Caitlyn's jaw dropped at his endearment, but Matt didn't wait for a response from either her or Brian. He headed into the house and scooped the diaper bag off of a nearby table.

"What was that 'honey' all about?" Caitlyn demanded, catching up to him in the hall.

"Bradley looks at you like he owns you."

"Well, *Brian* doesn't. And that's not because you called me honey."

She grabbed Emily's diaper bag out of his hand and walked up the stairs. "Come on."

"Can't we just do it down here somewhere?" Matt asked, not sure he wanted to see any more of Caitlyn's life. On second thought, judging by the stink of Emily's diaper, changing her on top of the mahogany dining table probably wouldn't be a good idea.

"In here," Caitlyn said, leading him into a bedroom.

It was a beautiful room, white walls, soft lacy curtains, and a large queen-size bed filled high with fluffy yellow pillows. A plush armchair and matching ottoman were placed comfortably by the window, offering a view of the trees outside. There was an array of feminine things in the room, perfumes, music boxes, and pictures. "This is your room," Matt said.

"*Was* my room."

He stopped by the dresser to check out a picture of a young Caitlyn. She was standing by a bus with a backpack at her feet and couldn't have been more than about ten.

"That's my fat picture," she told him as she walked into the adjoining bathroom to get a towel.

"Fat?" The girl was a little pudgy but certainly not obese.

"My mother told me she'd signed me up for this great camp in Santa Rosa," Caitlyn said as she returned to the room with a towel, which she spread over the bed. "It turned out to be a camp for fat kids. They fed us celery and carrots and made us hike ten miles a day. So much for the art, watercolors, and charades I was expecting."

"Doesn't sound like fun."

"It wasn't supposed to be fun, it was supposed to be good for me."

"Your mother knows what she wants."

"And goes after it full steam ahead," Caitlyn agreed. "She can be a little ruthless. I'll take Emily."

He handed her the baby and dug his hands in his pockets as he watched Caitlyn change Emily in record time.

"That's better, isn't it, sweetie?" Caitlyn fixed the tape on a new diaper. "Let's hope your mother doesn't try to change every last thing about you."

"Being smothered with motherly attention isn't the worst thing that can happen to you," Matt reminded her.

A guilty look flashed in her eyes, as well as a glint of irritation. "Maybe not the worst thing. You wouldn't understand."

And he didn't. How could he when he'd had absolutely no motherly attention? From where he stood, Caitlyn's life looked pretty damn good. "Look at your bedroom," he said with a sweep of his hand. "Who could be unhappy here? It's a room for a princess, a pampered princess."

"You think I'm spoiled?" she snapped.

"I think you got everything you wanted."

Caitlyn looked like she was counting to ten, and there was a thundercloud gathering in her eyes that told him he should probably shut up. But he'd never been very good at avoiding trouble. And in truth he wanted to fight with her. He wanted to remind himself that this would never be his world and a woman like Caitlyn would never be his woman.

He had to suck in a breath of air at that thought, because the real truth was he wanted her to be his woman.

"You're just like the rest of them," Caitlyn said.

It wasn't what he'd expected. "You're comparing me to your parents?" he asked in amazement. "That's a laugh."

"Why? You're just as ruthless, critical, judgmental, making comments about something you know little about but acting like you know everything there is to know."

"So what are you trying to say? You were the lonely little rich girl? No one understood you? You didn't get to go to a real camp? It still doesn't compare to growing up wondering where your next meal is coming from. That's trouble, Caitlyn. That's adversity."

"Fine, you win. Your mother was worse than my mother. Are you happy now?"

"It's not about winning," he grumbled, her comment making him feel like he was about ten years old.

"Then what is it about?"

"You and me," he said with a cryptic wave of his hand.

Caitlyn sat down on the bed and adjusted Emily's sleeper. "You're going to have to give me more than that."

"I don't fit in here."

"No man does," she said. "It's a girl's room. In fact, my mother designed it to make boys feel uncomfortable so they wouldn't think about sneaking up here with me."

"That's not true."

"It is true," she said. "But you're right. I did have an okay childhood. I certainly had more than the basics. Maybe I was due for a fall. Maybe that accident was a way for fate to balance the scales." Her face grew pensive. "Maybe I deserved what I got because I had so much and I didn't appreciate it."

"Whoa there. No one deserves to fall down a mountain or to be hurt. That wasn't my point."

"I'm not sure you had a point."

He wasn't so sure, either. But he didn't know why she didn't think she measured up to her parents. As far as he could tell, she was a very bright woman, perceptive, intuitive, compassionate. Okay, this wasn't working. He was supposed to be concentrating on the negative, not the positive.

She shrugged. "Well, it doesn't really matter. I am who I am, shaped by everything in my life, the good stuff and the bad stuff. And frankly, I've worried too much about what other people think of me, so whatever you think of me—so be it. I'm not going to apologize." She looked up at him and shook her head. "I can't believe the deep conversations we have. Haven't you ever heard of polite chitchat? Where you talk about the weather and the ball game and who's dating Gwyneth Paltrow?"

"Who *is* dating Gwyneth Paltrow?"

"That's better."

He sat down on the bed next to Emily, who was looking with delight at a couple of stuffed animals on top of Caitlyn's dresser. He wondered what kind of bedroom Emily would have. One like this, he hoped. What a hypocrite he was, condemning Caitlyn for having what every little girl should have, what he'd want to give his own little girl.

That thought hit him like a punch in the gut. He wanted his own daughter. He wanted a bedroom like this one in his house. He wanted pictures on the dresser, height marks on the doorway, stuffed animals on the bed.

"What are you thinking?" she asked, a curious note in her voice.

There was no way in hell he was going to tell her. "Nothing."

"I guess we should go downstairs."

"In a second."

"What? You're not ready to face my incredibly wonderful parents? Have brunch off China plates and sip on champagne cocktails? Didn't you just say I had everything? So why the hesitation?"

"Facing your mother is a bit like going before the firing squad," he admitted.

"My beautiful mother?" Caitlyn asked in mock wonder. "Really?"

"Okay, I'll admit that having material things isn't everything," he conceded. "But I always thought I'd like a shot at being rich and unhappy instead of poor and unhappy. At least I could sunburn my sorrows while I was sailing on a yacht instead of counting the cockroaches darting under my bed."

"There aren't any cockroaches in your apartment now. In fact, I bet you make a pretty good living—a single guy, a good job, no furniture. Oh, my God! I bet you even have a bank account." She put a hand to her mouth in horror.

"A small one, maybe." He liked the fact that she could give it right back, that his harsh words hadn't sent her into an all-day sulk, which would have occurred with many of the women he'd dated over the years. Not that he ever would have allowed himself to speak so freely or so openly. But there was something about Caitlyn that made him feel like he could be himself.

"And you have a nice car, too," she said with a growing smile. "Yeah, you're really suffering these days."

"I might be a little lonely."

"Well, lonely isn't real trouble, real adversity, Matt, it's just lonely. You can get over that. Get yourself a cat."

He laughed out loud. "You're enjoying yourself now, aren't you?"

"Pretty much."

Emily gave a little gurgle, as if she, too, were enjoying herself.

Matt shook his head. "Figures you'd both gang up on me. After all, you're both female."

"Caitlyn?" Brian's voice caught them both off guard. He stood in the doorway, a frown spreading across his face as he took in their cozy appearance on the bed. "Am I interrupting?"

"No," Caitlyn said.

"Yes," Matt said.

"I was hoping we could talk for a few minutes before brunch is served," Brian replied.

"I'm listening."

"Alone?" He sent Matt a pointed look.

"I can hardly ask Matt to leave. He's a guest."

At her words, Matt made himself more comfortable on the bed, ignoring Brian's look of displeasure. He probably should leave them alone, but he didn't feel like it. The guy was an ass, and he didn't deserve one second of Caitlyn's time.

"Fine." Brian took a deep breath, then continued. "I thought about what you said yesterday, about my impulsive comments in the hospital after your accident. I realize now how deeply I must have hurt you, which in turn must have influenced your reaction later on when the fellowship came up. I'm very sorry. I can't take my words back, but I wish I could."

Matt saw Caitlyn lick her lips and wondered if she was actually buying this load of crap. Damn. Her eyes were moist like she was about to cry, like she was about to jump off the bed and give Brian a big old reunion kiss. Couldn't she see that the guy wanted her back now because she was healthy and beautiful? What would happen when life knocked them down again? She wouldn't be able to count on this man.

"Maybe you should leave us alone," Caitlyn said to Matt.

Before he could tell her he wasn't going anywhere, Emily let out a sharp cry. Good girl, Matt thought with a small smile, as Caitlyn immediately turned her attention to the baby.

"What's wrong, sweetie?" Caitlyn picked Emily up and cuddled her in her arms.

"Can't you take her for a minute?" Brian said impatiently to Matt. "She is your niece, isn't she?"

"She's hungry," Caitlyn said to Matt. "I know that cry."

"Can't he feed her?" Brian asked.

"Emily likes Caitlyn to give her the bottle," Matt said.

"I don't think that's true," Caitlyn replied, but she didn't give up the baby. Instead, she turned to Brian and said, "I appreciate what you're saying, but this isn't the time or the place to have this discussion."

Matt frowned. Didn't she realize her statement was leaving the door open for future conversations? Brian, too, interpreted her words that way, his eyes lighting up with optimism.

"Would you at least consider having a meal with me one day this week, if for no other reason than old times' sake?"

"Why don't you call me?" Caitlyn stood up and walked to the door, pausing in front of Brian. "I know that on the outside I must look like the girl you used to love, but the truth is she's gone, and she's not coming back. The last year and a half changed me forever. You better think about that. There is the possibility that you might not want me back."

"I don't think so, Caitlyn. But let me get to know you now. That's all I'm asking."

"I'll—I'll think about it," she said as she left the bedroom.

Matt followed Caitlyn down to the kitchen, wanting to shake some sense into her. It was ridiculous to give that idiot a second chance. He'd left her once. That should have been enough to tell her he wasn't a man to be trusted.

"Why did you leave the door open?" he demanded as she entered the kitchen. Thankfully, they were alone, the cook or whoever she was having gone out to the deck to serve appetizers.

Caitlyn sent him a puzzled look. "What door? That door?" She pointed to the kitchen door.

"No, the door to your relationship. You should have cut him off at the knees. Instead you gave him hope."

She shrugged her shoulders helplessly. "I was engaged to the man. All he wants now is one meal. I didn't know what else to say."

"How about 'Hit the road, Jack'?"

"I couldn't do that."

"For God's sake, Caitlyn, the man left you in a wheelchair. How can you let him back into your life just like that?"

"I'm trying not to."

"You better try harder. Because right now I guarantee you he's calling around for dinner reservations."

"I just don't want to hurt him unnecessarily."

"You are too damn . . . nice," he said spitting out the word like it was foul tasting.

"You think I'm too nice?" She looked more pleased than upset.

"I didn't mean that as a compliment. You shouldn't let people take advantage of you."

"Oh, you mean like when someone knocks on my door and asks me to help him take care of a baby?"

"How long are you going to throw that at me?"

Caitlyn considered the question. "For a while, I think."

Her wicked smile took his blood pressure up a notch. How he wished they were alone—no baby, no family, no old boyfriends around—so he could wipe that smile off her face in his own very personal way. He couldn't help licking his lips, and saw Caitlyn follow the move with a pair of widening eyes.

"What are you doing?" she asked, a breathless note in her voice.

"Nothing."

"That's not nothing," she said. "You licked your lips like you were thinking about . . ."

"About what?"

"You know."

"Why don't you tell me?"

"Like kissing me. And if that's the case, you better stop thinking."

"And start acting? I agree," he said, moving swiftly forward to steal a brief but passionate kiss that left his mouth tingling.

"That was . . ."

"You're having trouble completing your sentences," he told her huskily.

"Too short," she finished.

He shook his head in disbelief. "You're one of the few people who doesn't say what I expect you to say."

"I'll take that as a compliment. And by the way, I'm taking the too nice thing as a compliment, too."

Emily gave a cry, reminding them that she was still hungry and they better get back to business. "I'll take her. You can make the bottle," Matt said, reaching for the baby.

"What's going on in here?" Jolie asked as she entered the room.

Caitlyn blushed. Matt saw it. So did Jolie.

"Just getting Emily a bottle," Caitlyn said hastily.

"Really?" Jolie sent them both a thoughtful look. "You three look like a family, you know that?"

"We're not," Caitlyn replied.

"No, we're not," Matt echoed, but he had a shocking feeling he wanted them to be just that.

 *Nine*

"*W*here are we going?" Caitlyn asked Matt as she drove through the streets of San Francisco at his direction, making turns that were inexplicably leading them away from their apartment building.

"I want to show you something," Matt said somewhat tersely.

She cast him a quick glance, but he was staring out the window, tapping his fingers against one thigh. He'd been quiet at brunch, too. In fact, after that kiss in the kitchen he'd pulled away from her, keeping a distance between them at all times.

It had been easy for him to do that, her mother having placed Brian next to Caitlyn with Matt at the other end of the table. The conversation had been carefully manipulated by her mother as well, as Marilyn discussed the highlights of Brian's year in Boston, accentuating each positive point for Caitlyn's benefit.

Did Caitlyn realize that Brian's research paper had

won an important award? That he was being courted by both Stanford and California University? And wasn't Caitlyn proud of him for all that he had accomplished?

Caitlyn had managed to nod and murmur appropriately, the only saving grace being Brian's own embarrassment. It reminded her of the man she'd once loved, a man who could be intellectually arrogant but also appealingly human.

She knew Matt thought she was an idiot for even considering giving Brian another chance. But he only knew part of the story. That was the problem. Everyone knew only a small part of the story, and she wasn't brave enough to put it all together for them.

"Turn right at the next light," Matt said.

"What are you planning to show me?" she asked, relieved to have something else to think out. Granted, she was quickly becoming the queen of denial, but like Scarlett in her favorite novel, *Gone with the Wind*, she'd think about that tomorrow.

"You'll see."

"How's Emily doing?"

"Fast asleep." Matt looked into the backseat, where they'd placed Emily's car seat. "I think she likes cars."

"You'll have to remember that the next time she wakes up at two A.M."

"So, now I'll be driving around the city in the middle of the night?"

"Or spending a lot of time on the roof."

He smiled, and she felt a welcome relief that the camaraderie between them had returned. As they drove down lower Market toward the theater district and the area known as the Tenderloin, Caitlyn noticed the growing numbers of homeless people on the streets, the graffiti on alley walls, the gradual deterioration of the neighborhoods.

"Hard to wear those rose-colored glasses around here, isn't it?" Matt asked, an edge back in his voice. His profile was etched in stone, his eyes hidden behind a pair of dark sunglasses that gave nothing away. "Turn left at the next block."

She drove down a residential street filled with cheap, old apartment buildings squished tightly together.

"Pull over," he said, staring at a building on the other side of the street.

Caitlyn parked the car and turned off the engine. "Who lives here?"

He swallowed, the pulse in his jaw beating overtime. "I used to live here."

His childhood home. She should have guessed. "Do you think Sarah is here?"

"No. I've had my investigator check it out every day, every hour practically. She hasn't been back."

Caitlyn remained silent for a few minutes. "Why are we here?"

"Since I saw where you grew up, I thought I'd return the favor."

She thought about that. "Another line in the sand? Do you think I'm a snob as well as privileged?"

"I think you're a girl from the other side of the tracks."

"The tracks don't run through this city."

"You know what I mean."

"I know you put way too much importance on circumstances. Neither one of us was responsible for where we grew up or how we grew up."

He turned in his seat to look at her. "Even so, you can't imagine what it was like to grow up here."

"Why don't you tell me?"

"I can't."

"You can't or you won't?" She looked toward the apartment building. "Which window was yours?"

For a moment she didn't think he would answer, then he said, "Fourth floor, last window on the end. That's where Sarah would sit and stare out at the stars. She was like you. She thought there was some answer to be found in the heavens."

"Have you been back inside?"

"No. God no! Why would I want to do that?"

"Maybe to see if anything has changed. Maybe to see if you've changed."

"I have changed. This place is just the same."

"How would you know if you haven't been inside?"

"I know."

"But there was a fire. They must have remodeled. Don't you want to see what they did?"

"No."

"You can't make yourself go in, can you?"

"I've tried," he grudgingly admitted. "My last memory of this building is watching the smoke pour through the windows and the flames leap out in long, monstrous fingers, trying to suck us back in."

Caitlyn felt a chill run down her spine at his words. She could only imagine a young boy and his sister, all alone, watching their only home burn. "Where was your mother at the time of the fire?"

"I have no idea."

"How did the fire start?"

"I don't know."

He was lying. For some reason, the man who loved the truth was lying. Why?

"Oh, my God," she said, jumping to the most logical conclusion. "Sarah started the fire, didn't she?"

"No."

"Yes. You're lying to protect her. I know it's the truth because you can't look at me and tell me it isn't, can you?"

He stared out the window, wrestling with the question in agonizing silence.

"Sarah was fascinated with fire," he said finally. "My mother used to light candles at night, and she'd let Sarah light them sometimes because—because she couldn't quite hold her hand steady enough to strike the match. It was something they did together. But sometimes Sarah picked up the matches when my mother wasn't home. I think she'd light the candles hoping they would bring my mother back."

"And one night they started a fire instead."

"I accused her of ruining what little we had left in our lives. Damn it, Caitlyn." The lines in his face tightened with guilt. "She was a little girl, and I screamed at her like a lunatic. And she just looked at me with her big dark eyes and said she was sorry. I never saw her again after that. I never had a chance to tell her I didn't mean it."

Caitlyn didn't know what to say. Some things couldn't be taken back or done over.

"Is it any wonder she dropped her baby in front of my door and ran like hell?" he asked bitterly. "She probably still can't face me."

Caitlyn wondered if that were true. Had Sarah left Emily with just a note because she couldn't face her brother? Because of some angry words spoken between them more than a decade ago? Caitlyn couldn't quite believe that Sarah would leave her baby with a man she didn't trust completely, which made any anger on her part illogical.

"I don't think that's it," she said slowly. "I think whatever caused Sarah to leave Emily with you has more to do with who she is now than who you were then."

"Maybe who she is now is because of who I was then."

How could she argue with a man who was so good with words? "I think you should do what you normally do—get the facts first, then decide."

"How do you know what I normally do?" he asked grumpily.

"Well, I figure that's what most good reporters do, and I think you did tell me you were a good reporter." She offered him a wheedling smile. "Come on, Matt. You know you won't be able to make sense of this until you find Sarah. Until then you have to be objective."

"I can't be objective about this. And I'm not sure I will find Sarah. It's been three days. Where the hell is she?"

Matt suddenly straightened in his seat. She followed his gaze, but didn't see anything that might have set his nerves on edge. "What's wrong?"

"That woman, the one wearing the straw hat and carrying a water can. Did you see her?"

"Where?" she asked.

"She was right there." He pointed down the street. "How could you not see her?"

"I was looking at you. Who was she? Someone you know?"

He hesitated. "Probably not. It's just that my mother used to water the plants in our apartment with an old-fashioned watering can. Sometimes, I thought she cared more about those plants than she did about us. Hell, maybe she did." He shrugged. "This place makes me crazy. I keep looking for the people who used to be here. Mr. Maloney's newspaper stand was on the corner over there by the liquor store, but he's gone now." Matt pointed to another abandoned storefront farther down the block. "That was a blues club. I'd lay awake in my bed at night with the windows open and listen to the music. It made it seem like there was something good about the neighborhood. I'm sure it was a drug den. There were fights and sirens blaring after midnight. But I just heard the saxophone."

Caitlyn could almost hear it, too, so vividly had he painted the scene. "Matt?"

"What?"

"Tell me again. Why are we really here?"

He shifted restlessly in his seat. "Things were getting out of hand at your parents' house."

She stiffened, having a feeling she'd rather talk about his past than hers. "So you thought this would scare me off."

"I know you wanted a buffer between you and Brian, but your friends and your family started wondering about us, thinking that you and I are something more. And we're not."

"I know that." She just wasn't sure she liked hearing it said so certainly, as if there were no possibility that they could be more. Well, that was a ridiculous way to feel, she told herself firmly. She was already confused enough about Brian, how could she throw another man into the mix? Matt's attitude was perfect. They wouldn't have any misunderstandings between them.

Of course, there was that physical thing that even now was turning the air into electrical currents flowing back and forth between them in the intimacy of the car. Caitlyn was acutely aware of how close Matt was to her, just an automatic gearshift between them, barely a foot. She could touch him if she wanted to. He could touch her— not that he would want to.

"I know you were just helping me out today, nothing

more." Despite her blithe words, she knew how easy it had been to pretend that Matt and Emily were something more. She'd already gotten too involved and emotionally attached to both of them, but she couldn't let Matt know. She wouldn't make her feelings his responsibility. "It's okay, really. You don't have to worry. I know where the lines are."

"Something tells me you don't know how to color within the lines."

"I can if I have to. But sometimes you get a better result if you don't paint by the numbers. It's called being imaginative and creative, and the result can be fabulous."

"Or it can be a mess. I like you," he said huskily, meeting her eyes. "That's not the point, you know."

Oh, Lord. If he was going to be nice, acting casual would be a lot more difficult.

"I thought bringing you here might make you see how far apart we are. But all I can think about right now is how close you're sitting to me and how much closer I'd like you to get."

Caitlyn sucked in a desperate breath. Then he leaned over, and her heartbeat came to an abrupt and shattering halt as he put a finger under her chin and turned her face toward him. She thought he was going to kiss her, but he surprised her by simply removing her sunglasses.

"I can't see what you're thinking," he said.

"I could say the same about you." She pulled off his glasses before realizing how much more unsettling his gaze would be without any barrier between them. Eye to eye, there was an even greater connection, one that seemed impossible to break.

"What am I going to do about you?" he murmured.

"I have no idea. You keep telling me we're not going to be more than friends, but we keep getting friendlier."

"You talk too much."

"And you're going to make me stop?"

"Oh, yeah." Not a man to ignore a dare, Matt's mouth came down on hers before she had a chance to reconsider her impulsive challenge.

Matt kissed with the same brutal honesty with which he spoke, not letting her retreat or hold back when her good-girl upbringing warred with her desperate need to slide her tongue into his mouth and taste him. And when Matt put his hands on her arms, pulling her deeper into his embrace, all she could think about was getting closer to all that heat.

"God," he swore as he released her, their breaths coming fast and ragged, steaming up the car in the middle of the afternoon. "What you do to me. I could forget everything."

Caitlyn sat back, suddenly realizing how much she'd forgotten, like the fact that they were parked on a busy street with a baby sleeping in the very backseat she would have liked to hop into with Matt.

"Well, that was . . ." She couldn't even think what it was—Fun? Wild? Stupid? All of the above?

"Yeah, it sure was. Want to do it again?"

Her pulse leaped in response, but she forced herself to shake her head. "No."

"Right. Can you open a window? It's hot in here."

Caitlyn started the engine so she could lower the power windows, flooding the car with cool air. For a moment they just sat there and breathed in and out until the tension between them began to dissipate.

"We could just go home," Caitlyn finally suggested, quickly realizing that her use of the word *home* hadn't exactly made things easier. She jumped back in with another suggestion. "Or we could do what I always do when I don't know what to do next."

"And what would that be?"

"Go shopping."

He groaned. "I hate shopping, especially with a female."

"Well, you're in luck, because you won't just be shopping with a female but for a female. Seriously, Matt, Emily needs some clothes. We can't keep changing her from one outfit to the other. And I was thinking maybe . . ."

"I'm not buying a crib."

The man was incredible at reading her mind. "Okay, how about a cradle, or one of those traveling cribs, so Emily has a more comfortable place to sleep?"

"She won't be staying long enough to need any furniture."

"Matt!"

"All right, a couple of outfits. We can always give them to Sarah when she comes back, but don't get carried away."

"Me? Get carried away? I wouldn't dream of it."

"How long has it been since you've eaten?" Jonathan asked Sarah as she pushed her empty plate away. She'd shoveled the food down as if she were afraid it would disappear before she'd had enough.

She looked guilty at his question and mumbled, "A while."

"It's okay, you know. Everyone gets hungry. We all need to eat." He rested his elbows on the white linen tablecloth covering his dining room table. "What else do you need, Sarah? Besides food?"

A dozen emotions flitted through her eyes in the seconds that followed his question. Finally, she shook her head, hopelessness settling over her face.

"Who hurt you?" He knew his question was abrupt, but he had a feeling giving Sarah too much time to think would be a mistake.

"I—I can't tell you."

"Just a first name."

She considered his words thoughtfully, and he realized he'd never met anyone so intensely serious and so desperately sad, for there was pain in her eyes, in every movement of her mouth, every tiny flicker of her eyelids. He had a feeling the sadness had come before the bruises.

"Gary," she said abruptly.

"And who is Gary to you? A boyfriend? A husband?" His eyes drifted to her hand, but there was no ring on her finger and no indication that there ever had been one. He couldn't stop the sudden tingle of relief that ran through him. He forced himself to remember that this wasn't personal, this was business, his business. Sarah was simply a lost soul he needed to save.

Sarah appeared confused by his question. In fact, she looked downright dazed. Not for the first time, he prayed that she wasn't on drugs. In his experience the power of the Lord couldn't always overcome the power of narcotics.

"He said he loved me."

"Violence isn't love," Jonathan said gently.

"Gary didn't hit me before. He just got so mad when I said I couldn't—" She stopped abruptly. "It doesn't matter."

"What couldn't you do?"

"Nothing."

"It had to be something important." He paused, waiting for her to continue, but she remained silent. "Do you ever pray?"

"No."

"Really? Not even once in a while, just in case someone might hear you?" He smiled at her reassuringly. "I won't get mad either way, I'm just curious."

"A long time ago I used to pray, but no one was listening."

"I'm listening now, if you want to talk."

She remained silent for so long he was about to give up when she finally spoke, slowly, haltingly. "Gary said I was a bad mother. And he was right. The baby was always crying. She didn't like me much. But I—I loved her like I never loved anyone." Her eyes pooled with moisture. "You have to believe me."

"I do. What did Gary ask you to do, Sarah?"

"I can't say. I've said too much already."

"But your baby is safe with someone you trust?"

He knew he had asked her before, but he had to be sure. If the baby was all right, he could take his time before he called anyone. It was a weak rationalization, but he made it all the same, for there was something about Sarah that touched him deeply. And what would a few hours mean in the overall scheme of things? If he could help her, he'd feel like he was doing something meaningful. It occurred to him that his feeling better was not nearly as important as Sarah's mental health, but he couldn't stop to examine his motives.

Sarah drew in a sniffly breath, her frail shoulders trembling. "She's with someone who can take care of her, probably better than I can. I turned out just like my own mother, totally worthless. I always knew I was like her, but I didn't know how much until I had Emily."

"Your mother wasn't supportive?"

Sarah shook her head. "She wasn't even around most of the time. She'd go off and leave me with my brother, even when I was a baby. She'd say she loved me, but she hated me, too."

"I don't believe that."

"Oh, it's true. I know it's true, because she . . ." Her voice drifted away. "Well, I just know."

Jonathan let that pass. "You can still be a mother to your child, Sarah. You can get help."

"From who?"

He wanted to shout "From me!" but forced himself to hold back. He was here to give advice and spiritual guidance, not to step in and solve problems, especially when he had no real idea just how deep Sarah's problems went. She was a confused young woman who'd obviously led a rough, uncertain life, but was there more? Was she too weak to take care of a child? Was she mentally ill? Or just tired and worn out and overwhelmed?

"There is help out there," he said. "Social services, welfare, transitional homes . . ."

Sarah immediately shook her head. "I've seen foster homes. The people in it do it for the money. They don't care about the kids."

"They're not all like that. You haven't met very many good people in your life, have you?" He didn't wait for an answer, making an impulsive decision. "Well, that I think I can do something about."

"What do you mean?" she asked warily.

"I could use some help today. Your help, if you're willing."

"I don't know how to do much."

"You can do this."

She stared at him doubtfully. "Why would you want me to help you?"

"Because giving can make you feel better at the same time it makes someone else feel better."

"Are you sure?"

"I've never been more sure of anything in my life." He paused, reaching across the table to cover her hand with his. "In my line of work, you realize early on that life is about taking one step at a time. Can you do that much for me, Sarah? Can you take one step with me?"

"Are you going to hold my hand?" she asked softly.

Her eyes met his, and he knew he should let go, but he couldn't.

 Ten

"We don't need a changing table." Matt rolled his eyes as Caitlyn ran her hand across the smooth surface of an oak changing table that would also serve as a dresser. "Or a stroller," he added as her eyes lit on a state-of-the-art stroller across the aisle. He would have to rein her in, he realized as he followed her through the crowded baby store with Emily in his arms.

"Look, this is one of those joggers," Caitlyn said with delight, stopping in front of a three-wheeler. "You can run with Emily. You said you haven't been able to run since she got here. This would be perfect."

"She's not going to be with me that long. And I don't think Sarah runs."

"How would you know? Oh, isn't that the cutest outfit?" Caitlyn ran down the aisle and pulled out a bright red dress that was only a little bigger than Matt's hand. "It has a bonnet to go with it. You have to get this one."

"This was a big mistake," he said, frowning at her unbridled enthusiasm. With Emily nuzzled against his chest and Caitlyn by his side, he felt like he was part of a family: a husband, a wife, a baby. But they weren't a family, and he couldn't let himself forget that. "Look at you," he said pointedly, finally getting Caitlyn's attention.

"What? I'm fine."

"You're out of control."

"It's one cute little dress," she said, putting it in the cart. "Diapers, we need diapers." She walked around the corner and tossed several large bags into the cart, followed by baby wipes, bottles, formula, bibs, socks, a couple of sleepers, a baby blanket, a traveling crib, and a pink hair ribbon that Caitlyn couldn't resist. By the time they headed down the last aisle, the cart was overflowing with items Caitlyn insisted that he needed.

"You know I'm not a rich man," he told her.

"Most of it is on sale."

"And most of it we don't need. I don't need," he corrected. "She doesn't need," he said, finally finding the right pronoun.

Caitlyn simply offered him a smile that told him she could see right through him. To distract her, he stopped and looked over at the shelves, determined to find something else that they didn't need, so she would coo over it and focus her attention anywhere but on him. That's when he saw it, an enormous chocolate brown teddy bear with soft, plush fur and black eyes that reminded him of Sarah.

"Emily would love that," Caitlyn said.

"It's bigger than she is," he replied gruffly.

"She'll grow into it." Caitlyn took the bear off the rack and sat it on top of the growing pile, daring him to take it off.

"Fine," he said with a long-suffering sigh.

"Oh, please, you don't fool me."

"I don't know what you're talking about."

"I'm talking about that sentimental streak that runs down your back."

"You're seeing things with those rose-colored glasses again, Princess."

"And you're a terrible liar. Why not just admit that you wouldn't mind giving this sweet bear a little hug?" Caitlyn leaned over and put her arms around the bear, her eyes lit up with mischievous playfulness.

He tried hard not to smile, but she was a picture with her long golden hair and her warm brown eyes. "I've got my arms full as it is," he said, adjusting Emily on his shoulder.

"I can take Emily."

"She's my responsibility."

"How kind of you to remember when it's convenient," she said dryly. "I'll remind you of that next time she has a poopy diaper."

Matt laughed out loud, thinking how long it had been since he'd heard himself laugh. Not that he'd admit that to her. It was one thing to confess a little lust to a woman, but genuine liking was going too far.

"You should do that more often," Caitlyn told him. "And maybe pick out some brighter clothes. You wear a lot of black."

"I like black. It suits my mood."

"It's depressing," she said, pushing the cart toward one of the checkout counters.

"That's me and the newspaper, depressing."

She made a face at him as they stopped at the end of a long line. "Life is too short to spend most of it dwelling on the negative."

"But it helps to be informed. You can make better choices, avoid costly, dangerous situations."

"Like opening your door at midnight when some man announces there's a baby in the hallway?"

He groaned. "There it is again."

"And how would reading the newspaper have prevented me from opening my door?"

"You might have read about the dangers of letting a stranger into your house."

"And where would you be then? I'll tell you," she said, not waiting for an answer. "You'd be here alone, buying Emily an entire wardrobe in black, I'm sure."

"All right, you win." He wrinkled his nose as a nasty smell assailed him. He didn't know why women raved about a baby smell. As far as he could tell, there was only one distinct odor, and it certainly wasn't rosy.

"Ooh," Caitlyn said with a frown. "Guess it's time to remind you about Emily being your responsibility."

"I have to pay for this stuff."

"That is a dilemma, isn't it?"

"You're going to make me ask, aren't you? Fine. Will you please help me by changing Emily's diaper?"

"Yes, I will, since you asked so nicely. I'll take her out to the car."

"I think there's one diaper left in the diaper bag," he told her. "If not, you'll have to wait until I pay for these."

"I think there is one left. I'll pick up a newspaper on the way out and lay it down over the upholstery," she said with a mischievous smile. "See, I knew those newspapers were good for something."

"Remind me to tell you how important wedding dresses are to national security."

"I was just kidding. Jeez, lighten up. And wedding dresses may not be important to national security, but they do add to the national gross product." She took

Emily out of his arms. "And more importantly, they make people happy. And that's priceless."

Matt was still smiling even after she'd left. A foolish grin no doubt, judging by the way the checker stared at him like he was looney. And maybe he was. Emily and Caitlyn were turning his world upside down. He just wished he didn't feel so damn good about it, because if he knew anything, he knew this: if something seemed too good to be true, it probably was.

Caitlyn hadn't enjoyed herself so much in a long time. After they'd finished their shopping, Matt had dropped her and Emily off at home, while he'd run out to pick up some food for dinner. Caitlyn had made herself comfortable in Matt's apartment, and after putting away the baby things, she'd given Emily a bath in her new tub.

Emily loved the water, smiling and gurgling every time Caitlyn drizzled streams of water over her body. By the time they were through, Caitlyn was almost as wet as Emily. They were both disappointed when Caitlyn decided enough was enough and wrapped Emily in a terry cloth towel and laid her down in the middle of Matt's bed. She had just finished dressing Emily in one of her new soft, fuzzy sleepers when she heard the front door open.

Caitlyn walked into the living room with a bright smile and offered Matt a flippant, "Hi, honey, you're home."

The expression on Matt's face told Caitlyn she'd probably gone a little too far in making herself comfortable. She'd known it, too. Every second of the afternoon a voice inside her head told her she was getting too involved, enjoying it all too much, losing sight of the fact that this baby, this man, were not hers to keep. But she'd ignored that little voice, concentrating on the here and now instead of the future. Unfortunately, the future seemed to have arrived in the form of one scowling male.

Caitlyn pushed a damp strand of hair away from her face. "We took a bath," she said.

"I can see that. Just out of curiosity, did you actually get Emily wet?"

"She likes to splash. In fact, she's a regular water baby. You should take her in the shower the next time you go. She'd probably love the water going over her . . . her head." Caitlyn added belated, suddenly aware that her mind had just conjured up Matt naked in the shower, and what an image that was. "Or you can just stick with the bath."

Matt didn't say anything to relieve her discomfort. Instead, the scowl was replaced by a small smile playing at the corner of his mouth. "Maybe you could join us in the shower."

She cleared her throat. "I don't think so."

"But you've been so helpful. Why stop with just—redecorating?" His gaze swept the apartment, noting how she'd spread everything out, including placing the big bear in Matt's favorite armchair.

"If you don't like things, you can move them around."

Matt walked over to the dining room table and set down the bag of Chinese food. "Has anyone ever told you that where you go, chaos seems to follow?"

"I didn't want to go through your drawers," she said defensively, "or I would have put things away."

"Maybe I'd like you to go through my drawers," he said with a wink.

"Matt, the baby!" she said in mock outrage, putting her hand over Emily's ear.

"If she hangs around here much longer, she'll hear a lot worse."

"You know, you're a lot cuter when you smile."

He shook his head in disbelief. "Do you actually think before you speak?"

"What? I'm not supposed to notice that your face takes on this amazing glow when you're amused by something?"

"You don't have to comment on everything you see. And men don't glow. Nor are they cute."

"You glow and you're cute. And I'm in a good mood, so don't spoil it." She rested her chin lightly on Emily's downy head, loving the feel of the baby in her arms.

Matt's expression softened as he gazed at them both. "You don't have to hold the baby every second."

"I like holding her."

"You're spoiling her."

"You can't spoil a baby, especially one who's missing her mother."

"Emily looks pretty happy to me. You make a good substitute."

Caitlyn drew in a sharp breath, once again reminded that this was all very temporary. "Right. Well, maybe I will put Emily down so we can eat."

"Good idea. You never know how long the quiet will last," he added as he set out the food. "I got chicken chow mein, sweet and sour pork, and an assortment of other stuff. I wasn't sure what you'd like."

"That's fine." Caitlyn placed Emily in her car seat, which was now adorned by a colorful mobile, giving the baby something to look at. In fact, Emily's eyes immediately fixed on the swinging teddy bears, allowing Caitlyn to back away without even a hint of protest.

Caitlyn was almost sorry that Emily was so happy. Without the distraction of the baby, it was just her and Matt, not in the couple sense, of course, although they did seem to have a very inconvenient and potent attraction for each other. But that was just chemistry. It wasn't like they had an emotional connection. It wasn't like they had anything in common—besides Emily.

Caitlyn simply had to keep things light and breezy, casual. They would just be two neighbors sharing dinner, nothing more, nothing less. She could do it. To do anything else, to imagine any other kind of relationship with Matt, would be foolish and dangerous to her heart. It was bad enough she was falling for Emily; she couldn't allow herself to fall for Matt, too.

Caitlyn sat down at the table as Matt retrieved plates and utensils from the kitchen and took a few calming breaths. Just dinner, she reminded herself, realizing that dinner actually sounded pretty good. There was a rumbling in her stomach that couldn't be denied.

"Chopsticks or forks?" Matt asked her, holding out both.

"Forks."

"Now, that surprises me. I would have picked you for the chopstick type, romantic versus practical."

"Or hungry versus trying to impress," she replied as she began dishing food onto her plate. The smells of ginger and soy made her take a long deep breath of delight. "This smells wonderful."

Matt sat down across from her, but instead of picking up his own fork, he watched her take a bite. "It amazes me sometimes how little it takes to make you happy."

"After the accident I realized that you have to enjoy the small moments, because sometimes that's all you have. Right now, at this place in this time, I'm happy." She shrugged. "In five minutes maybe I won't be, but now is good, so I'm going to enjoy it."

Matt picked up his fork and took a bite of the pork.

"While I hesitate to upset your apple cart . . . did I mention there's a bouquet of red roses sitting outside your apartment door? And before you ask, no, I didn't send them. In fact, I couldn't help glancing at the card. It was sitting right there."

"You snooped through my roses?"

"The handwriting was huge."

"Brian?" she asked, a knot forming in her stomach.

"Apparently he's even more sorry than he was earlier today."

Caitlyn set down her fork. "You couldn't have waited until after dinner to tell me about the flowers?"

"The guy doesn't give up; I'll give him that much. Of course, you now fit into his plans better than you did last year."

"What would you have done differently? Let's say the positions were reversed. You're in a wheelchair, and your fiancé has this fabulous job opportunity. Would you tell her to forget it, to stand by your side no matter what it costs her professionally?"

"No, I wouldn't, because I'm as noble as you are," he said. "But if she left, I'd probably figure she didn't love me as much as I loved her. I learned a long time ago that you can't make people stay. You can't make them love you, and you can't make them change their minds, not about the things that are important to them, the things they want more than they want you."

"You're saying Brian's career was more important to him than me?"

"Hell, yes, I'm saying that. Don't you feel the same way? Isn't that why you haven't jumped back into his arms?"

"That's part of the reason," she conceded. "It isn't just

that he left, though. When I think of him, I think of all the pain. It's like the last thing you eat before you get the stomach flu. All you remember is how bad you felt afterward, even discounting the fact that what you ate might have had nothing to do with the vomiting. They're coupled forever."

"Nice analogy while we're eating," he said dryly. "But I get your point. You can't think of Brian without thinking of the wheelchair."

"Exactly. I know that's not fair. But there you go." She paused, feeling a need to explain further. "I also know that a part of me wanted Brian to go. It was easier for me when he was gone. I didn't have to worry about him anymore, about how he was feeling, if he was spending too much time at the hospital, if he hated the way I looked, if he was only there out of pity. That's why I sound so ambivalent about wanting to blame him for leaving, because I know in my heart that I kind of pushed him away. I don't know if you can understand. Everything is so black and white with you, but I see all the shades of gray. You probably think I'm nuts."

Matt reached across the table and covered one of her hands with his. "I thought you weren't going to worry anymore about what people think?"

She sighed. "It's a habit I still have to break. You know that saying about hearing the beat of a different drum? I've always felt that was me, growing up out of step with everyone around me."

"Maybe the people around you were the ones out of step. After all, your father doesn't even appear to be on this planet at times, and your mother is so driven by what she wants that she doesn't understand what you want. And Brian, well, don't get me started . . ."

She looked at him in amazement. She'd never considered that angle. "But they're all brilliant, successful people, admired by many."

"So are you. Brilliant and successful."

She brushed the compliment aside. "Hardly."

"You run your own business. You have your own apartment. You live your own life. What do you have to apologize for?"

She hesitated, feeling the words begin to bubble up inside of her, words she couldn't possibly share. Fortunately, the phone rang, effectively breaching the growing confidence between them.

Matt was all business when he answered the phone with a simple, "Winters." His next words shocked her to the core. "You've got a lead?"

The question sent Caitlyn to her feet as well. The call had to be about Sarah. Oh, God. What if he'd found Sarah? Caitlyn looked at Emily, sleeping peacefully in her car seat, and was assailed by the sudden urge to grab her and keep her safe. But safe from whom? Her own mother? How could she do that?

Matt grabbed a piece of paper and jotted something down. "Maybe I should go there, too, ask some questions." He paused, then nodded. "All right. I'll wait for your call."

Caitlyn twisted her fingers together, feeling the tension rising within her. It was all she could do not to say anything until Matt had hung up the phone, then the words burst out of her. "Did he find Sarah?"

Matt's eyes blazed with excitement. "A woman with long black hair checked into a shelter in San Francisco last night under the name of Sarah Vaughn."

"Do you think it's her?" she asked tightly.

"Vaughn was my mother's maiden name."

Caitlyn wrapped her arms around her waist, feeling cold. This was supposed to be good news. So why didn't she feel good? "What happens now?"

"Blake assures me that Sarah is not at the shelter now, but he has an assistant who will be there tonight in case she returns. Blake also ran her name through the computers and came up with an address in Berkeley. That's where he is now. He says no one is home, but he will call me as soon as someone comes back." His eyes blazed with renewed hope. "I've never been this close, Caitlyn. I have half a mind to drive over there myself."

"I'm sure Blake will call you as soon as he knows anything."

"But what if Sarah sees him and runs? I'm not sure I should take the chance."

"You can't take Emily," Caitlyn said abruptly.

"Sure I can. She loves the car."

"No."

Matt raised an eyebrow in surprise. "Why not?"

Caitlyn swallowed hard, suddenly forced to come up with an explanation for her knee-jerk reaction, one based on logic and not emotion. Finally, she said, "For whatever reason, Sarah didn't want Emily with her. I don't think you should take Emily back to a place Sarah left."

He hesitated. "You might have a point."

"Of course I do. You should just let your investigator investigate. I'm sure he'll call you as soon as Sarah surfaces, if she does." Caitlyn walked away from his inquisitive eyes and paused in front of the window. She knew why she didn't want Matt to take Emily and go, and her reasons were purely selfish. In spite of telling herself a hundred times not to get attached, she'd gotten attached.

"Emily will go back to her mother, Caitlyn," Matt said

quietly from behind her. "You know that. It's the best thing for her. A baby needs its mother."

"A mother who left her in a hallway?"

"We don't know why she did that."

"I'm not sure I care why." A minute later, she felt his hands on her shoulders, and she couldn't help herself from leaning back against Matt's chest. "I'm sorry," she whispered. "I know you want me to be happy that you're close to finding Sarah, but I guess it just hit me that as soon as Sarah comes back, Emily goes."

"You really love kids, don't you?"

He didn't know the half of it. "Yeah," was all she said.

"You've been great with Emily." He turned her around to face him. "I will promise you one thing. I won't hand Emily over without having a discussion about why Sarah left her with me."

"You have to do that, Matt, even though I know you're dying to see Sarah. You can't let your feelings from the past overrule your common sense. You can't let your reunion with Sarah be more important than Emily's welfare."

"That won't happen," he replied, his face as serious as her own. "Emily is my primary concern. I know what it's like to be raised by a mother who shouldn't be a mother. I won't let Emily grow up in that situation. But I want to give Sarah a chance to explain, because if they can be together, they should be."

Before she could reply, the phone rang again. "You should get that," Caitlyn said, moving away from him. "It could be Blake."

The phone had awakened Emily, who began to whimper and stretch. While Matt took the call, Caitlyn picked up the baby. Changing Emily's diaper and getting a bottle ready gave Caitlyn a chance to put matters back into perspective. By the time Matt hung up the phone, she was convinced she could keep everything on an even keel. With her emotions safely locked away once again, she sat down on the couch and placed a bottle in Emily's mouth.

"Was that the investigator?" she asked.

"No, my editor, David Stern." Matt kicked the teddy bear out of the armchair and sat down, watching them both for a long minute. "You've got a natural touch with babies."

"It's easy when you have a bottle in your hand."

"It's more than that, and you know it. You have . . ." His voice trailed away, and she wondered what he was thinking.

"I have what?"

"A lot to give," he said somewhat cryptically. "Most people are more comfortable with taking than with giving."

"Which are you? A giver or a taker?"

"That's easy, a taker."

"I don't think so."

"Why not?"

"Well, for one thing, if you were a taker, I think you'd have more furniture."

He smiled at that and tipped his head. "Point taken. Speaking of taking, do you want me to take Emily?"

"No, I'm fine." She'd cuddle with Emily for a few minutes, then say good-night and go home. Tomorrow, she would get her life back to normal. "You can get me a fortune cookie, though."

"Deal." Matt got up and retrieved the bag of fortune cookies from the table. He handed her one and sat down next to her.

She cracked the cookie with one hand, careful not to jostle the bottle out of Emily's mouth. Then she pulled out the slip of white paper and laughed out loud.

"What?" Matt asked.

" 'When fortune knocks, you should answer.' "

"Words to live by." He surprised her by leaning over and giving her a quick kiss on the lips.

"What was that for?"

"I told you I was a taker. Your hands were full. I figured that was fortune knocking for me."

"Oh." She paused, her mouth still tingling. "My hands are still full."

Matt's eyes darkened as he answered her unspoken wish with his lips. This kiss was warm, tender, satisfying, like a long, cool drink after a long, hot day. Caitlyn could feel the passion checked carefully between them as only their mouths met in the promise of more—someday, but not this day.

When Matt pulled away, he brushed the hair from her face with a gentle caress. "You know those moments you were talking about, when everything seems perfect? I think this might be one of those."

"I think you might be right." She only wished the moment could last forever.

Eleven

$\mathcal{S}$arah glanced out the window of the church minivan as Jonathan pulled up in front of yet another apartment building. It was the tenth one they'd gone to since they'd started delivering dinners just after four o'clock. She'd begun to lose track. She had to admit that bringing food to people who couldn't get out of the house had taken her mind off her own problems for a while. She was still somewhat surprised that there were people like Jonathan who actually did this stuff. Certainly no one had ever cared enough to bring her and Mattie a meal, not even when they'd been really, really hungry.

Sarah didn't want Emily to ever know the kind of hunger pains that gnawed at you until you'd actually consider catching and eating one of the cockroaches that ran through your apartment. If she could protect her from that kind of life, wouldn't that be something? Wouldn't that mean that giving her up was the right thing to do?

"Ready for one more?" Jonathan asked, interrupting her thoughts.

She nodded. "Sure."

"You've been a big help today," he said.

"I haven't done much more than unwrap some plates."

"Some people never do that much."

She sent him a thoughtful look. "You're a good man. I guess you're blessed or something, huh?"

He smiled at her. "We're all blessed, Sarah. Even you."

"I don't know about that."

"I do. I wish I could find the words to make you believe. That's always been my biggest problem, finding the right words."

Sarah glanced at him, struck by the weariness in his voice.

"What good is a preacher who can't find the right words to preach?" he asked.

She didn't know what he wanted her to say. But then she'd never been that good with words, either.

"I thought somewhere along the way I'd find the words, that God would send them to me, not to help me, but to help the people around me, the ones I was meant to serve. But it hasn't happened, and it may soon be too late."

"What do you mean?"

"There's a possibility that the church may close if I can't increase the attendance at Sunday services. Real estate in this area has skyrocketed, and the land the church sits on is very valuable. The church could sell it and use that money to fund other programs, ones they think would reach more people than the empty church is reaching."

"But they can't tear down the church," Sarah cried, not even hearing the rest of his explanation. All she knew was that they couldn't close down her church. She grabbed his shirtsleeve and twisted it with her fingers. "You have to stop them."

He stared at her in surprise. "It's just a possibility. And I am trying to do something about it. Are you all right?"

She looked down at her hand and immediately let go.

"Why do you care if they tear down the church?" he asked, sending her a thoughtful glance.

"I don't care," she said, but he didn't believe her. And why should he after her reaction? It was just that the church, the steeple, it was one of the few things in her life that was still around, that meant something.

"You care. Look at you, there's a flush in your cheeks and a fire in your eyes. I like it."

Sarah turned away from him. She couldn't believe she'd shown she cared about something. It was a lesson she'd learned early on. Never let anyone know that you want something, because that's the thing they'll take away when they want to hurt you. Just like her mother had taken away the candles. . . .

She looked out the window at the nearby apartment building, so similar to the one she'd grown up in, which was just a few blocks away. Was there a little girl somewhere inside, on one of the top floors, who looked out her window at night and saw a steeple and felt hope? What would she see if they tore down the church? How would she feel then?

"Sarah? Tell me what's bothering you."

"I used to live around here."

Jonathan waited patiently for her to go on. That was something she liked about him. He didn't jump into a reply or an argument. Gary always said she was slow, but Jonathan didn't make her feel that way. He made her feel calm.

"I used to kneel next to my bedroom window at night,

and I could see the steeple of the church. Sometimes the moon would light it up, and I thought God or the angels were sending me a sign that it would be all right. The only times I couldn't see the steeple was when it rained or when the fog came in. Then I'd just crawl under the covers and wait for the morning to come so I could see it again, so everything would be all right."

"I'm glad the church called to you when you needed it the most."

"But if you tear the steeple down, what happens to the little girl or the little boy who lives up there?" She pointed to the building. "What will they see when they look out their window?"

She saw in Jonathan's eyes the same worry, the same fear. "I don't know if I'm good enough to save it, Sarah."

"But you are good." She knew that with a certainty that she couldn't explain. "Look at what you did today, bringing food to all these people who can't get out."

"I need to do more. I need to fill my church every Sunday with people who want to praise the Lord."

"Folks around here probably don't think they got much to praise. No offense."

"None taken. I know it's hard to see God in places like this." He sighed. "Maybe it's impossible. I could be beating my head against a wall. I hope if I keep showing up here, offering a helping hand, maybe they won't just see me when I come, maybe they'll see God, too. That sounds idealistic, I know."

"It sounds nice."

"Well, nice won't deliver the last of our Sunday suppers. Can you stand one more trip?"

"I think so."

Sarah followed Jonathan into the apartment building, down the dimly lit hallways that smelled like cigarette smoke and beer, a scent with which she was intensely familiar. A small child, barely two, played alone outside a half-open door. Inside, Sarah could hear the sounds of an argument. She wondered if anyone knew the little girl with the dirty face was outside the apartment.

She was suddenly assailed by the old feelings of fear, uncertainty, and loneliness. She didn't want to raise Emily in a place like this. She didn't want to see her child crawling around on a dirty carpet in a place where no one cared about anything or anyone.

Matt's hallway had smelled clean. The carpeting had felt soft under her feet, and there had been no graffiti on the walls, only pretty pictures. That's the kind of place where Emily belonged. Suddenly, the confusion of the past few days was gone. Sarah knew exactly what she had to do.

"I know what I have to do," Brian told Caitlyn as she answered her door early Monday morning.

Barely awake, Caitlyn blinked rapidly, trying to clear her head. Brian was the last person she'd expected to find in her hallway. She'd assumed the pounding on her door was Matt. She drew her terry cloth bathrobe more closely around her, distinctly aware of the less-than-sexy gray T-shirt underneath, not to mention her tangled mess of hair that she instinctively tried to pat down.

"I know what I have to do, what *we* have to do," Brian repeated, looking far too awake in his tan dockers and white polo shirt.

"What time is it?" she asked in confusion.

"It's seven-thirty. But that's not important. I have a proposition for you."

"Maybe you could come back later, when I'm awake."

"I don't think so. You've opened your door, and I consider that a victory. This is the perfect time."

"Perfect time for what?"

"Getting reacquainted. I'd like to take you to break-fast. How about Nini's? I know you love their vegetable omelettes, and I promise not to say a word if you order the greasy potatoes."

Nini's? Caitlyn suddenly realized how long it had been since she'd gone to the coffee shop near the univer-sity. In fact, she couldn't remember . . .

"I haven't been to Nini's since before the accident," she said slowly.

Brian appeared surprised. "Really? But you love that place."

Did she? Or was he the one who loved it? Or was it her mother? She'd been going there forever. Yet, once she'd broken away from her parents and Brian, she hadn't once thought of going there. It was an odd revelation but it seemed to mean something; she just couldn't quite figure out what.

"What do you say?" Brian persisted. "Your mother told me you don't usually go into the shop before ten on Mondays."

Caitlyn silently cursed her mother's helpfulness. "That's true, but—"

"You can't avoid me forever."

Maybe not forever, but she'd been hoping for at least one more day.

"We need to talk this out, Caitlyn, clear the air, so we can move forward. My mother gave me a book on male/female relationships, and I can see that we've had a communication problem in the past."

"You think you can figure me out by reading a book?" she asked him. She was both touched and amused by his plan.

"I think the book has already helped me. I have to admit you've been somewhat of a mystery to me at times."

A mystery he'd never tried that hard to solve, she thought cynically. Still, he was trying now, and she supposed she should be flattered by the effort.

"Why now, Brian? Why the sudden interest in figuring out what makes me tick?"

"Because I want you back in my life."

"Why? What did you miss about us?"

"A lot of things."

"Like what?"

"Well, I missed this." He placed his hands on her waist and pulled her against him, planting a determined and firm kiss on her lips.

Caitlyn was so amazed and dazed by the sudden action she didn't immediately pull away. Her brain was trying to register Brian, kiss, feeling . . . feeling what? It had been a long time between kisses. But there was a familiarity to the embrace that made her wonder deep down inside if there could still be something left to save.

Then a door slammed, and Caitlyn broke away from Brian like a guilty teenager.

Matt's face was grim and accusing as he stared at them both. "Maybe you should find a bedroom," he said tersely.

"Matt, I—" Caitlyn didn't know what to say, nor did she know why she felt like a guilty lover. It was none of Matt's business who she kissed or where she kissed. "What do you want anyway?"

"I heard a noise. I thought maybe Sarah . . ."

"She's not here."

"Well, don't let me interrupt." He stepped back into his apartment and slammed the door again.

"What the hell is his problem?" Brian asked, an un- usual anger in his normally calm eyes. "You keep saying you're just neighbors, but that looked like more than neighbors to me."

"You're imagining things," she said, still staring at Matt's door. Or was he? There had been a look in Matt's eyes, a look she'd never expected to see—possessiveness. Why? He barely wanted to be neighbors, much less any- thing more.

"Let me take you to breakfast, or at least let me come inside," Brian said. "We could use some privacy."

The last thing she wanted was privacy, not when she was feeling confused and unsure of what she wanted to do next. She needed coffee and a shower and her clothes on. Then she could deal with Brian—and Matt, too, for that matter.

"I can't do this now," she replied decisively. "You have to give me some time."

"We've had too much time as it is," he complained.

"Another day won't make a difference. I turned every- thing off when you walked out of that hospital room, Brian, and whether I told you to go or wanted you to go doesn't change the fact that you went, and I was alone, and it hurt." Her voice shook as she remembered in vivid detail the pain of that long, lonely day. "It hurt a lot. I know that things look better to you now. I'm walking. I'm healthy. You're back in town. So you think why not get back together—take two, as they say. But this isn't a movie. We can't just go for another shot and get the same emotion we had before."

"We can try." Brian took her hand in his. "Maybe it won't be like it was before. Maybe it will be better."

"What would make it better?"

He seemed confused by her question. "What do you mean?"

"What do you think you want out of a relationship with me?"

"I just want you. That's what I want." He paused, a frown settling across his features as he looked into her eyes. "That's not the right answer, is it?"

"There is no right answer—"

"I should have brought that damn book with me."

"So you can use it like a dictionary, translating my words for you?"

"If you'd speak in plain English, it would be easier for me. I'll admit that I'm a numbers man. Words are far more complicated." He squeezed her hand. "Why don't you tell me what you want? Why don't we start there?"

"I want you to already know what I want," she said, silently admitting that wasn't particularly reasonable, but it was the way she felt.

He sighed. "That's what I was afraid of. Look, I'm going to go read chapter seven again, but I will be back, because one thing I have learned is that *go* does not always mean *go*. So even though you've said no to breakfast, I won't assume that means you don't want another invitation. That's right, isn't it?"

This time it was Caitlyn who sighed.

"Never mind," he said. "I'll be back."

Caitlyn watched him walk down the hall. Somehow she didn't think relationships were supposed to be this hard.

"That's it," Matt told Emily as he wrestled her kicking foot into a new yellow sleeper. "We are out of here. I will not continue to sit around waiting for something to happen. I'm going to make it happen."

The waiting was driving him up the wall. Not to mention the crying. Emily had kept him up half the night. If he didn't find a way to muzzle the midnight crying, he would probably be evicted. His downstairs neighbor had leveled a three-o'clock-in-the-morning complaint about the music.

He'd tried taking Emily up to the roof after that, but it hadn't been the same without Caitlyn whispering stories about star-crossed lovers in his ear. Not that he needed that nonsense, he told himself. But Emily had seemed less enchanted with the night sky as well. Finally, he'd put her in the car and driven her around for an hour until she'd finally fallen asleep sometime around five, which made him tired and grumpy.

Not jealous, he decided. Definitely not jealous. That scene in the hallway had not bothered him one little bit.

Matt closed the last snap on Emily's sleeper and held her up to face him. She offered him a crooked smile, and he felt his anger slowly seep away. At least this female didn't have a hidden agenda. He couldn't say the same for Caitlyn—kissing him last night, kissing Brian this morning . . . talk about being fickle.

Talk about being ridiculous. He didn't have any rights over Caitlyn. She could kiss anyone she wanted, and he supposed her ex-fiancé probably had more in the way of rights than a neighbor she'd only met a few days earlier.

But that didn't stop Matt from feeling distinctly pissed off. Brian was an ass. And Caitlyn should have her head examined for giving him a second chance. How much more did she need to see? Matt would bet at least twenty bucks that the guy had some other motive for wanting her back now. He just hadn't figured it out yet, but he would. And then he would tell Caitlyn.

Why? A small voice inside his head asked. Why tell

her? Why not let her go back to him? Then you won't
have to worry about her. She'll get married and have ba-
bies and live happily ever after. And she certainly can't
do that with you, because you're not ready to settle down.
So why not let her go back to the boyfriend?

Because he couldn't. It was the only answer he had.

A tentative knock brought his head around in anticipation. Holding Emily in one arm, he opened the door, not
sure who he wanted to see more, Sarah—or Caitlyn.

"Hi," Caitlyn said. She was still wearing her bathrobe,
still appearing deliciously tousled and sleepy, making
him think of how she would look in his bed with her long
blond hair drifting across the pillow.

He cleared his throat. "What do you want?"

She straightened at his irritated tone. "Coffee. Do you
have any?"

It wasn't what he'd expected, but he tipped his head
toward the kitchen. "It's strong."

"Thank God," she murmured, heading toward the
kitchen.

He shut the door behind her and followed her into the
kitchen, leaning against the counter as she poured coffee
into a black mug and took a long, grateful sip.

"Better?" he asked.

"Slightly. You were a jerk, you know."

"I've been worse."

"Is that supposed to make it all right?"

"You surprised me."

"Well, Brian surprised me."

"So you kissed him?"

"Actually, he kissed me." She set the mug down on the
counter. "Why does it matter to you?"

"It doesn't. I told you I thought maybe Sarah was
outside."

She stared at him. "Was there any word from your investigator?"

"As of an hour ago, she hadn't gone back to the shelter or to the apartment."

"Maybe she isn't planning to go back."

"Maybe not, but it's the only lead I've got."

Emily started to squirm, and Caitlyn immediately reached for her.

Matt let the baby go into her arms, feeling an unexpected wave of tenderness as Caitlyn cuddled the baby against her breasts. This was the way it should be—a man, a woman, a child they both loved. He tried to shake the thought out of his head. But it wouldn't go. In fact, the voice in his head returned, stronger than ever.

You could have this, Matt. You could have Caitlyn and Emily. The three of you could be a family, the family you've always wanted.

Caitlyn sent him a funny look, and he hoped to hell she couldn't read his mind. "So what do you want?" he asked gruffly. "Besides coffee."

She raised an eyebrow. "I don't want anything."

"Then why are you here?"

"I didn't like the way things went in the hall."

"Well, lately nothing has gone right in that damn hallway. Every time I open my door I see something I don't want to see."

"Me, too," she said with annoyance.

He felt his temper rising along with his passion and everything else in his body. This woman was under his skin, and he wanted her out.

"So, are you and lover boy getting back together?"

"No."

"Why not? Hasn't he groveled enough yet?"

"Are you looking for a fight?"

"Maybe I am."

Caitlyn walked into the living room, carefully setting Emily in her car seat before looking back at him. "Gloves on or off?"

"Off."

"Fine." She put her hands on her hips. "Go ahead, get whatever it is off your chest."

"You should take Bradley back."

"Why is that?"

"Because he's perfect for you. Roses last night. Kisses this morning. Or did they come with something else, diamonds maybe?"

"He asked me to go to breakfast, not that it's any of your business."

"Breakfast, perfect. Well thought out. If things go well, you can spend the whole day together."

"I said no."

"Why? I thought you wanted him back. I thought you said it was all your fault for acting the martyr, that he was completely blameless."

"I didn't say that exactly."

"Well, it doesn't matter. Because whether you say yes today or tomorrow, we both know that you will eventually say yes."

"How do you know that?"

"Because you'll give in," Matt replied, desperately wanting to convince her as well as himself. "Bradley is smart, persistent, probably habitually punctual. I bet he writes poetry."

"He does not," she snapped, fire flashing in her eyes. "And his name is Brian."

"Your parents love him. He fits right in. Hell, you probably love him, too. He's the kind of man you were raised to love."

"You are so full of shit. You don't know how I was raised."

"You were raised to want stability, to vote Republican, to have a savings account, to never read the newspaper. With Bradley, you can have everything you ever wanted—the house in the suburbs, the husband, the baby—"

"Stop right there," she said, her face red with anger. "You and your know-it-all attitude. You don't know what I want or who I want."

"I know what you want," he interrupted. "I can see it every time you touch Emily. A look comes into your eyes that's incredibly maternal. You were born to be a mother. And I think Bradley would be very happy to make you one."

"Well, he can't make me a mother; no one can," she cried.

"What the hell are you talking about?" Her words didn't make sense to him.

"I can't have children, Matt. I can't ever have children. You wanted to know my big secret—there it is. Are you happy now?"

"What?" He couldn't believe what he was hearing.

"Don't make me say it again."

No, it wasn't possible. It wasn't right. Caitlyn was meant to be a mother. He knew that deep down in his soul. "God, Cait, I didn't know—" He felt like a complete scumbag. He'd never meant to hurt her, never ever wanted to see such a look of pain in her eyes. But his damn jealousy had made him say things he shouldn't have.

"Just shut up. You've said enough. More than enough."

He grabbed her arm as she tried to leave.

"Don't go. Let's talk about it."

"I don't want to talk about it. I don't *ever* want to talk about it."

"They don't know, do they? Not Brian or your parents or your friends? You haven't told them."

Tears filled her eyes. "They wouldn't be able to accept it. They couldn't accept *me*. Don't you get it, Matt? When Brian said I was damaged, he was right. Only he didn't know just how right he was." She looked down at his hand on her arm. "Let me go, Matt. Please let me go."

 *Twelve*

"**I**'m not letting you go," Matt said firmly. "Not like this."

Caitlyn tried to pull her arm away, but his grip was like a vise. That was the problem with Matt. He never let go. He never walked away. He was like a leech, she thought with annoyance, sucking every last bit of blood out of her. "Not like what?" she asked. "What do you think you could possibly say now that would make a difference?"

"I could start with I'm sorry."

"It's not your fault." The kindness in his voice caught her off guard, and she felt the anger begin to slip away. She tried desperately to hang on to what little control she had left. She wished she'd never told him the truth, because just as she'd expected, the words had created a freight train of emotions filled with anger, grief, and hopelessness, knocking her completely off her feet.

The weakness in her legs made her sway, and Matt reacted by catching her other arm and pushing her down on the nearby couch. He sat next to her, wrapping one arm around her shoulders as he pulled her against his chest, tucking her head under his chin.

His embrace was a warm cocoon of strength, security, and comfort. His shoulders were strong, his chest broad, and she thought maybe, just maybe, if she didn't move, he could make it all go away. Matt stroked her back, not speaking, not questioning, just letting her catch her breath. He wasn't making it go away, but he was making her feel better. For just a moment she was able to share the burden she'd been carrying, and it made her feel lighter.

Finally, she sat back. Adjusting her bathrobe, she was reminded that she still hadn't taken a shower, her hair was tangled, her feet were bare, tears stained her face, and she probably had red, puffy eyes. She'd never been a pretty crier. So much for putting on a front. With Matt she seemed to be baring her body and soul inch by naked inch.

"Are you okay?" Matt's eyes searched hers for the truth.

"I'm thinking about going back to bed and starting the morning over in about—oh, say, twenty years."

"I had no idea, Caitlyn. I knew you were hiding something, but I wasn't expecting that. I'm sorry I said what I did."

"It doesn't matter."

"It does matter. I hurt you." He looked angry with himself. "I had no right to do that. Frankly, I was pissed off because you were kissing Brian, and it looked like you were getting back together. And I didn't like it."

"You didn't like it?"

"No," he admitted.

She caught her breath at the look in his eyes, feeling the powerful pull of attraction between them. She glanced down at her hands, at the third finger where she'd once worn another man's ring. How could she consider taking Brian back into her life when she had such a strong reaction to Matt? But how could she take either one of them into her life when she couldn't have children? She knew Brian wanted children. And Matt would, too. She'd seen his paternal instincts blossom with Emily, and a man who cared so much about finding his sister—about pulling what little of his family was left back together— was a man who needed to have children of his own.

"What are you thinking about?" Matt asked. "Besides hitting me over the head with something heavy?"

She sent him a shaky smile. "That sounds appealing. Do you have one of those iron frying pans?"

"Sorry."

"I'm not angry with you, Matt. I just can't quite believe I finally said the words out loud. I don't think I've ever said them where anyone could hear."

"Why not? Why haven't you told your family?"

"Because it's too hard," she said with a helpless shrug.

"They love you. Knowing that you can't have kids wouldn't change that," Matt argued.

"Spending one Sunday morning with my parents doesn't make you an expert on them."

"It was long enough for me to see that they want the best for you."

"Which is marriage and children, which is what I can't have. That's the problem."

"Not all men want children."

"Brian does. He's the last of his family line. He's told me a number of times how eager his parents are to see him with a son to carry on the family name."

"You could adopt."

"It wouldn't be the same."

"Look, I'm not going to argue Brian's case. But to be fair, the guy has a right to know the real reason you sent him away. Because that *is* why you sent him away, isn't it?"

She hesitated, knowing it was pointless to prevaricate when Matt saw everything anyway. "After he left, it was easier, because I didn't have to think about it every day. The marriage was off. The issue of children was moot."

"You should tell him now."

"I know I should. I've thought about telling him a hundred times, especially since he's come back to town. I know that if I tell him I can't have kids he'll probably say he's sorry but he can't be with someone like me. And that will be the end of it."

"Maybe it will be the end, but you should stop putting words in his mouth. And what about your parents? What's up with that?"

"It would hurt them, Matt. Think about it. They won't ever have grandchildren," she said passionately. "I'm an only child. I'm it. There aren't going to be any more little ones around our Christmas tree. And my mother, who has driven both of us crazy by fixing every last little thing wrong with me, can't fix this. That will make her nuts."

"That's not the whole truth. Try again."

"Oh, for God's sake, you and the friggin' truth." She waved her hand wildly in the air. "Some things don't need to be shared with the world. I'm not hurting anyone with this secret."

"You're hurting the people you say you love. They don't understand why you're acting the way you're acting. They must sense you're holding something back. That lack of trust will hurt them more than the truth."

He was making her feel like a fool, and not just a fool but someone cruel and uncaring. "You're turning this all around," she said in confusion.

"Am I?" He cupped her face with his hands and gazed

into her eyes. "I don't think you're keeping this secret to protect anyone but yourself. If you say it out loud, it will make it true, won't it, Caitlyn? And that's why you can't say it, because it's not your parents who can't accept it, it's you, isn't it?" he asked, giving her a little shake.

"Yes," she confessed. "It's me. I don't want it to be true." She pushed his hands away from her face and stood up as angry, hurt tears welled up in her eyes. "When I was a little girl all I ever dreamed about was growing up and getting married and having children. I was lonely as an only child with parents who were always at work. I used to make up families in my head with lots of kids so I wouldn't feel so alone. I'd play house and make everyone else play house with me until they were so bored they wouldn't come over anymore. And every time we played house, I was always the mother." She pointed to herself. "Me. I was the mother."

Her voice faltered. "But I'm never going to be a mother, and it just . . . it just rips me apart every time I think about it, much less say it aloud. I'm not just a liar, Matt. I'm a coward. Is that what you wanted me to say? Because that's the truth, the whole truth. And if you want to shout it to the world, I can't stop you."

Matt stood up to face her. "I'm not going to tell anyone."

"Really? Isn't that what you do in the newspaper? Strip someone bare, tie them to a post, and let the world stare at them?" She saw him pale under her attack, but it didn't slow down the anger that was running away with her good sense. She shouldn't have to defend herself. She was the victim, not the villain.

"That's not what I do, and you know it."

"I know you think I was wrong not to tell Brian. And

you're the Robin Hood of truth, so why don't you run and
tell him?"

"Because it's not my secret."

"You tell people's secrets every day."

"Not people I care about."

Shocked by his words, she forgot what she was going
to say next. "You c-care about me?" she stuttered.

He hesitated, then said, "I do, yes." He moved closer
to her, shaving the distance between them to just a breath.
"I don't give a damn about Bradley or your parents, but
you . . ." He put his hands through her hair and pulled her
face toward his. "You."

"What?" she whispered.

"You've become important to me."

"I have?"

He answered her with a passion-filled kiss that sucked
the last bit of anger out of her. And when he would have
moved away, she pulled him back, desire fueled by the
pounding blood in her veins, and the need to take something back from him. He was so many things she
wasn't—strong, courageous, brutally honest—and she
needed those traits. Maybe in the taking she would give
him something back like compassion, tenderness, understanding of the frailties that made them both human.

Then the phone rang, once, twice, persistently, until
they could no longer ignore it.

Matt groaned. "I'm going to have to unplug that damn
thing." He planted one last kiss on her mouth before
reaching for the phone.

Still shaking, Caitlyn returned to the couch in a daze.
Emily slept peacefully in her car seat, sleeping the sleep
of angels while Caitlyn's life was unraveling. Why
couldn't she have that kind of peace? Why couldn't she

sleep without want, without regret, two emotions that were never far away?

Matt hung up the phone, his eyes alight with excitement. "Someone is in Sarah's apartment."

"Sarah?"

"No." He frowned. "Some guy. But he used a key, so . . ."

"So he must know Sarah."

"I hope so."

"Will Blake talk to him?"

"Only if he tries to leave before I get there. This might be my best chance to find Sarah. I have to go."

She nodded in agreement. "I'll take care of Emily for you. She can come to work with me. All those brides dreaming of babies will love her."

His eyes darkened. "What about you? How will you feel?"

Caitlyn hesitated, deciding there was no more need for secrets or even half-truths between them. "I'll feel the way I've been feeling the last couple of days—like her mother."

He frowned. "I can't ask you to do it. Now that I know—"

"You're not asking me. I'm offering. It's too late for me to pull away. I knew when I took Emily out of her car seat Friday night that I would fall in love with her." Caitlyn sent Emily a tender glance. "And I did. What will a few more hours matter?"

Matt didn't have an answer. And neither did she. He would do his best to get Sarah back. And Caitlyn would help him, even if Sarah's coming back meant Emily would have to leave.

Matt was still thinking about Caitlyn when he drove across the Bay Bridge toward Berkeley. He realized he'd pushed her harder than he should have. He had a problem with backing out of something once he was more than halfway in. And Caitlyn had let him in. That fact both pleased and disturbed him. He'd never shared so many confidences with anyone, much less a woman he'd known only a few days.

But there was something about this woman that spoke to him, a rare connection he'd never experienced with anyone else. And he'd hammered into her like a battering ram, goading her into telling him a secret she had not wanted to share. And what a hellish secret. He'd never expected the sad look in her eyes to be tied to something so tragic.

He'd thought of Caitlyn as a golden girl—beautiful, smart, funny, rich—a woman who had everything. Only she didn't have everything, and she never would. There wouldn't be a child with her smile, or her hair, or her incredible eyes. The truth tore him apart. It was just plain and simply wrong. And he wanted to—God help him— he wanted to fix it.

Maybe Caitlyn was right. Maybe telling her parents would leave them with the same helpless feeling of wanting to make it right but unable to do so.

Matt took the University Avenue exit, following the directions that Blake had given him on the phone and trying to refocus his attention on the task at hand.

There was nothing he could do to help Caitlyn right now, but maybe there was something he could do to help Sarah. His eyes narrowed as he drove farther away from the university and parallel to the freeway. The neighborhood was not the best, and it made him wonder what kind of life Sarah had led during the years they'd been apart. He'd hoped for her sake that she'd been adopted by some nice suburban family with a big house and clean sheets and a safe neighborhood. He had a terrible feeling that hadn't happened.

As he turned the corner, Matt spotted Blake in his forest-green Jeep Cherokee parked near the corner. After parking his own car, he walked down the street to the Jeep and slid into the passenger seat. The car smelled like tacos, and judging by the fast-food wrappers piled up in the backseat, Blake had passed the boring hours of his watch by eating. Not that the man showed an ounce of fat on his muscular frame. In his mid-forties, at six foot five, two hundred plus pounds, Blake, an ex-marine with a couple of ex-wives and an ex-drinking problem, was not a man to be messed with. Matt had met him while covering a political story in Washington ten years earlier, and over time Blake had conducted several investigations for him, including the long-running search for Sarah.

"He hasn't come out," Blake said, his eyes fixed on the apartment down the street.

"What did he look like?"

"A punk. Skinny, stringy hair, tank top, blue jeans falling off his ass. You know the look."

Unfortunately, he did. Matt felt more depressed by the second. Was this really where Sarah had lived? And who was this guy? A friend? A lover? A stepbrother? He didn't know which possibility disturbed him the most.

"Let's go," Matt said decisively. "I'm tired of waiting."

"You and me both." Blake got out of the car with Matt, and they walked down the block to the apartment building that Sarah had apparently called home. Her apartment was on the second floor with a sticker that said *Beware of Dog* in the window. Matt didn't believe that one for a second. He rapped on the door. No answer. He knocked again—louder.

The door was thrown open with a resounding "Shit."

The guy facing them wore baggy blue jeans hanging past his crotch, a pair of yellow boxers sticking out at the waist. His skinny chest was bare save for a snake tattoo across his abdomen. Judging by the blank look in his eyes, he was either stoned or hung over, Matt couldn't tell which.

"We're looking for Sarah," Matt said.

The guy's dull, vacant gaze sharpened somewhat at this piece of information. "Who are you?"

"We're friends."

"Sarah don't have no friends."

"Where is she?"

"Don't know. Don't care."

"Well, you're going to care." Matt pushed past him and entered the apartment. It was a pit, beer bottles, wine bottles, smoke so thick you could barely see.

"What the fuck are you doing, dude?" the guy asked. "You can't just come in here, and—"

His words were cut off as Blake pushed him up against the wall, one hand encircling his throat. "He wants to know where Sarah is, and you're going to tell him."

"She ain't here," he gasped. "Let me go."

"Where is she? When did you last see her?" Matt asked.

When he didn't reply, Blake said, "Maybe I can squeeze it out of him."

"She split a couple of weeks ago," the guy said hastily. "That's all I know, dude."

"Then you won't mind if I take a look around, will you?" Matt didn't wait for an answer but headed into the bedroom.

"She ain't in there."

No, she wasn't, Matt realized, but there was something more telling inside—a cheap bassinet sitting next to the bed. His stomach turned over. Had Sarah and Emily really lived in this dump? He walked over to the bassinet and saw an old blanket inside, nothing more.

He stepped back and took note of the rest of the room, the double bed with tangled sheets, a battered dresser, clothes everywhere, and then he saw something on the floor, something he remembered vividly, a small gold heart on a thin chain. *Sarah.* He picked it up, his pulse speeding with the memories. He'd given her the necklace for her fifth birthday. It was nothing more than a drug-store trinket, but she'd loved it.

Taking a breath, he told himself with renewed determination that he would give it back to her, that he would find her and make everything right again. He walked over to the dresser and ran through the drawers, discovering three pieces of paper lying loose on a pile of underwear. They all had one name in common, Sarah Vaughn.

The first was a pay stub from Laree's Hair Salon in Sacramento, the second a bill for a prenatal visit at Oakland County Hospital, and the third was a bus schedule for travel through the Bay Area. He stuffed all of them into his pocket and returned to the living room to find Blake searching through a desk while Sarah's friend smoked a cigarette and acted like he didn't give a shit. Hell, maybe it wasn't an act.

"What's your name?" Matt asked.

"John Smith."

"Very original."

The guy sneered at him, and Matt had to resist the urge to put his fist through John Smith's smart-ass mouth. "When did you last see Sarah?"

"I don't remember. Why do you want her? She ain't good for nothing."

"I just want her. If she comes back, tell her to call her brother."

The guy didn't even blink. "She don't have no brother."

Matt stared back at him. "What happened to the baby?"

"Dead." And he smiled a slick, nasty smile. "Sarah's probably dead, too."

Matt lunged for him, but Blake pulled him back. "Don't do it, man," he said, pulling him out of the apartment.

"You shouldn't have stopped me." Matt freed himself from Blake's grip as they hit the sidewalk.

"Seeing you arrested on assault charges won't help us find Sarah. He was yanking your chain. You know that. Now, what did you find in the bedroom?"

"Sarah was definitely there." Matt pulled out the necklace. "This was hers."

"Anything else?"

Matt handed Blake the hospital bill and the bus schedule. "Why don't you take these? I'll check out the pay stub. I need to do something. I can't just sit around and wait."

Blake nodded. "Did you happen to notice the scratch marks on our friend's arms? Looked like some woman with long fingernails got tangled up with him."

Matt felt sick. He'd barely looked at the guy, so intent had he been on finding something of Sarah's. "If he hurt her, I'll kill him."

"Well, let's find her first."

"She has to be all right," Matt said, trying to convince himself. But all he could remember was that asshole's parting words: *Sarah's probably dead, too.*

Thirteen

*S*arah hovered outside the doorway to Jonathan's home office. Two men were with him; Jonathan had introduced them to her as board members. They'd gone straight back to his office, their expressions very serious, and as the minutes passed, their voices had gotten louder. She wondered what was wrong. She hoped she hadn't gotten Jonathan into trouble. But as she listened, it didn't appear they were talking about *her*.

"Yesterday's numbers were appalling," one of the men said. "Pauline told me you had seven people sitting in the pews."

"I think there were ten," Jonathan said calmly.

"You're preaching to no one, Jonathan, and it isn't that we blame you, but we can't keep the church open for the few that come," the other man said.

"Why not? I believe one soul is just as important as twenty. And by the way, I think the Lord is on my side in this."

Sarah felt her lips curve into a small smile at Jonathan's dry tone. Good for him, she thought. He was fighting back. The board members were not amused.

"The budget is not on your side. I don't want to argue with you. This is the bottom line. We'll give you two more weeks to find a way to fill this church on Sunday. If you can't do it, then we'll close. We don't want you to think we're blaming you for any of this. In fact, there's a wonderful church in the South Bay. Reverend Davis is planning to retire next month. We think you might fit in very well there."

Sarah caught her bottom lip with her teeth as their words sunk in. They were going to send Jonathan away.

"Two weeks is hardly enough time. I've barely gotten to know this community. I still have work to do."

"You can tie up whatever loose ends you have in the next few weeks. This church in the South Bay is wonderful—teen choirs, ladies' groups, picnic suppers, fund-raisers, and a congregation that comes every Sunday rain or shine. It's a wonderful opportunity for a young minister."

"I like it here. This community needs a church."

The other man spoke up in a gruff voice. "If they needed a church so bad, they'd show up on Sunday and thank God for one."

Sarah frowned. These two men didn't seem religious to her at all. They were talking about the church like it was a grocery store that wasn't selling enough bread.

"It's not that simple," Jonathan answered. "The poverty in the neighborhood takes a toll. Some of the people here work two jobs and on Sunday all they want to do is sleep."

"Exactly. They don't need a church."

"Of course they do. And so do their children."

"You tried to start a youth group. No one came."

"These things take time. I've been here less than a year."

"I'm sorry, Jonathan. We've simply run out of time. All we can give you is two more Sundays. Talk it over with your father. Perhaps he can help."

Sarah heard their chairs move, and she darted back into the living room before they could catch her listening in the doorway. Her pulse was racing and she was having trouble catching her breath. She hadn't realized until just this second how dependent she'd become on Jonathan and his church.

He had been so kind to her. Last night he'd offered her a bed in his guest room instead of forcing her to go to a shelter. For a split second she'd cynically wondered if he'd be paying a late-night visit, but he simply said good night with the gentle smile that was beginning to warm her as much as the sight of any church steeple, and she'd slept peacefully for the first time in a long time.

When she'd gotten up in the morning, she'd found a pile of clean clothes outside her door, nothing fancy, just blue jeans, a T-shirt and some underwear, but she'd appreciated the thought. After taking a shower and brushing her hair, she felt almost normal again.

Jonathan had made her pancakes for breakfast, saying his housekeeper wouldn't be coming in until the afternoon, but he wasn't bad with Bisquik mix, a couple of eggs, and some milk. The pancakes had been spectacular, the best she'd ever eaten. The rest of the morning had passed by in a blur as he'd given her errands to run—a trip to the post office and the office supply store down the street for some file folders.

Jonathan made her feel like she was important, as if she was worth something. Sarah wanted to keep that feeling alive. She wanted to believe in the good things he said instead of the bad things that kept running around in her head, telling her she couldn't do it, couldn't make it, couldn't be anything.

Maybe she could take care of Emily. Maybe she could be a good mother.

Even as the glimmer of hope tried to flop its wings and catch flight, it quickly died. She had no education, no job, no money, no place to live, and it looked like the church and Jonathan would be gone in a few days. She wouldn't even have a friend then. She'd be right back where she started—nowhere.

The front door to the house opened. A black woman came down the hall. It was the same woman she'd seen with the reverend that first day, the one who'd looked at her breasts and known right away she'd had a baby. Sarah self-consciously crossed her arms in front of her chest, even though her breasts had finally given up on nursing and flattened out the way they'd always been, another reminder of her failure to be a mother.

The woman raised her eyebrow when she saw Sarah standing in the room. "Well, you came back. You feeling better?"

"Yes."

"That's good. Where's Reverend Mitchell?"

"He's in a meeting."

The woman's lips drew together in a sharp frown as she looked down the hall. "Oh, dear. They came early."

Sarah wondered if the woman was worrying about Jonathan or the church or maybe just her own job. She seemed to serve some purpose, although Sarah wasn't sure what.

"Do you need something?" the woman asked.

Obviously, she wondered why Sarah was standing in the living room. "Jonathan, I mean Reverend Mitchell asked me to wait."

"I see. You can sit down if you want."

"Oh, all right." Sarah took a seat on the couch. She self-consciously clasped her hands together as Pauline stared at her from the doorway.

"My name is Pauline," the woman said unexpectedly. "If I can help, let me know."

"I'm all right."

"What happened to your baby?"

Sarah was taken aback by the abrupt change in subject. Apparently, now that they were on a first-name basis, Pauline wanted more information. "She's with some friends."

"You don't look like you have many friends."

Sarah didn't know what to say in reply. She doubted Pauline would believe anything she had to say.

"I hope you'll take whatever help Reverend Mitchell offers you," Pauline said. "It's not any easier out on the streets. You might run away from one bad situation only to find yourself in a worse one. Well, you give a holler if you need something."

Sarah nodded and let out a sigh of relief when she was alone again. The meeting down the hall was still in progress. Too restless to stay seated, Sarah got to her feet and walked quickly to the front door, slipping out of the house as quietly as she could. It struck her that she was always leaving, always escaping, always trying to run away from her problems, just like her mama. But where to go next? That was the question that plagued her as she walked down the sidewalk.

Maybe she should go to Mattie's, see if she could spot Emily. Just the thought of her baby made her stomach contract in a deep hungry yearning. How badly she wanted to hold Emily again, to touch her soft head, to whisper to her that everything would be all right, the way she'd done every night when she'd lain in bed, her hand pressed against her stomach, feeling the baby's tiny feet kick and flutter within her.

Sarah gasped at the rush of emotion that hit her. The suffocating pain stole her breath right out of her chest, and she put a hand to her heart, wondering if it would ever stop hurting. She tried to tell herself that it didn't matter if she was hurting, as long as her baby wasn't.

As she drew in long, calming breaths, torn between going and staying, she saw the woman with the watering can again. She was almost a full block away, her big straw hat hanging low on her head. Sarah suddenly had the urge to catch up with her. There was something so familiar about the woman, the way she walked, the way she concentrated so intently on her watering, and yet it couldn't be. It was impossible, or was it?

Sarah jogged down the street, almost as afraid of catching up with the woman as she was afraid of losing her.

"I think you'd look perfect in an off-the-shoulder dress, something simple, sleek, sophisticated," Caitlyn murmured as she studied the slender woman in front of her. For the first time in a long time, her fingers itched for a sketch pad and a pencil. But she wasn't anywhere near her drawing board. Instead she was standing in front of a rack of gowns that came from every top designer in the country, reminding her that her dreams had been put on hold for far too long.

"None of these are right," Danielle Slawson replied. "And I don't want what everyone else has."

Caitlyn didn't think many people did, but that was the way of the world.

"I'd like my own dress, something made just for me. Do you know a designer I could work with?"

Caitlyn hesitated. If she said yes, she might actually have to design a dress, and she hadn't completed one drawing since before the accident. What if she still couldn't do it?

"I see something with a long line of tiny pearls going down my back, intricate lacework, but nothing too poofy or trite," the woman said with a wistful note in her voice. "You see, I've waited thirty-eight years to find the right man to marry. I didn't want to settle for second best in a man, and I certainly don't want to settle for second best in a dress."

Caitlyn felt something inside of herself shift at Danielle's heartfelt words. She wondered if she hadn't settled before, if Brian hadn't been a little too easy. He'd slipped into her life like one of the family. She'd been innocent, wanting the basics—someone to love her, someone to promise she wouldn't ever be alone, someone to hide all the bad stuff away so she wouldn't have to see it. But Brian had left her to deal with the bad stuff on her own, and she'd become a woman who wanted more than the basics.

"I want everything in this wedding to be real and honest and not off of a rack," Danielle added, bringing Caitlyn's attention back to the matter at hand. She smiled apologetically. "I know I'm getting carried away. My friends can hardly believe it. I've always been a career-driven woman, but Travis makes me feel all gooey inside."

Caitlyn offered her a smile. "You should get carried away. Getting married is one of the most important things you'll ever do. You should have your wedding just the way you want it. Would you let me design a dress for you?" Caitlyn asked impulsively as Danielle started to turn away.

She looked surprised. "Can you do that?"

"I think so. You can approve the design and be involved every step of the way. But since we have some time, I'd love to try and come up with something you love."

"That would be fabulous. When can we start?"

"I already have some ideas. Why don't I come up with something, and if you like the basic idea, we'll talk price and deadlines, okay?"

"Sounds perfect. This will be great. I knew this was the right place to come. I had a good feeling about it. Another by-product of this thing called love—good feelings. I used to plan everything out. Now I'm working on instinct."

"I'll try to keep the lucky streak alive," Caitlyn said.

"Terrific. I'll call you next week."

Caitlyn said good-bye, then walked up to the front of the store, where Jolie was tallying receipts while Emily sat in her car seat nearby. Thankfully, Emily had been a peach of a baby all morning, gurgling and smiling and happily going from bride to bride when they asked wistfully if they could hold her.

"Are you being good?" Caitlyn asked as she picked Emily up.

"I'm being very good," Jolie replied with a smile. "Oh, you mean Emily. She's perfect. You, however, let someone go without making a sale." She tipped her head toward the departing Danielle. "I thought you had a fish on a hook with that one."

"I thought I'd design a dress for her instead of selling her one off the rack," Caitlyn said casually, as if it were no big deal, as if it weren't the breakthrough they'd been waiting for.

Jolie's eyes almost popped out of their sockets. "No freakin' way. Can you really do it?"

"I sure hope so," Caitlyn said fervently. "My fingers were actually tingling while I was talking to her. I wanted to draw something right then and there."

Jolie reached under the counter and pulled out a pad of paper. "Well, hell, get started."

Caitlyn laughed. "Jeez, give me a little pressure."

"I'm just thrilled you're even considering the idea. You are so gifted, Caitlyn. I hate to see you wasting that gift."

"Whoa, slow down. I said I would try. I don't know if I'll be successful." Already, the fear was infiltrating her mind. What if nothing came to her? What if her hand froze on the pencil? The woman didn't want second best. She wanted the ultimate wedding dress, and Caitlyn had just told her that she could deliver that when in fact she had no idea if she could.

"You can do it," Jolie said, reading her mind. "You've changed the last couple of days. In fact, I noticed it yesterday morning at brunch when you were hanging all over Matt."

"I wasn't hanging all over him."

"It's not a crime to like someone else."

"I don't think Brian or my parents would agree with you."

"They're not living your life. Trust your instincts."

Caitlyn was touched by Jolie's unending loyalty and support. "You're a great friend." She paused, looking around the busy shop, knowing this wasn't the time to share but determined that it would be soon. "I do want to talk to you about some things."

"Whenever you want, Caity. You don't owe me any explanations." Her gaze softened as she studied Caitlyn and Emily. "You're crazy about that baby, aren't you?"

"I tried to keep my distance, but it didn't work."

"Big surprise there. I knew the second I saw you with

her that you would fall in love. What are you going to do when her mother comes back?"

Caitlyn sighed. "Say good-bye, I guess."

"I don't think it will be that easy."

"I won't have a choice. If she does come back, that is."

"What does that mean?"

"It's possible that she might not return." Caitlyn felt guilty as the words left her mouth. Matt would hate her for losing faith in Sarah, but Caitlyn couldn't imagine how a woman could leave her baby for so many days without a word. Either something had happened to Sarah or she wasn't fit to be a mother. Neither scenario spoke well for Emily's future. Unless Emily's future could be with Matt. He would be a good father, Caitlyn thought, feeling a wave of sadness rise up and grab her around the throat. That was the problem with the truth. It didn't just hurt once. It hurt over and over and over again, every time she thought about it.

"What happens to Emily if her mother doesn't come back?" Jolie asked.

"I don't know. I guess Matt might have to raise her."

Jolie nodded, her expression thoughtful. "That would make sense. Would you . . . never mind."

"What?"

"How would you feel—raising someone else's baby?"

Caitlyn swallowed hard, knowing inside that that was the only way she ever would raise a child.

"I don't know." She looked away from Jolie's questioning gaze. "But this baby will be Matt's responsibility, not mine."

Caitlyn looked up as the subject of their conversation walked into the shop. As their eyes met, she felt the inevitable jolt of desire hit her body, making her heart pound and her palms sweat. Sharing her worst secret with this man had only made the intimacy between them that much greater.

Jolie cleared her throat as the glance between Caitlyn and Matt went on far too long. "Nice to see you again, Matt," she said pointedly.

He started, looking over at Jolie for the first time. Caitlyn felt a small rush of pleasure that for a second Matt had only had eyes for her.

"I hope Emily hasn't been too much trouble," he said.

"She's been a peach," Jolie replied. "But all this baby talk is making my uterus hurt, so I'm going back to work."

"Any luck?" Caitlyn asked Matt when they were alone.

"A little. The apartment was a pit, booze everywhere, probably drugs if you looked hard enough." His mouth wrinkled in disgust. "And there was a bassinet next to the bed."

"Emily's?" Caitlyn whispered in dismay, hating the thought that the baby in her arms had once slept in such a place.

"I think so. I can't believe Sarah lived there. Although why I'm surprised I really don't know. It's not like she grew up in a palace."

"Did the man who lived there tell you anything?"

"Not even his real name, but that shouldn't be too hard to find out. I picked up a few papers she left behind."

"So you were in the right place."

"I'm afraid so."

"I don't understand something, Matt. Sarah knows where you are, even if you don't know where she is. Why doesn't she come back and get Emily?" Caitlyn couldn't help voicing the question, even though she knew it made

Matt uncomfortable. Well, tough. He'd played hardball with her earlier this morning about telling the truth. Maybe he'd needed to tell himself the truth.

"I can't answer that." Matt held up a hand as she started to interrupt. "I know what you're going to say, but just don't, okay?"

She hesitated, but she was nowhere near as tough as he was. She could already see the worry and doubt in his eyes and she couldn't add to it. "All right, I'll shut up for now. I guess you're entitled to bury your head in the sand once in a while."

Matt reached for Emily, and Caitlyn let the baby go into his arms, sensing that he needed the hug more than she did.

"Has she driven you crazy today?" he asked.

"No, she's been perfect."

He raised an eyebrow. "Perfect? Our Emily?"

She felt another gut-wrenching twist at his use of the word *our*, but she tried not to let it show. "I think the mornings are better for her; she does a lot of sleeping."

"Tell me about it. It's the middle of the night she doesn't like. I guess you want me to take her home."

Caitlyn sighed at the word *home*. No matter what he said, no matter how casual she tried to act, she was still allowing herself to be pulled into his life, deeper and deeper, until she doubted she'd be able to get out on her own. And he'd want her out eventually. She didn't doubt that. This fantasy they were living would come to an end. Sarah would come back. Emily would return to her mother and Matt would just be her neighbor, someone she might occasionally pass in the hallway, not someone she would kiss or share moonlit stories with on the roof. She couldn't start thinking there would ever be anything more.

"Don't forget to dodge Mrs. Pederman," she said as he put Emily in her car seat.

"I'll try. When will you be home?"

"I can leave early. Mondays are usually slow. And I have a sketch I want to get working on." She offered him a beaming smile. "I told a bride I'd try designing a dress for her, and I think I might be able to do it. I don't know what changed. . . . Actually, that's not true. I do know what changed."

"The truth will set you free," he quoted with a grin. "Just think what you might be able to draw when you finally tell your parents and Brian."

She made a face at him. "Don't push it."

"I wouldn't dream of it."

"Ha! That's all you do is push."

"I've never gotten anything by being patient." He leaned over and pressed a hot kiss against her lips.

"Matt!"

"I figured you weren't going to kiss me first," he said without apology.

"I wasn't planning to kiss you at all."

"That's the difference between us. I don't like to plan. I like to live in the moment."

She felt a shiver run down her spine as the gleam in his eyes took on new meaning.

"Listen, my editor, David, and his wife, Jackie, are expecting a baby," he continued. "They'd like to meet Emily and they've invited us to dinner."

"Oh, well, that's good. You won't have to cook."

"Neither will you."

"They don't want to meet me."

"Yes, they do. David specifically said he wanted to meet the woman who'd gotten me into a baby store."

Caitlyn felt ridiculously pleased by the invitation. It

wasn't a date. It wasn't even close to a date, but it felt good, better than good. And she wasn't planning to examine that feeling any more closely.

"Will you come?" Matt asked.

"Sure."

"Good." He put the diaper bag over his shoulder. "By the way, David and Jackie thought they should get some baby practice while they have the chance. They've offered to keep Emily overnight, so I can get some sleep . . ." He smiled wickedly at Caitlyn. "Or not, depending on if I get a better offer."

A better offer . . . The words were still running through Caitlyn's mind several hours later as she put on a casually elegant black shift dress. She had no idea if Matt's friends were the dress-for-dinner type, and she wanted to fit in either way.

Of course, whatever his friends were or weren't shouldn't have affected her underwear choice, but Matt's parting shot . . . *a better offer* . . . had certainly made her consider pulling out the new silk undies. Not that Matt would be seeing her underwear. They did not have that kind of relationship. They were friends, just friends, she told herself firmly as she took one final glance in her bedroom mirror and saw a woman who had dressed up for a man, a very special man.

Who the hell was she kidding? She was attracted to Matt in a way that was far more friendly than friendship required. In fact, she had the hots for him, plain and simple. And every time he kissed her only made her want to do it again, longer and slower, and over and over and over.

She put a hand to her hot cheeks as she turned away from the mirror, somewhat embarrassed by her own lust. She'd never considered herself a passionate person. Her sex life had not been overwhelming. While Brian had been attentive and caring, in retrospect it had never been all that hard to sleep in the bed with him without having sex. In fact, they'd spent a lot of nights sharing the same space without making love. Why? She wondered now. Why hadn't she been overwhelmed with need and desire?

Maybe because she hadn't realized just how strong those emotions could be. Because Brian had never made her want him as much as she wanted Matt. She let out a breath, another truth rearing its ugly head. And the worst part was that Matt didn't even try for the most part. Oh, sure, a few teasing kisses now and then, but he got to her just by walking into a room. And his smile literally made her knees weak. Was this love, then?

No, it couldn't be. It shouldn't be. It was too damn confusing and unsettling. This wasn't comfortable and safe. This was scary and . . . and exciting . . . and wonderful. Maybe it was just lust. That's it, pure, unadulterated lust. She'd heard about it before. She'd just never experienced it until now. But everyone knew that lust wasn't love. You couldn't compare the two—could you?

Before an answer could register in her brain, she heard Matt knocking. She grabbed her purse and walked into the living room, her pulse already in overdrive, and she hadn't even opened the door yet. She was in trouble, big trouble.

"For once, you're on time—" she said, then stopped abruptly, shocked to find yet another unexpected visitor in her hall.

 *Fourteen*

"*M*om. What are you doing here?" Caitlyn asked.

Marilyn Devereaux stood in the doorway wearing a stark black suit with a silky white blouse. Her power suit, she liked to call it, the one she reserved for faculty dinners. Caitlyn felt her heart sink down to her stomach. Marilyn wanted something, and Caitlyn had a feeling her mother wouldn't be leaving until she got it.

"I came to speak to you, of course," Marilyn replied. "Can I come in?"

"I'm actually on my way out."

"I can see that." Marilyn's brows knitted into a thoughtful frown, as if Caitlyn's attire had suddenly thrown her plans off kilter. "Are you going to see Brian?"

"No."

"Oh. Well, I won't keep you long."

"All right." Caitlyn stepped back and let her mother into the apartment, feeling a bit like a child who had just been caught with a messy bedroom.

"My goodness," Marilyn exclaimed. "This looks more like a sweatshop than an apartment."

"Since I'm the one doing the sweating, I guess that's okay."

"Jolie told me that your customer base is growing and that the shop is very successful. You must be proud."

"I am proud for both Jolie and myself. We're still taking it day by day, though. We don't want to get overconfident, but for the most part things look good."

Marilyn picked up a piece of lace and fingered it thoughtfully. "You're so different from me," she mused. "I was never interested in sewing. I can't even hem a pair of pants. In fact, not many of the womanly arts come naturally to me. Thank goodness for housekeepers," she said with a quick smile.

"You didn't come to talk to me about housekeepers, did you, Mom?" Somehow Caitlyn didn't think her mother had come to talk about her wedding business, either.

"No. I wanted to speak to you about Brian."

Caitlyn sighed, knowing what was ahead. "I know how you feel, Mom. I know you and Dad love Brian."

"You used to love him, too. And I saw the care you took planning your wedding, designing your dress, the invitations we picked out together."

"What's your point?"

"I know that you were angry when Brian left to take the fellowship. You thought he was putting his career before you—the way your father and I had done."

Caitlyn couldn't quite believe her mother would admit to that.

"I'm not stupid," Marilyn said, catching her eye. "I know I'm not the mother you wanted. I remember when you used to visit Stacey Dempsey. You would describe Mrs. Dempsey's homemade after-school snacks ad nauseum. And the lunches Mrs. Dempsey made for Stacey always had Tupperware containers in them with roast beef and carrots and all the little things that made a lunch special, including silly notes from her mother. And Mrs. Dempsey made Halloween costumes and volunteered at school and even made her own candles. You wanted to be her little girl so badly. I was terribly jealous."

"I don't think that's entirely true," Caitlyn said, somewhat uncertain and wary of her mother's odd reflective mood. They'd never shared many confidences over the years; her mother had been far too busy for such conversations. In fact, she was surprised her mother even remembered Mrs. Dempsey.

"Oh, it was true, all right. You wanted me to be the kind of mother I didn't know how to be."

"I suspect you didn't get the daughter you wanted, either."

"I wish I could fix this breach between us, dear."

"I know you do. You always want to fix everything."

"It's been worse since the accident," Marilyn continued. "Nothing I said was right. And after Brian left, you grew even more distant. I wish you would have seen a therapist. Although it's not too late."

"A therapist wouldn't have made me feel differently about Brian, because the truth is . . ." Caitlyn hesitated, realizing how big a place the truth had come to demand. "The truth is that I feel differently about myself, and I have since the accident."

"You're just the same, Caitlyn, more beautiful than ever. Even the scars have faded. No one would ever know."

"But I know. And I can't sweep it under the rug even though that's what the rest of you want to do."

"We don't want to do that. We just want you to get on with your life."

"I have gotten on with my life. I'm just not doing it in the manner you'd like to see. But you know what, Mother, that's okay, because I don't hear the same tune you do."

Marilyn looked confused. "What does this have to do with music?"

Caitlyn smiled, feeling more self-assured than she had in years, maybe because for the first time in her life she wasn't trying to defend herself. "I march to a different beat than you and Dad and Brian. I've tried forever to keep up with you, but I can't. I've only just now realized that it's all right. You're a great Marilyn Devereaux. You don't need a clone. I don't have to be you."

"I never wanted you to be me."

"Didn't you? Why all the repairs, then? The extreme efforts you took to make me better?"

"I just wanted you to be the best you could be."

Caitlyn looked into her mother's eyes and saw that she really believed what she was saying. "Maybe that was your motive, but your repairs always made me feel like a very ugly work in progress. When I had a problem I was afraid to tell you, because I knew you'd criticize whatever choice I'd made."

Marilyn shook her head in amazement. "All these years you've felt this way, and you've never said anything?"

"I tried about a thousand times."

"Well, you didn't try hard enough."

Caitlyn smiled with exasperation. "Did you just hear yourself?"

Marilyn started, then stopped. "Oh, that didn't come out right, did it?"

"Nope."

"Well." Her mother nodded. "I guess it was good we

had this little chat." She turned her head as a knock came at the door.

Matt, Caitlyn realized with dismay. She'd hoped to get rid of her mother before Matt arrived.

"Who's that?"

"Matt."

"Your neighbor? You're going on a date with your neighbor?"

"Not a date, just dinner with some friends."

Matt rapped more impatiently this time, and Caitlyn moved over to answer the door.

She'd already felt unsettled by her mother's arrival, but seeing Matt fresh from a shower with damp hair and clean-shaven cheeks, smelling of something deliciously sexy, took the rest of her breath away. Not to mention the fact that this ruggedly handsome male was holding a baby in his arms, a baby dressed all in pink and wearing a slightly askew hair ribbon that Matt had obviously tried to attach.

A pleased smile spread across Caitlyn's face as she reached out and straightened the ribbon. "You put it on her even though you thought it was silly for her to wear a ribbon when she didn't have much hair."

"Well, you liked it," he said huskily. "And this is her first evening out."

"She's beautiful."

"So are you." Matt's gaze shifted as he looked past Caitlyn. "Oh. I didn't realize your mother was here. Hello, Mrs. Devereaux."

"Hello, Matt. Please call me Marilyn."

"Marilyn," he acknowledged.

A silence fell between them—an awkward silence, Caitlyn thought.

"I can wait for you," Matt said. "Just knock on my door when you're ready."

"I'm ready now."

"Yes, she's ready." Marilyn moved close enough to Matt to stroke Emily's head. "Where did you say her mother is?"

"Uh, my sister had to go away for a few days."

"I hope your sister doesn't suffer for her absence. Children have a way of blaming their parents for everything that goes wrong in their life." Marilyn looked back at Caitlyn. "You may have thought I didn't need you in my life or want you there because you weren't perfect. Strangely enough, I've felt the same way." She let the words sink in for a moment, then said, "But no matter what you think, Caitlyn, I do love you, and that will never change."

Caitlyn felt a suspicious moisture in her eyes as she watched her mother say good-bye to Matt and walk down the hall. She wanted to say something back, but the words wouldn't quite come.

"It's not too late," Matt said. "You can catch her at the elevator."

Caitlyn debated, then shook her head. "Not tonight."

"Did you tell her—"

"Not that. But other stuff." She drew in a breath and forced a smile on her face. "Let's go to dinner."

"Did I tell you that you look incredibly sexy tonight?"

"You mentioned something about beautiful, but I don't think I heard sexy."

"Sexy and beautiful. By the way, don't be surprised if my friends try to do some matchmaking. Like your parents, they'd love to see me happily attached to a woman."

Caitlyn was beginning to think she'd like to see the

same thing—but not just attached to any woman, attached to her.

Jonathan couldn't believe Sarah had left him without a word of good-bye. He'd quizzed Pauline like a prosecuting attorney, knowing he was completely over the top by the astonished expression on her face. But he couldn't stop the feeling that in losing Sarah he was losing a precious piece of himself that he might not ever be able to get back.

He'd spent the afternoon looking for Sarah instead of considering his probable transfer and the closing of the church. Now it was almost seven, getting dark, and he was sitting in the living room of a house that felt as cold as his heart. Why couldn't he hang on to things? Why couldn't he make people do what he wanted them to do? Why couldn't he find the right impassioned words to persuade?

His gaze drifted to the photograph on the mantel, his mother and father on their wedding day. It was a photo no one had wanted but him.

His mother had left his father just after Jonathan's thirteenth birthday, saying she couldn't come in second to God for the rest of her life. And since Jonathan was almost a teenager, she thought it was best if he lived with his father and visited her on the weekends. He'd wanted to protest, but his father had agreed with the arrangement, and Jonathan hadn't found the words to persuade them to do otherwise.

Now he was losing the church he'd come to love because everyone thought it would be better for him to go somewhere else. And if he didn't speak up, if he didn't say no, he'd be in the South Bay in less than a month, leaving this neighborhood and the friends he'd made here without a church, without a minister, and maybe without a friend. But was he strong enough to fight for the church he served? Could he find the right argument to convince the board that the church needed to stay open?

And Sarah . . . where had she gone? Why had she left when he'd asked her to wait?

He didn't know why he felt so strongly about this woman. Well, maybe he did. Maybe he saw in her a little bit of himself, a lack of confidence, a big heart, but the uncertainty of how to use that heart. He looked to the ceiling and prayed. "Lord, I could use some help here. How can I help Sarah if I can't keep her close to me?" He paused. "Maybe I'm not meant to help her. Is that it? Has she come into my life for some other reason?"

Not even God seemed to be speaking to him these days, Jonathan thought with a depression that weighed heavy on his heart. But then the Lord probably didn't have much patience for self-pity, and neither did Jonathan. He was acting like he had to save the church himself, and all by himself. It occurred to him that that wasn't the way it was meant to be. The only way to save the church was for the people of the community to do it, and he hadn't asked them. The answer was suddenly glaringly clear, so loud in his head he wondered if someone else had spoken, a greater voice perhaps, he thought, directing another glance at the ceiling. "Thanks," he muttered.

Jonathan got up and reached for the telephone. Maybe he couldn't inspire a crowd, but he could influence people one by one. He dialed the number of Martina Petrovka, one of the few loyal churchgoers they had.

"Hello, Martina," he said when he heard her distinctively accented voice on the other end of the phone. "I need a favor."

"Whatever you need, Reverend Mitchell."

"I need you to call everyone you know," he began, his voice growing in fervor with each passing word, until Martina was almost as excited by the challenge as he was himself. He only had two weeks to turn things around. Well, the Lord had created the world in seven days. Surely he could save one small piece of that world in the next fourteen.

The doorbell rang through the house, lighting another spark of hope in his heart. He opened the door and breathed out the name that had been on his lips all day. "Sarah."

"Jonathan," she said, calling him by his first name. They were suddenly no longer minister and supplicant, they were man and woman.

Caitlyn had never been so aware of a man's touch than on this night. It had begun with Matt's hand on the small of her back as he ushered her into the Sterns' home, then the brushes of their hands as he took Emily out of her arms, the reassuring caress of his fingers on her thigh as they sat next to each other at the dinner table.

Every time he touched her, a foolish little tingle ran down her spine. She couldn't stop her pulse from speeding up when he smiled at her, couldn't keep her heart from skipping a beat when he laughed or smiled. She just hoped no one else was noticing.

"Caitlyn?"

She started, suddenly aware that everyone at the dinner table was looking at her. So much for going unnoticed. "Did I miss something?"

"You aren't eating your dessert," Jackie said. "Is it all right?"

"It's fine. I was just thinking about . . ." Caitlyn darted a quick glance at Matt, who had a little smile teasing the edge of his mouth, and it occurred to her that all those innocent touches might have been deliberate. "I was just thinking about the beautiful china in your cabinet," she prevaricated.

"It was my mother's," Jackie replied. "She gave the entire set to David and me when we married. Part of that 'something old' tradition. She said she was more than happy to turn over the family dinners to me, and I might as well have the plates, too."

"They're beautiful. And I like that they're passed down. It makes the setting more special."

"Oh, I agree. You must know a lot about weddings, Caitlyn. I bet you'll have a spectacular one when you get married."

Caitlyn shrugged, seeing Jackie and David exchange a conspiratorial look.

"That's the problem with married people," Matt broke in. "They want everyone else to get married so they can share their misery, I mean happiness."

"Very funny." Jackie made a face at him. "Marriage does not equal misery. David and I are blissfully happy. Aren't we?"

"Uh, yeah," David said, sending her an annoyed look. "That is my leg you're kicking, in case you hadn't noticed."

"Of course it's your leg. Tell Matt how happy you are."

Matt laughed. "Don't bother. It's written all over your face, buddy."

"I am happy." David smiled tenderly at his wife. "I never thought I could be this happy. Even though I take a lot of bruises on my shin when we have dinner guests."

Jackie leaned across the table to kiss him. "I'll make it up to you later."

"The best part of marital fights," David said with a wink in Matt's direction.

"I'll let you in on a little secret. You don't have to get married to have sex," Matt said dryly. "Despite what they told us in gym class."

Caitlyn picked up her spoon and took a bite of her dessert as the conversation flowed around her. The confection of chocolate mousse and whipped cream slid down her throat in heavenly delight. "This is fantastic."

"A recipe from my mother," Jackie said. "I'm glad you like it."

"I love it."

"So do I. I've been eating far too much of it the past nine months." She rested her hand on her pregnant belly. "The only good thing is I have a little table now to catch all the crumbs that drop from my mouth."

Caitlyn stared at Jackie's stomach, and a gnawing ache developed in her own abdomen. Why couldn't she have lost the urge to have kids along with the ability to do so?

"So, how do you like those Giants?" Matt asked, changing the subject with a deliberation that did not fool Caitlyn for one second. A pleasing warmth spread through her as she realized he'd seen her discomfort and acted on it without her even asking. That was the difference between Matt and Brian. Brian needed a book to figure her out. All Matt had to do was look at her.

"We are not talking sports," Jackie interrupted. "This is a dinner party. Do you want to hear the names we've picked out for our baby?"

"Oh, honey, they don't want to hear that," David protested.

"Abigail if it's a girl and Matthew if it's a boy," Jackie said.

Matt looked stunned. "You're naming your kid after me?"

"It's not after you. It's after, uh, it's after David's Uncle Matt," Jackie said haltingly, correctly interpreting a pointed look from her husband.

"It's just a coincidence," David said.

Matt didn't look like he believed either one of them, and Caitlyn couldn't blame him. They were pathetically transparent.

"How did the three of you meet?" Caitlyn asked, deciding it was time to save Matt from a little discomfort.

"I saved Matt's life," David replied.

"Correction, I saved his life," Matt said.

Caitlyn looked to Jackie, who groaned. "This could go on for the next three hours, trust me. The short version is they met in a bar. Someone insulted a woman. Matt took a swing at the guy. The guy took a swing at Matt and hit David by accident."

"I swung back just in time to save Matt from getting his head bashed in," David added.

"Then I saved him by throwing the guy over the bar."

"And they became best friends," Jackie finished. "Actually, they found out they were both journalists, and David got Matt a job at the paper, and the rest is history."

"Except Matt almost got me fired from that job by refusing to reveal a source," David said grumpily. "Come to think of it, you've caused me nothing but trouble."

"You love trouble."

"That's true," David agreed, a smile breaking across his face. "All I can say, Caitlyn, is that Matt is the kind of guy who can give you a tremendous migraine headache, but when you need someone to back you up, there's no one better."

"Thanks, I think," Matt replied dryly.

Caitlyn smiled. "Believe me, I've already had to replenish my aspirin supply since Matt knocked on my door last Friday."

"Not to mention earplugs," Matt added just as Emily let out a scream of distress. "Speak of the devil—"

"She's not a devil, she's a baby." Caitlyn rescued Emily from a blanket they'd spread on the floor so she could kick and stretch out of the confines of her car seat. "She's wet."

"Of course she is. She drinks like a sailor on three-day leave," Matt said.

"Can I change her?" Jackie asked. "In fact, can David and I do it? We need the practice."

"Speak for yourself," David said, but he got up and obediently followed his wife out of the room.

Caitlyn sat down next to Matt and eyed her dessert plate suspiciously. "Did you take a bite?"

"No way." A tiny spot of chocolate on his top lip made a lie out of his words.

She put her finger to the corner of his mouth and wiped it off and held it up for him to see the evidence. "Really?"

"You got me." Then he grabbed her by the wrist and raised her finger to his mouth so he could lick off the chocolate.

Caitlyn caught her breath as a jolt of desire swept through her. His tongue caressed her finger as he sucked it between his lips in a movement so highly erotic she felt the heat rise through her body, every nerve ending on fire, and the last thing she wanted was to put out that fire. No, she wanted to add another log and take the flames even higher.

"I—I think it's gone." She forced herself to pull away.

Matt's eyes had darkened to a dangerous black. "You taste better than the chocolate."

She swallowed, unused to seeing such naked lust in a man's expression. "Oh, Matt, what are we doing?"

"It's what we're *not* doing that's bothering me. Do you want to go home with me?"

"Well, you did drive," she said, striving for lightness.

"That's not what I meant, and you know it."

"Do you think it's a good idea?"

"Probably not," he admitted, sneaking a kiss on the corner of her mouth, then another on the other corner, finally sliding over to take her in a full, open-mouth kiss that sent what little doubt was left right out of her head. "I want you," he added with the honesty that was so much a part of him.

"You're not supposed to say things like that," she said somewhat breathlessly.

"Why not? Because the words scare you? Because you can't run and hide from them?"

"Well, technically, I could run and hide, but . . ."

"But you can't make yourself move. I know the feeling, Caitlyn. It washes over me every time I see you."

"It's crazy. A few days ago we didn't know each other. Now we're spending every second together. For a man who didn't even want to know his neighbor's name, your attitude has certainly changed."

"We've gone way past being neighbors, Caitlyn."

"What happens when it's over? Will we be able to just pass each other in the hall again, say an occasional hello?"

"I don't know. At the moment, I'm not thinking much past unzipping your dress and seeing if your breasts taste as good as your finger."

Her jaw dropped open. She'd never had a man state his intentions so boldly. And she couldn't believe how much she liked it, how turned on she was by a sentence. They weren't even touching, and she was going up in flames.

She cleared her throat, trying to gather her wits about her. "Most people say those kinds of things with the lights out."

"I can turn out the lights, but it won't change how I feel—or how I could make you feel."

Caitlyn looked into his eyes and saw his promise. "I don't know what to say."

"Just tell me what you want."

"Do I have to?" she whispered. "Or do you already know?"

 *Fifteen*

"**W**hat do you want from me?" Sarah asked Jonathan as she stood in the middle of his living room. She didn't know why she kept coming back, why her feet couldn't seem to move in any other direction than toward him. Who was this man and why couldn't she seem to let go? She'd tried to walk away all afternoon, following the woman in the straw hat halfway across town, then losing her just around the corner from Matt's apartment. It was odd how the woman had taken her there, almost as if she'd known that's where Sarah needed to go.

She'd lingered in front of Matt's building, catching a bittersweet glance of Matt kissing Emily on the cheek as he'd taken her out of his car. Emily hadn't been crying. She'd been happy, happier than Sarah ever remembered her being.

She'd done the right thing leaving Emily with Matt. Her baby was in good hands, healthy, happy. Sarah could leave now with a clean conscience. Only she couldn't leave. Because seeing Emily again had only made the terrible ache in her soul turn into a sharp, stabbing pain.

She'd wanted to run up to Matt and take Emily out of his arms and promise she'd never leave her again. But she'd waited too long, and he'd gone inside the building. She'd lost her nerve then, imagining what she could possibly say. *Hi, how are you? How have you been for the last thirteen years? You don't mind that I dropped my baby off without even asking, do you?*

How ridiculous would that have sounded? It would have sounded crazy—crazy like their mother. Matt would have taken one look at her and seen the resemblance. And then what would she have done? And maybe Matt would think Emily would go crazy, too. But her baby wouldn't, because she wouldn't grow up the way they had. She'd have a better life—a life with Matt.

"Sarah?"

It was a moment before Sarah realized that Jonathan was talking to her. "What?"

"You asked what I wanted from you. The answer is nothing."

"That can't be true. Everyone wants something."

"What do you want?"

She'd backed herself into that corner. "I don't know."

"Yes, you do. You're just afraid to say it out loud. Actually, I do want something. I want you to trust me. I want you to stop guarding your words, to feel free enough to be yourself."

"I don't even know who that is."

He smiled. "No time like the present to find out. So, tell me what you want."

"I want the Christmas card family," she said impulsively, the words coming out of her mouth before she could stop them. "The one with the roaring fire and the kids hanging the stockings and the cat playing with the ribbons on the Christmas present. Mattie gave me a card like that once." Matt was the only one who'd ever given her anything. She reached for the necklace that was usually on her neck, reminded again that she'd left it behind in her desperate flight from Gary.

"Why can't you have it?"

"Because people like me don't have things like that."

"When you look in the mirror, you see limitations, but when I look at you, Sarah, I see possibilities." The warmth in his eyes took the chill from her bones. And when Jonathan led her over to the couch, she didn't resist.

They sat in silence for a few moments. Sarah was grateful that he didn't rush into speech. She couldn't think when things moved too fast. She needed time for all the words to get to her head in the right order. One of her teachers had said she had some learning problem, but she couldn't remember the name of it. Not that it mattered. There were lots of reasons why she hadn't finished school, and none of them had to do with her brain.

"Tell me about this Mattie you speak of so fondly," Jonathan said.

"He's my brother. My older brother."

"Where does he live?"

She tensed, still not sure how much she should trust him. But as she looked into his encouraging eyes, she knew that if she was ever going to take a chance on a man, this was the man.

"He lives here in town," she answered.

"Why didn't you go to him when Gary hurt you?"

"I did. He's the one who has my baby."

A light of understanding came into his eyes. "I see."

"No, you don't see. I left Emily in the hallway with a

note. I didn't give Mattie a chance to say no. I just left her. Now you know what a terrible mother I am."

"Is she safe with Matt?"

"Yes."

"Then you're not a terrible mother. Let me ask you this, would she have been safe with you?"

"I don't know. She kept crying. I felt so helpless. And Gary couldn't stand it. He talked to some friends of his, and he found a lawyer who would pay us ten thousand dollars to give Emily to him." Her mouth trembled, and she bit down on her lip to stop herself from crying. "I said I wouldn't sell my baby, but Gary said he didn't need my permission because he was the baby's father and I'm not a good mother. He could find people to say that was so if I tried to stop him. And there was a part of me that believed him, that I was a bad mother."

"Sarah, no, that's not true. You protected your child. That was the right thing to do, the courageous thing to do."

"But what am I going to do now? I don't have an education. The only job I ever had was as a shampoo girl at a beauty salon. If I don't stay with Gary, who's going to pay for everything? I feel so tired, so overwhelmed. I don't think I can do this by myself."

"Sh-sh," he said, putting a finger against her lips. Then his hands slid to her shoulders and she was suddenly resting her head on his chest. "You're not by yourself anymore."

Oh, how she wanted to believe him, to close her eyes and be swept away into a beautiful dream where a man and a woman and a child lived happily ever after.

"I can help you if you let me," he told her.

She lifted her head to look at him. "Why would you want to?"

"Because I want to."

"That's your reason? I thought you'd say because God wanted you to."

"Well, he probably does. Actually, I'm not sure if you were sent to me so I could help you or so you could help me."

"Me? What could I do to help you?"

"You're not the only who feels helpless to change things. And you're not the only one who feels alone sometimes."

"But you're a minister. You have God for company."

He chuckled. "Sometimes, the conversation is a little one-sided."

She sent him a tentative smile. "I guess that's true."

He put his hand on the side of her face, his fingers gentle as they traced the fading bruise around her eye. A second later he dropped his hand with a guilty frown. "Sorry."

Jonathan stood up abruptly and walked around the room. He picked up a photograph on the mantel, then set it back down again.

"Who's in the picture?" she asked, wondering why he suddenly seemed so uncomfortable.

"My parents on their wedding day."

"Can I see it?"

He hesitated, then picked up the frame and handed it to her.

"Your mother is pretty. She looks happy."

"She was then. It didn't last. They divorced when I was thirteen."

"I didn't think ministers could get divorced."

"It's frowned upon, but my father is such an incredible preacher that he can talk most people into forgetting what he wants them to forget and remembering what he wants them to remember."

"You make him sound like God."

"Do I?" Jonathan shifted his feet, then took the photo out of her hand and set it on the mantel. "Let's talk about you."

"I told you everything."

"Not about your parents. What about your father?"

"He died when I was a baby."

"And your mother?"

"She wasn't around much. Mattie used to take care of me. Then we were split up into foster care after a fire in our apartment. I never saw him again after that. I didn't even know where he was until a few days ago when I picked up a newspaper and saw his name. I thought it was a sign."

"You need to talk to him, Sarah. Tell him you're all right. Tell him what happened with Gary."

She shook her head. "I can't do that."

"Why not? You miss your baby, don't you?"

"So much," she said, a tear spilling out of one eye. She wiped it away but it was quickly followed by another and another. Some days she thought she might drown in her own tears.

Jonathan handed her a Kleenex from the box on the end table. She wiped her cheeks. "Sorry."

"You don't have to apologize for loving your baby or for wanting her to be with you." His gaze was so piercing it went straight through to her heart.

"I do want her, but I'm scared."

"Of Gary?"

"And myself. You see . . ." She twisted the tissue in her fingers, wondering how much she should tell him, but she couldn't stop the words from coming straight out of the scariest part of her mind. "My mother was crazy. Most people thought she was just a drunk, but I knew different. And I'm afraid I might be crazy, too."

"I don't think you're crazy, Sarah," Jonathan said as he sat down next to her.

"You don't know me well enough to say that."

"I know that people who are crazy are usually the last to know," he said bluntly. "Did your mother ever say she was crazy?"

"No. She never said that. But she was. She'd say things that made no sense, and the things she did . . . Well, I don't want to talk about this anymore." She got to her feet, the memories making her restless, making her feel like she should run again. Because she'd been running from them her whole life.

"You have to talk about your past. You have to bring your fears out of the shadows, flood them with light, so they won't scare you anymore."

She wondered if it could really be that easy. Deep down she didn't think so. This man hadn't seen what she'd seen, hadn't lived the life she'd lived. He wanted to believe that there was good in everyone, but she knew that some people just weren't good.

"Have you ever hurt anyone, Sarah?" he continued, his eyes intent on hers. "Have you? Look at me, dammit."

She was startled by the first swear word she'd ever heard cross his lips. She turned her head to face him.

"Have you ever committed a crime?" he asked.

"No."

"Done drugs?"

"No! I never did drugs. I swear. I used to drink when I

was in high school but I quit as soon as I got pregnant. And I haven't had anything since."

"Because you were worried about hurting your baby. That sounds pretty smart to me. I don't think you're crazy, Sarah. I think you're scared. You're twenty-two years old, and you've had a rough life so far. Now, you have a baby and no way to support that child, no home and no job. If you weren't scared, there would be something wrong with you." He got up and walked over to her, putting his hands on her shoulders. "We are not our parents, Sarah. Not for the good stuff, not for the bad stuff. It's taken me a long time to learn that."

"Some things are hereditary."

"And a lot of things are not. Believe me, I wish I had my father's fire, his passion, his ability to make things happen, but I don't. And I happen to look just like him, too," he added with a smile. "Maybe you see your mother in the mirror, but she's not there, you are."

She wanted to believe him, wanted to feel better, but it was difficult to let go of the fear. "After I had Emily, she cried all the time, and I couldn't make her stop. I tried rocking her, singing to her, feeding her. But she hated to nurse, and she hated me. It got harder and harder to get up out of bed to take care of her. I was so tired, and Gary wouldn't help. He'd just say it was time to give her up. He almost had me convinced, but then I couldn't— couldn't let her go. I love her," she said passionately, knowing it was the one truth she could speak freely. "I love her so much. But I have to do what's right by her, which I think means letting her go, but then I miss her so much I can't stand it." She put a hand to her heart. "It hurts in here, Jonathan. It hurts worse than anything." She couldn't keep the agony out of her voice, because now that the dam had burst, she was swamped with regret for having let Emily go. The baby was the only good thing that had ever happened to her in her whole life. "Tell me what to do. Please tell me what to do."

"I can't tell you what to do," Jonathan said slowly. "But I do have an idea."

"What?"

"These feelings that you have of depression and terror, did you have them before Emily was born?"

"Sometimes, but they got worse when she was crying all the time. I didn't know babies could be so hard or that I would feel so overwhelmed."

He nodded. "Come with me."

"Where—the church? Because praying hasn't gotten me anywhere."

He smiled at her, the smile that told her things would work out. "Prayer got you here," he said. "But now you have to come with me to the office, to my computer."

"Your computer is going to help me?" she asked doubtfully.

"A little faith can be a wonderful thing."

"Emily won't stop crying," Caitlyn told Matt as they waited in the Sterns' living room for Jackie and David to get Emily to sleep so they could go. "I know they want to help you, but Emily doesn't know them. We can't leave her here overnight."

"You're right. Emily doesn't even like us much once the witching hour hits."

"It was nice of them to offer . . ."

"But we should take her home with us."

Caitlyn liked the fact that there wasn't any real doubt in his voice, no edge of irritation that he wouldn't get the night off he'd expected.

David came out of the bedroom with a harried look on his face. "My God, that baby can cry. I had no idea a little thing like that could make so much noise."

"Tell me about it," Matt said, starting toward the bedroom.

"I'll go," Caitlyn said as she put a hand on his arm. "You better talk to David about some of the joys of fatherhood before he decides to call the whole thing off."

"Hey, can I do that?" David asked.

Caitlyn smiled as she entered the bedroom and saw Jackie frantically trying to bounce Emily out of her bad mood. "Do you want me to take her?"

"I think you better," Jackie said, more relief than dismay in her voice. "I don't think she fits too well with my pregnant stomach. She can't get comfortable. And David doesn't know how to hold her. He acts like she's a football and he's looking for a receiver to pass to."

Caitlyn took Emily and placed the baby in her favorite position, which was against Caitlyn's chest, Emily's head tucked under Caitlyn's chin. Her cries turned into sobs, then whimpers, then breaths of relief as exhaustion claimed her into sleep.

"Wow, you have the magic touch," Jackie said, her eyes worried as they studied Caitlyn and the baby. "What were David and I thinking? We can't take care of a kid. We don't know the first thing about babies. What if our child doesn't like us? What if we do the wrong thing?"

"You won't, and you'll learn about your own baby very quickly. You'll start to distinguish between real cries of distress and just cries of irritation."

"Do you really think so?"

"Yes, absolutely. And don't think Matt and I are experts. Emily cries with us all the time. Ask Matt what he did last night to get her to sleep."

"What?" Jackie asked.

"He drove Emily around in the car for an hour until she fell asleep."

"That's not exactly making me feel better."

"Sorry; I just didn't want you to think it was you. Emily doesn't like the nighttime. She's fussy. But I'm starting to figure out what makes her happiest."

"She's lucky to have you."

"Lucky to have Matt. I'm just helping out."

"Matt is lucky to have you. Although, he has taken to this child like I never expected. The way he looks at her, the way he talks to her . . . it amazes me."

"It gets to me, too," Caitlyn admitted. "I never thought a man and a baby could be so beautiful together, but Matt and Emily—sometimes they take my breath away."

Jackie smiled knowingly, and Caitlyn had a feeling she'd been a little too enthusiastic. "I'm speaking objectively, of course."

"Of course."

"You'll see what I'm talking about the first time David falls asleep with your baby in his arms."

"I can't wait. Sometimes it seems to take forever."

Caitlyn felt a rush of emotion as she watched Jackie rub her stomach in a loving gesture. She wondered what it would feel like to carry a baby inside your body, to feel its feet and hands kicking against you, to know that you were giving life to a human being. But she would never know any of that. Her body would always be barren. Such an awful word that was, like a dry, parched, deadly desert, where nothing could grow, nothing could live. What kind of a person did that make her?

Logically, she knew she was a good person, that having a baby wouldn't validate or invalidate that. But she still felt like she was missing something important. And somehow, some way, she had to find purpose and meaning in the rest of her life, in her other relationships, because whatever version of family she ended up with, it wouldn't be the one she had always wanted. And she'd have to reconcile with that.

That sense of reconciliation had grown in the minutes and hours since she'd shared her secret with Matt. She didn't know why really. But saying it out loud had made her face it in a way she hadn't done before. It was the first step. Now she just needed to take the next one and the one after that. But not today. Maybe tomorrow or some time in the future.

"I never thought of Matt as a family man," Jackie mused, her gaze still fixed on Emily, who had drifted off to sleep. "I used to think he'd never settle down. It was more likely for him to have a different woman on his arm every Friday night than the same one two weeks in a row." Jackie stopped, suddenly looking guilty. "That wasn't the smartest thing to say, was it?"

"It doesn't matter. Matt and I are just friends." Caitlyn said the words automatically, although Jackie seemed disinclined to believe them. Of course, she was having a little trouble herself, but that was beside the point.

"He watches you when you're not watching him," Jackie said.

"Really?" Caitlyn couldn't stop the irrepressible tingle that ran down her spine at this piece of information.

"Yes, really. You like him, don't you?"

"Sure, I like him, but—"

"Don't worry, I'm not asking your intentions. But Matt is a great guy, and I know deep down that he really wants a family of his own. He had a hard childhood, very little love or support, and he's spent most of his adult life focused on his career, which has made him a great reporter, but I'm not sure it's done much for his loneliness. And I do think he's lonely. He acts like he doesn't care, like he's the proverbial rolling stone, but he never refuses a dinner invitation with us, and since I got pregnant he's been so interested and concerned. I sure would like to see him surrounded by a wife and kids of his own."

Caitlyn swallowed hard as a picture of Matt sitting on a couch with a couple of kids on his lap came into her head.

"I'm sorry," Jackie said quickly. "I just made you uncomfortable, didn't I? Me and my big mouth."

"It's fine, really."

"I'm a little protective where Matt is concerned. I don't want to see him get hurt. He really has had more than his fair share of pain."

"He told me a little about his childhood," Caitlyn admitted. "But I think I'm in more danger of getting hurt by Matt than vice versa."

"Don't be so sure. A man's heart can break, too, no matter what they say. In fact, I think we're the stronger of the two sexes. Look at me. In three weeks, I'm going to have to squeeze an eight-pound baby out of my body. What man could do that?"

Caitlyn laughed. "I don't know any."

"Talking about me?" Matt asked as he and David walked into the room.

"We've got better things to do than talk about you," Jackie lied. "I'm just sorry we can't give you that night off. I think Emily wants Caitlyn."

"Well, everyone wants Caitlyn," Matt replied.

Caitlyn felt a rush of heat flow across her cheeks at the look in his eyes. Didn't he realize he was giving his friends the wrong impression? Didn't he realize he was giving her the wrong impression? "I'm sure Emily would probably just as soon have you holding her," Caitlyn said. "She likes Matt's big strong chest."

"All the women do," he replied with a grin. "But I'm not taking Emily. Rule number one is never disturb a sleeping child."

"Should I write this down?" David asked. "I didn't know there were actual rules to parenting."

"Absolutely," Matt replied.

"What's rule number two?" Caitlyn inquired.

"Never answer a woman when she asks you what rule number two is."

David laughed. "That goes along with never answer a woman when she asks you if she looks fat."

"Ha-ha," Jackie said, slipping her arm around her husband's waist. "You just have to know the right answer, sweetie."

"You look incredibly thin, beautiful, and drive me wild with desire," David replied.

"Ah, I have taught you something." Jackie planted a smacking kiss on his cheek.

They were so perfect together, Caitlyn thought wistfully, and in a few weeks they would have a baby to make their family complete. The thought jabbed at her like a knife. When would it end? When would she stop looking at happy families and wonder, Why me? When the real question was, Why not me? What made her so special? Nothing. She was just like everyone else. She'd had an accident. It was no one's fault, except maybe her own. And she had to find a way to live with it.

"Let's go home," Matt said quietly, putting his arm around her and Emily.

They were a family, Caitlyn thought suddenly. The three of them were a family. Her body tightened with an impossible wish—a wish that it would last. But where would that leave Sarah? And where would that leave Matt? They were the true family, Matt, Sarah, Emily. Caitlyn was the interloper, the one who didn't belong, but she wanted the wish anyway.

"Let's go home," she agreed. Maybe she wouldn't have tomorrow, but she still had tonight. And if her accident had taught her anything, it was that every moment counted.

Sixteen

$\mathcal{E}$mily was still asleep when Caitlyn and Matt stopped in front of their respective doors. The silence that had grown between them on the car ride home lengthened and deepened. It was no longer comfortable but tense, edgy, filled with unspoken questions, unanswered desires.

"Think Emily is out for the night?" Matt asked as he unlocked his door.

"Probably. She was up all evening."

"That doesn't mean anything."

"I'll keep my fingers crossed for you."

"Does that mean you won't be staying?"

She met his eyes and nervously licked her lips, drawing his attention to her mouth, which was a big mistake. Because then she thought about kissing him. And she was trying not to think about that.

"Well, since you have Emily . . ." Her voice drifted away, knowing it was just an excuse. Emily was a tiny baby and was also fast asleep. As far as chaperones went, she wasn't much of one.

Matt pushed open his door. "Running away again, Caitlyn?"

"Hardly. I'm not even moving," she said defensively.

"But in a few minutes you'll be on the other side of that door with the chain pulled safely across."

"Where do you want me to be?"

"You know where I want you to be, naked, under me, on top of me, all around me."

She blew out a sharp breath, her nerve endings fired up by his blunt response. "God, Matt, how can you just say things like that?"

"It's the truth." His gaze bored into hers. "But you're afraid of the truth, aren't you?"

"No," she said, although he was partly right. She wasn't just afraid of the truth, she was afraid of the way she was feeling about him, like she was in quicksand, going under without any hope of being saved.

"It's your move, Caitlyn. You know where you can find me." He walked into his apartment and shut the door.

"Good night," she muttered crossly. "I had a great time. Thanks for the invitation."

She stood there for a long minute and stared at that closed door. It was not the way she'd expected things to end. At the very least, she'd thought maybe a kiss on the cheek, a "Thanks for the nice evening," a smile. But no, Matt had to make his point. Well, he could wait forever for her to act.

She unlocked her door and stepped inside her apartment. She threw her purse down on the table and kicked off her heels. Going to bed would be a good decision, she told herself. Only problem was she didn't feel tired, more like wired, jittery, frustrated. Matt had been warming her up all evening only to give her the cold shoulder now. Why? Because he wanted her to come to him.

Well, she could do that if she wanted to. But did she want to? Matt wouldn't be easy. He wouldn't play by the rules. He wouldn't let her hide in the shadows, where she was most comfortable. He probably wouldn't even stay on his side of the bed. Not that she was planning to go to bed with him. Good heavens! How crazy would that be?

Crazy in love . . . there was that pesky word again. Not love, lust. Okay, maybe a little liking, but that was it. Then she remembered the way he'd asked her about her day earlier, listened to her design plans for Danielle's wedding dress, and he'd never looked bored. And she thought about how he'd pulled out her chair at the dinner table and changed the subject when she'd become uncomfortable, the little proprietary touches that made her feel protected . . . She didn't just like him a little. She liked him a lot.

Too much. She had a feeling this one could hurt bad. She also had a feeling that this one could be spectacular.

"Oh, Matt, why did you have to leave it up to me?" she whispered.

Brian would have either kissed her or said good-night. He wouldn't have left this indecision between them. But then Brian wasn't here. He was at home reading some book, trying to figure out how to get her back. As if a book could explain her actions; she couldn't even explain her actions. Nor could she explain how a lone wolf bachelor with a lot of rough edges had completely stolen her common sense and replaced it with overwhelming desire.

This wasn't her—this woman who wanted to strip naked and make wild passionate love with the sexy man across the hall. She wasn't wild or passionate. Or was she? The woman before the accident had certainly not been those things. But those were the days of innocence, when she'd happily anticipated everything's ending up happily ever after. Now she knew she'd have to find her own happy—even if it didn't last forever. She wondered what Brian's book would make of that.

Of course, Matt didn't need a book. He knew exactly which buttons to push. He probably knew what she was thinking right now, no doubt writing her off as someone who couldn't make a decision, couldn't take a risk, a scared little girl who couldn't say she wanted a man to his face. Well, she'd show him.

Throwing open the door, she found Matt leaning against the doorway to his apartment.

"What took you so long?" he drawled.

"You are too annoying to sleep with," she replied, both hating and loving the fact that he could read her mind.

"I wasn't planning on sleeping," he said with a sexy smile.

She opened her mouth to speak but nothing came out. There was such a predatory male look in his eyes, she was torn between running back into her apartment and closing the door and taking the last three steps to bridge the gap between them.

"We sure are spending a lot of time in the hall," he said. He crooked his finger for her to come forward. "Come here."

And she went, God help her. Straight into his arms, directly into his kiss. His arms came around her as he explored her mouth with a warm sweep of his tongue. He tasted like the chocolate they'd eaten earlier, deliciously spicy, dangerously addicting, and her arms crept around his neck, keeping him close as she wantonly plastered her body against his.

"Uh, Caitlyn, we're still in the hall," he murmured against her mouth.

"So?" She looked him straight in the eye. "I want you, Matt, right here, right now. What do you say?"

The pulse in his throat leapt at her words, and she felt a feminine surge of power.

"Uh . . ."

"You want truth, Matt. Here it is." She took a deep breath and looked straight into his eyes. "I want to make love to you. But there's a part of me that's really afraid that at the end of it all I'll be in love with you. And you won't like it, and I probably won't like it either."

"I can't make any promises, Caitlyn," he said in a husky voice.

"I'm not asking for any. I don't have a lot to offer a man—not for the long-term future anyway."

"You have more than enough to offer any man." He pulled her into his apartment and backed her up against the door, then kissed her until she couldn't think straight. His hands ran through her hair, trapping her in a passionate prison from which she didn't want to escape. She just wanted more, more of his mouth, more of his hands on her body, more of him.

Caitlyn pushed up his shirt, spreading her hands across his abdomen, running her fingers up through the fine black hairs on his chest.

Matt groaned. "Slow down, honey, we're not even in the bedroom."

Despite his protest, Caitlyn felt the zip on her black dress hit the bottom of her spine and a second later the dress was pooled around her ankles, leaving her in the sexy underwear she'd chosen earlier. Thank God for a little forethought.

Matt lifted his head and looked at her.

She held on to his arms, trying to keep him close, but he wasn't going anywhere, he was just staring at her, his gaze drifting from her mouth to her breasts, to her belly button, and below . . .

"Wow," he murmured.

She smiled. "That's the best you can do? I might have to get you a dictionary."

"You might have to get me oxygen," he said with a groan, filling his hands with her breasts, his thumbs drifting across her nipples, raising them into tender, pulsating points that demanded even more attention. His mouth pressed against her lips, then dropped to her cheek, his tongue sliding along her jaw, dancing past the edge of her ear, his breath sending shivers from her head to her toes. And then he was peeling back the straps of her bra, unhooking the front clasp, his lips, his tongue nuzzling the valley between her breasts, circling closer and closer, as he licked his way slowly to the heart of her, his mouth finally closing over her breast in a kiss of desire, possession . . .

Caitlyn eagerly pressed her body against his, his denim jeans brushing roughly against her thighs, arousing her even further with proof of his hardness. She dropped her hands to his waistline, to the top snap of his jeans.

"Yes," Matt murmured, leaving her breast to plant a quick kiss on her lips before grabbing her hand and whisking her across the room. She stumbled after him, not at all steady on her feet, but she didn't need her feet when he pushed her down on the king-size bed in the middle of his bedroom. Dazed, she simply lay there, watching him as he stood at the edge of the bed, his ragged breaths raising his chest up and down. He was all male, tall, strong, muscular. And her heart stopped as he reached for his jeans and slowly undid the snaps.

One by one they popped open as if in slow motion, each click giving her a chance to run ... or not. She raised herself up on her elbows, barely aware that her breasts were bare and she was wearing nothing more than a tiny black bikini. She was mesmerized by Matt, by the way he was watching her, by the sight he was revealing. She'd never seen a man strip before, and certainly not one with such slow deliberation.

He slid the jeans down his hips, taking his briefs off along the way, leaving nothing to the imagination. Not that her imagination could have sculpted such a handsome specimen.

"Now you," he said huskily, tipping his head toward her underwear.

She hesitated, thinking it would be easier if he stripped her. But then she realized that was what this was all about, choices, truth. He wanted her to come to him without hiding anything. She lifted her hips and pulled off her panties. "Is this the way you want me?"

"It's one of the ways," he said as he came down on the bed, covering her body with his. "But I'm open to suggestions."

She loved the feel of his skin against hers, his hands in her hair, his hardness pressing between her thighs, and she wanted him so bad she didn't think she could wait one more second.

"Why don't you come inside," she invited as his mouth drifted against her ear.

"What about foreplay?" he asked, his fingers sliding up her thigh.

"Haven't we been playing all night?" she asked on a sigh as his penis pressed against her hot spot.

"I want you to be ready," he whispered.

"I was ready three days ago."

He looked into her eyes and said, "You're going to kill me."

"I'm going to try."

He reached over her and opened the drawer in the nightstand and pulled out a condom. His hand shook as he ripped open the package, and it was that tiny tremor that told her this was absolutely meant to be, for Matt was as nervous and as needy as she was.

Caitlyn put her hand over his and smiled into his eyes. "Let me." She pressed him down on his back and slid the condom on, then straddled his legs. His hands moved from her waist to her hips as she took him into her body, delighting in the breaching of the final barrier between them.

They moved together in delicious friction, her breasts against his chest, her mouth against his mouth. Each movement drew her muscles tighter and tighter and tighter, until she burst with pleasure, her cries mingling with his as they caught each other on the way down.

Matt put his hand around her neck and pulled her face into the crook of his shoulder. "Don't move."

"I wasn't planning on it."

"Good. Because I'm not leaving until you kick me out."

Caitlyn sighed with satisfied pleasure. Kicking him out was the last thing she wanted to do.

Matt awoke, bewildered at first by the fragrant womanly scent surrounding him. Then he realized Caitlyn was curled up next to him, her head resting on his chest, her arm flung across his waist, one of her legs tangled up with his.

She was all woman and all his . . . the thought came to

him unexpectedly, shocking him with the truth. He wanted her to be all his, and only his. How had that happened? He'd slept with women before and not awoken with this possessive need to keep her close throughout the rest of the night. In fact, he was usually the one who got up and dressed in the dark of the night and went home to his own bed. But this time Caitlyn was in his bed, and he didn't want to leave.

She'd touched him in ways he'd never imagined, not just great physical sex, but mind sex, too. She'd made him laugh. She'd made him shake. She'd made him want more. Damn.

What had she said—that she might fall in love with him after sleeping with him. Well, he had a feeling she wasn't going to be in love alone. Jesus! What was he thinking? He wasn't in love. He was . . . Well, he didn't know what he was, but love . . . What was love anyway? It had always been a transient emotion in his life at best. He didn't know how to handle it, and he sure as hell didn't know how to keep it.

"Are you awake?" Caitlyn asked in a soft voice as she lifted her head off his chest.

He only wished the shadows weren't so deep. He wanted to see her, really see her. They would have to make love in the sunshine so he could watch every expression travel through her eyes. She hid nothing from him. This woman who'd been living with secrets had bared her body and her soul to him. And the gift humbled him in a way he'd never imagined.

"I'm awake," he replied, even though it was unnecessary, because she was smiling into his eyes with a love that took his breath away. At least he thought it was love. Maybe it was just the aftermath of great sex. How could he be sure?

Her hand slid down his thigh, and he caught his bottom lip with his teeth. "Don't start something you can't finish, honey."

"Who says I can't finish it?"

"Apparently, Emily does," he said with a groan as the baby began to cry. "It must be the witching hour." He glanced at the bedroom clock. "Two A.M. Right on schedule."

Caitlyn laughed. "Do you want me to get her?"

"Would you?"

"But I'm naked."

"So am I."

"I'd rather see you walk across the room naked. It turns me on."

"Caitlyn, there is a baby in the next room. Where is your sense of propriety?"

"I left it in the hallway." She kissed him on the cheek and sat back so he could get out of bed.

He heard her whistle in appreciation at his obvious arousal. That was the problem with being a man, nowhere to hide. He ruthlessly pulled on his jeans, Emily's piercing cry helping to deflate his libido. And by the time he reached her crib, which he'd placed in the living room, he was back under control.

Caitlyn joined him a second later, wearing one of his T-shirts. In companionable silence, she made a bottle while he changed Emily, and it struck him how good it all felt, how normal, how familylike. He sat down on the couch and propped his legs up on the table as he placed a bottle in Emily's mouth. Caitlyn sat down next to him and rested her head on his shoulder.

"This is nice," she said.

"Aren't you tired?"

"Not really. What about you?"

"I'm okay." It was a massive understatement. He was better than okay, better than he'd been in his whole life. He had Caitlyn. He had Emily. He had it all. Until this moment he hadn't really known just how much he wanted it all.

"Do you want me to go home?" Caitlyn asked a few moments later, her voice sounding a bit unsure.

"Do you want to go home?"

She hesitated. "I want to stay."

"Then stay." *Stay forever if you want.*

A while later, they went back to bed and the next time Matt awoke sunlight was pouring through his window, the smell of bacon was coming from his kitchen, and he could hear Caitlyn talking to someone. He stumbled out of bed, grabbed his bathrobe off the hook in the bathroom, and walked into the living room.

Caitlyn sat on the couch, a sketch pad propped up on her knees. Emily was playing with the mobile over her car seat which was carefully placed on the coffee table next to Caitlyn. It was a scene out of a storybook, he thought, wondering how this particular scene had ever come to happen in his supposedly bachelor apartment.

Caitlyn looked up and saw him standing there. A smile of delight, of intimacy, of awareness spread across her face. One look from her and his whole body tightened. He remembered every kiss, every touch, every incredible moment that had passed between them, and he wanted to do it all over again.

"Good morning, sleepyhead," she said with a smile.

"Oh, God, you're one of those."

"Cheerful as a morning blue jay," she agreed. "Emily and I have already had breakfast, but I kept some eggs and bacon warm for you. Are you hungry?"

He had the sudden desperate feeling that he should say

no, that he should somehow put a stop to it all before he started believing he could actually have all this. Apparently, Caitlyn sensed something was wrong, because the smile faded out of her eyes.

"I overstepped, didn't I? I'm sorry. When I'm happy, I feel like cooking and eating . . ." Her voice drifted off in apology. "I guess you're not quite as happy. When you said stay, you probably just meant until morning, right? And you were hoping when you woke up that I'd be gone."

"No." He ran a hand through his hair. "No. I meant stay as long as you like. I'm not awake yet, that's all."

"Are you sure?" Her eyes pleaded with him to be honest. "Because this feels kind of strange to me, too. I haven't woken up next to a man in a long time. I'm not sure how to act."

"I don't want you to act with me. Just be yourself."

She stood up, setting the pad down on the table. "Can I get you breakfast? And you don't have to worry. I didn't sneak out and pick up a wedding ring while you were asleep, hoping to plant it in your scrambled eggs as a surprise."

"Do I look worried?"

She nodded. "Oh, yeah."

"Sorry."

"It's just eggs. There is no hidden agenda."

He offered her an apologetic grin. "Then I'll have some eggs."

As Caitlyn disappeared into the kitchen, Matt picked up the sketch pad and studied the dress she'd drawn. He didn't know anything about dresses, especially wedding dresses, but he liked the bold lines, the sway of the skirt . . . and more than anything, he liked that Caitlyn had drawn something.

Caitlyn came out of the kitchen with a plate of food and a glass of orange juice. She set it down on the coffee table. "Here you go."

"Thanks." He held up the sketch pad. "This is the dress you're designing for that bride?"

"Yes. What do you think?"

"It looks like a dress."

"That's good, since I was trying to draw a dress."

"I don't know anything about this stuff. But tell me this, did it feel good?" He saw the answering light in her eyes.

"It felt wonderful, like the cold layers of winter melting into summer. It's as if I had so many clothes on, I'd lost myself. But I'm slowly coming back." She paused, her eyes meeting his. "You had something to do with it, you know."

"I've always been pretty good at peeling off clothes," he replied lightly.

"I noticed. By the way, you snore."

"I do not."

"Yes, you do, cute little snores, you could almost make a tune to them. I was going to sing along, but I didn't want to wake you."

He frowned at her, not feeling entirely comfortable with the intimacy between them. It was one thing to make love to a woman, it was another to share jokes at the breakfast table. "Well, you talk."

"I do not."

"Cute little words that make no sense."

She laughed. "As long as I'm not spilling my guts in my sleep, I'm okay with it. Not that there's anything you haven't heard yet." And then she surprised him by throwing her arms around his neck and pressing a kiss against his lips. "I had a great time last night, in case you hadn't noticed."

"Me, too."

"I'm going back to my apartment to get dressed and go to work. You can have your space, get your bearings, pretend that nothing changed last night. But don't get too comfortable, because I will be back."

"I'm counting on it," he said, surprising both of them with his answer.

She paused in the doorway. "You aren't scared I'll ask too much of you?"

"Are you scared I'll ask too much of you?"

"I'm scared that you won't ask me for anything. You're a very self-sufficient man."

"I used to be," he muttered as she left the room. "I used to be."

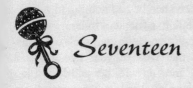

Seventeen

"Do you really think I have postpartum depression?" Sarah asked, stumbling slightly over the words. Jonathan sat next to her on the couch, the papers they'd printed off the Internet spread out before them on the coffee table. They'd spent most of the night going over the subject.

"It's a possibility," Jonathan said. "What do you think?"

She'd never heard of having a baby making someone sad, but she certainly felt like a lot of the women in the articles. "I'm not sure."

"If your depression is related to the fluctuation of your hormones, it could explain why you've felt so over-whelmed since Emily was born, especially if she was a difficult baby."

Sarah felt a kernel of hope take root and grow. Maybe she wasn't like her mother. Maybe she wasn't crazy or bad. Maybe she could take care of her baby.

Jonathan put his hand on her thigh, and she relished

the growing closeness between them. They'd parted for a few hours during the night to get some sleep, but other than that they'd been together every second. She'd never known a man to take such an interest in her problems, to want so badly to help her when he had nothing to gain.

"I think you should talk to a friend of mine," Jonathan continued. "Her name is Karen Harte, and she's a psychiatrist. Now, don't get that look in your eye. She's a friend, not an enemy. I grew up with her and I trust her completely. Besides that, she had a baby about six months ago. If anyone will understand how you're feeling, it's her."

"But I don't have any money," she said.

"I'll take care of the first consult. We'll figure something out after that."

Sarah hesitated. How could she tell her problems to a complete stranger? A voice inside reminded her she'd already told her problems to one complete stranger, why not two? And if she really did have something that could be cured, maybe . . . "All right," she said, making her first real decision in weeks. That step alone made her feel better, like she was taking control over something. "I'll go see her."

"Good. I'll call her right now."

"Right now?"

"No time like the present." He flung her a smile as he walked out of the room and down the hall to his office.

Sarah stacked the papers into a neat pile, again pleased with her ability to perform the simple task. It had been so long since she'd felt like her feet were under her, like she could stand up without swaying. She tested it out just to be sure, and it was true. She could stand up. She could stretch her arms above her head. She could . . . smile.

Sarah felt the smile spread across her face, and she

couldn't stop it. Nor did she want to. This feeling was better than the one she'd been carrying around the last two months, actually longer than that, the last thirteen years, since she and Mattie had said good-bye. She let out a sigh as she flopped back down on the couch.

"It's set. I got you an appointment for Thursday morning at eight A.M.," Jonathan said, returning to the room.

"That fast?" she asked in alarm.

"Yes, that fast."

"Oh." She looked down at her hands, feeling his gaze lingering on her. She didn't really know what Jonathan saw when he looked at her, and she was afraid to ask. There was something growing between them, and it was probably wrong. He was a minister, and she was just someone who needed his help. They weren't . . . they couldn't be anything more. But it was odd to have a friendship with a man. In her experience the only thing a man had ever wanted from her was sex.

"Sarah?" Jonathan inquired.

She looked up into his blue eyes and felt her heart jump into her throat. The fog in her head seemed to be lifting, letting in all kinds of other feelings.

"I have a favor to ask of you," he said. "I know you think I'm selfless, but I am human."

So he did want something from her. It only made sense. He'd helped her out. Now he wanted payback. She got to her feet and began to unbutton her blouse.

His jaw dropped. "What are you doing?"

"Giving you a favor."

He put his hand over hers. "No. That's not what I meant."

"It's not?" So he didn't want her, then? She felt horribly embarrassed.

"I mean I do, but I won't," he said cryptically. "I can't."

He tilted up her chin with his finger. "You're a very attractive woman. Don't think I haven't noticed."

"You don't have to say that."

"It's the truth. But I'm a minister and you're in trouble. I won't take advantage of that. I want you to trust me, and you won't be able to do that if . . ." His voice trailed away as he seemed to get lost in his thoughts. "You have incredible eyes." He gave a shake of his head. "Sorry. Where were we?"

"You weren't taking advantage of me," she said, feeling a shy pleasure at the look in his eyes.

"Right. I won't do that."

"I believe you."

"Good. Okay, then. Now, back to my favor. . . . You know that the board members are planning to make their decision about closing the church in the next week or so. Well, I have a plan." He paused, offering her a wry smile. "It occurred to me that I've been praying for a miracle instead of trying to make one happen. I may not be good with the masses, but I'm pretty good one on one. And I've helped a lot of people over the past year, good people. I think they'll want to know that the church may close, that I may leave."

She smiled at the very unreverendlike look in his eyes. "You want to make them feel guilty."

"I want to get them in my church this Sunday, whatever the motivation. That's the first step. Then I'll try to keep them coming back. Because I don't just need them. They need each other, and they need this church."

"What do you want me to do?"

"Help me make calls, and tell me not to quit when I get discouraged."

Jonathan was so endearingly uncertain. It wasn't a

trait she'd ever seen in a man. Most thought they knew exactly what to do and when to do it.

"I can do that," she said.

"And one last favor."

She eyed him warily this time, noting the change of tone in his voice.

"I want you to make a phone call."

"Me? Who do I have to call?" She knew the answer even before he said it.

"Your brother. You have to talk to him, tell him you're getting help and that you miss your daughter."

"I do miss her," she whispered. "But what will he say?"

"We won't know until you call." He took her hand in his. "I'll be right here beside you. You're not alone anymore."

Sarah took a deep breath and walked back to the office with him. He waited while she dialed the number she'd already put to memory. The phone rang, once, twice, three times, then the machine picked up.

"He's not there," she whispered.

"Leave a message."

Sarah heard the beep but what could she say in thirty seconds that would make any sense? She hung up without saying a word. "I'll call back," she told Jonathan defensively.

"I know you will, because you're a good mother."

"If you keep saying that, I might start believing it."

"And so you should. There's another place I want to show you today, too. It's a transitional home for mothers and children who are trying to start over for whatever reason."

"They wouldn't want someone like me."

"Sarah, you're exactly the kind of person they want.

But I won't force you into anything. I just want to show you that there are options and there is help out there."

"Do you really think Emily and I can be together again?"

"I do," he said with a passion in his voice that couldn't be denied.

Jonathan thought he didn't have the power to persuade. But he'd just about convinced her to believe in the future, something she hadn't been able to do for a very long time.

Matt pulled up in front of Laree's Hair Salon in downtown Sacramento and shut off the engine. The salon was in a strip mall next to a thrift store and a doughnut shop. He had no idea what Sarah had been doing in Sacramento, which was an hour and a half's drive from San Francisco, but he had a pay stub to prove she'd been there sometime in the last year. It was the best lead he had, and he hoped it would be worth the drive.

Matt glanced at Emily, who was entertaining herself by blowing drooling bubbles out of her mouth. He took the edge of his sleeve and wiped her chin.

She tried to push his hand away with her tiny fingers, but he simply smiled. "I know you think you're the boss, but I am. And Caitlyn says you'll get a rash on your chin if it's always wet. I don't know how she knows that, but I believe her. She's smart, you know. Not to mention beautiful. Sexy." His body tightened at the memory of the night before. "Pretty damn wonderful, in fact."

Emily blew him another bubble, and he smiled. He had never thought he was a sucker for kids, but this child got to him, probably one reason why he hadn't been able to leave her with a baby-sitter. How could he trust her with someone he didn't know? He couldn't, so he'd told

David he needed a few more days off work and decided he might as well drive to Sacramento. At least he was doing something instead of just sitting around. And Emily had enjoyed the ride.

He took her out of her car seat and automatically checked her bottom for any wetness. It was amazing how things he'd never anticipated doing last week had become habit to him, like checking for a soppy diaper. Fortunately, she was dry. So he got out of the car with Emily in his arms and walked up the path to the salon.

There were five women in the salon: two stylists, a receptionist and two customers. All five turned to look at him the minute the door clanged. He cleared his throat, feeling uncomfortable in the definitely female environment.

"Would you like a cut?" the woman behind the desk asked.

"Actually, I'm looking for someone named Laree."

"Hey, Laree," she called to the stylist who had just taken her customer to the back room of hair dryers. "He wants you."

Laree, a tired-looking brunette with a blond streak through one side of her hair, came forward with a towel in her hands and a wary expression in her eyes.

"Can I help you?" she asked.

"I'm hoping you can. I'm Sarah Vaughn's brother. Do you remember Sarah?"

Laree didn't even blink. "Sure, I remember Sarah. Why?"

"I'm looking for her."

"She's not here."

"Do you know where she might be?"

"No."

Matt forced himself to be patient. Laree looked like

she was hiding something; he just had to figure out what it was. But he needed something to barter with—make that someone. "This is Sarah's baby, Emily," he said. It was a gamble to share the information, but he took it anyway.

Laree's whole face changed. "This is Sarah's baby?" She stepped forward. "She's darling." A frown settled across her features. "Why do you have her?"

"Because Sarah left her with me. She wanted Emily to be safe. But now I want to make sure that Sarah is safe. To do that I have to find her. And I know that she worked here about six months ago."

"She worked here," Laree admitted. "But she left without any notice. I figured Gary's band got a new gig somewhere. I didn't like the guy, but Sarah wouldn't leave him, especially not after she got pregnant."

"Did you ever see him hurt her?"

"Not physically, but he had a nasty tongue. Sarah just took whatever he said like she thought she deserved it. I hope she's okay, but I don't know where she is."

"Do you remember exactly when she left? It might help me to pinpoint some dates."

Laree thought about his question, then nodded. "It was mid-February, right after Valentine's Day. I remember because it was the day the fire truck blocked our driveway, and Sarah had to meet Gary down the street because he couldn't get his car in the parking lot. That's the last I saw of her."

Matt's mouth went dry. Another fire? It had to be a coincidence. But then he remembered Sarah's fascination with candles and matches, and goose bumps ran down his arm. "Where was the fire?"

"In the doughnut shop next door."

Of course, that was easy to explain, donuts, ovens, fire.

Matt tried to shrug off the uneasy feeling that continued to cling to him. "Do you know how it started?"

"I think someone threw a lighted cigarette into the trash. Why?"

"No reason. So that's the last you saw of Sarah. She didn't quit or tell you where she was going?"

"Just disappeared. Her baby sure is pretty," Laree said. "I hope Sarah comes back soon."

"So do I." Matt walked outside, stopping to take a look at the doughnut shop next door. It looked freshly painted, all evidence of a fire completely erased, just the way it had been erased at the old apartment building, like it had never happened. But Matt couldn't erase the fire from his memories. And he wondered how Sarah must have felt to see flames coming out of the building next door. Had she panicked? Had she run? Had she been responsible?

A part of him wanted to believe in his sister, in the good things he remembered about her. Another part of him was telling him to face the facts: Sarah was just like his mother, a loser. She'd run out on her baby. And she probably wasn't coming back. And even if she did come back, how long would it take before she ran again? What kind of a life could she give Emily?

His arms tightened around the small baby in his arms. He had to protect her. But protect her from her mother? Could he really do that? He hadn't been able to protect Sarah from her own mother. And look how that had turned out.

Matt opened the car door and settled Emily in her car seat. By the time he'd slid behind the wheel, Emily was starting to whimper for the bottle he'd packed earlier. He pulled it out of the diaper bag and popped it in her mouth. Fortunately, she wasn't particularly fussy about whether or not it was warm. With one hand propping up her bottle, Matt opened his cell phone and dialed information for Caitlyn's phone number. He knew he shouldn't be calling her at work or anywhere else. But when the number came up, he had the operator dial it for him. A second later he heard Caitlyn say, "Devereaux's."

"It's me," he said.

"Hi me."

Her voice dropped down a notch, reminding him of the husky way she'd talked to him last night, telling him how good he felt, how good she felt. He swallowed, trying to remember why he'd called her.

"Are you all right?" she asked.

"I'm fine. I'm in Sacramento. I found the hair salon where Sarah used to work."

"Did they give you any more information?"

"Not really." He hesitated, not sure why he felt compelled to confide in her. He'd carried stories of huge ramifications in his head for days, weeks, months without needing to share. "There was a fire next door to the shop," he blurted out. "The day Sarah left. She never came back."

"What kind of a fire?" Caitlyn asked quietly.

"It was in a doughnut shop. It had nothing to do with Sarah."

"Of course not. A kitchen fire could happen anywhere, Matt."

"Yeah. I think I just wanted you to tell me that. I want to believe in her, Caitlyn. I want to believe in the sweet little girl whose image I carry around in my head."

"You should. Innocent until proven guilty, remember?"

"I'm trying. I just don't like the way the puzzle pieces are coming together. The way people talk about Sarah, it makes me remember how they used to talk about my mother."

"Sarah isn't your mother."

"Maybe she is." He hated to say that, hated to even think it, but he couldn't stop himself.

"Don't say that, Matt. You have to keep the faith, for Emily's sake if not your own. How is she, by the way?"

"Fine. She's drinking a bottle and kicking her feet in the air. Oh, great. Now she's dribbling formula down the side of her neck." He reached out with his sleeve and tried to wipe it off. Matt could hear Caitlyn laughing on the other end of the line. "It's not funny," he told her.

"Yes it is. You are so cute with her." She paused. "I better get back to work. Jolie is giving me the evil eye."

"Can I knock on your door later? I might need to borrow a cup of sugar."

"I've got plenty of sugar for you, sugar," she said with a laugh. " 'Bye now."

Matt smiled to himself as he ended the call. He felt better already and even more determined to find Sarah. With that thought, he punched in a second number.

"I've got another job for you," he said briskly when Blake answered. "I want you to see what you can find on Kathleen Vaughn Winters. That's right, Kathleen, my mother." It felt strange to say the word *mother*. He hadn't said it in a long time, hadn't felt the need of a mother or the love for a mother. But now . . . now he was thinking about her again, wondering if the answer to Sarah's disappearance could somehow be tied to his mother.

"You told me you didn't care where your mother was," Blake reminded him.

"I've changed my mind. She's the only other link I have to Sarah. It's probably a long shot, but see if you can find anything on her. Oh, and by the way, start checking the hair salons in San Francisco. Sarah used to work as a shampoo girl. She might be doing that now."

"I'm on it."

Matt closed the phone and turned to Emily. "Ready to go home, kid?"

Emily gave him a sloppy smile. Matt took a moment to pick her up and burp her, then set her back in the car seat with an efficiency he'd never dreamed he'd own. Just went to show you could never say never.

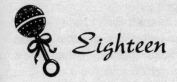

Eighteen

*C*aitlyn flung open her apartment door later that afternoon as Matt came down the hall. "You're finally back. It's about time." She grabbed his arm, dragging both him and Emily into her apartment. "What took you so long? You called me hours ago."

"I stopped at the paper," Matt explained with a quizzical look in his eye. "Has something happened?"

Caitlyn took the car seat out of his hands, planted a quick kiss on Emily's cheek, then set the seat on the floor and backed Matt up against the door. "Yes, something happened." She smiled helplessly at him. "I missed you." She pressed her hands against his chest and stood on tiptoe to kiss him on the lips, a hungry, yearning kiss that couldn't even begin to tell him how much she'd missed him.

Matt slid his arms around her and pulled her up tightly against him, devouring her mouth with the demanding intensity she'd come to expect from him. He wasn't a man to do anything halfway, especially when it came to kissing a woman.

"Better?" he asked her a few minutes later.

"Slightly," she said breathlessly.

"Give me another chance?"

She'd have given him a dozen if Emily hadn't started to whimper. Caitlyn looked over her shoulder to see Emily's mouth puckered up in dismay. "I think she's jealous."

Matt laughed. "I think she stinks. I didn't want to change her in my car," Matt said, rescuing Emily from her car seat. He held her out with a grimace. "You want to take over?"

"And ruin the bonding I see between you two—not on your life." But she did follow him across the hall to his apartment and stood by while he changed Emily. When he was done, he sat back on the couch and rubbed his hand over Emily's bare stomach, bringing a coo of delight.

Caitlyn could hardly blame her. The man had magic hands. But that was another matter. Right now, despite his earlier enthusiastic response to her kiss, he seemed a bit distracted. "Did you find out something more?"

"Not really."

"You don't sound sure."

He shrugged. "Probably just another coincidence."

"What is another coincidence?"

"When I was at the paper David was following up on a suspected arson fire in an apartment building in the Tenderloin. A woman was seen leaving the scene."

Caitlyn frowned. "What are you trying to tell me, Matt? Do you think Sarah is setting fires all over the city?"

"I didn't want to say that out loud."

"But that's what you think?"

He ran a hand through his hair. "How can I think that? It's crazy. I've never been one to believe in coincidence."

"Maybe you need more information about the fire to assure yourself that it has nothing to do with Sarah."

"Maybe," he conceded. He picked Emily up and set her on a blanket on the floor. Then he got up and walked over to the window. "I hate this, Caitlyn. I hate not knowing. I hate not having control over when and if Sarah comes back for Emily."

"I know." She walked up behind him and slid her arms around his waist, resting her head on his back as she held him against her. She wished she could fix this for him. And the thought startled her. She'd never been the fixer, just the fixee, yet here she was . . .

"Thanks for not saying everything will be fine. I hate platitudes that don't mean anything," he said.

"Me, too." And she simply held him tighter, happy that he was letting her into his life, not just into his bed. She knew she wouldn't be satisfied with anything less. Although she couldn't tell him that. Theirs was supposed to be a casual relationship. So why couldn't she feel casual about him?

Even now their embrace was changing from comforting to caressing, the air between them tingling with a sense of anticipation as Matt turned around, bringing her up hard against his chest.

"I just got a shock off you," he murmured.

"You shouldn't rub your feet on the carpet."

"I didn't get it from my feet but from your breasts. I want to feel them against my skin without anything between us."

Caitlyn swallowed hard at that piece of information. "It's five o'clock in the evening."

"So?"

"It's still light out."

"It is," he agreed, holding her slightly away so he could look at her. "I want to see you in the light, Caitlyn. I want to watch your eyes when we come together, when you can't take it anymore."

"You're really good at this foreplay stuff."

"I'm not even touching you yet."

"And you don't have to," she whispered. "The way you talk, it makes me feel like . . ."

"Like what?"

"Like taking all my clothes off," she confessed.

"I'll help you."

Her heart leapt against her chest as she wondered if she really had the nerve to do this. "Uh, Emily," she said, suddenly remembering that they weren't exactly alone.

They turned in unison to look at the baby.

"Asleep," Matt said in triumph, a wicked light coming into his eyes. "Sometimes, the kid has good timing."

"If we do it again, it won't be a one-night stand," she warned him. "Have you considered that?"

"I never thought it was a one-night stand," he replied on a more serious note. "And neither did you."

There was no humor between them now, only a quiet, purposeful passion.

"All I could think about today was you," Caitlyn said. "It's never been so fast for me before."

"Hey, wait a second," he said in mock outrage.

She grinned. "I didn't mean that. I meant us, falling into bed together, and not just making love, but sharing so much of ourselves. You know more about me than people I've known my whole life."

"And you know more about me. But I think we should stop talking and start . . ." He finished his words with a kiss that made Caitlyn understand the expression "swept away." She was caught up in the texture and taste of his mouth, the feel of his hands, the beauty of his male strength and hard body against her softness. He made her feel beautiful, feminine, and wanted—unconditionally. There were no pretenses, just a naked longing that was as honest an emotion as she had ever felt. This time she was the one to take his hand and lead him into the bedroom.

They made short work of their clothes, stripping each other with smiles of delight and groans of pleasure as their hands roamed without restriction.

"You are such a beautiful man," she told him, running her hands along the muscles of his chest.

"These are beautiful," he replied, cupping her breasts with his hands, molding the tender globes with his fingers. "And this is a beautiful mouth." He traced her lips with the tip of his tongue as his hands slid downways. "And this is a beautiful—"

"Sh-sh," she whispered, taking possession of his mouth. "Make love to me, Matt." And together they sank into the soft mattress, their bodies merging so completely that Caitlyn had a feeling she'd lost herself somewhere in him.

A while later Matt heard Emily stirring and knew that they couldn't spend the next few hours in bed as he would have liked. Although he doubted a few more hours with Caitlyn would be enough. He needed days, weeks, months, even years.

It surprised him to want to be with someone that often. He'd always guarded his privacy. Letting anyone in had been dangerous in the early years and unacceptable in the latter. But Emily's arrival had opened up the gates to his past, and the walls he'd been building for more than a decade were slowly crumbling.

He had two females to thank for that, Caitlyn and Emily. Maybe he should add Sarah, too. For if she hadn't left her baby with him, none of this would have happened. Caitlyn would have stayed on her side of the hallway.

But she wasn't across the hall, she was lying next to him, in what he was already learning was her favorite position, one arm and one leg over his body, as if she would keep him close even in sleep. Some men might have seen it as needy, as too much, but he liked it. No one had ever wanted to keep him close, to protect him while he slept. But this small, feminine woman had more heart than most. Maybe too much heart.

He knew she was crazy about Emily. And he was beginning to realize how hard it would be for her to let Emily go.

Maybe she wouldn't have to let Emily go.

The thought hit him over the head like a sledgehammer. He hadn't wanted to consider the possibility that Sarah wouldn't return. But what if she didn't? What if he had to raise Emily?

Maybe he wouldn't have to let Caitlyn go either.

Whoa! He couldn't start thinking that way. A couple of nights of sex was a long way from a long-term relationship. And sure he wanted a family someday, but now? He wasn't ready. At least he hadn't thought he was ready. Things were changing. He was changing.

Emily gave a little cry from the living room, disrupting his thoughts. It was her waking-up cry, Matt realized. He was beginning to be able to distinguish between waking up, being wet, and wanting food. Another sign that he was no longer the same man who knew every score of every sports game being played but one who was listening for the fine nuances of a baby's cry.

"Is she awake?" Caitlyn murmured, stirring beside him.

"I think so."

"I'll get her." She sat up, a chill hitting his body as she got out of bed.

He would have argued, but the view was just too good to pass up. Caitlyn tried shyly to hide her nakedness as she slipped on her black pants and rose-colored sweater, but her quick movements only made him smile. He'd already traced every inch of her body with his tongue. They were hardly strangers. Caitlyn's lack of casualness reminded him that in many ways she was such an innocent. He should be protecting her—protecting her from himself.

But protection was the last thing on his mind as he watched her hair flow past her shoulders, wild and tangled from his fingers. When she looked back at him, her brown eyes were bright, her face still flushed from their lovemaking.

"You're staring," she told him.

"No judge on this earth would convict me. Come back to bed."

"Later," she said with a laugh. "Emily waits for no man."

Matt lay back and stared at the ceiling after she left the room. He could hear her talking to Emily, and he thought how much he liked this moment, this sense of satisfaction, this feeling of peace that everything was as it should be.

They were becoming a family, the three of them. He couldn't deny it. He was falling in love—with Caitlyn, with Emily, with the idea of being the man in their lives.

"Matt?" Caitlyn called to him, then appeared in the doorway with Emily in her arms. "Someone is knocking on my door. Could you get Emily a bottle while I answer it?"

He was already out of bed and putting on his jeans by the time she finished speaking. Throwing on his T-shirt, he took Emily out of Caitlyn's arms while she went across the hall. He heard her talking to someone through the half-open door. Their voices grew louder, then the sound of music followed.

After grabbing a bottle for Emily, he walked out to the hall to find a young man, with a bouquet of red carnations in one hand, singing to Caitlyn.

"Forgive me, Cait, for making you wait, I love you true, so don't make me blue. I'll be by soon, near the end of this tune."

Caitlyn looked at Matt with amazement and embarrassment in her eyes. "He won't stop."

"Hey, buddy," Matt said. "What's this all about?"

The man got to his feet and handed Caitlyn the enormous bouquet of flowers and a card. "Have a nice day."

Caitlyn opened the card. " 'Chapter three said don't forget to send presents to show how much you care. I still love you, Caitlyn. Call me, Brian,' " she read aloud.

"Chapter three?" Matt asked.

"He's reading a book so he can figure me out."

"He should have saved his money. No one is going to figure you out by reading a book."

She raised an eyebrow. "Is that a compliment or an insult?"

He laughed. "It's a compliment. You're one of a kind."

She didn't smile. "What am I going to do? I think he's on his way over."

Matt didn't like her question or the note of indecision in her voice. What was there to do but call Brian and tell him she wasn't interested any more, that she loved . . . okay, maybe not loved, but liked, or at the very least was having sex with, someone else.

"What do you want to do?" he asked somewhat tersely.

"I don't know."

"Well, hell, if you don't know . . ." He stalked back into his apartment.

She followed him into the room. "What is your problem?"

"I don't have a problem. You're the one who has a problem."

"You're mad."

"I'm fine. I'm just going to give Emily her bottle and turn on the ball game. You can do whatever you want." Matt sat down on the couch with Emily in his arms and flipped on the television. He wanted Caitlyn to sit down next to him, preferably after she dumped Brian's flowers into the trash. He wanted her to put her head on his shoulder and play with Emily's toes while the baby drank her bottle. He wanted them to be as close as they'd been fifteen minutes ago. He wanted Brian out of her life.

Caitlyn kept turning the flowers around and around in her hand. "I need to call Brian, stop him from coming."

"Sure, fine, whatever." He turned the volume up louder.

"Don't you want to know what I'm going to say to him?"

"Not particularly."

"Can I come back?" Caitlyn asked.

"Do what you want." He banged his head against the couch after she left. What an idiot he was. What if she didn't want to come back? Shit! What would he do then?

Caitlyn entered her apartment and immediately picked up the phone, but she didn't dial right away; she was still thinking about Matt. Was he jealous? Upset that she hadn't tossed Brian's flowers away? Was that why he'd acted like such a jerk? Didn't he know it was so much more complicated than just throwing some flowers in the trash?

She didn't want to hurt Brian. He was trying so hard to make things right, and there was something endearing about his efforts. For a man who had devoted himself completely to his intellectual pursuits, it was somewhat gratifying to Caitlyn to have Brian suddenly devoting himself to her. She knew deep down, however, that it was too little, too late. But she did owe Brian something; she owed him the truth.

Before she could dial, there was a knock at her door. Brian. She took a deep breath and opened it.

He tipped his head toward the phone in her hand. "Were you calling me?" Brian asked with a hopeful smile.

"As a matter of fact, I was."

"I told you I was on my way. I have this feeling that if I don't get you back now, I won't get you back at all."

"You better come in." She stepped aside so he could enter her apartment. "Do you want to sit down?"

"I was thinking I might kneel."

"Brian—"

"Wait, before you say anything." He pulled a small velvet box out of his pocket. "This is for you."

She knew what it was; she knew *exactly* what it was. And she didn't want it. Couldn't take it. "I can't."

"Please," he said. "Just open it."

After a moment, she took the box out of his hand and opened it. She expected to see the ring she'd given back to him eighteen months ago, but this one was different. The other ring had been an old-fashioned setting for an old-fashioned girl. This diamond was at least two carats, a square blunt cut, a setting that emphasized how large the diamond was. It was modern, sophisticated, expensive, and just as wrong as the other one had been.

"I know you've said a number of times how much you've changed," Brian said. "I understand that. I'm not trying to go back; I'm trying to go forward—with you. That's why I got you a new ring, one to go with the new us." He paused, his eyes anxious. "Did I get it wrong?"

"It's beautiful," she said, for it was a spectacular ring. Any woman in her right mind would like this ring. And if she'd been madly in love with him, she probably would have liked it, too.

"Can I put it on your finger?"

She snapped the lid shut.

"I guess not," he said with disappointment.

"We need to talk. Please sit down."

He sat at one end of the couch; she sat at the other end.

"I want you to know that I really appreciate the effort you've put into trying to get our relationship back on track, but I haven't been entirely honest with you," she said.

"There is someone else," he interrupted. "That's it, isn't it? Your neighbor, Matt."

"No, that's not what I'm talking about." She hesitated, wondering if she had the courage to do this. It had been different telling Matt; she'd known the secret would stay with him. But once she told Brian it would be out in the open. Her parents would have to know. Jolie would have to know. And Caitlyn would have to live the rest of her life with everyone knowing that she couldn't have children. They'd look at her with pity. They'd guard their words or watch their actions when a baby came by.

"Whatever it is," Brian said. "You can tell me. It won't change the way I feel about you."

"I think it might." She forced herself to look into his

eyes. "After the accident, I got some bad news. I didn't tell anyone, because it hurt so much, and I couldn't talk about it, so I tried not to think about it."

"You're not sick?" he asked tentatively.

"Not exactly. I can't have children, Brian. When my pelvis was crushed, everything inside was damaged, irrevocably damaged. I won't be able to get pregnant or carry a child."

He stared at her blankly as if the words hadn't registered. "There must be something they can do," he said slowly. "I can't believe that there's not something they can do. Have you talked to your mother? Have you seen specialists?"

She cut him off before he could get even more wound up. "I had a second opinion, Brian. And there isn't anything my mother can do that I didn't do already."

"But Caitlyn, there are so many new scientific advances. There may be something you have overlooked. We need to research the possibilities, talk to specialists, go on the Internet."

"Brian, please. I have looked into the possibilities."

"But you're not a scientist. No offense, Caitlyn, but this is my area. Let me talk to some people for you. Let me get a copy of your medical file." He paused, looking confused. "Why didn't you tell me before? Or even after? You could have written or called me or even come to Boston, for that matter."

"Because I didn't want to deal with it. I didn't want to talk about it. I didn't want to listen to all of the suggestions you just threw out. It was easier after I gave you back your ring and you left to take that fellowship. I knew it was over between us."

"It wasn't over. I never thought it was over."

"But you do now. I can't give you a baby. Don't you understand?"

Her words hung between them for a long moment.

"I understand what you're saying, but—"

"You think I'm wrong. You think you can fix this. You can't. I'm finally starting to accept the truth. I can't have a child of my own, and I know that you want children. That's why I can't accept this ring." She pressed the box into his hand. "I can't marry you, Brian."

He shook his head in confusion, looking much the way she'd felt eighteen months earlier, as if he'd just had the rug pulled out from under him. "What if . . . what if I said it didn't matter?"

"But it does matter. Why would you say otherwise?"

"I've never thought of marrying anyone but you. Our families are perfect together. I can't imagine starting over with anyone else. We're good together, Caitlyn. We fit into each other's lives. There must be a way out of this."

"I know that it's hard to grasp; it's taken me a long time. But you have to understand one thing before you go. Our relationship is over."

"Are you saying you don't love me anymore? Or are you giving me an easy way out?"

She thought about his question. "When we first met, I was a young girl, barely out of my teens. I loved the fact that you spoke my parents' language. Bringing you home made me feel smart and accepted and right in the middle of things, the way I'd never felt before. You took charge. You made decisions for us. Frankly, you took up right where my parents left off. I was happy to go straight from living with my parents to living with you.

"Then the accident happened, and everything changed. I realized that bad things could happen to me and no one could fix them. Living through the pain, the rehabilitation, and the uncertainty about being able to walk again made me look at my life in a different way. Finally, knowing that I couldn't have children changed me forever."

She took a breath as the words poured out of her. "I grew up, Brian. I grew up in a way I never imagined. I didn't have a choice. I had to learn how to take care of myself and stand on my own two feet, and I had to think about what I wanted from life and how I could get it. I believe that most men in this world want children of their own. And I know that you're one of those men. Family has always been important to you and your parents. I can't take that away. And I won't let you sacrifice for me."

"It's my decision. You should have told me before. You should have told everyone."

"I was hiding. Matt made me realize that it wasn't fair—"

"Matt?" he asked in shock. "You told Matt? You told this neighbor that you met last week a secret you couldn't tell me?"

She cleared her throat, realizing her error. "It just slipped out."

"Sure it did." Brian stood up. "This is all a bunch of bull, Caitlyn. You're not thinking of me. You're thinking of yourself. You want the guy who lives across the hall." An angry gleam appeared in his eyes. "Or is it his baby you want? That's it, isn't it? He's got a ready-made family, just waiting for you to step in and play mom."

"The baby belongs to his sister," she said tightly, knowing what he was saying wasn't true. She was attracted to Matt. She cared about Matt. It didn't have anything to do with Emily. Well, maybe a little, but not the way he made it sound, like she was using Matt, like she was expecting them to be a family.

"What do you want me to do, Caitlyn? Do you want me to go? Or do you want me to stay and see if we can work this out? I would like children. I'll admit to that. Maybe I won't be able to come to terms with the fact that you can't have any. But maybe I will. We'll never know if you don't give us a chance.

"One thing I won't do is share you with another man. You have to decide who you want. I love you. You used to love me. Do you want to throw all that away on a casual affair? On a man and a baby who don't belong to you?"

He let the words sink in. "Or do you want to try again with me? I can promise you that I won't leave you again. I won't put my job before you. You weren't the only one who changed in the last year. I realized when I got to Boston that I'd left something important behind—you. It was the biggest mistake I'd ever made. So what's it going to be?"

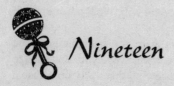 *Nineteen*

 att lay in his bed and stared at the ceiling. It was five-seventeen in the morning, Thursday morning. It had been more than twenty-four hours since Caitlyn had left his bed to call Brian, and he hadn't heard a word from her since. He'd never anticipated she'd stay away so long.

He felt better being outside, doing something instead of waiting, so he'd spent most of Wednesday cruising his old neighborhood with Emily in tow, hoping to see someone, maybe Sarah, he didn't know.

But waiting was what he'd done all evening, hoping to hear Caitlyn's knock at his door. He'd listened for her footstep in the hallway, but either she'd stepped lightly or she'd never come home, because he hadn't heard a thing. Maybe she'd gone to Brian. Maybe Matt had blown the best thing that had ever happened to him.

Emily began to cry, and he glanced over at the portable crib, which he'd moved into his bedroom. She'd been crying off and on all night. He'd already given her two bottles and changed her diaper, even taken a quick foray up to the roof, but nothing had helped. It was a different cry tonight, not so much a mad cry as one of discomfort. Hell, maybe she missed Caitlyn, too.

Matt got up and padded over to the crib, picking Emily up as she began to cry in earnest. That's when it struck him how red she was. Her head was hot and sweaty—too hot, he thought. It wasn't that warm a night, and she was only wearing a small t-shirt with her diaper. He wondered if she had a fever.

Carrying Emily into the living room, he dug through the pile of stuff Caitlyn had convinced him to buy. Sure enough, there was a baby thermometer. He read the directions, relieved when one of the options was to place the thermometer under the baby's arm. Emily didn't like it much, but he managed to get a reading, one hundred and four. His heart began to race. Emily wasn't just fussy; she was sick. Damn! How long had she been sick?

He was out the door and across the hall before he had time to consider whether or not Caitlyn was home. Emily continued to sob, and when Caitlyn didn't answer his knock, Matt felt a rush of anxiety. What should he do? Who should he call?

He was just about to panic when Caitlyn opened the door wearing a short bathrobe and a scowl. "What do you want?"

"She's sick," he said.

Caitlyn's expression immediately changed to one of concern as she took Emily in her arms. "Oh, my God, she's so hot."

"A hundred and four. What should we do?"

"I—I don't know."

"You have to know."

"Okay. All right. She doesn't have a pediatrician that we know of. And it's—what time is it?"

"Just after five."

"I guess we should take her to the Emergency Room."

"You'll come with me?"

"Of course I will. Just let me throw on some clothes, and you better, too."

It was only then he realized he was wearing nothing but a pair of boxers. He returned quickly to his apartment, putting Emily down for just a second while he threw on some clothes. He grabbed a bottle on his way out the door just in case she was hungry. But she didn't seem interested in sucking on the bottle, which only worried him more.

Caitlyn met him in the hallway wearing a pair of jeans and a sweatshirt. "You drive, and I'll watch over Emily."

The trip across town to the nearest hospital was tense. Emily continued to cry intermittently. Neither the car ride nor the fresh air calmed her down. Finally, they reached the Emergency Room. Matt parked the car, then put a hand on Caitlyn's shoulder as she started to get out.

"She has to be our baby," he said.

"What?" she asked in confusion.

"Emily is our daughter. We're Mr. and Mrs. Winters, and this is our daughter, Emily," he said slowly and deliberately. "If we don't have the authority to get her treated, we're going to run into all kinds of red tape."

"What about insurance?"

"I'll give my insurance information. By the time they figure out she's not covered, it will be later in the day, and then I'll give them a check."

Caitlyn nodded. "I understand. Let's just get her inside."

Their rush to get Emily help was slowed down by a busy Emergency Room. They spent nearly forty-five minutes in the waiting room, then another thirty in an examining room. The waiting was driving Matt crazy. He wanted to track down a doctor and drag him into the room, so they could stop Emily's suffering, because she did seem to be suffering, her little eyes looking at him for help. And he didn't know what to do.

"She'll be all right." Caitlyn patiently stroked Emily's back. "I'm sure it's nothing."

He wanted to believe her. If anything happened to Emily while he was taking care of her, he'd never forgive himself. He checked his watch. "It's after seven. What good is calling this an Emergency Room if they don't treat you like an emergency?"

"The nurse said Emily's temperature was a hundred and two, which isn't that bad for a baby."

Matt was unconvinced. "She probably says that so you don't complain."

"Matt, sit down." Caitlyn leaned back against the wall with a sigh.

"Are you all right? Do you want me to take Emily?"

"She's dozing now. Let's not disturb her."

"I couldn't have done this without you."

"Sure you could have."

"Well, I'm glad I didn't have to." He sat down next to her on the bench. "You're one hell of a woman, Caitlyn. In case I haven't mentioned it."

"What a difference a day makes," she said dryly.

"I'm sorry about the other night. I don't know what came over me."

"Don't you?"

"All right. You jumped out of my bed and went to Brian," he said grumpily. "That's what came over me."

"I didn't jump out of your bed. Emily was crying and then that singing telegram arrived, and I knew I couldn't just let things drift along."

"So, did you talk to Brian?"

"Yes."

"And?"

She hesitated. "Let's not get into that right now."

For a moment he thought about forcing the issue, but he changed his mind. What could he offer Caitlyn in the way of a relationship? He didn't know what would happen with Emily, if Sarah was coming back, or if he'd have a child to raise. If Sarah didn't come back, he would raise Emily as his own. Because he loved her, he realized, staring down at her small head. He loved Emily. And as he raised his gaze to Caitlyn's eyes, he had a feeling he loved her, too.

"You all right?" she asked.

"Not really."

"Do you want to talk about it?"

"Not right now."

"Okay." She scooted over on the bench and rested her head on his shoulder. "Then we'll just be together, you and me and Emily."

"Yeah, you and me and Emily," he muttered. What a great family they could be. There were still too many variables—Sarah, for one; Brian for another. But for now he was just going to hold Caitlyn and think about everything else tomorrow.

Jonathan pulled into the hospital parking lot just after seven-thirty. "Ready?" he asked Sarah. He smiled at her stiff posture. She was sitting in the passenger seat with her fingers pressed tightly together, her hair combed neatly into a ponytail. At least the bruises were fading and the horrified look in her eyes had disappeared.

They'd been busy the past two days, talking to as many possible churchgoers as they could find. In between, they'd spent some time at a transitional home where Sarah had met another young mother who was trying to get back on her feet. She'd begun to realize she wasn't the only woman who'd been completely overwhelmed by the responsibilities of motherhood.

"I'm still not sure about seeing a psychiatrist," she said finally. "What if the doctor thinks I'm crazy, too?"

"Then you'll deal with it."

"I won't be able to get Emily back if someone puts me away."

"You don't have Emily now," he gently reminded her. He knew that Sarah was missing her baby, that she was torn between doing what was best for Emily and what was best for Sarah. That she had put Emily's welfare before her own, told him how much she loved her child. Protecting a child was a mother's most important job, and in his book Sarah had done what she needed to do. Now he needed to help her get on track, so she could get Emily back in her life. It still disturbed him that she hadn't made contact with her brother, but one step at a time, he reminded himself.

Sarah sighed but still made no move to open her car door. "Do you really think I could be a good mother?"

For the first time he saw a hopeful look in her eyes, and it pleased him. "I do."

Her mouth slowly blossomed into a smile, and it stirred his heart in a way he'd never imagined. Maybe if she smiled more, he'd be used to it. Maybe then it wouldn't make his heart skip or his stomach turn over. He kept telling himself this was business, his business of helping people, but it was getting more personal with each passing day.

"I've never known anyone who believed in me," she told him. "I don't know why you do."

"You're young and smart and you have a good heart. This is the beginning of your life, Sarah, not the middle or even the end. There is so much ahead of you."

"You make it sound like it will all be good."

"Maybe not all, but hopefully, with some support, some friends, the bad times will be easier to handle. You're not alone anymore."

She drew in a breath for courage. "All right. I'm ready."

"Let's go." Jonathan stepped out of the car and walked with her through the front doors of the hospital. He felt confident that his friend would be able to give Sarah peace of mind. And then maybe he could do the rest, get her a place to live and reunite her with her baby. He wondered if Emily had her mother's beautiful eyes, her mother's incredible smile.

Emily threw up all over the doctor's sleeve. Matt looked away as the doctor bit back a curse and moved over to the sink to wash away the damage. As he dried off, he picked up his chart and jotted down some notes. "It's an ear infection," he said.

"Is that serious?" Matt glanced at Caitlyn, who was holding Emily in her arms now that the examination was over.

"It's very common in babies," the doctor replied. "Is she allergic to any antibiotics?"

"Uh . . ." How did he know what she was allergic to? What if he said the wrong thing?

"She hasn't been on any antibiotics," Caitlyn said quickly. "Is there something very mild you could start with?"

"Sure. Amoxicillin should take care of this. Give her the medication for its entire course. And then take her to your pediatrician in about two weeks and make sure everything is back to normal. Any problems before then, see the pediatrician."

Matt nodded as he took the prescription slip from the doctor. "That's it?"

"That's it," the older man said with a knowing smile. "First child?"

"Yeah."

"You'll get used to it. I've got three of my own at home. They always get sick in the middle of the night. You can give her some baby Tylenol for the pain. But in a few days the antibiotics should take most of the discomfort away. Any questions?"

Matt shook his head.

"Great. Have a nice day."

"Have a nice day," Matt echoed wearily. "It must be daytime, huh?"

"Almost eight," Caitlyn said, glancing at the clock on the wall which had been ticking ever so slowly the past two hours. "Are you ready to get out of here?"

"More than ready."

They walked through the hallway toward the Emergency Room entrance. That's when Matt saw something that caught him completely off guard. It was just a flash at the end of the hall, but a very familiar flash.

"Hold on a second," he said abruptly.

"What's wrong?"

"I thought I saw someone." He dashed down the hall which led into the main part of the hospital. It was her;

the old woman with the straw hat and the watering can. He was too far away to see her face, but he had a terrible feeling he knew who she was.

Fifteen minutes with Jonathan's psychiatrist friend had already made Sarah feel better. The woman, Karen Harte, was easy to talk to, very understanding, and had baby pictures all over her desk. Every time Sarah looked at one, she thought of Emily, wondering how she'd changed in the past week, if she'd stopped crying, if she'd begun to smile.

"You miss your baby," Dr. Harte said sympathetically.

"So much." Sarah felt the emotion clutch at her heart. Sometimes she thought she'd die if she didn't touch or hold Emily again. She'd thought she could break the connection between them simply by walking away, but the bond was as strong as ever.

"The mother-child relationship is very powerful," Dr. Harte continued.

"That's what worries me the most, that my mother may have passed down her craziness, I mean mental illness, to me."

"That's not an uncommon fear, Sarah. But not all mental illness is hereditary. And like other predispositions, such as alcoholism or obesity, an individual can make conscious choices to avoid those pitfalls. Understanding yourself, your strengths and weaknesses, can play a big part in a healthy mental life."

"But I left my baby just like my mother left me," Sarah argued, still not sure she could believe in herself the way the doctor was telling her to.

"Having a baby can be overwhelming, especially when you don't have any support. The physical changes in your body, the lack of sleep, they can play havoc with your mental health. What I'd like to suggest is that we see each other again, spend some time talking about your past and hopefully your future. Unfortunately, today's schedule is packed, but if you'd like to make an appointment for the next day or two, we could begin to explore some of your concerns on a deeper level. What do you think?"

"I don't have any money," Sarah said bluntly. "Jonathan said he'd cover today, but I can't ask him to do that again."

"I understand, Sarah. You're in a difficult situation. But I would like to speak with you again. So why don't we set up an appointment for one more session, and then perhaps I can steer you in the right direction for additional help."

"You would really do that?"

"I would," Dr. Harte replied with a smile. "I didn't become a psychiatrist just for the money." She paused. "My grandmother was sick, Sarah. I know what it's like to have mental illness in the family and how it affects those who live with it. You were a little girl at the mercy of your mother's erratic behavior. And you took steps to protect your child from a similar situation. I think the fact that you took those steps says quite a bit about your mental health."

"I hope you're right."

"Where is your mother now, Sarah?"

"I don't know."

"That's a shame. It might be good for you to talk to her again. Sometimes the monsters we create in our mind are far more powerful than the ones that actually exist. Please make an appointment on your way out, Sarah. I'd like to see you again."

"All right. Thank you." Sarah got to her feet and

walked through the door. As she debated which way to go, she caught a glimpse of a woman, the same woman she'd seen by the church. What on earth? She walked quickly down the hall. She had to catch up with her. She had to pull that straw hat off her head and look into her eyes.

Jonathan lifted his head as a man came into the reception area and glanced impatiently around the room, then at Jonathan.

"Excuse me," he said. "Did you see a woman with a straw hat come through here a second ago?"

"No, I've been reading. I haven't seen anyone."

The man let out a sigh. "Thanks anyway."

"No problem."

Jonathan looked down at his magazine and flipped idly through another half dozen pages of business news. He had just closed the cover when Sarah came into the lobby. She wasn't smiling, and he felt a sudden worry. Had he done the wrong thing by bringing her here, encouraging her to speak to a doctor? Most people would have told him to point Sarah in the direction of Social Services and let them help her weed through her problems. And those people might have been right.

"Are you okay?" he asked, getting to his feet.

She nodded, somewhat distractedly. "Did you see a woman come through here? She was carrying a watering can and—"

"Wearing a straw hat?"

"Yes." Her eyes lit up. "You saw her?"

"No."

"But how did you—"

"A man just came through here asking me the same question."

"Really?" Sarah looked around the room in much the

same way as the man had done. Jonathan felt an uneasy chill race down his arms. It was the kind of feeling he often got when things couldn't be explained.

"I wonder where she went," Sarah murmured.

"I don't know. I never saw her."

"But you have seen her—by your church?"

"I don't recall anyone of that description."

"She's been there twice this past week, watering the weeds along the sidewalk and the curb. She wears a bunch of clothes, like someone who lives on the street," Sarah added.

"It doesn't ring a bell."

"Really?"

"Nope. How did your meeting with Dr. Harte go?"

"Good." She smiled warmly at him. "She's very nice. She wants to see me again, and she said she won't charge me."

"Even if she did charge you, we'd find a way, Sarah."

"I'm beginning to believe you could find a way for anything."

He felt a rush of unexpected emotion. The confidence in her voice gave him renewed faith in himself. He had a feeling Sarah was doing as much for him as he was doing for her.

"Can we make a stop on the way home?" she asked him as they turned toward the door.

"Sure. Where do you want to go?"

"I want to go to Matt's house." She looked him straight in the eye. "I want to see my brother and my baby."

Twenty

"I know you're probably exhausted," Matt said as he started the car and pulled out of the hospital parking lot.

"But?" Caitlyn asked, sensing there was more to his statement than met the eye. In fact, he'd been acting odd since his mysterious dash through the hospital.

"I was wondering if you'd make a little side trip with me."

"Where?"

"Back to the old apartment building."

Caitlyn studied him thoughtfully. His face was tense. Gone was the relief he'd shown after learning Emily had a simple ear infection. Something had happened in the interim, and she didn't know what. "Where did you go?" she asked him. "Back at the hospital, when you took off so suddenly?"

"I thought I saw someone I knew. Do you remember that day when we were sitting in the car outside of my old building?"

"Sure."

"And there was a woman walking down the street with a watering can, and I said she reminded me of someone."

Caitlyn nodded. "Yes."

"Well, I have this strange feeling she could be my mother."

Caitlyn's eyes widened in surprise. "Really?"

"Yeah, and what's even stranger is that I saw her in the hospital. That's why I took off, but she disappeared before I could find her." He tapped his fingers impatiently against the steering wheel as he stopped at a red light. "Why was she in the hospital, Caitlyn? Why was she by my old building? Why do I keep seeing her?"

"I have no idea," she replied, even though she had a feeling all of his questions were rhetorical.

"Maybe she's connected to Sarah. Maybe they're together. Maybe they're watching me or something. . . . Damn! I wish I knew what was going on."

"So you want to go back to your neighborhood and do what?"

"I'm not sure. It sounds nuts, and I know you're tired. We should just go home."

"I don't mind coming with you. Emily has dozed off since we gave her the sample medication, and I don't have to be at work for a while."

He turned his head to smile at her. "I really appreciate it. I know I could drop you off, but . . . and this sounds ridiculous . . . I'm a little concerned about going back there by myself."

"Concerned?" she repeated with a grin. "You're scared out of your mind."

"That obvious, huh?"

"Yep."

"How do you know me so well?"

She shook her head, wondering exactly the same thing. "I don't know, Matt. I just do."

"And that scares the hell out of you, doesn't it?"

"Maybe a little."

"Are you ever going to tell me what you said to Brian the other night?"

"I told him that I couldn't have children, for one."

"How did he take it?"

"He had a lot of suggestions for ways I could follow up on the problem."

"I'm sure they're probably valid."

"No doubt they are. Brian has a scientific mind, and he sees unlimited possibilities where science is concerned. He feels in this day of medical advances nothing is impossible."

"Sounds like he still wants to be with you."

"He says so."

"What do you say?"

"Isn't that the street you're supposed to turn on?"

Matt made the turn as directed. "If you want to go back to him, hell, I've got nothing to say about it. I mean, you and I were just . . ."

"Just what?" she demanded, not liking his tone.

"I don't know exactly. What I do know is that you were in love with this guy, and I don't want to stand in your way."

"So you're being noble? Telling me to go because you think it's in my best interest?"

He shot her a dark look as he got her point. "I am not acting the way you acted before when you sent Brian away."

"Sure you are. You're playing the martyr, just like I did."

She could tell by the expression on his face he knew

she was right. Caitlyn just wished he could tell her how he really felt about her. But since she was having trouble doing the same thing, she could hardly judge him for remaining silent. It was just all too fast. Her mind couldn't keep up with the constant changes; she needed to think, maybe even sleep for a few hours and clear her brain.

"Here we are," Matt said, pulling into a parking place in front of his old building. He turned off the engine, his gaze sweeping the long block. "I know she couldn't be back here this fast, since I just saw her at the hospital."

"She could if she had a car or someone was driving her."

"True." He drummed his fingers against the steering wheel. "Why can't I go in there, Caitlyn? Why can't I just go into that damn building, walk up those stairs and down that hall?"

"Would it help if Emily and I came with you?"

"I know Sarah isn't there. I know my mother isn't there."

"But the monsters under the bed still are," she said softly.

He turned his head, his eyes filled with uncertainty. "The monsters were never under the bed, Caitlyn. They—I mean *she* was right there in front of me."

She put her hand on his thigh. "I'll come with you. We'll take a little walk, you and me and Emily. We'll go as far as you want, as slowly as you want."

Another moment's hesitation, then he nodded. "All right."

Caitlyn got out of the car and waited for Matt and Emily to join her. They walked up to the front door and then stepped inside. Matt paused, his hand seeking Caitlyn's in the dusky interior. She tightened her fingers around his, and together they turned toward the stairs.

* * *

As Sarah walked with Jonathan down the hall toward Matt's apartment, she replayed every second of her last trip. She'd called Matt from a pay phone on the corner to make sure he was at home. Then she'd slipped into the building and taken the elevator to his floor. That had been the easy part. Putting Emily down on the floor, tucking her blanket around her, saying good-bye, that had been the hard part.

Sarah felt the pain return as they approached Matt's door, as she stared down at the spot where she'd left Emily, the spot that was now empty. She had the sudden terrifying thought that her daughter might be lost to her forever.

"I can't," she muttered.

"Yes, you can." Jonathan took her trembling hand within his solid, comforting clasp. "You had the courage to leave her. Now you must have the courage to ask for her back."

"Is that what I should do?"

"It's up to you."

Sarah lifted her hand and, after another small hesitation, rapped sharply on the door. When there was no reply, she knocked harder. For there was suddenly a burning need inside her to hold her baby again.

"Just knock," Caitlyn told Matt as they stood in the hallway outside his old apartment.

"Why? There's no one inside I know."

"Wouldn't you like to take a peek?"

"What will I say?"

"Oh, for heaven's sake. I thought you were the intrepid investigative reporter who goes where other men fear to go."

He sent her an annoyed frown. "This is different."

"It's not. You're investigating your sister's disappearance. This is a place she used to live. It makes sense to check it out. Maybe she came back. Maybe she knocked on the door. Maybe the person inside will remember or know something."

"How do you know so much for a wedding dress designer?"

"I have a good imagination."

"Yeah, well, mine is working overtime right now. I feel like I'm sixteen again."

"You're not," she said gently. "Look at Emily. She should remind you that you're all grown up, and so is Sarah. Whoever or whatever hurt you in this apartment is gone."

She took the car seat from him. "Go on, Matt. Knock."

He raised his fist and knocked. Caitlyn held her breath, suddenly worried that her advice might be completely wrong, that Sarah might be inside, or his mother. Who knew? And if they were, if they saw Emily . . . Her grip tightened on the car seat. Well, someone would have some explaining to do before she handed over this innocent child.

There was no answer. They both turned their heads as footsteps came down the hall. It was a woman, looking tired and suspicious.

"What are you doing there?" she asked.

Caitlyn didn't know what to say. She felt like she'd been caught with her hand in the cookie jar.

"I used to live here," Matt said.

"Since when? I've been the manager here for ten years, and I don't remember you."

"It was longer than that. There was a fire . . ."

"Oh, yeah, I heard about that fire, some kids playing with matches almost burned the place down." Her eyes narrowed. "The fire started in that apartment. Was it you who started it?"

"No."

"Hmph." She didn't look like she believed him.

"Can you tell me who rents that apartment now?" Matt asked.

"No one. That apartment has been empty for the last three weeks."

Caitlyn saw a light flash in Matt's eye. "Can you tell me who rented it before?" he asked.

"An older woman."

"Do you remember her name?"

The woman thought for a minute, then asked warily. "Why do you want to know? I don't want no trouble here."

"I'm looking for my sister."

"This woman couldn't have been your sister. She was sixty if she was a day."

"What about her name?" he asked impatiently. "Do you remember her name?"

Caitlyn wondered why he was pressing so hard, and then it hit her. He thought the apartment had been rented by his mother, the woman in the straw hat, the one he kept seeing everywhere.

"Katherine Vance," the woman said. "Yeah, that was it."

"Are you sure? It wasn't Kathleen Vaughn?" he asked tightly. "They're awfully close."

"No. I'm pretty sure it was Vance."

"Did she wear a straw hat? Carry a watering can?"

"She kept to herself. I don't know what she wore."

Caitlyn could tell Matt was frustrated with the woman's short answers. "Since the apartment is empty," she interrupted. "Do you think it's possible we could go inside?"

The woman hesitated. Even Matt looked taken aback by the suggestion. But Caitlyn didn't waver. Matt was so big on facing the truth, well, here was his chance to face his past as well.

"Why not?" the woman said. She pulled out a thick ring filled with keys. "Just close the door on your way out."

Matt stared at the partially open door, not making a move to open it.

"You can do it," Caitlyn told him. "Just put one foot in front of the other." She gave him a gentle push on the back and finally he moved through the doorway.

Walking into the apartment where he'd lived with his mother and sister was one of the hardest things Matt had ever done. The first thing he saw when he walked through the door was the past, his mother's light blue sofa against the wall, stained with liquor spots and ciga-rette burns, the old television set, the old beat-up coffee table in front of the couch. On the table there had been dozens of candles of all different sizes and shapes, can-dles that his mother and Sarah would light every night. And then there were the plants, filling every corner of the apartment.

Matt blinked the memories away. In reality, the apart-ment was actually completely empty, a dull green carpet that had obviously come with the remodel, squares of lighter paint where pictures had once hung, empty hooks hanging from the ceiling. In one corner was a stove and sink in what passed for a kitchen. Next to that was a small bathroom and a door into the bedroom where his mother and Sarah had slept.

It wasn't a big room. It wasn't even a scary room. It was just beaten up, the way he'd felt all those years ago. He let out the breath he'd been holding as he realized there was nothing here for him, absolutely nothing. It was a relief in a way. One he couldn't even explain.

Matt glanced at Caitlyn, who had placed Emily's car seat on the floor but was standing protectively nearby. Caitlyn's brown eyes were filled with concern, caring, compassion, all the things he'd come to expect from her. She wasn't judgmental; he liked that. He felt like he could be himself, maybe for the first time in his life. For here was Caitlyn standing right smack in the middle of his past, the only woman he'd ever let into his life in such a way.

Caitlyn opened her arms to him, and he moved into her embrace, burying his face in her sweet-smelling hair, loving the feel of her body molding into his. She fit him—fit him perfectly. And here in this cold, dark room, Caitlyn surrounded him with warmth and light, promising a future he'd never allowed himself to believe in. But here with her, he could almost picture it.

I love you. The words jumped into his brain. He almost thought he'd said them out loud, but then Caitlyn was talking, slipping out of his arms, and he knew that the words still remained safely locked in his heart.

"I was thinking that maybe there is some clue in this apartment," Caitlyn said, walking toward the window. "Something brought us here today, but what is it?"

He shook his head, trying to clear the haze of love out of his brain. He couldn't believe he'd almost told her he loved her. They'd known each other a week. A week, for God's sake. How could he love someone that fast? How could he even trust someone that fast?

"Matt, are you listening to me?"

"Sorry. What did you say?"

"Where did you sleep?"

"Couch usually. Sarah and my mom had the bedroom."

"What was it you told me about her?" Caitlyn snapped her fingers. "I remember. She used to kneel by her bedroom window and look out at the stars at night." Caitlyn walked into the bedroom. "Come here," she called.

Matt grabbed Emily's car seat and took her with him into the bedroom. He couldn't leave Sarah's baby alone, not in this place.

"What did you find?" As far as he could see, the room was completely empty.

Caitlyn stood by the window. "Look out and tell me what you see."

Matt gave her a skeptical look, but joined her at the window. "I see the building across the street, and the sign for the liquor store, some clouds."

"Look harder. Look past the building. Look past what you remember, Matt, and think about what Sarah might remember."

He wondered what she was trying to tell him. Focusing on the view out the window, he tried to note every detail, and that's when he saw it, the sun glinting off the shiny white peak. It was the steeple of a nearby church, and as he stared at it, he could have sworn that a beam of light went from that steeple straight into the heavens.

"Sarah believed in angels," Caitlyn said.

"Oh, my God." A sudden shiver ran down his spine. "I know where we need to go." Matt took one last look out the window and saw what had drawn Sarah to the window every night of her life. It was hope.

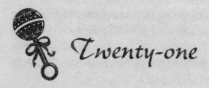

Twenty-one

It took only a few minutes for Matt to find the church they'd seen from Sarah's window, but in those few minutes Caitlyn felt a dozen different emotions. They seemed so close to finding Sarah now. Just standing in the apartment where Sarah had lived, looking out the window where she had knelt night after night, had made Caitlyn feel like Sarah was only a breath away. And Caitlyn wasn't sure she wanted to find Sarah. It would change everything.

She turned around in her seat to check on Emily, who was waking up with a yawn. "She's awake," she told Matt as he looked for a place to park near the church. "You know what that means."

"Do we have any bottles left?"

"No. Maybe we should go home. Emily isn't feeling well, and I don't want her to be hungry on top of everything else."

Matt frowned, obviously torn between finding Sarah and taking care of Emily.

"What's another hour?" Caitlyn asked. "Besides, there's nowhere to park. We can come back later."

He braked at the stop sign at the corner. "We're right here. It will just take a minute to ask if anyone has seen Sarah." He whipped a U-turn and pulled into a spot that blocked the driveway leading up to the house that sat next to the church. "I'll be right back."

"Matt," she said in protest.

He stopped halfway out the door and looked back at her. His eyes were understanding but determined. "I have to do this, Caitlyn. It will just take a minute."

"Not if you find Sarah. That will take more than a minute."

"We'll deal with that if it happens."

"Are you sure you want to find her?" The impulsive words left her mouth before she could stop them.

"She's my sister. She's all I have left of my family."

"You have Emily. You *love* Emily. I know you do. I can see it in your eyes. Have you thought about what will happen if you have to give Emily back to Sarah?"

He stared at her for a long moment, the pulse in his neck beating rapidly. "I can love Emily as her uncle."

"What if Sarah takes Emily and runs again? What if you never see either one of them again?"

"That's a chance I have to take."

"Well, *I* don't want to take it."

"I know this is unfair to you, Caitlyn." He sighed, glancing from her to the church. "But this is the right thing to do. Emily needs her mother."

Caitlyn blinked back the moisture that filled her eyes. He was right. Emily needed her mother. All children needed their mother. They certainly didn't need a substitute.

"Shit!" Matt swore. "I don't want to hurt you, Caitlyn."

"Just go," she said tonelessly. "I'll be fine."

He looked like he wanted to argue, but Emily began to whimper, and they both knew they were short on time. "I'll be right back."

Caitlyn turned around and saw Emily trying to wake up, her little eyes squinting at the bright sunlight. Well, no wonder she was crying. The poor thing was probably confused as to where she was, who she was with. Her life so far had been pure chaos. She deserved better than that. Emily deserved a good home, parents who would be there for her, parents like her and Matt.

Caitlyn couldn't stop the thought from running through her mind, even though she knew it was selfish. She didn't want the home for Emily; she wanted it for herself, and not just the house but the husband, the baby, maybe even a dog.

She reached over the seat and played with Emily's tiny toes. Such a perfect little creature she was, so untouched, so innocent, so lovely. Her life was a blank page upon which she could draw whatever she wanted. The possibilities were endless.

Caitlyn wanted those possibilities back for herself. She didn't want the lines that told her she couldn't go here or couldn't go there. She wanted the wide-open spaces, the free, unlimited choices. She wanted what so many other women took for granted—children. It was heartbreaking that she couldn't have them.

Anger swamped her soul like a tidal wave taking down the beach and everything on it. She hadn't let herself feel the anger, the bitterness, the sorrow—and she didn't want to feel it now, but she couldn't stop it. She wanted a baby of her own. She wanted it more than anything else in life.

The tears slid down her cheeks in a relentless stream until she couldn't see, which was why she didn't notice Matt had returned until he slammed the door and pulled her into his arms.

"It's okay. It's all right," he muttered. "She wasn't there. No one answered the door."

"I'm sorry. Sorry," she repeated hopelessly as she tried to pull herself together.

"You don't have anything to apologize for. I kept you up half the night. I've dragged you all over town to look for someone you don't even know. I'm the one who's sorry."

She sat back in her seat and wiped her eyes and cheeks with the back of her hand. "It's not you. It's me. I want what I can't have, and I think I just realized how much I want it."

He nodded, his eyes filled with compassion.

"It's not fair, Matt. It's not fair that I can't have kids, and yet here is this beautiful baby that your sister doesn't seem to want. Why could she have kids, but I can't? I'm sorry if that hurts your feelings, but it's the way I feel."

"You have a right. What happened to you is tragic. I wish I could make it go away, but I can't."

"Yeah, I know."

"Let's go home. We can get Emily a bottle and get ourselves some sleep."

Caitlyn nodded as Matt started the engine. She wanted to go home, to a home with Matt and Emily. Maybe Sarah could just stay lost.

Matt knew they were close to finding Sarah. His instincts had always been good, and right now those instincts were telling him that Sarah was nearby. Seeing that steeple out of Sarah's window had reminded him of how many times she'd talked about the angels nearby. It made sense that if she were seeking a refuge, she'd go to the church. It was unfortunate that no one had answered the door. But they'd have to come back sometime and so would he.

Glancing over at Caitlyn, he saw the tenseness in her face, the worry in her eyes, the tightness in her shoulders. She was thinking about losing Emily. For Caitlyn there was nothing to gain by finding Sarah.

For him it would be different. He would have his sister back, his family back. It was what he had always wanted, what he'd thought he'd probably lost forever, but now it was almost within reach.

But while he would gain a family, Caitlyn would lose the baby she'd grown to love. That didn't seem right, either. He wondered why there couldn't ever be two good things in a row, why it was always one up and one down.

There was no question that Caitlyn had gotten a raw deal. And why her? She was such a sweetheart, a natural-born mother. Her kids would have had it great. They would have been lucky to have her for a mother. But there weren't going to be any kids. Not unless she married someone who already had a child, a ready-made family.

They would have made a great family, Caitlyn, Emily and himself. Maybe . . .

No, he couldn't think that way. Sarah was Emily's mother. He had to find her. He couldn't stop trying to reunite them, no matter what the cost to Caitlyn or himself. But one thing was for sure, he would make certain that Sarah could take care of Emily before he let her go. There was no way in hell Emily would grow up with the same awful uncertainty he and Sarah had lived through with their own unstable mother. He wouldn't allow that to happen. Because Emily was the most important, and it was her welfare he had to consider over everyone else.

Fifteen minutes later, he pulled the car up in front of the apartment building that had begun to feel more like home since he'd discovered Emily and Caitlyn. He'd always moved around a lot, careful not to settle down. But he was starting to want roots, starting to desire things like stability and consistency, like waking up with the same woman every morning and saying good-night to that same woman every night. And maybe seeing a baby smile when she saw him, or hear a small child call him *Daddy*.

He shook his head, trying to dislodge the disturbing thoughts. For he'd learned a long time ago that loving or wanting something or someone was pretty much a guarantee that that something or someone would disappear.

Caitlyn let out a sigh that turned into a yawn.

"You must be exhausted," he said.

"I am," she agreed.

"Are you going in to work?"

"Maybe later. What about you? Will you go back to the church?"

"I know you want me to say no, but—"

"But you can't leave any stone unturned. I understand." She offered him a tentative smile. "I know I was upset back there for a second. And since you're so big on honesty, I'd have to say it's probably going to happen again, as soon as you find Sarah, and as soon as I have to say good-bye to Emily. But I'll try to keep it together. This isn't your problem. It's mine, and somehow I'll find a way to deal with it."

"I wish you didn't have to deal with it."

"Me, too. Things would have been a lot easier if you hadn't knocked on my door last week."

"Easier, yes, but better?" he queried, wondering if she regretted getting involved with him as well as with Emily.

Her eyes darkened. "Not better, just easier. You know that."

"The good things are always hard."

"Maybe not just the good things."

Emily, having grown weary of their conversation, let out a cry. They quickly exited the car and dashed up the steps to the apartment building.

"Someone should fix this," Caitlyn said as Matt held open the front door. "This is supposed to be a security building."

Matt felt the same prickle of uneasiness he'd felt a few nights earlier when he'd first noticed the jammed lock. Had Sarah done it?

He'd become so suspicious where Sarah was concerned. Maybe he was looking for a reason to keep Emily, too. That little truth jumped into his head, and once there, refused to budge. Like Caitlyn, he had become attached to Emily, maybe too attached. He needed to keep his objectivity. It was the only way any of them would get through this.

Caitlyn pushed the button for the elevator, tapping her foot impatiently as she tried to keep Emily quiet. Matt hoped Mrs. Pederman wouldn't suddenly appear. A nosy neighbor, on top of everything else, he could definitely live without.

"Where is the damn elevator?" Caitlyn muttered.

Matt looked up at the lighted numbers. "It's on ten." As soon as he said it, his heart skipped a beat, and when he turned to Caitlyn, he saw the same look in her eyes. Whoever was coming down in that elevator was probably someone who had come to see one of them, as the other wing had a separate elevator.

"Probably Bradley," he said shortly. "Or your mother. Or one of your other many visitors."

"Right. I'm sure it's someone for me. No one ever comes to visit you."

No one except Sarah. His throat was suddenly too tight to speak. It was ridiculous. It wasn't her. It couldn't be her. But he saw Caitlyn's arms tighten around the baby and knew she was thinking the same thing. And suddenly he was the one who wanted to run.

But the silver doors were opening, so slowly he wanted to thrust them apart with his bare hands. He saw a man's trousers first. Brian, he thought with relief. Then the doors opened farther, and he heard Caitlyn's small gasp as the woman standing in the back of the elevator stepped forward. She was small and thin with long black hair that reached down to her waist. Her eyes were as dark as the night and as familiar as his own.

"Sarah," he breathed. "Oh, my God!"

No one moved. They were suddenly frozen in time, and it wasn't until the elevator doors began to close again that Matt reached in and held them back.

"Is it really you?" he asked.

"It's me."

"Sarah," he breathed, feeling an incredible sense of reunion. His sister was back. He could hardly believe it.

The elevator doors hammered his hand again, impatient to close. The man standing next to Sarah put his hand in front of the other door. Matt gave him a cursory glance, enough to know it wasn't the same man he'd met in Sarah's old apartment, thank God for that. Then he looked at Sarah. "You finally came back."

"I've been waiting for you," she answered.

"Have you? I'd almost given up."

"Why don't we go upstairs?" Caitlyn suggested from behind him.

Suddenly realizing where they were, he stepped into the elevator, followed by Caitlyn and Emily. The three of them stood on one side of the small car, Sarah and her companion on the other, the air thick with tension, with questions, with curious looks. Every muscle in his body was tight, but there was a surge of adrenaline coursing through him, making it impossible to stay still.

"This is Caitlyn Devereaux, my neighbor," Matt said. "She's been helping me take care of Emily."

"Is Emily all right?" Sarah asked. "She's crying."

"She's hungry," Caitlyn said shortly. "And it's about time you came back."

Sarah looked stricken by Caitlyn's sharp words and moved closer to the man who was with her.

"I'm Jonathan Mitchell," the man said, slipping his hand through Sarah's. "I'm the minister at the All Souls Church."

The church they'd just visited. "We were there fifteen minutes ago."

"You were?" Sarah asked, sounding amazed. "How did you know I was there?"

"I went back to the old apartment and looked out your window. I saw the steeple, and I knew." He gazed into her eyes and saw that she knew, too, that they both remembered all those nights she'd stared out at the sky, looking for angels.

Then Sarah's gaze turned back to Emily, to the baby held tightly in Caitlyn's arms, the baby who was beginning to fuss yet again. Matt suddenly didn't know what to do. Should he give Sarah the baby so she could comfort her? Should he take Emily? Should Caitlyn hold on to her?

Fortunately, the elevator had reached their floor, taking the decision out of his hands. They walked down the hallway, a solemn quartet of adults with one crying baby. He found his keys and opened the door as quickly as he could, knowing they needed to feed Emily before they did anything else. And it was that practical thought that calmed his churning stomach. This wasn't the time or the place for emotion. He had to take care of business in a logical, practical way.

"I'll get her a bottle," Caitlyn said as they walked into the apartment. "You can talk to your sister."

The way she said the word *sister* left no doubt in his mind that Caitlyn wanted him to grill Sarah on why she'd left the baby alone in the hallway. And he would do that—in a minute. First, he needed to just look at her.

As his gaze slid up and down her slender frame, settling back on her face, he saw some fading bruises. He caught his breath at the sight, reminded of a time when he'd seen similar bruises on his mother's face. His own hands clenched into fists. "Did that bastard hit you?"

Sarah started, lost in her own bit of staring. "It's a long story."

"I'm going to need to hear all of it."

"Yes, I know. But first I want to say that I'm sorry for dumping Emily on you the way I did. I was desperate, and I didn't know what else to do." Her gaze traveled to the kitchen door where Emily had disappeared. "Is she all right?"

"She has an ear infection," he said. "Caitlyn and I spent half the night at the hospital."

"Oh, no," Sarah said in dismay.

"But she's all right now." Matt was relieved to see the

worry in his little sister's eyes. She cared. Sarah cared about her baby. It was a start. "Maybe we should sit down."

Sarah hesitated, taking some sort of silent encouragement from her companion. Matt didn't know what to make of her relationship with the minister, but he'd deal with him later. Right now he needed to concentrate on Sarah.

He turned his head as Caitlyn returned to the room. He motioned for her to sit in the armchair while he got to his feet. He was too tense to sit.

"Why don't you tell me why you left Emily in such a rush and why you ran away from that apartment in Berkeley?"

"How do you know about that?" Sarah asked with alarm. "Did you see Gary? Did you tell him you had Emily?"

"I didn't tell him anything. Relax," he added as Sarah looked ready to take Emily and bolt.

She took a deep breath. "I don't want Gary to know where Emily is."

"Why?"

"Because he wants to put her up for adoption."

"He's the father?" Matt's stomach turned over at the thought of that punk's being Emily's father.

Sarah nodded. "Yes, but Gary didn't really want to have a baby. It was an accident. He couldn't stand her crying, and his friend told him about this lawyer who put babies up for adoption. Gary said he'd give us a lot of money if we gave him Emily. I told him no, but he wouldn't listen to me, so I took Emily and ran away." She paused for a moment, then said, "I didn't know where to go. And then like a miracle I saw your name in the newspaper. I couldn't believe it. I couldn't believe it was you. But I went to your workplace and saw you come out of the building and I knew it was you, and I knew it was a sign that I should take Emily to you."

"Why didn't you knock on the door? Why leave without talking to me?" he demanded.

"I was going to, but I was afraid you'd say no, and I had nowhere else to take Emily. You were my last hope. Otherwise, we would have spent the night on the street."

"Sarah was beaten up," Jonathan interjected. "When I found her she was in pretty bad shape."

"That bastard hit you?" Matt asked again, realizing she'd never answered him the first time.

"Yes," she whispered. "But I'm okay now."

For a moment Matt was so filled with fury that her words barely registered, but finally they sank in, and he knew he'd have to deal with Gary later. Right now it was about Sarah and Emily. "Tell me the rest. Where did you go after you left Emily? The church?"

"Yes."

"And you've been doing what?"

"I—I've been trying to figure out what to do."

"How about taking care of your daughter."

Sarah looked taken aback by his harsh words, but he wouldn't take them back. They needed to face the truth.

"I wanted to, Mattie. I did. But I didn't have any money or a place to stay and no friends. I was a mess, and I was ashamed for you to see me . . . to see me acting like . . ." She drew in a deep breath of courage. "Acting like Mama. I didn't want you to think I'd turned out like her, but I was terrified that I had."

Matt felt his anger deflate as her words took him back to a time when they'd both been ashamed, both been a mess, both been afraid. And he supposed on some level he'd always been afraid of ending up back where he started. It was one reason why he'd become career-driven and stayed on the move, afraid to settle down, afraid to find himself alone in an apartment with nowhere to go and no one to care about him.

"I was trying to be a good mother," Sarah said, interrupting his thoughts. "Before Emily came, I kept the apartment clean and took my vitamins and drank my milk. But after she was born, it was so hard. She cried all the time, and I was so tired I couldn't think straight. Gary wouldn't help at all. Then he wanted to give her away, and I couldn't do anything but run. When I saw you, I knew you'd take care of her for me."

"How could you know that?" he muttered.

"Because you always took care of me," she said simply, a trust shining out of her eyes that he'd never thought he'd see again, not after the way he'd let her down.

"That was a long time ago."

"I still remember. And I still love my baby. I know it might not look like that to you, but I did what I did to protect Emily, to keep her safe, until I could figure out a way to take care of her myself."

"Which is why you're here now?"

"Yes." She glanced at Jonathan again. "I've learned a lot about myself in the last week. And I'm willing to do whatever I need to do to be a good mother to Emily." She paused, her gaze traveling to where Caitlyn was trying to pat a burp out of Emily. "Do you think I could hold her?"

Matt hesitated, not sure what he should say. Caitlyn didn't look like she wanted to let go of the baby, but Sarah was Emily's mother. How could he not let her hold her baby?

"Sure," he said finally. "Caitlyn?"

She hesitated for a long second, then she stood up and

walked over to Sarah, who immediately got to her feet and took Emily into her arms.

Emily went to her mother with a big smile, looking like she'd just arrived at the Promised Land, and Sarah wore the same joyous expression. Mother and daughter were back together.

When Matt turned to Caitlyn, he saw a shimmer in her eyes and knew she'd seen the same thing he had.

"I should go," Caitlyn said abruptly.

"Right now?"

"Yes."

"I'll be right back," Matt said to Sarah as he followed Caitlyn into the hallway. "Are you all right?"

"No." She held up a hand as she looked at him with an expression that was a mix of anger and sadness and resignation. "This isn't about me. It's about Emily and Sarah and you. I don't belong in the middle of this."

"I put you in the middle."

"Well, I didn't try that hard to get out. But it's time, past time."

"I will keep my promise. Sarah won't take Emily until I'm sure she'll be all right with her."

Caitlyn nodded. "I know you'll do the right thing, Matt. Do you realize you finally have your family back? You've found Sarah. And you have Emily, too, now. I'm so happy for you."

She didn't sound happy. "You should get some sleep," he said.

"I will."

"You'll come by later, right?" He tried to make the question sound casual, but he suddenly needed the reassurance that she would be back, because she no longer had a real reason to return.

"Sure, later. After all, I live just across the hall. We're

neighbors, remember?" The reality of her words cut through him like a knife. With Emily gone, would they be anything else except neighbors?

Shaking his head, he returned to his apartment to find Sarah crying over Emily. "Is she okay?" he asked worriedly.

"I got her to sleep," Sarah said.

Matt sensed this was a victory for Sarah, and he could hardly blame her for feeling jubilant. "You should be smiling then, because getting your daughter to sleep is an amazing accomplishment. Believe me, I know."

"She cried with you, too?"

"All the time. Frankly, I think she likes the sound of her own voice."

"I thought it was just me. And I felt so alone."

"Didn't you have any friends you could talk to?"

"No. We moved around a lot."

"What were you doing with a creep like that anyway?" He held up a hand. "Never mind about that. We have a lot of catching up to do."

"Are you sure you want to? I realize I didn't give you a choice when I left Emily with you. And I wondered afterwards if you were sorry I'd tracked you down, if you wished I'd stayed gone."

"Are you kidding? I've spent the last thirteen years wondering what happened to you, worrying if you were happy or safe or in trouble. I tried to find you a dozen times, hired private investigators, but I couldn't get a clue. Where did you go? Where have you been living all these years? Were you adopted? Did they take good care of you?" The questions shot out like bullets from a gun. "Sorry," Matt said hastily. "I didn't mean to sound like an interrogator. I just can't quite believe you're standing in front of me."

"I didn't know you were looking for me. I thought you were angry with me for starting the fire, for burning us out of the only home we had."

"I shouldn't have said that. You were a little girl. You didn't know what you were doing."

Jonathan cleared his throat, and the minister and Sarah exchanged a look that set Matt's curiosity on edge.

"Am I missing something?" Matt asked.

"I'm going to leave you and your brother to talk," Jonathan said, getting to his feet. "All right, Sarah?"

"You're leaving?" she asked in dismay, the same dismay Matt had felt with Caitlyn's departure.

"You have a lot to discuss. Why don't you call me when you're done or if you want to come home."

"Home? Where is home?" Matt caught a slightly guilty look in Jonathan's eyes. "She's been staying with you and your wife?"

"I'm not married, and she's been staying in the guest bedroom at my house. Although we have made arrangements for Sarah and Emily to stay at a transitional home beginning on Monday." Jonathan met Matt's gaze head-on, as if he had nothing to hide. Matt still wondered if there was more going on between the minister and his sister than met the eye. But it was just another question he had in a very long list, and he had to take them one at a time.

Jonathan walked over to Sarah and squeezed her hand. "You have more courage and strength than you know. That's what brought you here. Listen to your heart. It won't steer you wrong."

Matt saw a nervous gleam in Sarah's eyes after Jonathan left the room. "Well, it's just the two of us again. Amazing. Oh, wait a second . . ." He walked into his bedroom and returned with the gold chain he'd found at her apartment. "I think this is yours."

Sarah's mouth trembled as she took the heart necklace out of his hand. "I couldn't find it when I left. I wanted to look for it, but I was afraid to take the time."

"I'm glad you kept it all these years. Now, tell me, are you really all right?" He searched her eyes for the truth. Sarah wasn't as easy to read as Caitlyn. There were dark shadows in her eyes, shadows of pain, betrayal, and the sadness he remembered. But her eyes were also clear and alert, no trace of drugs or confusion. She looked like a woman who knew what she wanted.

"I'm fine now that I'm holding Emily again."

"You can put her down. Or at least sit down; she gets heavy after a while."

Sarah took his advice and sat down on the couch, settling Emily more comfortably in her arms. "She's the best thing I ever did," she murmured, looking from the baby to Matt. "And I want her to have a good life, better than the one I had."

"What happened to you, Sarah? Where did they take you after the fire?"

"They took me to a foster home, the Rodgers. They were okay. They had a bunch of foster kids. I stayed there for about four months."

"Then what?" She looked away, and he didn't like her expression. His stomach muscles tightened to the point that he thought he might get sick.

"Mama came to the school one day and told me we were going to be together again."

Matt felt his heart stop. "Mama came back for you?"

"She told me we would get you, too, but we never did."

"Do you think she tried?" Matt tried to stop the question from sliding out of his mouth, but he couldn't.

Sarah's eyes turned more sorrowful. "I don't think so, Mattie. She said you always reminded her of Daddy and that made her sad. She also said you'd criticize her, and you were almost a man anyway. You didn't need a mother."

Matt had to turn away as he struggled to keep his emotions in check. It shouldn't matter that his mother had gone back for Sarah and not for him. He'd always known she disliked him for criticizing her. Not that there hadn't been plenty to criticize. But still, he was her son. And he could have helped. He could have taken care of Sarah.

"Maybe I shouldn't have told you."

He took in a breath and let it out, wondering how many more shocks were headed his way. It had been a hell of a morning. "You caught me by surprise. I thought our mother had disappeared forever."

"No. We went to Sacramento after that. Mama found a new boyfriend. His name was Tommy. He just ignored me, but that was okay, because the next guy . . ." She licked her lips. "Well, there were others, lots of others. We moved around all the time, L.A., Las Vegas, Reno, then back to Sacramento. When I was sixteen she left and never came back." She paused. "I used to think you were old, Mattie, but I realized later on that you were just a kid like me."

"I'm not sure either one of us was a kid. What happened to you after she left?"

"I stayed with friends, some girlfriends, some boyfriends," she added, looking into his eyes with shame. "I saw how Mama had survived, and I copied her."

He shook his head, feeling so much anger, so much regret, he couldn't even speak.

"That's when I first realized how much like her I was," Sarah continued. "And when I had Emily, I got scared. I was afraid I would lose control like Mama did. I can still hear her that night, the yelling, the screaming, the scrap-

ing of those matches against the box, the sparks crack-
ling, the smoke blowing through the air."

"What are you talking about?" he demanded, suddenly
afraid he knew where this was going.

"The fire," she said, meeting his gaze head-on. "Mama
started the fire."

"No!" He shook his head. "No. She wouldn't have
tried to hurt you."

"I was bad, Mattie. I played with her matches."

"Oh, my God!" He put a hand to his mouth, feeling
sick to his stomach and sick at heart. All these years he'd
thought Sarah had started the fire, but instead she'd
watched their mother try to burn down their life.

"She was sorry, though. She told me later she was
sorry and that she wouldn't do it again. But . . ."

"But what?"

"She started other fires, here and there, mostly small
ones, I think, but I never knew when I heard the fire engines nearby if Mama was involved. Once I asked her,
and she got all guilty looking and said she always felt better when the flames were dancing."

He stared into his sister's eyes and realized that she'd
suffered far more than he had. "Do you know where she
is now?" he asked, suddenly remembering the woman
he'd seen earlier that morning in the hospital.

Sarah visibly stiffened. "I don't know. I thought for a
long time she was probably dead. But last week and this
morning I saw someone who reminded me of her. It was
so odd."

"Me, too," he said in a rush. "In the hospital."

"Yes, in the hospital," Sarah agreed. "And by the
church."

"And in our old neighborhood. She looked like a
homeless person. She was carrying a watering can and—"

"Wearing a straw hat like the one she used to wear when the sun was too bright for her pale skin. She hated to burn."

Their eyes connected, their expressions mirroring each other's.

"Do you think that was really her?" Sarah asked.

"I couldn't see her face. I tried to catch up to her, but she disappeared."

"I lost her, too."

Matt blinked, another oddity suddenly registering in his brain. "You were at the hospital this morning? Why?"

"Jonathan took me to talk to a psychiatrist friend of his. She helped me to see that I might be suffering from post-partum depression and that I might not be like Mama."

"You're not," Matt said forcefully. "You're nothing like her. You aren't high, for one. You don't do drugs, do you?"

"No, never, honestly. I used to drink, though, but I stopped when I got pregnant. Gary thought I was a big drag. I know I should have left him, but it was easier to stay than go. He wasn't bad all the time. And I didn't really think I deserved better."

"You do, a lot better."

"Mama made me feel like we were trash. She only came and got me because it was easier for her to get welfare with a kid. She used me, Mattie. I don't want to do the same thing to Emily. I'd rather give her up than raise her the way we were raised."

Matt let out a breath, his mind reeling with her story. He still couldn't believe she'd been with their mother for such a long time. He'd thought they'd all been split up, but he had been the only one on his own. Maybe he'd actually drawn the long straw and never known it.

"I don't know if you can believe me," Sarah said. "But I'm going to get my act together."

"I believe you," he said. "And I can help you." He could protect her now the way he hadn't been able to protect her before. "You and Emily can stay with me," he said decisively, feeling better now that he was taking charge.

Sarah hesitated. "Maybe for a few days, Mattie, but come Monday I'm moving into the transitional home Jonathan found for me."

"But why? I can take care of you."

"I know, but I need to take care of myself and my baby. I can't keep drifting from one man to the next, always looking for someone to solve something for me. If I'm going to be a good mother, I need to solve my own problems. It's not that I'm not grateful. I know you could be really mad at me for dumping Emily on you. I'll try to pay you back."

"That's not necessary. Emily brought you back to me. That's all I ever wanted."

Her mouth turned down as she struggled for composure, reminding him of how Emily looked before she burst into tears.

"Whoa," he said quickly, not sure he could take any more water works today. "Don't get all mushy on me."

She gave him a watery smile. "I don't deserve you."

"Hell, you deserve more than me. I let you down before by not believing in you. That won't happen again."

"I feel so much better. No more running away, Mattie. I know that now. I won't repeat Mama's mistakes. She told me once right before she left that last time that she'd never known what to do with us after Daddy died. And that sometimes she'd look up in the sky and wonder if he was watching her and if he was sad because she was screwing up so bad. It was one of the few times she seemed really clear and really sorry. And she said, Someday you'll be happy, Sarah. Someday you and Mattie will be together, and you'll be happy. She left the next day and I never saw her again. After that I drifted into living her life, but that's over. I'm going to live the rest of my life differently. And I'm starting now."

He liked her positive attitude. "I'll be right behind you every step of the way."

"Thanks." She studied him for a moment. "Your friend, Caitlyn—she's nice."

"Very nice."

"But she doesn't like me."

"It's not that. She became attached to Emily. It's hard for her to let go. But she'll come around." At least he hoped she would. Because it would be hard enough saying good-bye to Emily without saying good-bye to Caitlyn, too.

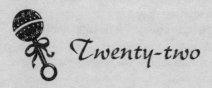 *Twenty-two*

*L*ater that afternoon Caitlyn picked up the phone and dialed. "Mom," she whispered. Her voice was shaky, her insides still in turmoil from watching her future evaporate before her very eyes. She'd tried to talk herself into a better mood most of the day but the pain wouldn't go away, and she couldn't take it anymore.

"Caitlyn? What's wrong? I can hardly hear you."

"Emily is going back to her mother," Caitlyn said with a sob.

"Is that bad?" Marilyn asked after a long pause.

"She's not going to be my baby. I'm not going to be her mother." The realizations poured out of her mouth, each one hurting her heart a little more.

"Oh, honey, I didn't know you'd gotten so close."

"I'm never going to have children," Caitlyn said baldly. It wasn't the way she'd intended to tell her mother, but it came out, just like that. The words she'd been hiding for a year and a half had come out in a rush.

"That's not true, Caitlyn. You'll have a baby of your own one day. You can have one with Brian. Or if you really don't want him, with someone else."

"You don't understand, Mom. You have to listen really carefully right now, because I don't think I can say this again. I can't ever have children." Caitlyn let the words sink in. "The accident crushed my ovaries. There was permanent damage. I wanted to tell you before, but I couldn't." She closed her eyes and tried to prepare herself for her mother's reaction.

"My God, Caitlyn. Why didn't you say something? Are you sure?"

"I'm positive. I'm sorry, but you're not going to be a grandmother." The tears ran down her cheeks.

"I can't believe it."

"You have to believe it, because it's true."

Silence filled the phone line. "Well. Well," her mother said finally.

"Don't say you'll fix it, because you can't," Caitlyn said, trying to ward off any suggestions. "No one can fix this."

"What do you want me to say?" Marilyn asked cautiously, as mother and daughter waded into unfamiliar territory.

"Nothing. I just want you . . ." Caitlyn drew in a deep breath. "I just want you to be my mom."

"I'm coming over. I'll be there in fifteen minutes."

"What about your classes?"

"They can wait. My daughter needs me."

And she did. Caitlyn hung up the phone and rested her head on her arms. A few minutes later she heard a knock on her door. She knew it was too soon for her mother to have traveled across town. That left Brian or Matt, and she didn't feel in the mood to talk to either one of them.

She'd just let whoever it was knock. She wasn't going to answer the door. No good ever came of opening that door. She'd learned that the hard way.

"Caitlyn, come on, open up. I know you're in there," Matt shouted, knocking relentlessly against the door frame.

Caitlyn put her hands over her ears, trying desperately to ignore him. She didn't want to talk to him, didn't want to see him, didn't want to hear anything about him or Sarah or Emily, about the family he would have without her.

"I'm not like Brian. You can't just tell me to go and I'll go. I'm not leaving." The pounding began again, beating in time with the pain in her head. Finally, she got up and opened the door.

"What do you want?"

He stared at her, then reached out his hand to touch her face. She jerked away; she couldn't help it. The thought of his touch was too painful.

"I wanted to make sure you're all right."

"I'm fine. Any other questions before you go?"

"Just one." He put his hands on her waist and yanked her up hard against his chest, crushing her mouth with his. She tried to resist him, but his kiss was like a steamroller, knocking every piece of her resistance out of the way.

"Stop," she gasped, breaking away from him.

"I'm not the enemy. Why are you treating me like one?"

"You are the enemy," she cried. "You made me believe in the impossible. You made me feel things I didn't want to feel. You melted the ice around my heart, and then you broke it."

"I didn't mean to. You knew Emily had to go back to her mother. You knew that."

"But I was her mother this past week. I was there with

her, with you, on the roof, in the car, at the Emergency Room. And now I just have to back off and say good-bye and pretend I don't love her." Her voice broke. "But I do love her, Matt. I love her like she was my own baby. And I have to watch some other woman take my place."

"Not some other woman, her mother. Her mother, Caitlyn." He gave her a little shake. "Emily needs Sarah."

"I know that. I know," she added when he didn't look like he believed her. "It still hurts."

"Let me help you with the hurt."

"You can't."

"Just because Emily goes back to Sarah doesn't mean you and I aren't . . ."

He hesitated for a second too long, a very telling second. "Aren't what?" she asked. "Aren't neighbors? Friends? Lovers? What am I to you, Matt? What am I to you without Emily between us? Well, I'll tell you what I am—I'm nothing. The only reason you crossed that hallway was to get a baby-sitter. Now you don't have a baby. You don't have a reason to come over here."

"That may be how it started, but that's not how it is now, and you know it." His eyes narrowed. "You're looking for a reason to push me out that door. Just like you did with Brian."

"This is not the same thing."

"This is exactly the same thing. You want me to tell you it was nothing. Is that how you feel, Caitlyn? Because what am I to you without a baby attached? Answer me that. Do you want me at all if I can't offer you a child to take care of?"

"That's not fair."

"Life isn't fair. You of all people should have figured that out."

"I think I hate you," she said with all the passion in her

soul. Because she didn't just hate him, she loved him. And she hated him even more because of that.

"When you're sure, let me know. For what it's worth, you were everything, neighbor, friend, lover . . . everything. But I don't have a baby to offer you. So if I'm not enough, then I'm not enough."

"And I don't have a baby to offer you," she said, her heart ripping in two.

"I don't have to have children."

"Don't lie to me, Matt. I saw you with Emily. I saw you acting like a father. I saw you falling in love with that baby. I didn't go there alone; you went with me." And she saw the answering truth in his eyes. "But the difference is, you can have a baby with someone else. And you should. Because you would make . . ." She stumbled over the words. "You would make one hell of a father."

"Caitlyn—"

"Go home, Matt. I can't do this anymore." And she shut the door in his face, putting him where he should have been all along, on his side of the hallway.

Caitlyn's mother convinced her to come home and spend the night with them, and too tired to hang on to her independence for one second longer, Caitlyn agreed. She needed the distance. She didn't think she could stand to see Matt or hear Emily's cry. It would hurt too much. So she packed a bag and let her mother drive her home.

To her credit, Marilyn said next to nothing on the way there, just reaffirming her support. Back at the house, Caitlyn excused herself, climbed the stairs to her old bedroom, and collapsed on the bed. She slept for five straight hours, waking up a little after nine o'clock that night.

For a moment, she was disoriented by her surroundings and the darkening light. She found herself reaching for Matt, listening for the baby, only to realize that neither one of them was there. All she could do was wrap her arms around herself and hope that the chill would eventually go away.

"Caitlyn, are you awake?" Marilyn pushed open the door to the bedroom. "I thought I heard you stirring."

"And I thought I was being quiet."

"I still have a mother's ears." Marilyn sat down on the end of Caitlyn's bed. "I'm glad you called me today."

"Thanks for coming."

"Thanks for asking."

Caitlyn picked at the top sheet, wondering if the lectures would now begin, the endless suggestions on how she could repair her body, fix her little problem, but her mother remained oddly quiet. Finally, she looked over at her. "Well?"

"I was going to ask you the same thing."

"I had all sorts of tests, Mom. I even had a second opinion. There is no miracle cure. I simply can't have a baby."

"There's nothing simple about what you just said. I only wish you had told me sooner. Why did you keep it a secret?"

"I told myself I didn't want you to try to fix me, and I knew you would try. Just like you fixed everything else about me, my hair, my eyes, my teeth, my body."

"Caitlyn—"

"No, wait, let me finish. That isn't really why I didn't tell you. Just what I told myself. The other reasons included not wanting to hurt you, not wanting to tell you that you couldn't have grandchildren."

"You're more important than grandchildren."

"Well, that wasn't really why I didn't tell you, either."

"Good heavens. Are you going to make me guess?"

Her exasperation drew a reluctant smile from Caitlyn. "I couldn't accept it, Mom. I knew if I said it out loud, if I told people, it would be real, and I didn't want it to be real, so I pretended it wasn't there."

"And you sent Brian away." Marilyn nodded her head as it all became clear to her.

"It was easier with Brian gone. There wasn't any wedding to plan, no future to think about, at least not one that included children. I didn't have to deal with any of it. But that changed when a man knocked on my door one night and told me there was a baby in the hallway."

"Matt."

"Matt," Caitlyn echoed. "His sister had dropped the baby off, asking for help. It's a long story, but he wasn't sure where she was or if she was coming back. I knew I should keep my distance. But one look at that baby and I was gone. I fell in love with Emily, head over heels in love." She shook her head at the hopelessness of it all.

"Are you sure Emily is the only one you fell in love with?"

"Of course." Caitlyn looked away from her mother's sharp gaze.

"We've come this far, Caitlyn. Don't you think you could tell me the whole truth, especially if I promise not to point out why Matt is completely unacceptable."

Caitlyn looked at her mother in surprise. Was that a teasing note in her voice? Was there a smile trying to fight past her cool expression? "Is something funny?" Caitlyn asked suspiciously.

"No. Nothing is funny. Tell me about Matt."

"He's my neighbor."

"And he's very good looking in that rugged, dangerous, bad boy sort of way."

"Mother! What do you know about bad boys?"

"I've been around the block a few times. And I'm not blind. I did notice that Matt is a very attractive man and that the two of you couldn't keep your eyes off each other. At the time I still had hopes that you and Brian would get back together. I realize now I never had a chance. Neither did Brian."

"Brian is a good man," Caitlyn said, the truth of that situation becoming stunningly clear. "But I can't marry him to make you and Dad happy, or even to make Brian happy. It wouldn't be fair. I'm not in love with him. And I'm not the same girl he loved."

"No, I don't suppose you are."

"As for Matt . . ." She let out a long weary sigh. "Maybe it's love. I don't know. We weren't living in reality. Emily was just borrowed. It was a mistake to start thinking that Matt and Emily and I were a family. I kept telling myself to remember it would all end. But every moment was so wonderful that I didn't want to back away. I knew I was heading straight off a cliff, but I couldn't stop myself."

"That's the way love is, Caitlyn. It's madness. It's wonder. It's crazy and beautiful and dangerous, all at the same time."

Caitlyn had never heard her mother speak with such passion. "Is that the way you feel about Dad?"

"All the time. Love will change your life forever, and it's no use pretending it will go away just because you want it to."

"But it is over, Mom. Whatever we had is gone. Matt has the family he missed all those years, and now I'll go back to being his neighbor. There won't be any reason to cross the hall, no crying baby, no mystery to solve, no nothing."

"How about love? That's a good reason to cross the

hall. Are you so sure Matt didn't fall in love with you the same way you fell for him?"

Caitlyn knew Matt had feelings toward her, but she also knew they were tied up with Emily. "I think he liked the way we made up a family, because he'd missed that in his life. But without Emily, I don't know who we are to each other."

"Maybe you should find out."

"I thought you said Matt was completely unacceptable."

Marilyn smiled. "Believe it or not, I'm going to let you figure this one out on your own."

"You're awfully calm about all this," Caitlyn said suspiciously. "Why?"

"Don't you think one of us should be calm? I figure right now it should probably be me."

"I'm still sorry there won't be any grandchildren for you."

"Oh, Caitlyn. It's you I feel bad for. I know how much you love children. But there are other options. Maybe as time passes, you'll be able to consider them."

"Adoption?"

"Why not? You fell in love with Emily. And she wasn't yours. She wasn't Matt's, either, but that didn't stop the two of you from making a family. Why couldn't you do it again?"

"That was different. Matt had no choice in that situation, but now he does have a choice. What man wouldn't prefer a baby of his genes, his blood?"

"The only one who can answer that is Matt."

"I can't deal with it right now. Everything has happened too fast. It's too much. I need a break."

"You can stay here tonight, Caitlyn. But tomorrow you should go home, because whether Matt is across the hall or across town, it won't change how you feel about him. And as much as I would like to fix this for you, I'm afraid the only person who can fix this is you."

Late Friday morning Sarah walked into Jonathan's office with Emily in her arms. Already, she had changed, her face a rosy pink, her eyes alight, her posture optimistic. The reunion with Emily and her brother had done amazing things for her confidence. Jonathan almost didn't recognize the lost soul who had broken into his church only a week earlier.

"Hi," she said simply.

"Hi yourself. You look like you had a good night."

"Emily still cried, but Matt sat up with both of us, and he told me that she's been crying with him, too. Then he took me up on the roof of his building, and Emily quieted right down. She likes being outside."

"No one should have to take care of a baby alone. I'm glad you don't have to anymore."

"I don't want to get in Matt's way. I want to be able to make it on my own. That's why I've decided to take that spot in the transitional home, if it's still okay."

He smiled warmly at her. "It's still okay. They'll help you with baby-sitting and job hunting, and you'll have other women to talk to who've been in your shoes."

"That will be nice," Sarah replied, but her tone, the expression in her eyes, told him she'd already moved on to something else in her head. But what? He couldn't read her anymore. She'd gone from someone who was hurt and helpless to a woman who was slowly taking control of her life. He wondered if there would be any room left for him in that life. Not that it should matter. He'd done his job. Only now he realized just how personal that job had been.

"Can I still come and see you?" Sarah asked him.

He felt his pulse jump. "Do you want to?"

"Yes."

Their eyes met, and he saw an awareness there that had begun to grow in the past few days.

"You've been a good friend to me," she added. "I'd like to be a friend to you now."

"I'm not sure that I can be friends with you."

The light in her eyes vanished. "Oh, I guess not."

"Not because you're not worthy. That's not it." He took a big breath and stepped over the line he'd been straddling for the past week. "It's because I'd like to be more than your friend."

"You would?" The light came back on along with a slow wondering smile.

"Yes."

"I would, too."

"Really?" He paused, trying to keep a lid on the joy that was racing through him. "I don't want to take advantage of you, Sarah. I don't want you to confuse gratitude with anything else. That's why I didn't say anything before."

"I am grateful to you, Jonathan. I can't help that. But I like you as a man, not just as a minister. In fact, the whole minister thing kind of scares me, because I've never been very holy. And maybe a holy man should have a woman who has lived a better life than I have."

"It's not where you've been, it's where you're going."

"Where we're going?" she asked hopefully.

He nodded but there was still a worry in his heart. "I don't know where I'll end up, though, Sarah. If we don't see a miracle at Sunday service, I may be transferred somewhere else. I don't want to take you away from your brother."

"Maybe there will be a miracle on Sunday. I'm beginning to believe anything is possible." Emily woke up and stretched in Sarah's arms. "Isn't she beautiful, Jonathan? Sometimes I look at her, and I am completely awed."

"I know the feeling. I've been in awe since I found you in my church. I thank God he sent you to me."

"Would it be wrong to ask if I can kiss you?"

"You don't ever have to ask." He met her halfway, his mouth closing over hers with a sigh of satisfaction. In a few days he might not have a church to serve, but if he could keep Sarah in his life, he wouldn't need anyone else. For she had taught him to see the people instead of the crowd, the human faces of each individual instead of the masses he'd once longed to preach to. He knew his calling now, for he'd finally seen the trees instead of the forest.

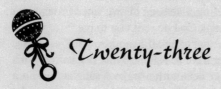

Twenty-three

Friday before work Matt dropped Sarah off at the church, where she planned to spend the day. He had a feeling he'd be losing his sister again—and to a minister, no less. Who would have thought someone in his dysfunctional family would end up with a man of the cloth? The Lord certainly worked in mysterious ways, he thought with amazement. But now that he had Sarah and Emily back in his life, he wouldn't let them go too far. He had a family again. He could hardly believe it.

Unfortunately, as he tried to get excited about digging into a new story, his mind kept returning to Caitlyn, to the awful pain he'd seen in her eyes. He'd hurt her. He'd let her get close to Emily. Even after learning that she couldn't have children, he'd still encouraged the attachment, because he liked having her attached, and not just to Emily, but to him.

Now what?

It was the same question Caitlyn had asked him. Could

they have a relationship without Emily? Caitlyn thought he'd only wanted her because he needed a mother figure for his niece. But did she want him if he didn't come with a baby in his arms? Had the attraction been Emily or himself? The answer eluded him. Or maybe he was just afraid to find it.

He'd never really thought long and hard about whether or not he wanted children. Having kids had always been on the distant horizon, after he found Sarah, after he got his career going, after he found the right woman. But suddenly all those things had fallen into place, and here he was, faced with the possibility of loving a woman who couldn't have children.

Taking care of Emily had turned him into more of a family man than he would have ever imagined, and he knew he didn't want to spend his life without ever holding a baby again. But did the child really have to have his blood? His lines were less than stellar. And there were children in the world who needed homes, babies like Emily, kids like Sarah who'd gone to a foster home for a while. Maybe those kids needed him. Maybe they needed Caitlyn, too. Maybe they all needed each other.

He leaned back in his chair, knowing that coming to work had been a pointless exercise. He couldn't concentrate. For the first time his personal life was more important than his professional one. He'd always defined himself as a newspaperman. Now he found himself wanting the other titles, the titles that belonged to men with wives and children.

Matt looked up, jolted out of his reverie as David stopped by his cubicle, his tie loose around his neck, his shirtsleeves rolled up to his forearms. "I'm glad to see you back at work."

"If you can call it that."

"I gave you several leads."

Matt shrugged. "Nothing that exciting."

"So make it exciting. Dig up some dirt for me. Rattle some cages. Do what you do best."

Matt ran a hand through his hair. "I'm not sure what that is anymore."

"She really turned you inside out, didn't she?"

"Who are you talking about?"

"You know damn well who I'm talking about—Caitlyn, the babe with the blond hair and the great—"

"Don't say it. Don't even think it."

"A little possessive, aren't you?"

Matt tried to brush off the comment as completely incorrect, but it wasn't. He couldn't imagine Caitlyn with another man. Which reminded him that Brian was still lurking in the wings. If Caitlyn went running to Brian . . . well, he didn't want to think about that. She deserved someone better. *She deserved him.*

"Yo, Matt, where did you go?"

Matt started as he realized David was trying to get his attention. "What did you say?"

"Look, why don't you go home, get your head together? You're no good to me this way."

"What way?"

"Crazy in love," David said with a wide grin. "Never thought I'd live to see the day when you'd crumble."

"I have not crumbled."

"You're completely gone."

"Well, it may not matter. I'm not sure Caitlyn wants me."

"Are you nuts? The woman couldn't take her eyes off you the other night. I thought you were going to set the room on fire there were so many sparks between you."

"That's when I had a baby for her to love. Now, I don't."

"So have your own baby."

"She can't. Caitlyn can't have children."

David's smile disappeared. "Oh, man, that's rough."

"She loves kids, too. She'd be a fantastic mother."

"Maybe she could adopt."

"Maybe." He stood up. "You're right about one thing, I'm good for nothing today. I'll be back Monday." Matt was about to leave when a coworker stopped by his cubicle.

"Our firebug struck again, Chelsea Street. Someone saw a woman leaving the area. Connie is checking it out."

Matt's body stiffened as a sudden, terrifying possibility occurred to him. Chelsea Street was right around the corner from his building. "What did the woman look like?"

David sent him a curious look. "Hey, isn't Chelsea Street by your place?"

"Do you know what the woman looked like?" Matt repeated.

"No description yet."

Matt grabbed his keys. "Give me the address."

The reporter rattled off the numbers, and Matt's anxiety heightened as he realized how close it was to his home. Please don't let it be a woman with a straw hat and a watering can, he muttered silently as he ran down to his car. Although he had the sinking feeling that this was yet another downturn in the rollercoaster he called his life.

"So that's it," Jolie said, handing Caitlyn yet another Kleenex.

"That's it." They sat in the back room of Devereaux's

surrounded by wedding dresses and other wedding para-
phernalia while one of their assistants worked out front.
Caitlyn had just finished telling Jolie the whole horrible
story—for the last time, she hoped. There was no one else
left to tell.

"I knew something was bothering you, I just didn't
know what. I thought maybe Brian had cheated on you."

Caitlyn shook her head. "No, he didn't do anything
wrong."

"Well, he did leave you at a rotten time in your life."

"I told him to go."

"Yeah, yeah, yeah, but that didn't mean he had to listen. I know this must be killing you, Caity. You love
kids."

"I do, but it's not meant to be. Now that I've said it
out loud four times, no less, I'm starting to come to
terms with it."

"You know, I would have a kid for you if you wanted
me to."

Caitlyn's mouth dropped open. "What? Are you
crazy? You couldn't do that."

"Actually, I could. I wouldn't want to raise it, of
course, but I'd carry it for you."

"Wow." Caitlyn was awed by the offer, and when she
looked into the eyes of her very best friend, she saw nothing but love and a need to help. "That's an incredible
thing to suggest, and I would really need to think long
and hard about it, but thank you. You're amazing."

"You'd have to be my personal slave for nine months,
though."

"I'm sure. But at the moment this conversation is pre-
mature. I don't exactly have a father figure lined up."

"Sure you do." Jolie smiled her wise little smile that
drove Caitlyn nuts.

"Don't say Brian."

"I wouldn't dream of it. I never thought Brian was good enough for you."

"Hello. You were going to be my maid of honor, and you never said anything."

"Because you seemed happy. In retrospect, I think you were lucky you didn't marry him. Especially now that you're in love with Matt."

"I am not in love with Matt."

"You are so in love with him."

"I might have a little lust, but that's it."

"That's bullshit, Caity. You've never in your life slept with a man you didn't care about."

"How do you know I slept with Matt?"

"Because you looked loved two days ago. I must admit you look more depressed now, but love and pain tend to go hand in hand."

"We had a great time together." Caitlyn tried to make it sound casual. "But it's over."

"Why does it have to be?"

"Because Emily is gone."

"So what? Matt is still living across the hall, as hunky as ever. Frankly, I think you could have even more fun making love without a two-month-old chaperone in the next room ready to bawl her eyes out at any second."

"But Emily is the only reason Matt ever asked me over."

"So ask yourself over. You're a modern woman, Caitlyn. Are you going to let a little hallway between you hold you back?"

"He'll want children. I saw him with Emily. He was a great dad. I can't give him that."

"That's his decision. Stop trying to make it for him. That's what you did with Brian when you sent him away.

That's what you did with me by not telling me the truth.
Let Matt decide for himself if he wants you or if he
doesn't."

"I'm not sure I can handle the 'if he doesn't' part. It already hurts so much to lose Emily, and I've known her a
week. How can I take a chance on losing Matt, too, if not
now, but in the future? It would hurt even more then."

Jolie took Caitlyn's hand in hers. "You'll lose him if
you don't tell him how you feel. That's the one thing I do
know. But whatever happens, we'll get through it together. Now, go home and get your life straightened out."

"Are you sure?"

"I'm sure. And give Matt my love," she called after
Caitlyn with a cheerful smile. "On second thought, just
give him yours. That will be more than enough."

The fire engines were lined up down his block, smoke
turning the sky to black, ash blowing in the wind. Matt
had tried to get closer, but the police had kept everyone
back. There was nothing he could do now but watch and
wonder.

Fire seemed to be a theme that ran through his life,
and Sarah's too—the fire that tore them apart, the fire
next to her hair salon, and now a fire practically in his
backyard. . . . Was something going on? Or was it all just
coincidence?

"Matt?"

He turned to see Jonathan and Sarah walking up the
sidewalk. Sarah had Emily in her arms; Jonathan had his
arm around both of them. Matt felt his body tighten with
jealousy. Yesterday the family had been his, his and Caitlyn's. Now it was Jonathan, Sarah, Emily. He was surprised at how much he didn't like the idea, not for Sarah's
sake but for his own.

"What's happening?" Sarah asked.

"A fire in the apartment building at the corner."

"What are you doing out here?"

Matt looked into her eyes and realized she knew exactly what he was doing out there. "Just checking things out."

"Did you see her?"

"No, but I heard a woman was seen leaving the building shortly before the fire. I don't know any more than that." He paused. "What's up with you?"

"I wanted to tell you that I can get into the home tomorrow. A space opened up earlier than they thought."

"I thought you could stay with me for a few days."

"I won't be far away. But I need to do this, Mattie. It's time I took charge of my own life."

He understood, but he didn't like it. Sarah had just returned to his life, now it felt like she was leaving again. And as his expression drifted to Emily, he knew he would miss her, too, more than he had ever dreamed possible.

As Matt looked away, he saw Caitlyn standing by the front door, watching them. He didn't know if the longing on her face had to do with him or with Emily; it was impossible to tell, and his confidence took another big hit.

Caitlyn started, suddenly realizing they had caught her staring.

"Hi," she said, her gaze sweeping over all of them.

Sarah and Jonathan said hello. Matt simply nodded.

"Do they have the fire under control?" she asked.

"It looks that way," he replied.

And there was nothing left to say—only there was everything to say. He just didn't know where to begin.

"I want to thank you," Sarah said to Caitlyn. "Matt told me how much you helped him, how much you cared for Emily."

"It was nothing. She's a good baby."

"I'm lucky to have her. And I'm going to work really hard to make sure she feels lucky to have me."

"Are you going somewhere, then?" Caitlyn asked.

"To a home for single mothers and kids. They help you with baby-sitting and job hunting. I'm moving in tomorrow."

Caitlyn licked her lips. "I hope it works out for you. I should go upstairs."

"Hang on a second, Caitlyn," Matt said.

She stopped, but she didn't look like she planned on staying. Before he could think of something to say, his cell phone rang. "Just wait," he said as she started to edge away.

"Winters."

"I think I found your mother." Blake's abrupt words shocked Matt to the core. Would they never stop coming, the unexpected surprises? He didn't think he could take one more.

"Where is she?" he asked curtly, not sure he wanted to know. Except that he did, because he couldn't keep chasing fires, wondering if his mother had started them, and he couldn't keep following old ladies in straw hats just to catch a glimpse of a familiar face. He needed to end it. He needed to end it now.

"Meet me at 472 Dolores Drive in South San Francisco. Take the Orange Drive exit off 101 and turn right."

Matt didn't recognize the address. "Is that where she's living?"

"Just come," Blake said.

"I'll be there in twenty minutes." He hung up the phone and found the others watching him expectantly. "Blake thinks he found our mother."

Sarah was horrified. "You were looking for her?"

"I have to know, Sarah. I can't keep wondering if she's going to pop up somewhere, especially now that I know she came back and got you. I think you should come with me. I think you should all come."

Caitlyn immediately shook her head. "This is family business. You don't need me."

"I do need you," he said, moving toward her so he could look directly into her eyes. He wanted her to see how deep his need was. He couldn't do this alone. He needed her by his side. Maybe it was selfish. Maybe Caitlyn was wondering when it would ever be her turn. He just hoped she would say yes anyway.

She hesitated, obviously torn. "Is it that important to you?"

"More than I can say."

"All right."

"Sarah?" he asked, turning to his sister.

"If you really feel you need to see her, I'll go with you. But don't expect too much, Matt. I don't think she got better with age."

Twenty-five minutes later Matt pulled up in front of the address Blake had given him. The black numbers were painted broadly on the white wall in front of the Bayview Cemetery. Matt was stunned. He hadn't expected this, not this. His mother was dead? It didn't seem possible. But of course it was. Only, in the past week he'd thought he'd seen her. He'd thought he'd felt her presence in his life again.

Blake was waiting just inside the gates. He motioned for Matt to follow him, then got into his car and led them about a half mile into the cemetery. Matt parked his car along the road and stepped out, the others doing the same.

"Why didn't you tell me on the phone?" Matt asked Blake. "I could have prepared Sarah." And he could have prepared himself.

"You won't believe this," Blake said. "Remember that woman you told me you kept seeing, the one holding the watering can?"

"What about her? Obviously, it wasn't my mother, if you're going to tell me she's dead."

"Follow me." Blake led them through a clump of trees. Just on the other side was a grave with a plain headstone and something next to it—a watering can.

Matt felt his heart skip a beat, and he instinctively reached for Caitlyn, who steadied him by placing her hand in his.

"It's okay," she whispered. "You can do this."

He moved closer to the grave, his gaze traveling first to the watering can; it was exactly like the one he'd seen the old woman carrying. Then his gaze moved to the headstone, where he read his mother's name and the dates of her life, the last date being one year, almost to the day, earlier.

Matt sank down to his knees on the ground. Sarah knelt beside him. "I can't believe she's dead," Sarah said.

Leaning over, Matt picked up the watering can. "A gardener probably left this behind."

Sarah didn't answer him as she turned her gaze toward the sky. Matt couldn't help but follow her lead, not knowing what he was searching for, but he still felt compelled to look up.

"Maybe it's a sign," Sarah whispered.

"Of what?"

"She could be an angel."

"An angel? I doubt that. If she ended up anywhere, it

was hell. Sorry, Reverend," he mumbled, glancing back at Jonathan.

Sarah looked at Jonathan, too. "Do you think it's possible? Could Mama have been trying to make up for everything bad by bringing us back together? I saw her. You saw her, too," she said to Matt.

"What do you think?" he asked Caitlyn.

"It is odd that I never saw her."

"Jonathan didn't see her either," Sarah added.

The four of them stared at each other, then one by one their gazes drifted back to the simple headstone.

"Well, at least we won't have to worry every time we hear a fire engine. I wonder who buried her," Matt said as he and Sarah got to their feet. "I guess we'll never know. I guess we'll never know a lot of things."

"Can you live with that?" Caitlyn asked him. "Can you live with not knowing all the details?"

He gave her question a moment of thought. "I think I can. It's over now. It's all over." He looked at Blake. "You were right. I needed to see this for myself."

"I don't think you'll be needing me anymore." Blake tipped his head. "I'll see you around. Enjoy your family."

"I will." Matt took one last look at his mother's grave, then walked back to the car. He knew where everyone was now. Maybe he could finally find peace.

Caitlyn was glad she'd gone with Matt to the cemetery, happy she'd seen him put to rest the last of his demons. But when they walked down the hallway to Matt's apartment, she knew she couldn't go any farther. Sarah, Jonathan, and Emily went inside the apartment, leaving the two of them alone in the hallway—again.

"This is where it all started," Matt said.

"Right here."

"I don't want it to end."

She wasn't sure she'd heard him correctly. "What did you say?"

"I don't want it to end, you and me, Caitlyn. That's what I don't want to end."

"There is no you and me without Emily," she argued, feeling she had to point it out to him one last time.

"There could be." He moved closer to her, putting his hands on her waist, burning her with his touch. "We were good together even when we weren't changing diapers. I know you know that, even though you're not willing to admit it. We clicked on a lot of levels. I've never known a woman like you. I never knew I could feel the way I feel when I'm with you."

She swayed slightly, torn between pushing him away and pulling him closer. "How do you feel?"

"I love you, Caitlyn," he said slowly, deliberately, purposefully.

Her breath caught in her chest. "You do?"

"Yes. I love the way you smile at the silliest little things, the way you light up a room when you walk into it, the way you insist on seeing the good things in life and in people and in me. I don't know if I deserve to have you, but I sure as hell want you. Now, tell me how you feel, and remember that you can't lie to me. I'll see right through you."

She looked into his eyes and saw a man who spoke only the truth. How could she do anything but the same? "I love the way you can read my mind, the way you don't need a book to figure me out, the way you boost my confidence and make me feel stronger and braver than I've ever felt in my life. I love the way you accept me for who

I am without trying to change me. I love you, Matt, with all my heart."

"Thank God," he muttered, pressing his mouth against hers.

She took him in, all the way in, into her mouth, into her heart, into her soul. He was everywhere, in every molecule of air that she breathed. Love had never been so all-consuming. And she knew without a doubt that this was meant to be.

"We'll figure out the kid thing," Matt muttered against her mouth as he continued to press kisses along her lips, her cheek, and the sensitive spot behind her ear. "We can adopt. There are hundreds of kids out there who need the kind of love we can give them."

She pulled slightly away so she could look into his face. "Are you sure, Matt? It's all so fast. I don't want you to make any promises now. It's enough to know that you love me. The rest I want you to think about. If you want children of your own, you should have them."

"I don't have to think about it, Caitlyn. I know what I want, and it's you."

"Think about it anyway," she said, placing her finger against his lips as he started to interrupt. "I don't want either of us to have any doubts. I want to take it slow."

"How slow?" he asked with a sexy smile. "Because, believe me, I can go as slow as you want."

"Well, not that slow," she said with a laugh. "You'll drive me crazy."

"That would be my pleasure. Now, as for our next date . . ."

"We're going to date?"

"If we're going slow, we are. Our next official date will be Sunday morning."

Her eyes narrowed suspiciously. "Sunday morning? What happens then?"

"You'll see."

Caitlyn couldn't believe Matt was taking her to church. She was still in shock when they stepped through the doors of Jonathan's church two days later.

"This is where you wanted to go for a date?" she whispered.

He smiled lovingly at her. "We're not just here to date, we're on a mission. I figured the church saved Sarah, so we need to save the church."

Caitlyn nodded, having heard both Jonathan and Sarah talk about the problems at the church over the weekend. But Matt had never mentioned any mission to her until now.

"I hope you don't mind, but I invited your parents and Jolie, too."

Caitlyn's mouth fell open again as she saw her parents chatting with Jolie. "What on earth are you up to?"

"You'd know, Caitlyn, if you ever read the newspaper," he replied with a smug smile.

"Caitlyn!" Her mother came rushing over to her, giving her a hug of delight, followed by her father and Jolie, who were all muttering congratulations.

Caitlyn turned to Jolie when her parents were finally distracted. "Did you see the paper this morning?"

"Of course I did," Jolie said with a laugh. "Didn't you?"

"No, I did not. You know I don't read the paper."

"And you're in love with a newspaperman—shame on you." Jolie slid away to talk to more and more friends, people Caitlyn hadn't seen in years.

"Matt is amazing," Jonathan told her, as he joined her at the back of the church. "He did what I couldn't do. He filled this church to the rafters. We may have a chance at saving it."

"How did he do that?" Caitlyn asked.

"Didn't you read the paper this morning?"

"Okay, that's it. I'm going to get one right now."

"You don't have to," Sarah said, sidling up with Emily. She handed Caitlyn the front page of the paper.

Caitlyn was almost afraid to look, but she saw Matt watching her and knew that this was one paper she'd have to read.

And there it was . . . down in the right-hand corner, where Matt usually wrote about politicians and corruption . . . a story about a church that needed saving, a community that needed to pull together. And at the bottom of the short article, in large bold print, were the words, *"Will you marry me, Caitlyn? Because I love you, and if you read it here, you know it must be true."*

Her eyes blurred with tears of joy. A year and a half ago she'd thought her life was over, but now she realized it was the new beginning she'd needed. She'd come full circle, happier now than she'd ever been in her life.

"Yes," she said, shouting across the crowded vestibule, as she waved the paper in her hand. "Yes, I'll marry you."

Matt had her in his arms before the last word crossed her lips. "You won't be sorry, Caitlyn. I'll make you happy. I swear it."

"I thought we were going to take things slow," she said with a teary smile.

"I've been waiting my whole life for you. I don't want to wait another second. Do you?"

"No, I'm sure. You know me better than I know myself."

"I feel the same way. I won't try to fix you, Caitlyn. I won't even make you read the newspaper."

"Now I know you love me."

He cupped her face with his hands and looked deep into her eyes. "We'll make up the rest as we go along. Don't say it," he said, putting a finger against her lips. "If we decide to open our lives up to another small soul, we'll decide together how and when and all the rest. But the truth is, I don't need anyone else, Caitlyn. I found my other half in you."

Her eyes welled up with tears. "That's the nicest thing anyone has ever said to me."

"Hey, I'm just getting started. I've got a way with words, you know."

"A way with me," she said. "And you're my other half, too, the half that is bold and filled with attitude. You make me want to spread my wings and fly."

"And you make me want to put down some roots. We'll be good together, Caitlyn. We may not have the storybook ending"—he smiled at her with love and joy in his eyes—"but we will have some kind of wonderful. I promise you that."

Six Tips for Finding Mr. Right
From the Avon Romance Superleaders

Meeting Mr. Right requires planning, persuasion, and a whole lot of psychology! But even the best of us needs help sometimes ... and where better to find it than between the pages of each and every Avon Romance Superleader?

After all, Julia Quinn, Rachel Gibson, Barbara Freethy, Constance O'Day-Flannery, Cathy Maxwell, and Victoria Alexander are the experts when it comes to love. And the following sneak previews of their latest tantalizing, tempting love stories (plus a special bonus from Samantha James) are sure to help you on the path to romantic success.

So when it's time to find the man of your dreams (or, if you've already got him, to help your friends find equal success) just follow the lead of the heroines of the Avon Romance Superleaders. . . .

Tip #1:
Ballroom dance lessons really can pay off.

Miss Sophie Beckett longs to believe that her dreams can come true. However, this Regency miss seems destined to be at the beck and call of her wealthy relations. But when she secretly attends Lady Bridgerton's annual masked ball, she's swept into the strong arms of handsome Benedict Bridgerton. Sophie knows that when midnight—and the unmasking—comes she must leave or risk exposure. But she won't do so before she accepts . . .

An Offer From a Gentleman

Coming July 2001
by Julia Quinn

Sophie hadn't seen him when she'd first walked into the room, but she'd felt magic in the air, and when he'd appeared before her, like some charming prince from a children's tale, she somehow knew that *he* was the reason she'd stolen into the ball.

He was tall, and what she could see of his face was very handsome, with lips that hinted of irony and smiles and skin that was just barely touched by the beginnings of a beard.

His hair was a dark, rich brown, and the flickering candle-light lent it a faint reddish cast.

He was handsome and he was strong, and for this one night, he was hers.

When the clock struck midnight, she'd be back to her life of drudgery, of mending and washing and attending to Araminta's every wish. Was she so wrong to want this one heady night of magic and love?

She felt like a princess—a reckless princess—and so when he asked her to dance, she put her hand in his. And even though she knew that this entire evening was a lie, that she was a nobleman's bastard and a countess's maid, that her dress was borrowed and her shoes practically stolen—none of that seemed to matter as their fingers twined.

For a few hours, at least, Sophie could pretend that this gentleman could be *her* gentleman, and that from this moment on, her life would be changed forever.

It was nothing but a dream, but it had been so terribly long since she'd let herself dream.

Banishing all caution, she allowed him to lead her out of the ballroom. He walked quickly, even as he wove through the pulsing crowd, and she found herself laughing as she tripped along after him.

"Why is it," he said, halting for a moment when they reached the hall outside the ballroom, "that you always seem to be laughing at me?"

She laughed again; she couldn't help it. "I'm happy," she said with a helpless shrug. "I'm just so happy to be here."

"And why is that? A ball such as this must be routine for one such as yourself."

Sophie grinned. If he thought she was a member of the *ton*, an alumna of dozens of balls and parties, then she must be playing her role to perfection.

He touched the corner of her mouth. "You keep smiling," he murmured.

"I like to smile."

His hand found her waist, and he pulled her toward him. The distance between their bodies remained respectable, but the increasing nearness robbed her of breath.

"I like to watch you smile," he said. His words were low and seductive, but there was something oddly hoarse about his voice, and Sophie could almost let herself believe that he really meant it, that she wasn't merely that evening's conquest. . . .

Tip #2:
Mothers across America proven wrong—
sometimes looks do count!

The gossips of Gospel, Idaho, all want to know—who is Hope Spencer and what is she doing in their town? Little do they suspect that she's a supermarket tabloid reporter on the run from a story gone terribly wrong . . . all they can learn is that she's from Los Angeles, which is plenty bad. Even worse, she's caught the eye of Dylan Taber, Gospel's sexy sheriff—the only good looking man in three counties. He's easy on the eyes and not above breaking the laws of love to get what he wants. And before you know it, there's plenty to talk about in the way of . . .

True Confessions

Coming August 2001
by Rachel Gibson

"Can you direct me to Number Two Timberline?" she asked. "I just picked up the key from the realtor and that's the address he gave me."

"You sure you want Number Two Timberline? That's the old Donnelly place," Lewis Plummer said. Lewis was a true

363

gentleman, and one of the few people in town who didn't outright lie to flatlanders.

"That's right. I leased it for the next six months."

Sheriff Dylan pulled his hat back down on his forehead. "No one's lived there for a while."

"Really, no one told me that. How long has it been empty?"

"A year or two." Lewis had also been born and raised in Gospel, Idaho, where prevarication was considered an art form.

"Oh, a year isn't too bad if the property's been maintained."

Maintained, hell. The last time Dylan had been in the Donnelly house thick dust covered everything. Even the bloodstain on the living room floor.

"So, do I just follow this road?" She turned and pointed down Main Street.

"That's right," he answered. From behind his mirrored glasses, Dylan slid his gaze to the natural curve of her slim hips and thighs, down her long legs to her feet.

"Well, thanks for your help." She turned to leave but Dylan's next question stopped her.

"You're welcome, Ms—?"

"Spencer."

"Well now, Ms Spencer, what are you planning to do out there on the Timberline Road?" Dylan figured everyone had a right to privacy, but he also figured he had a right to ask.

"Nothing."

"You lease a house for six months and you plan to do nothing?"

"That's right. Gospel seemed like a nice place to vacation."

Dylan had doubts about that statement. Women who drove fancy sports cars and wore designer jeans vacationed in nice places with room service and pool boys, not in the wilderness of Idaho. Hell, the closest thing Gospel had to a spa was the Petermans' hot tub.

Her brows scrunched together and she tapped an impatient hand three times on her thigh before she said, "Well, thank you, gentlemen, for your help." Then she turned on her fancy boots and marched back to her sports car.

"Do you believe her?" Lewis wanted to know.

"That she's here on vacation?" Dylan shrugged. He didn't care what she did as long as she stayed out of trouble.

"She doesn't look like a backpacker."

Dylan thought back on the vision of her backside in those tight jeans. "Nope."

"Makes you wonder why a woman like that leased that old house. I haven't seen anything like her in a long time. Maybe never."

Dylan slid behind the wheel of his Blazer. "Well, Lewis, you sure don't get out of Pearl County enough."

Tip #3:
If he's good to kids,
he'll be good to you.

Most men, when confronted with a baby, do one of two things: run the other way or fall for it. When a beautiful baby girl is left on journalist Matt Winters's doorstep, he turns to his neighbor, wedding gown designer Caitlyn Deveraux, for help. After all, she's a woman . . . shouldn't she know everything about babies? Soon, Caitlyn and Matt must confront their deepest desires—her longing for a child, his wish for a family—and a passion for each other that's . . .

Some Kind of Wonderful

**Coming September 2001
by Barbara Freethy**

"Oh, isn't that the cutest outfit?" Caitlyn ran down the aisle and pulled out a bright red dress that was only a little bigger than Matt's hand. "It has a bonnet to go with it. You have to get this one."

"This was a big mistake," he said, frowning at her unbridled enthusiasm. With Emily nuzzled against his chest and Caitlyn by his side, he felt like he was part of a family—a husband, a wife, a baby. It was the American dream.

"It's one cute little dress," Caitlyn said, putting it in the cart. "Diapers, we need diapers." She walked around the corner and tossed several large bags into the cart, followed by baby wipes, bottles, formula, bibs, socks, a couple of sleepers, a baby blanket, and a pink hair ribbon that she couldn't resist. By the time they headed down the last aisle, the cart was overflowing with items Caitlyn insisted that he needed.

"You know I'm not a rich man," he told her.

"Most of it is on sale."

"And most of it we don't need—I don't need," he corrected. "She doesn't need," he said finally finding the right pronoun.

Caitlyn simply offered a smile that told him she could see right through him. To distract her he stopped and looked over at the shelves, determined to find something else that they didn't need so she would coo over it and focus her attention anywhere but on him. That's when he saw it: an enormous chocolate brown teddy bear with soft, plush fur and black eyes that reminded him of Sarah.

"Emily would love that," Caitlyn said.

"It's bigger than she is," he replied gruffly.

"She'll grow into it." Caitlyn took the bear off the rack and sat it on top of the growing pile, daring him to take it off.

"Fine," he said with a long-suffering sigh.

"Oh, please, you don't fool me."

"I don't know what you're talking about."

"I'm talking about that sentimental streak that runs down your back."

"You're seeing things with those rose-colored glasses again, princess."

"And you're a terrible liar."

Tip #4:
Sometimes it's good to take charge!

Charles Garrity is a man out of time . . . one moment it was 1926, the next, 2001! But he doesn't have a single minute to figure out what's happened, because he's faced with rescuing his rescuer—a very beautiful, very pregnant woman who says her name's Suzanne McDermott. Charles quickly realizes that all has changed except for one thing: Love is an emotion that can transcend time, and that nothing else matters but what you feel . . .

Here and Now

Coming October 2001
by Constance O'Day-Flannery

"Who are you anyway?"

"Charles Garrity, ma'am. And thank you again . . . for pulling me out of the river." He didn't know what else to say to this confusing female, and he certainly had no idea what to do with a woman about to give birth.

"I'm Suzanne. Suzanne McDermott. Now let's just make it to the car so both of us can get some help."

Charles kept looking at the odd automobile. "You drove this?"

"Of course, I drove it."

Charles shrugged, then reached down behind her legs and, with a grunt, swept her up into his arms.

"No! Wait! You'll drop me!" she yelped.

"Just stay still, ease up, and we'll make it," he gritted out.

As they approached the machine Charles took one last step and set her down as gently as he could next to it.

He pulled on the metal latch on the automobile and stared in wonder as the door opened easily and exposed the luxurious interior.

"You're going to have to drive us to the hospital," she said.

"I am?" he asked.

"Yes, you are. You have driven a car before, haven't you?"

"I've driven an automobile," he insisted, straightening his backbone.

"Good," Suzanne answered. "Let's get out of here. I want a doctor when my baby arrives."

"Let me help you," he said, wrapping his arm around what was left of her waist and assisting her. When they managed to get her onto the back seat, he stood panting.

She felt like she was instructing a child as she patiently began rattling off instructions. A wave of relief swept over her as the engine cranked and the motor began humming.

"This is astounding," he said with a breath of awe.

Suzanne knew now was not the time to ask questions.

The car lurched forward. He must have hit every single rut on the back country path, and he stopped when they finally came to the main road, even though there were several times when he could have safely merged.

"What's wrong?" she asked.

Charles Garrity stared at the unbelievable spectacle before him. Automobiles of every color and size whizzed past him with more speed than he'd ever imagined. Something was wrong—*very* wrong—for this was no place he'd ever been before.

Tip #5:
Sometimes men like it when you play hard to get.

When pert, pretty Mary Gates gets her chance for a London Season, she sets her cap on someone far more lofty than Tye Barlow, the local rake. The insufferable man thinks he's the world's gift to women! But though he drives her crazy when they're together, she finds herself longing for him when they're apart. Then a daring bet between them ends in matrimony, and Mary must decide whether she's lost—or won . . .

The Wedding Wager

Coming November 2001
by Cathy Maxwell

Tye Barlow's hand came down on top of hers, pressing it flat against the horse's skin. He held it in place. In spite of the beast's impressive height, Barlow glowered down at her from the other side.

Mary wasn't one of his silly admirers. She knew better than to trust a man who could make a woman's brain go a little daffy. But when he was angry like this, she had to concede he was rather good-looking. He boasted sharp, cobalt blue eyes, straight black hair, broad shoulders, and a muscular physique that made other men appear puny.

However, Mary knew what sent female hearts fluttering was not his perfections, but his imperfections. His grin was slightly uneven, like that of a fox who had raided the hen-house. A scar over his right eye added to his devil-may-care expression, and there was a bump on his nose from the day years ago when he, Blacky, David, and Brewster had brawled with a neighboring village.

They'd won.

Now her face was inches from Tye's, and she could make out the line of his whiskers and smell a hint of the bay rum shaving soap he used. For a guilty second she was tempted to blurt out the truth . . . then pride took over.

How *dare* he manhandle her. And the state of her affairs was her business, not his.

She gave his black scowl right back at him. "I can afford the horse, Barlow, and I've bought him. He's mine. And you are a sore loser."

Her words hit their mark. His hold on her arms loosened as if she'd struck a physical blow. She jerked away. Two steps and she could breathe easily again.

"Your stubborn arrogance will ruin you, Mary."

His accusation stung. She wasn't arrogant. Proud, yes; arrogant, no. Calmly, forcibly, she said, " 'Twas a business decision, Barlow. Nothing personal."

The daggers in his eyes told her he didn't believe her. "And how do you think you are going to find the funds to pay the horse's price?" His low voice was meant for their ears alone.

"I have plenty of money," she replied stiffly.

"God, Mary, stop this pretense. You're done up. It's not your fault. Your father—"

"Don't you dare mention my father. Not after what your family did to him—"

"I did nothing and if you think so, then you're a fool."

His blunt verdict robbed her of speech. They were back in each other's space again, almost toe-to-toe.

"If I was a man," she said, "I'd call you out and run you through."

"But you're not a man, Mary. Yes, you are good with horses, but damn it all, you are still a woman. . . ."

Tip #6:
Sometimes fainting isn't such a bad idea.

Lady Jocelyn is no shrinking violet, but even she knows that sometimes a lady has to fall into a swoon—and if you're caught in the arms of sexy Randall, Viscount Beaumont, so much the better. Of course, Jocelyn had always dreamed she'd be marrying a prince . . . or at least a duke. But Randall's strong embrace and tempting kisses are far more enticing than she'd ever imagined. And then a surprising twist of events makes it possible that she just might become . . .

The Prince's Bride

Coming December 2001
by Victoria Alexander

He caught her up in arms strong and hard and carried her to a nearby sofa. For a moment a lovely sense of warmth and safety filled her.

"Put me down," she murmured, but snuggled against him in spite of herself.

"You were about to faint."

"Nonsense. I have never fainted. Shelton women do not faint."

"Apparently, they do when their lives are in danger."

373

Abruptly, he deposited her on the sofa and pushed her head down to dangle over his knees.

"Whatever are you doing?" She could barely gasp out the words in the awkward position. She tried to lift her head, but he held it firmly.

"Keep your head down," he ordered. "It will help."

"What will help is finding those men. There were two, you know. Or perhaps you don't." It was rather confusing. All of it. She raised her head. "Aren't you going to go after them?"

"No." He pushed her head back down and kept his hand lightly on the back of her neck. It was an oddly comforting feeling. "I have my men searching now, but I suspect they will be unsuccessful. One of the rascals is familiar to me. I was keeping an eye on him tonight. He is no doubt the one who threw the knife."

"Apparently, you weren't keeping a very good eye on him," she muttered.

He ignored her. "I have yet to discover the identity of his accomplice and I doubt that I will tonight. It's far too easy to blend unnoticed into a crowd of this size." He paused, the muscles of his hand tensing slightly on her neck. "Did you recognize him?"

"Not really," she lied. In truth, not at all. They were nothing more than blurry figures to her and dimly remembered voices. "He could be anyone then, couldn't he?"

"Indeed he could."

It was a most disquieting thought. Well matched to her most discomforting position. "I feel ridiculous like this."

"Quiet."

It was no use arguing with the man. Whoever he was, he obviously knew what he was doing. She was already feeling better.

She rose to her feet. "Who are you?"

He stood. "I should be crushed that you do not remember, although we have never been formally introduced." He swept a curt bow. "I am Randall, Viscount Beaumont."

The name struck a familiar chord. "Have we met then?"

"Not really." Beaumont shrugged. "I am a friend of Lord Helmsley."

"Of course." How could she forget? She'd seen him only briefly in a darkened library, but his name was all too familiar. Beaumont had taken part in a farcical, and highly successful plan to dupe her sister, Marianne, into marriage with Thomas, Marquess of Helmsley and son of the Duke of Roxborough. "And an excellent friend too from all I've heard."

"One owes a certain amount to loyalty to one's friends." He paused as if considering his words. "As well as to one's country."

At once the mood between them changed, sobered. She studied him for a long moment. He was tall and devastatingly handsome. She noted the determined set of his jaw, the powerful lines of his lean body like a jungle cat clad in the latest state of fashion. And the hard gleam in his eye. She shivered with the realization that regardless of his charming manner, his easy grin, and the skill of his embrace, *this* was a dangerous man.

And because you can never have enough handy tips
when it comes to meeting a man,
we give you a bonus!
In case you missed it, it comes from
The Truest Heart
by Samantha James
Available now from Avon Books

Bonus Tip #7:
A good man is hard to find . . . and
sometimes a bad man is better.

When Lady Gillian of Westerbrook discovers a near-
mortally wounded warrior, she takes him in and
nurses him back to health. He has no memory of his
past, but as Gillian tends to him he begins to remem-
ber . . . and she realizes he is none other than Gareth,
lord of Sommerfield, the man sworn to betray her to a
vengeful king. As Gillian succumbs to his masterful
touch, she is forced to choose—between her family
honor and her heart's truest desire.

"You are a man who knows little of piety and virtue."

There was a silence, a silence that ever deepened. "I do
not know. Perhaps I am a thief. An outlaw."

Gillian looked at him sharply, but this time she detected
no trace of bitterness. "I think not. You still have both your
hands."

"Then perhaps I'm a lucky one. Now come, Gillian."

Outside lightning lit up the night sky. The ominous roll of
thunder that followed made the walls shake. In a heartbeat

Gillian was across the floor—and squarely onto the bed next to him.

He laughed, the wretch!

"Perhaps you are not an outlaw," she flared, "but I begin to suspect you may well be a rogue!"

He made no answer, but once again lifted the coverlet. Her lips tightened indignantly, but she tugged off her slippers and slid into bed. He respected the space she put between them, but she was aware of the weight of his gaze settling on her in the darkness.

"Are you afraid of storms?"

"Nay," she retorted. As if to put the lie to the denial, lightning sizzled and sparked, illuminating the cottage to near daylight.

She tensed, half-expecting some jibe from Gareth. Instead, his fingers stole through hers, as had become their custom. Comforted, lulled by his presence, it wasn't long before she felt her muscles loosen and her eyelids grow heavy. 'Ere she could draw breath, long arms caught her close—so close she could feel every sinewed curve of his chest, the taut line of his thighs molded against her own.

There was no chance for escape. No chance for struggle. No thought of panic. No thought of resistance, for Gillian was too stunned to even move . . .

His mouth closed over hers.